Parker's Folly

Doug L. Hoffman

Published by
The Resilient Earth Press
www.theresilientearth.com

Preface

This is a work of fiction, a science fiction novel of the type sometimes called a space opera. Over time that term has often been used derisively, though sometimes lovingly. I use space opera to denote a particular type of science fiction that I read as a youth; works penned by such old masters as Arthur C. Clarke, Issac Asimov, L. Sprague de Camp, Robert Heinlein and E.E. "Doc" Smith. Smith in particular defined this genre for me with his *Skylark of Space* series, the first novels I recall purchasing for my own reading pleasure.

Many, though certainly not all, of the novels from these giants of SF started on Earth, more or less in the present day. Not long ago, in a galaxy far, far away; not star-date 24-something-or-other; but in the here and now. That is what hooked me on Smith's first *Skylark* novel—the heroes were contemporary human beings that, through their own intelligence and effort, managed to construct a spaceship and blast off into the Galaxy on an amazing adventure. In short, the reader could imagine such a thing happening to them.

Few books are written like that anymore. Most seem set in a distant future and the ones that are set in the near term are usually dark, gloomy portrayals of post industrial dystopias. What a bummer. So here is my modest attempt at an old fashioned space adventure, an adventure that anyone could find themselves in the midst of with a little luck. The science within is either based on present knowledge or is possible without violating current understanding. The boundaries are stretched a bit, after all this is a work of science *fiction*.

Having explained my motivation and hopefully set the stage for the reader, I must thank the multitude of friends and family members that were sucked into the literary maelstrom I created while writing the book. Heartfelt thanks go out to Clayton Ward, David Metheny, Stuart White and Brandon Willis, who each provided page by page corrections and suggestions. Also Dr. Erin Willis, who checked my medical details for plausibility. As always, Dr. Rik Faith kept me honest with regard to the science and physical aspects of adventuring into space. The book was much improved by their efforts.

With any such enterprise, it is customary to dragoon one's family into reviewing (or at least listening to readings of) the book in progress. My mother Mary and sister Melinda both offered enthusiastic support while my brother David and sister-in-law Brenda both reviewed the final product. The number of early readers is far too large to list them all here, but I did appreciate every review and word of encouragement.

Lastly, I would like to thank Allen Simmons, my coauthor on two previous works of non-fiction: *The Resilient Earth* and *The Energy Gap*. In fact, Al must be credited with getting me addicted to writing in the first place. He was my constant sounding-board, despite not being a real fan of science fiction. So, if you enjoy Parker's Folly, at least some of the credit belongs to Al and the others mentioned above.

This, of course, brings us to the obligatory disclaimers: all the characters in this book are fictional, not representations of any real person, living or dead; Any mistakes in the science, engineering, etc. are purely my own and not the responsibility any of those thanked above. The verse recited by the Captain in Chapter 15 is from *A Pirate Looks At 40* by Jimmy Buffett. The verse from *Arriving Somewhere But Not Here* by Steven Wilson, © Warner/Chappell Music, Inc. The book was written using OpenOffice and the cover art done using the GIMP. I do hope you enjoy this book. It is the first of a planned trilogy—the second book, *Peggy Sue*, has been written and I have started on the third.

Regards,

Doug L. Hoffman

Conway, AR

September 25, 2012

Prologue

Arabian Peninsula, 1986

He could see them at the mouth of the ravine, where it emptied into the wadi. Arabs. At least they were dressed as Arabs, in long, flowing thobes with red-checked ghutras covering their heads. Each man also displayed that indispensable middle-eastern fashion item—an AK47. Even at this distance the curved magazines and distinctive forestocks were hard to miss.

They might be from the government or just some passing Bedouins, it made little difference. Here, in the wilds of the empty quarter, any group of armed men was a law unto themselves. As the armed party began the climb from the dry river bed, the observer zipped up his fly, turned and hurried back up the ravine. *Got to warn the Professor,* he thought.

Hustling up the steeply pitched gully was harder than it looked. The mountain was made of purple-red basaltic rock—unusual in the eastern part of the peninsula where most of the bedrock belonging to the Nubian-Arabian shield was buried under a covering of limestones and sandstones—ancient strata that formed when dinosaurs still roamed the planet. But that was not the source of the difficulty.

It was the sand that impeded his upward progress, sand blown in from the surrounding desert that collected in the mountain's ravines and crevasses. The color of dried wheat stalks, Arabian sand had little in common with beach sand. It was gritty with a tendency to cling and possessed an almost greasy quality that seemed to hint at the oceans of crude oil buried beneath the rock below. Even as sand it was particularly useless: concrete made from it soon crumbled and fell apart. Arabia, a land synonymous with sand, had to import the stuff to build with.

Now, the useless stuff was tenaciously sucking at his boots as he scrambled for the cave near the top of the ravine. The entrance was lost in shadow, beneath a small overhang—perhaps the men climbing up the gully would miss it.

Fat chance, he thought. *I hope they're friendly.*

1

Crouching down to clear the low entrance, he duck walked into the cave that had been his workplace for the past three weeks. Inside there was an older man hunched over a collection of boxes. The faces of those boxes were aglow with numbers, moving squiggles and illuminated dials—an indication of electronics within.

"We are about to have company, Professor," the younger man said, partially out of breath from his hasty ascent of the ravine. "They're dressed as locals and they're armed."

"They probably just want to shake us down for a little baksheesh," the older man said, not looking up from the instruments. "I think we're ready for another test. Go to the other station and shout when you are ready. Maybe we can run the test before we have to deal with the native problem."

"But Professor, they'll be here any minute!"

"Go!"

The young man moved deeper into the cave, careful not to step on the wires running along the floor of the passageway. About 25 meters in, the curving tunnel ended. There stood another pile of softly glowing electronics. Wires led to probes, stuck on a smooth metallic surface about the size of a house door. That surface, or rather what that surface was a part of, was the reason why he and the Professor were in this cave, deep in the wastelands of Arabia, in the first place.

There was no logical explanation why there should be a smooth metallic surface embedded in volcanic rock that had formed several hundred million years ago. The surface appeared to be part of a larger object—more probes were attached to a similar, though smaller, exposed surface at the Professor's station. Neither of the researchers knew what the object was, how big it was or why it was here—they simply referred to it as the "artifact."

And an artifact it was. Whatever its origins, the object embedded in the mountain before them was most certainly a made thing. If a light was played across its exposed surface cryptic symbols could be seen on or, more accurately, within the material. Symbols that shifted and moved with changes in the observer's viewing angle, much like the hologram embedded in a charge card.

Deciphering those symbols had consumed the Professor for the past several years—this was not his first foray into the desert wastelands or, indeed, to this very cave. He now claimed to have figured out at least some of the enigmatic symbols. As best he could tell, the markings were a puzzle: a collection of hints, possibly providing instructions for unlocking the artifact.

According to the Professor, the instructions said that a specific series of electrical pulses had to be applied simultaneously to different locations on the artifact's surface. But there was a catch: the transmission spots had to be more than 20 meters apart and the signals needed to be synchronized to within a few femtoseconds. Forced to look up the unfamiliar term, the assistant discovered that a femtosecond is one millionth of a nanosecond. In other words, a millionth of a billionth of a second.

Given that light travels nearly 300,000,000 meters per second, it takes about 70 nanoseconds to cross a distance of 20 meters. That delay was far too large for the required signals to be synchronized by simply running a wire or fiber-optic cable between the two transmission spots. Even using a central transmitter and two cables of exactly the same length proved problematic—the tolerances were just too exacting. Particularly considering that the transmission equipment would have to survive being hauled across the wastelands of the Arabian peninsula.

Here was a puzzle that seemed to require sending a signal faster than the speed of light—something human science said was impossible. Could the artifact be an alien version of a time capsule and the puzzle a test to make sure only sufficiently advanced beings could open it? No stupid ape-men need apply. Naturally, it took the professor quite a while to come up with a solution, but solve it he did.

The solution was quite elegant. He found a paper describing a device called a salphasic clock. The paper explained a method that used the properties of standing waves to substantially reduce clock skews due to unequal length transmission paths. Originally intended for use in computer systems, it was soon adapted to help synchronize the (hopefully) artifact opening signals.

The salphasic clock did not make it possible to send a signal faster than light. What it did was provide a heartbeat signal that

3

occurred at exactly the same time at both ends of a cable regardless of length. This, in theory, would allow other equipment to slowly shift the offset between the two signals until the required synchronization was achieved. In theory.

"Ready, Professor," the young man called out, his voice echoing down the passageway.

"Clock up, starting synchronization run," came the answer.

They had been through this dozens of times before with little success. Some small glitch would always mess up the procedure. And it was hard to concentrate on the equipment with a party of armed men about to burst in on them.

As if his thoughts triggered the event, a new voice shouting in Arabic could be heard echoing within the cave. He heard the professor greet the strangers.

"Salam alaikum." Peace be upon you.

The reply was a rapid stream of Arabic, from which the young man only understood *kafir*—unbeliever. And then the unthinkable.

There was a burst of sound—loud, flat cracks that could only be gunfire. More yelling in Arabic and another burst of gunfire, felt as much as heard within the confined space of the cave.

My God, he thought, *they've killed the Professor.*

Then it dawned on him that he was trapped in the cave with no way out and no place to hide. As sure as the intruders had killed the Professor, his own death would follow shortly.

This was not the way his life was supposed to end. His academic career had barely started when he signed on to be the professor's assistant. This trip to the desert mountains of eastern Arabia was a way to build his resume, to get some field time, to begin a life of scholarship. Instead his future was about to be taken from him.

His head was spinning. To steady himself he raised an arm to head height and placed it cross wise against the artifact's smooth, unyielding surface. Squeezing his eyes tightly shut in a vain effort to stop the hot tears that ran down his cheeks, he could hear the killers making their way down the tunnel toward him. Feeling a weakness born of utter helplessness, the young man leaned his head against his arm.

As he moved to lean against the artifact, signals from the two sets of electronic instruments achieved that which had previously eluded the two scientists. Synchronization.

Within the artifact an intelligence awoke. Within a few hundred femtoseconds it had evaluated the entrance code. Signals were sent, subsystems activated, sensors aligned. The situation outside of the hull was analyzed at length, several nanoseconds past as the intelligence weighed options.

Quantum entanglements formed, probability fields collapsed and finally, a decision was reached. More signals were sent. The material properties of a portion of the hull were altered. What had been impenetrable became permeable.

The young man, still in the act of leaning against the artifact's surface, fell through it into darkness.

Part One

Leaving West Texas

Chapter 1

West Texas, USA, present day

Peggy Sue gazed out of the window of the KWTEX news van at the passing West Texas countryside. Like it or not, this was her home. "A whole lot of nothing," as the locals would say. Scrub brush, tumble weeds and a few cattle scattered across table top flat country. Occasionally a rock or small mountain poked up to give some sense of distance, but otherwise it just looked like the flat went on forever.

From Odesa west to Pecos, and from Kermit, up near the New Mexico border, south to Fort Stockton, that was her beat. Mainly the triangle of land formed by Interstates 10 and 20. Oh, it wasn't all as flat as the heart of the Permian Basin area. There were the seemingly endless sand dunes near Monahans, the Guadalupe Mountains to the west and the Stockton Plateau to the south. But it was still one of the most uninhabited areas in the continental United States.

For example, take Mentone, county seat and only community in Loving County, where they had been that morning to interview the local mayor. Loving County has the distinction of being the least populous county in the entire contiguous United States. In 2000, its population was 67. By 2006, the population had risen to 71 but by 2010 it had dipped to only 45. That's the way things are in far West Texas—boom or bust.

Thinking of Mentone brought a fleeting smile to her face.

"You seem particularly pensive today, Miss Susan," said JT, her driver and cameraman.

"I was just thinking about Mentone," she replied, "and Kermit." On the air she went by Susan Write, but everyone back home still knew her as Peggy Sue Whitaker. That's how it is when you come from the land of Billy Joes and Jim Bobs. She liked to blame her two part "good 'ol gal" name on Lubbock native Charles Hardin Holly.

Since no one else in her family was named Peggy Sue and it was not really a common name, even in Texas, Susan credited her unusual christening to Mr. Holly. Though he died in a plane crash long before her mother was born, Holly left behind a song about a girl called Peggy Sue. Of course, he preferred to be called Buddy. Lucky for her, nobody in Texas went by their given name.

"Kermit? The green sock puppet?"

"What?" Her train of thought interrupted, it took a few seconds for the question to register. "No, Kermit my home town. Back in 1966, the town moved the last working wooden oil derrick in the Permian Basin from Loving County to Pioneer Park. People say things in Loving County haven't been the same since."

"Not very kind to the folks in Mentone," JT snorted. "You sure your home town wasn't named after the frog?"

"Actually it was named after Teddy Roosevelt's son. He visited back around the turn of the last century."

"How do you know all this stuff? I mean, you're a walking encyclopedia of West Texas trivia."

"I'm running for Historian of the Permian Basin," she quipped.

They lapsed back into silence as the endless flat countryside scrolled by. Her relationship with JT was good—better than the two cameramen that preceded him. He at least understood that nonstop chatter was not a desirable thing when traversing the endless flat terrain surrounding them. Spare use of both water and conversation was the West Texas way. Out of the corner of her eye she could see JT wrinkle his brow in thought.

"Permian Basin?" he asked, curiosity getting the better of him.

"I forget that you weren't born around here," she sighed, switching to her on-air narrator's voice: "The Permian Basin is named for the geologic formation that is buried under this area—rock strata that was laid down during the Permian Period more than 250 million years ago, before the dinosaurs evolved."

"OK, and that's important because?"

"It's important because deep down that old rock is as buckled and wrinkled as the surface is flat. It created traps for oil and gas to form, and without oil and gas there would be even fewer people in West Texas than there are in Loving County."

"Ah, oil. That I understand. But I still don't get it."

"Get what?"

"Why you act the dumb blond when you interview these local yahoos. You are obviously smarter than you let on."

"Smart doesn't necessarily get a woman what she wants in West Texas, but pretty and dumb often does." And that's the truth she thought, bitterly.

Peggy Sue had been blessed by nature with cornflower blue eyes, honey blond hair, and a tall curvacious body—a natural Texas beauty. She was also gifted by nature with a keen intellect and a sharp wit. In her youth that wit often resulted in sarcastic remarks and the intellect a knowing air that many interpreted as smugness. As a child she was called precocious, but by the time she reached high school her blessings were more of a curse.

The football and cowboy crowd were put off by her intelligence and sharp tongue while the smart, nerdy boys were intimidated by her physical beauty—it was lose-lose in the romance department. She had to ask a boy to take her to the senior prom in order to get a date. Two things taught her how and when to hide her intellectual gifts and when to use her feminine wiles: the Miss Texas beauty contest and going to college.

She came in third runner up for Miss Texas, which taught her that she couldn't depend on being the prettiest girl in the room to get her what she wanted. But third runner up was good enough for a scholarship that allowed her to earn a degree in communications and journalism from Texas A&M.

That degree, along with being telegenic and smart, had gotten her a job as a roving reporter for KWTEX, the "West Texas News Authority." Not that bouncing around the Permian Basin dust bowl in a news van was where she wanted to be, but it was a start.

Reality intruded on her reminiscence in the form of Stevie Ray Vaughn blasting out the opening of "Texas Flood." Stevie Ray was another Texan musician whose life was cut short by an aeronautical mishap—*what was it with rock stars and airplane crashes?* In this case, the smoking hot blues song indicated an incoming call from her boss, station manager Ed Stanton.

"Yes, Ed?" she asked, bringing the iPhone to her ear.

11

"Suzy, I need you and JT to get on down to Upton County and check out a rancher who's building a rocket ship on his spread," her boss said without preamble.

She sighed. She hated it when he called her "Suzy" but he signed her paychecks. "Are you going to tell me who this rancher is and where he's located? Or do you intend for us to just start asking about him at the next roadside diner?"

"Terrance Kinkade Parker, goes by TK," her manager replied, ignoring Susan's sarcasm. "Made a fortune in oil and the last gas boom. He's rumored to be worth billions."

"Imagine that, a rich, eccentric Texas oilman. We've never done that story before."

"Not one with his own space program we ain't. I want this for the six o'clock tonight, so tell JT to hustle y'all on down there." The line went dead.

"Great, he didn't give the address." Sometimes she really hated that overbearing old redneck.

"What's up, Miss Susan? Are we off on a hot new assignment?"

"Yeah, Big Ed has heard a rumor about some billionaire oilman who's building his own rocket ship in Upton county."

"OK," he replied, leaning over to play with the satnav system between them. "You know that may not be as far out as it sounds. With NASA pretty much out of the manned rocket business there are a number of rich private investors trying to get into the astronaut transport business."

"Yeah, you know you're right? Ever since the shuttle was retired our astronauts have had to hitch rides to and from the ISS with the Russians."

"Un huh, damned humiliating for NASA. And expensive."

"Looks like this guy's ranch is northeast of Castle Gap, pretty much in the middle of nowhere," Susan announced, consulting the Internet via her iPhone. "You need to head for Crane, then south on state road 385."

"Ah, Crane, another thriving metropolis," JT muttered, as he turned the van south, off of Interstate 10 and onto the state highway.

"County seat of scenic Crane County, and right next to the Upton County line," she replied. Oh well, she thought, it was better than talking to some podunk town's mayor about his plans to revitalize the local golf course. "Then look for Ma Earp Road heading east past Castle Gap to county road 300."

"And just what is Castle Gap?"

"Castle Gap is a mile-long break in the Castle Mountains 12 miles north-northwest of Horsehead Crossing. It's bordered by King Mountain on the southern end and Castle Mountain to the north." Susan smiled her best beauty contest smile and brightly announced, "Why everyone who was anyone in West Texas history visited the Gap at one time or another."

"This," JT said, "sounds like more fun than when we covered the Pecos Cantaloupe Festival."

"You keep driving, I'll fiddle with the navigation system." She put the phone away and turned her attention to the in-dash map display. *What did people do before we got these things*, she wondered? *Wander around lost a lot, most likely.*

Goodfellow AFB, San Angelo, Texas

There are no Marine bases in the state of Texas, but there is a Marine presence in the form of an air wing and pilot training facility co-located with the Corpus Christie Naval Air Station. As with all branches of the military, since the winding down of the wars in Iraq and Afghanistan, it was a time of tight budgets and threatened program cutbacks. As a result, public relations had become an even more important part of the Marine Corps' daily mission.

One of the programs that had been in jeopardy since its inception was the V-22 Osprey, a twin rotor, tilt-wing aircraft that was intended to become the Corps' primary rotary wing asset. The V-22 Osprey takes off and lands vertically like a helicopter but flies like a plane by tilting its wing-mounted rotors to function as propellers. The idea behind its design was to combine a helicopter's operational flexibility with the greater speed, range, and efficiency of a fixed-wing aircraft.

Begun in 1982 by the Army and funded in part by the Air Force, the V-22 became primarily a Marine Corps program paid for by the Navy. Development had been troubled from the start, with a number of deadly crashes that claimed the lives of 34 men, 30 of them Marines. Even so, attempts to kill the program—including one by then Secretary of Defense Dick Cheney—all failed. Eventually, after almost 20 years in development, the first Ospreys entered the service.

The Marine version, designated the MV-22, can transport 24 fully-equipped troops some 200 nautical miles at a speed of 250 knots, significantly exceeding the performance of the CH-46 "Battle Phrog" medium-lift assault helicopters the MV-22 was meant to replace. In Afghanistan, the MV-22 was able to fly two missions to every one flown by the more conventional CH-53 heavy-lift helos. Faster, farther, higher and with more lift capacity, the Osprey was intended to be the backbone of Marine Corps Aviation Assault Support for the 21st Century.

The Corps now had several hundred of the aircraft in service and planed on buying several hundred more, assuming its critics and congressional budget cutters could be held at bay. And that was why the Corps sent an Osprey and a squad of Marines to the yearly Air Fiesta at San Angelo Regional Airport. It was hoped that seeing one of the multimillion dollar beasts up close and personal would make civilians think more kindly of both the Corps and its primary aerial transport. Reminding Texas voters that the Osprey was assembled in Amarillo couldn't hurt either.

The Osprey had been in the Corps longer than Gunnery Sergeant Jennifer Rodriguez, and the way things look it would outlast her as well. Soon to be discharged from the service, this could be her last ride in one of the cantankerous aircraft. All she could think of when she had been ordered to form a squad of soon-to-be-separated Marines for "special duty" at the San Angelo air show was the term "vortex ring state."

VRS was a technical term for exceeding the Osprey's flight envelope by descending too fast. Essentially, the craft could fly into its own downdraft and lose control. The result was generally dead

Marines. According to Marine Corps scuttlebutt, this was what happened when your transport tried to perform unnatural acts on itself during flight. All Rodriguez could think of was that it would be a real bitch to die at an air show after spending twelve years in the Corps.

"Where are we going again, Gunny?" asked Lance Corporal Feldman. Like the Gunny and the seven other Marines and one Hospital Corpsman on Operation Air Fiesta, Jon Feldman was due to muster out of the service in less than a week. The military was cutting back everywhere, including personnel. That didn't mean they were only letting the screw-ups and misfits go, but you couldn't prove it by this group.

"Mathis Field," Gunny Rodriguez shouted back, "by way of Goodfellow Air Force Base. Now shut up and enjoy the ride." At least one good thing could be said about the MV-22, it was about 75% quieter inside than a CH-46 Sea Knight or the heavier CH-53 Sea Stallion.

Established long ago as Carr Field, the squads' eventual destination had been a military training center since before World War II. Over the decades, it was known by a number of names, including at one time Concho Army Air Field and San Angelo Army Air Field. Finally, after WWII, it was designated Mathis Field in honor of Jack Mathis, a B-17 pilot who was posthumously awarded the Congressional Medal of Honor for some now forgotten act of aerial daring-do. The airport was now owned by the City of San Angelo and was classified by the FAA as a commercial primary, non-hub airport. In other words, it was the local regional airport. Still, it was the only commercial airport serving the Concho Valley and its three runways stayed open for operations 24 hours a day to commercial, private and military aviation.

Nearby Goodfellow Air Force Base was a non-flying Air Force installation, meaning there were no active flight squadrons stationed there. Instead, as part of the Air Education & Training Command (AETC), Goodfellow's main mission was cryptographic and intelligence training for all four main branches of the US military. There were Army, Navy, Air Force and Marine Corps personnel stationed there for training purposes. The MV-22 would be stopping at Goodfellow to pick up some lucky Marine Lieutenant who would be in-charge of what was basically a PR mission.

15

The squad Rodriguez had assembled was a sorry bunch: a Corporal, three Lance Corporals, and three Privates First Class. The number of PFCs was an indication of her charges' underachiever status. In the Corps all ranks below Corporal (E-4) were promoted at the company level. In theory, unit commanders decided who got promoted and who didn't. In practice, because there are no quotas for promotion to PFC (E-2) and LCpl (E-3), commanders pretty much promoted everyone after they meet the "promotion criteria," essentially time in grade without screwing up.

This meant that a newly minted Private should be a PFC six months after boot camp, and a LCpl after an additional nine. In fact, there were twice as many LCpls in the Corps as there were PFCs. This implied that these PFCs either screwed up or did not perform their duties in a satisfactory manner. Of course, the Gunny herself had not managed to qualify for one of the few open, highly competitive, E-8 slots.

"Hey Gunny," PFC Sanchez shouted from the rear of the compartment, interrupting the Gunny's train of thought. "How come we got rifles but no ammo on board?"

"Because the Corps doesn't want one of you maggots shooting any civilians by mistake." The thought of this squad of misfits running around with live ammo near a crowd of civilians gave her the willies.

"Then why do we have to lug the rifles around?"

Rodriguez gave him "the eye," but the PFC continued to stare back with a puzzled look on his face. No wonder Sanchez was getting the boot, a Marine was expected to be a rifleman regardless of his MOS, military occupational specialty. As such, he was expected to grab his rifle, say "aye aye" and get on with it—not play 20 questions with his Sergeant.

The Osprey's attitude shifted, signaling the beginning of their descent into Goodfellow, where they were to pick up one Lt. Ernest Merryweather. Merryweather was to command the non-aviation personnel for the duration of the airshow assignment. Rodriguez wondered what he had done wrong to be shanghaied into airshow duty. "All right, Marines. Listen up."

"We are about to land at Goodfellow Air Force Base. We will not be dismounting. I will exit the aircraft to report our status to Lt. Merryweather, who will be assuming command of this detachment for the duration of the operation. You will sit here until I return. Do not play with your weapons or yourselves. As soon as the LT is on board we will take off for Mathis Field.

"Do not talk to the Lieutenant unless spoken to. When we get to the airshow we will exit the aircraft by the aft cargo ramp, fan out and form a perimeter. You will keep your weapons pointed at the ground. Do not under any circumstances point your weapon at the civilians or anyone else for that matter. Look sharp and remember that you are Marines. The Lieutenant is in command but your asses belong to me until we are back in Corpus Christie. Do you understand me?"

The weak chorus of mumbled replies could barely be heard over the background noise.

"I SAID, DO YOU UNDERSTAND?"

"YES, GUNNY!" came the reply, as the Marines sat up, eyes forward, as close to "attention" as they could come and remain seated.

At least they still have Marine reflexes Rodriguez thought, when an NCO shouts at them they straighten up and sound off. Not that it mattered, in less than a week both she and her squad of misfits would be civilians. Oh well, one last goatfuck for the Corps—Oorah!

Parker Ranch, Upton County, Texas

TK Parker was getting a status report from his Captain and First Officer, John "Jack" Sutton and Gretchen Curtis. Which is to say, he was leading them around the old converted airship hanger that housed his pride and joy, haranguing them to get things ready faster. It was difficult for Capt. Sutton and Lt. Curtis to keep up because Parker was riding in his custom electric wheelchair, which could easily move at faster than walking speeds.

"We have to get a move on. I have it on good authority that word of our little project has leaked to the press," TK was saying as he rounded the front of the raised platform, passing under the nose of what might have been mistaken for a dirigible at first glance. "Just got a call from some damn lady reporter who's on her way to interview me."

"And just how did the news media find out about the project?" asked the Captain. "We've managed to keep the curtain drawn tight for 18 months. It's hard to believe that now, with the ship almost ready, we've had a security breach."

Jack Sutton was a tall man, 6'2" with intense brown eyes and sandy brown hair starting to go silver at the temples. A short, dark beard framed his jaw. Trim and erect, he was having trouble maintaining a dignified stride keeping pace with the speeding wheelchair. *He does that on purpose,* the Captain thought, slightly annoyed.

"Who knows? One of the workers gone into town and got a snoot full," snapped TK. "Can't stand a man—or a woman, for that matter —that can't hold his liquor. Or anyone can't keep their yap shut."

"I doubt it was any of our people, Sir," Curtis interjected. She was designated the ship's first officer and was also responsible for site security. "I suspect it was someone from one of the supply deliveries. We started provisioning food and medical supplies this past week and plants for the hydroponics section yesterday."

Gretchen Curtis was not as tall as the Captain but she was certainly near six foot. Her roan red hair was pulled back in a tucked French braid, her trim figure projected a military bearing. A graduate of the US Naval Academy and former Lieutenant in the US Navy, the green-eyed first officer took her duties very seriously indeed—perhaps to the point of overcompensation. In the Navy she had felt the need to constantly prove herself as good or better than her male counterparts. It was a habit she had not dropped since becoming a civilian.

"Damn outside contractors!" continued TK, "ain't none of them worth a shit." TK was famous for his colorful language. Pushing 80, confined to a wheelchair and with billions in the bank he once told a Dallas society matron who criticized his vocabulary, "I don't give a rat's ass what you think, woman, and neither does anyone else!"

Fact was, the only thing TK did care about was looming above him in the brightly lit vastness of the old airship hanger. The hangar itself was his primary reason for purchasing this particularly worthless piece of ranch land. The object of his affection was a long cigar shape, crafted from crystal and silver, whose curving flanks disappeared into the distance of the huge hanger.

Looking vaguely like an unpainted submarine hull with the glass nose of a vintage bomber, TK Parker's spaceship was overwhelming at first sight. Gleaming metal with a number of rounded rectangular openings along its flanks, it looked like something out of a science fiction story or a Hollywood film. A number of viewing ports, some large, some small, dotted the ship's flanks along with several teardrop shaped metallic blisters. But it was the nose that drew an observer's eyes back.

The bow of the ship was made of transparent panels that conformed to the curve of the ship's hull. Like on a vintage WWII B-29 bomber, the transparent sections continued back along the sides and top creating a greenhouse effect. Unlike the more or less rectangular glass panels of a B-29, the transparent sections forming this ship's nose were of seemingly random shapes, separated by curvacious silver strips where the panels adjoined. It was Superfortress meets Star Wars meets modern art.

This was the ship Hollywood would have given Buck Rogers in the 1930s serials if they had the budget and better construction methods. One of the assembly workers called it an art-deco space sausage. In fact, most of the workers thought the ship an old eccentric's fantasy or a prop for a new outer space TV series. Some of them referred to the vessel as Parker's Folly, though never in earshot of Parker. Very few of the workers actually expected the thing to ever fly, or even leave the hangar, for that matter. Little did they know how wrong they were.

Not that their doubts were unjustified, the aft end contained no giant rocket engines like the now defunct space shuttle or the even older Saturn 5 rockets that had launched astronauts to the moon. After a modest tapering, the ship ended in a slightly convex, featureless expanse of metal. There were no nozzles, no orifices, nothing to suggest an outlet for hot rocket gasses. The ship's aft was more like a gigantic boat-tailed artillery round, and for much the same reasons.

Parker's Folly was intended to be a spaceship, but a spaceship that could readily enter and leave a planetary atmosphere. It was what advanced rocket designers would call a SSO—single stage to orbit. There were no parts to be discarded during ascent or material to be lost to ablation on reentry, what went up came back down all in one piece. That was how the few people in the know expected the ship to function.

Among those in the know were TK, the Captain and Lt. Curtis, along with a handful of engineers. If Parker's Folly worked as planned it would change everything. No more rockets rising on columns of fire, throwing away large expensive chunks of themselves while expending millions of pounds of fuel to place a few thousand pounds of payload into orbit. At least that is what they all fervently hoped.

TK reached out and ran his hand across the curving hull above him in a loving caress. Then his high-tech wheelchair suddenly whipped about, rotating in place to face his ship's captain and first officer. "I got a bad feeling about this. If the news media knows about our little project there's sure to be some government snoops coming around. Damn government always looking for something to steal from honest folk."

Captain Sutton and Lt. Curtis stood at parade rest, both with their hands clasped behind their backs—they had heard TK's opinions about the government many times before.

"I'm going to go handle the busybodies from the fourth estate," the old man continued. "You two get the Folly ready to fly, and I mean now!"

His use of the name Folly for the ship caused Curtis to blink and the Captain to raise his eyebrows questioningly.

"What? You think I don't know what the workers call her? Well I've got no better name for her than Parker's Folly and it will just help rub their noses in it when she blasts outa' here." Without further comment he again pivoted his electric wheelchair in place and headed off toward the exit ramp and the path back to the ranch house a half mile away.

"Well," said the Captain, "I believe we have been given 'prepare for imminent departure' orders. We still need to run a successful full-power system test—hopefully Dr. Gupta has the muonium problem solved."

"I'll head back to the engine room and inform him we are about to run another test," replied the First Officer. Sutton nodded tacit approval as they walked up the ramp to the forward airlock together. Entering the ship, she headed aft through officer country while the Captain climbed up a level to the bridge.

* * * * *

Upon reaching the aft engineering spaces, Curtis sighted the slender form of Dr. Rajiv Gupta hunched over a glowing display panel. Gupta, who had PhDs in both Chemistry and Physics, was, for lack of a better title, the ship's chief engineer. If anyone understood how the mysterious devices in the aft portion of the ship functioned it was Rajiv.

His dark skin, black hair and dark brown eyes reflected his Indian heritage, though he had been born in San Jose. As with many children of immigrants, Rajiv was an academic overachiever, earning degrees from Stanford (elemental particle physics) and Cal Tech (physical and theoretical chemistry). He also picked up an undergraduate degree in Electrical Engineering and a masters in Computer Science along the way, both from Berkeley. After bouncing around various universities, high-tech companies and government research labs he had somehow been enticed into working on Parker's Folly.

"Dr. Gupta, how are things going?" asked Curtis.

"Oh, it is you Gretchen," said the scientist, looking up. "What brings you to my mad scientist's lair?" Dr. Gupta was gregarious and outgoing by nature, tending to call everyone by their given name. The ship's officers, all having some form of military background, tended to be more formal, but that did not affect Gupta in the slightest—everyone was the equivalent of a colleague or at least a graduate student in his world view.

At some institutions, particularly in undergraduate programs, the professors insisted on being called Doctor or Professor, but most graduate schools took the approach that everyone, student and teacher alike, were all scholars working together and hence on a first name basis. This made sense to Rajiv and he saw no reason to change his attitude.

"Mr. Parker has expressed a desire to have the ship ready for imminent departure. The Captain is on the bridge and sent me here to see when we can run a full-power system check."

"Well, I have made a number of changes to the calibration settings but I have not been able to verify that the spurious production of muonium has been overcome. As you know, the power plant's reaction rates depend on the isotopic identity of the reactants and products. Basically, it is a manifestation of the role quantum zero-point energy plays in chemical kinetics and is a consequence of the Born-Oppenheimer separation of electronic and nuclear motion in molecules."

"Of course, Doctor," said Lt. Curtis. She had a masters in aeronautical engineering but Rajiv's words may as well have been Martian. No matter, he was in full lecture mode and she would just have to wait until he wound down before asking another question. She nodded encouragingly.

"You see, we need negatively charged muons to catalyze a fusion reaction within the quantum channel matrix. A muon weighs 207 times as much as an electron and can act as either a very heavy electron or a very light proton, depending of course on the muon's charge. Replace a deuterium or tritium atom's single electron with a negative muon and the *1s* orbital shrinks down to only 0.2 picometers. When a pair of these atoms try to form a molecule of H_2 their nuclei are brought close enough together for fusion to take place.

"The presence of muonium, which is essentially a hydrogen molecule with the single nucleus proton replaced by a positive muon, is an indication that the muon generator is making both positive and negative muons. As a result, the reactor is making power but not at peak efficiency and there may be other side effects if allowed to run under these conditions."

"And have your adjustments fixed the problem, Rajiv?" Gretchen knew he liked it when she used his first name.

"I hope so," he said, turning back to the battery of displays, "I truly hope so."

"So I can tell the Captain to run the test?"

"Yes, yes. By all means, I was ready to suggest running another test myself."

* * * * *

On the bridge, the Captain was making ready to power up the ship's main systems. They had gone through this several times before, but had never reached full sustained power without an alarm sounding or a cluster of warning lights flashing.

"Bridge, Engineering."

"Go Engineering."

"Captain, we are ready for a full-power system test. Dr. Gupta has recalibrated some of the reactor settings and is hopeful that the previous problem has been corrected."

"Affirmative, Engineering. Test commencing in 10."

The Captain activated the exterior PA system. "Attention, all personnel in the hanger space. Please proceed immediately to the closest radiation shelter, there will be an engine check in 10, repeat, 10 minutes." The ship's power system was not supposed to produce any detectable radiation, but the last two tests had resulted in small bursts of gamma rays and some errant neutrons. Everything inside the ship was well shielded, but those outside could be exposed. The levels were probably not high enough to be dangerous but there was no sense taking any chances.

"Attention Control," he said, activating the ship's voice command system. "Prepare for full-power system test in 10 minutes. Verbal notifications at five and one minutes prior to test."

"Yes, Captain," came the immediate reply in the androgynous voice used by the ship's computer.

Outside, technicians and construction workers rapidly evacuated the platform surrounding the ship. Looking forward, through the ship's transparent nose, a vertical line of light could be seen marking the crack between the two closed hangar doors. The hangar was originally constructed during WWII to house Navy lighter-than-air craft. Made mostly of wood, the egg-shaped arch of the roof shell was stiffened with a series of transverse metal ribs.

The building was 525 feet long, 148 feet wide and 87.5 feet high, a half scale version of similar structures built at Tillamook, Oregon, and Tustin, California.

The huge pair of doors opened by sliding sideways in the overhead tracks that they hung from. Aside from the light leaking in from the doors, the only natural light came from the twin rows of vents along the peak of the roof. *A large, imposing man-made space, housing a mysterious, otherworldly machine—a scene worthy of a James Bond movie villain,* he thought to himself.

TK in his hot-rod wheelchair might just fit that image, but Jack could not see himself in the role of Captain Nemo or Dr. Evil. His life had been full of adventures, and not a few misadventures, but he never thought that he would command a spaceship, even one sitting in a construction hangar on good old Mother Earth.

On a whim, he addressed the ship's computer again, "Control, would it be possible for me to give you an alternate name?"

"Of course, Captain, you may call me anything you like."

"I would like you to respond to the name 'Folly' from now on, if you don't mind." Why not he thought, even TK had used the name, and it would be a lot more natural than using 'Control'.

"Very well, you can address me as 'Folly' from now on. It does seem quite apropos."

Apropos? That darn computer was acting more human every day. Both sailors and airmen claimed their vessels developed their own unique personalities over time. This, however, was taking things to an extreme.

"Attention all personnel, five minutes to power system test" the PA announced.

Chapter 2

Upton County, Texas, Near the Parker Ranch

The KWTEX news van pulled up at the gate to TK Parker's ranch. In front of the idling van was a nondescript but sturdy looking gate. Beyond the gate was a dirt road that showed little sign of maintenance. Off in the distance there appeared to be a low ranch style house and farther beyond that, obscured by haze and blowing dust, a much larger structure.

"You want to get out and look for a doorbell or should I," asked JT, flexing his arms and back against the seat and steering wheel.

"I'll do it," Susan replied, "I see a box on the gate poll on my side. Besides, I need to get the kinks out of my back and stretch my legs."

Hopping out of the van, she arched her back and then twisted her torso from side to side. *This is truly the back-end of nowhere,* she thought, *what would motivate a billionaire to buy such a place, let alone live here? I guess you couldn't build a space ship in your backyard in Austin or Dallas without the neighbors complaining, no matter how rich you were.*

The box had a grill, presumably hiding a speaker, and a single large button. "Here goes nothing," she called to JT, then pressing the button and speaking loudly into the box: "Hello, anyone there?"

"Hola, who is there?" came the answer in a female voice with a pronounced Spanish accent.

"Hola Señora, this is Susan Write with KWTEX news. I called earlier and made an appointment to see Mr Parker."

"Si, please drive up to the house. I will tell Señor Parker that you are here."

"Thank you," Susan said, but the only answer was a burst of static. "OK, now what happens?" she shouted to JT on the other side of the still idling van. With a clank, the gate opened and swung smoothly, almost silently aside.

"That gate may look like crap, but it is obviously well maintained," JT observed, adding with mock seriousness, "perhaps things around here are not what they seem."

"If you mean a broken down ranch in the middle of the West Texas desert scrub, I reserve judgment until we see the inside of the house. Now drive, before the gate swings back shut."

* * * * *

As they pulled up to the front of the ranch house the front door opened. A middle aged Hispanic woman wearing a kitchen apron appeared in the doorway and beckoned them in. Exiting the van, JT went around to the back to get his camera rig. Then, together they approached the portal.

"Hi, I'm Susan Write and this" Susan said, motioning to her partner, "is JT, my camera man."

"Welcome," the woman said, "I am Maria, Señor Parker's housekeeper and cook. Please follow me. Señor Parker is in his study."

Maria led them through the living room, past a breakfast nook and adjoining family room and to the door of Parker's study. The house was much larger than it appeared from the outside, probably around 4,000 sq ft. They also noticed that all of the doors were wider than normal and that all the sills in the doorways were almost flat.

Knocking on the study door, then opening it without waiting for a response, Maria announced them. "Señorita Write and party, Señor Parker." Smiling, she turned and motioned them inside.

An old man with an unruly shock of white hair looked up from the papers on his desk and waved with one hand. "Welcome" he said. There was a muted whine of electric motors and the man pivoted sideways. Then he smoothly moved around the heavy wooden desk, rolling forward to greet them. If that was not enough of a shock—they had not been warned that TK Parker was wheelchair bound—when the chair stopped in front of them Parker, wheelchair and all, stood up and extended his hand.

Susan, news professional that she was, didn't miss a beat. She grasped the proffered hand with a firm grip and shook it, the way

Texan's do. The firm handshake was something she had learned early in life. Some women just stick their hand out like a limp, dead fish when shaking hands. Susan shook hands like she meant it, like she was the other man's equal. She could see Parker sizing her up, with a twinkle in his pale blue-gray eyes.

"Mr. Parker, I'm Susan Write from KWTEX News, and this is my cameraman Jim Taylor," she said motioning to JT who was standing behind her, camera dangling from his left hand.

"Nice to meet you, Jim," Parker said. As he leaned forward to shake JT's hand the motorized chair, now balancing on two wheels, moved closer to him as if by telepathic control. "Welcome to my spread, have a seat. As you can see, I already have one."

As he uttered the last sentence, his wheelchair collapsed on itself, lowering him back to a seated position. Parker whirled about and reclaimed his position behind the desk.

"Call me JT, Mr. Parker," said the camera man. "That's some wheelchair you have there. I've never seen anything like it."

"Call me TK, son, everybody does. Yeah, this little beauty is an iBot. It was design back in the 00s by Dean Kamen, same guy who designed the Segway."

"Segway, that two wheeled, standup scooter you see mall cops whizzing around on?" asked Susan, trying to reclaim control of the conversation. It was obvious that Parker was a gear-head and JT loved gadgets. If they started talking about technology they could be here for hours.

"Yes indeed. He made a bunch of these things—an electric, motorized wheelchair that can go from four wheels to two wheels lifting the rider in the process, and it can climb stairs too. Unfortunately, the damn things cost a fortune and they discontinued making them in 2009. Insurance companies and Medicaid didn't want to foot the bill, cheap bastards."

"If they were discontinued in 2009 you must have owned it for some time."

"No, when they were for sale I hadn't had my accident yet, but you can find nearly anything on the Internet. Managed to pick up a couple of busted ones on eBay. And given a boot full of cash, I managed to get one of the original engineers to build me a working one using the broken chairs for parts. Had him hop it up a little bit, too.

"I'm one of the few people in the world that has a hot rod four wheel drive without owning a truck," TK chuckled, "but I don't think you're here to talk about my wheelchair."

"Well, no sir," started Susan.

"I said call me TK, girl. No need bein' so formal."

"TK then. We got a tip that your wheelchair is not the only futuristic vehicle you own. Word on the street is that you are building a rocket ship in your barn."

"Ain't a barn, its a dirigible hanger. And it ain't a rocket ship, it's a spaceship."

"Dirigible hanger?" said JT.

"Not a rocket ship?" said Susan.

"Right" said TK.

On Board Parker's Folly, Parker Ranch, Texas

"Attention, power system test commencing," announced the ship's voice, followed almost immediately by a cascade of flashing red lights and blaring klaxons.

"Excessive radiation emissions detected, test terminated," said the unruffled ship's voice.

Well, at least the warning system works, thought Jack. "Engineering, Bridge. Dr. Gupta, what just happened?"

"Well, it would appear that something different happened this time. My readings no longer indicate an excess of muonium. There is, however, a very strange indication of some anomalously heavy hydrogen atoms poisoning the fusion reaction and causing the quantum grid to generate an excess of radiation."

"Heavy hydrogen? I was under the impression that the ship's engines required deuterium and tritium to run."

"Oh no, this is much heavier than tritium," said the ship's engineer. "This seems to be heavy enough to be hydrogen 4, quadrium. Or an atom of helium. Really quite fascinating."

The Captain sighed silently. To Jack it was a failed system test, to Gupta it was an interesting experimental result. "The fusion process normally makes helium, correct? And you're telling me we are now making heavier hydrogen isotopes instead?"

"Highly unstable nuclei—hydrogen 4 through hydrogen 7—have been synthesized in the laboratory but their half-lives are on the order of a few picoseconds. What we are seeing are much longer lived atoms. I know the muon beam initiators are not making positively charged muons anymore, this new problem makes little sense."

"Dr. Gupta, could you tell me about the radiation emissions? What effect did this test have on the people in the area and on board?"

"What? Oh, the radiation—anyone who was in one of the shelters or inside of the ship should be perfectly safe. Beyond a hundred meters it would not be dangerous either."

"That's a relief, Doctor. I take it we cannot run the ship under these conditions, could you please get back to me when we are ready for the next attempt? Bridge out." *Great*, Jack thought, *another delay. TK will not be pleased.*

* * * * *

In the engineering compartment, Lt. Curtis stood staring at the flashing warning indicators and scrolling columns of numbers on the monitor readouts. Gupta was pacing back and fourth, obviously in deep thought. As she understood the problem, each muon needed to catalyze a few thousand fusion reactions to generate a usable amount of power. Since muons only lived a couple of microseconds this meant channeling the muons so they struck a sufficient number of hydrogen atoms.

Since muons had a tendency to "stick" to the resulting helium atoms it was also a good idea to remove the helium byproduct from the reactor area as soon as possible. All of this was the job of the quantum grid matrix. Somehow things were going wrong inside the grid—power was way down and excessive amounts of neutrons and gamma rays were being emitted. From what they had seen in earlier tests, it was like the waste helium was not getting removed.

"Rajiv, this seems similar to the helium removal problems we were having earlier," she ventured.

It took Gupta a few seconds to realize that someone had spoken to him. "Yes, yes it does Gretchen. But we eliminated that problem and the readings are not showing any helium buildup in the reaction matrix. It is so strange... OF COURSE!"

Gretchen was startled by the sudden outburst. She had never seen Rajiv having an "ah ha!" moment before. As all good scientists know, the words that come just before a great discovery are usually "that's strange?"

"Of course what, Rajiv?" she asked.

"My dear Gretchen, the heaviest usable isotope of Hydrogen can be created by using a negative muon (μ^-) to replace an electron in Helium to form $He\mu$, with an atomic mass of 4.116. Because the muon is much heavier than an electron, its $1s$ orbital is very close to the nucleus, effectively screening one proton charge, so that $He\mu$ may be considered a virtual isotope of Hydrogen. The matrix is filtering out all the helium but it thinks these hybrid atoms are hydrogen!"

"Wow, that's exciting, Rajiv," Lt. Curtis said, trying to be supportive. "Is there a way to filter those out as well?"

"Why yes," the diminutive scientists said, almost bubbling over with excitement. "It should be a simple matter of recalibrating the charge gradient across the quantum matrix..." His voice trailed off as he attacked the control panel keyboard, rapidly adjusting the reactor's calibration parameters once again.

* * * * *

"Bridge, Engineering"

"Go Engineering," replied the Captain. Fifteen agonizing minutes had passed since the failed power test and Jack was still trying to figure out how to tell TK that his ship remained earthbound.

"I have good news, Captain. Rajiv, er, make that Dr. Gupta has identified the problem and has already started implementing a fix. We should be ready to retest in about ten more minutes."

"Do I want to know what the problem was this time?" he asked.

"Hybrid muon helium masquerading as very heavy hydrogen. Seems that it confused the quantum matrix's helium extraction process."

"Hm, naturally. Glad I held off on telling Parker. Let me know when we are ready to give it another shot. It's near the end of the day so I am going to tell the workers to go home. No sense having them resume what they were doing just to be sent back to the shelters for another test."

"Yes, Sir. I'll let you know soonest. Engineering out."

AFTAC, Patrick AFB, Florida

Senior Airman Robinson stared with a mixture of frustration and despair at the sensor display in front of him. *Great, shift's almost over and we get a malfunction. Either that or someone just set off a small nuke somewhere in the Southwest. No, make that western Texas. More than likely just the sensor array misfiring.* He sighed, he wouldn't be going off shift until the sensor reading was explained.

The Air Force Technical Applications Center (AFTAC) performs nuclear treaty monitoring and nuclear event detection. To accomplish this, AFTAC operates a global network of nuclear event detection sensors called the U.S. Atomic Energy Detection System. Once the USAEDS senses a disturbance, whether underground, underwater, in the atmosphere or in space, the event is analyzed for nuclear identification and findings are reported to national command authorities through U.S. Air Force Headquarters.

"Oh crap!" The sensor display now had Robinson's full attention. The high-energy neutron sensors just registered an event in the same vicinity as the gamma ray hit. That confirmed the gamma ray sensor alarm wasn't just a fluke or a stray cosmic ray—something highly irregular was happening southwest of Midland, Texas.

Naturally this would happen at the end of his shift, a holiday shift at that. Normally, Tech Sergeant Anderson would be manning this console. Instead Anderson was enjoying the day off and he was stuck here. *Well, protocol says to call the watch officer.* Raising his voice, Robinson called out, "Lieutenant, could you come here please?"

Lt. Jefferies was in the same position as SrA Robinson, he pulled holiday duty instead of the Captain—rank hath its privileges, as they say. "What is it Robinson? Not another cosmic ray cascade, I hope. We've had to run down enough false alarms for one day."

"No Sir. I've got coincident earthbound events on both gamma ray and neutron detection arrays. Looks to be about 150 kilometers west of Goodfellow Air Force Base."

The National Nuclear Security Administration (NNSA), a semi-autonomous agency within the U.S. Department of Energy, provides operational sensor payloads for integration onto USAF satellites. For example, IIF series Global Positioning System (GPS) satellites, carry improved nuclear detonation detection instruments built by Sandia National Laboratories and Los Alamos National Laboratory for the NNSA.

The sensors look for the tell-tale signs of a nuclear detonation, monitoring optical, electromagnetic pulse (EMP), X-ray, gamma ray and neutron emissions. All are part of the United States Nuclear Detonation Detection System (USNDS) which is designed to detect, locate, and report nuclear detonations (NUDETs) on Earth and in local space in near-real-time.

"Goodfellow? That's in Texas, right?"

"Yes Sir, right here on the display," he said, calling up the sensor estimated positions on the overhead map display.

"What about visual? Double hump?" All nuclear detonations emitted a characteristic double flash of light. Orbital detection systems that monitor for atmospheric nuclear explosions look for such double flashes. In fact, bomb yield can be determined from the interval between the two flash peaks. If this was a bomb going off on the surface or in the atmosphere, optical sensors should have picked up the telltale 'double hump.'

"No double hump, Sir, and no EMP either. If it was a NUDET it must have happened underground."

"If it was an underground detonation there should be shock waves. What does the seismological monitoring network say?" *Maybe some Texas oil men are using nukes for fracking gas wells,* the Lieutenant mused.

"I've got nothing on the seismic net. It must not have been a detonation. Let me search the recent log entries" the airman said, typing furiously on the keyboard in front of him. "Oh wow. There was a similar event logged two days ago, though not as strong, and another one seven days ago. All emanating from the same location. Sir, this cannot be a coincidence."

"Christ on a crutch," Jefferies muttered. "You're right Robinson. I'm going to bounce this upstairs to the Major—let her call the Colonel on his day off and tell him we have a Pinnacle event in West Texas." Pinnacle was a reporting flagword used in the U.S. National Command Authority structure. The term 'Pinnacle' denotes an incident of interest to the Major Commands, Department of Defense and National Command Authority.

Lieutenant Jefferies picked up the phone receiver from the console and punched speed-dial for the command post. "Major Bledsoe? This is Lt. Jefferies in the monitoring center. We have an unexplained anomalous event, Ma'am..."

Parker Ranch, Upton County, Texas

JT was standing with his mobile high-def camera rig on his shoulder, recording Susan with the towering bulk of the old dirigible hanger in the background. They had walked about half a mile from the ranch house and were just outside the hangar. Approaching the old building, it became evident just how large the structure was.

The station had called demanding a short clip that they could use to pique the public's interest. So, using the giant hanger as a backdrop, Susan and JT were recording a teaser spot that would be shown during the early news show—a preview of more to come on the main six o'clock news.

33

"What you see behind me is a World War II era dirigible hanger that supposedly contains something out of this world," Susan said into her hand mike while gazing intently into the camera. "Does a local rancher have his own private space program? Tune in tonight at six to see if the rumors are true." Then, with a practiced head toss, "Susan Write, KWTEX News, reporting live from the Parker Ranch in Upton County."

"Zooming out and panning left, and we're clear." JT lowered the camera from his shoulder.

"How was it?" Susan asked.

"Good, the sun is in the right place and the building looks huge—very impressive. You'll have them tuning in for sure."

"Great, that should get Ed off our backs. Now let's rejoin our host and see if there really is something worthwhile in the hangar."

As Susan turned toward the imposing structure, JT quickly punched the buttons that would send the short video through the relay in their van and on to the station. One of the station techs would cut it down and clean up the sound before broadcast. He had already sent some interior footage of Susan interviewing TK in his study. All the story lacked, he thought, was a spaceship.

Following Susan through a side door in the massive structure, it took a few seconds for his eyes to readjust to the light—the West Texas sun is bright even on a hazy day. As his vision faded in, JT saw the old man in his wheelchair and standing next to him a tall figure in black.

TK was addressing Susan, introducing the newcomer, "...and this is Lieutenant Curtis, the ship's First Officer. She'll give y'all the VIP tour. I've got to get back to the hacienda, we'll probably have more guests coming." With that prophetic statement, he exited down the door ramp and back down the trail toward the ranch house. Freed from his two legged entourage, TK put the hammer down on his hot rod wheelchair. Its rear tires threw up twin rooster tails of sand as he sped across the scrubby brushland.

JT barely noticed the old man's exit. He was staring at the Lieutenant—tall, broad shouldered, narrow waisted looking both very trim and very sexy in her midnight black jumpsuit. *Now there is a first officer I would love to serve under*, JT thought, a wide smile slowly spreading across his face, brilliant white against his mahogany colored skin.

"...and this is my camera man, JT," Susan was saying.

JT quickly juggled the camera and extended his hand, "Very nice to meet you, Lieutenant," he said. "We really appreciate you taking the time to show us around." Her handshake was firm and business like.

"My pleasure," said the red haired First Officer, "if you will please follow me."

Wow, I wonder if they are taking applications for crew on this voyage, the bedazzled camera man thought, watching the two women as they walked up the ramp leading to the interior of the hangar. As a former Special Forces operative, JT was a trained observer. It was a habit that had been drilled into him first as a paratrooper, then as an Army Ranger and finally as a Green Beret. Being observant, paying attention to details, is what made him a good camera man and it had literally saved his ass when he was deployed in Afghanistan.

What he was observing now was much more pleasant than trying to spot Kalashnikov toting towel-heads along a desolate Afghan ridgeline. Still, he could not help but compare the two women walking ahead of him. Susan, who was a truly stunning beauty, walked with an alluring sway that could stop traffic in any city in Texas—hell, anywhere for that matter. It was, as one of his physics professors described it, the coupling of rotational and translational motion in perfect harmony. Not all women knew the secret, the walk was definitely something that pretty women learned, a walk that says "I know you're watching me—eat your heart out!"

The Lieutenant, on the other hand, did not walk with movie starlet grace. She strode forward with determination, not wasting energy on extraneous motion. Definitely feminine but no nonsense, and with a hint of "I can kick your butt" as well. Her rank here was obviously a civilian label, but something in the back of JT's mind whispered *military*. Where Susan exuded sexuality, Lieutenant Curtis walked like a warrior princess.

Steady boy, don't get carried away, he thought, giving his head a slight shake. For almost a year, he had been riding in the news van with Susan, and though he was as appreciative of her physical charms as any man, he had never been tempted to make a play for her. He had decided at the beginning of their partnership that she was a team member, a colleague not a prospective date. Time had proven that approach to be the right one—Susan didn't get romantically involved with people at work—and he felt they now enjoyed a strong mutual friendship. That put Susan off limits in the romance department. The green-eyed amazon walking next to her, now she was fair game.

As they emerged into the brightly lit interior of the hangar, Lt. Curtis was speaking in a military issue brief-the-VIPs voice: "This, ladies and gentlemen, is the ship—she has yet to be formally christened. Overall hull length is 135 meters, beam 12 meters amidships, with tapering at both bow and stern. That would be 440 feet by 39 feet for the metrically challenged. There are two decks forward and aft, with three decks in the mid section except for the main cargo hold aft of midships. If she were a naval vessel she'd displace 7400 metric tons. In all, she's a bit bigger than a Seawolf attack submarine."

Lt. Curtis turned to find her audience standing with mouths agape, staring down the ship's curving flank toward the back of the hangar. "Sorry, I forget how overwhelming she can be to newcomers."

JT quickly recovered his wits, shouldered his camera and began recording the long silver ship in front of him. Panning left slowly, toward the front of the ship, light glinted off its gleaming crystal nose. *This was not just some crackpot building a mockup or model in his garage—this was an honest to God spaceship!* Then, reining in his wildly racing thoughts, he tried to regain his objectivity.

Sure, its big and shiny, but that doesn't mean it will fly. And why is it laying on its side? Aren't spaceships supposed to be launched straight up? For that matter, is there anything inside the hull? Impressive as the exterior is, it could still be a hoax. He concentrated on the camera, not trusting himself to speak.

"Oh. My. Goodness," Susan managed. "This will most certainly make the six o'clock news."

A hint of a smile on played across the First Officer's previously stoic face. "If you will please follow me, I'll take you inside," she

36

said, with obvious pride. "Come, we'll enter through the main cargo door and work our way forward."

AFTAC, Patrick AFB, Florida

"Sir, it looks like we have a Pinnacle *Faded Giant* event in the western part of Texas. No EMP or seismic activity has registered but we have confirmed neutron and gamma ray hits," Major Beldsoe told her boss, the commander of AFTAC, over the secure phone line. A Faded Giant is a nuclear event not related to a weapons detonation and not considered likely to start a nuclear war.

Faded Giant not withstanding, he had been barbequing in the back yard and was less than pleased to have his family holiday interrupted. "No Sir. We are dispatching an atmospheric sensor drone from Detachment 45 in Denver, but it will take several hours to arrive on station."

Though AFTAC was attached to the Air Intelligence Agency for administrative support, the center reported directly to the Deputy Air Force Chief of Staff for Air and Space Operations. That meant escalating the problem required a call to a Major General at the Pentagon, who was probably also enjoying the holiday with his family.

"Sir, I've talked with the Chief Scientist and he thinks this may be someone running some sort of particle collider or possibly, given the particle and X-ray spectra, an attempt at igniting a fusion reaction." Many of the people working at AFTAC were civilians, including more than thirty scientists with PhDs. "Yes Sir, he's coming in now."

If it were not for the previous event occurrences at the same location they would have probably just logged the event and ignored it. But this was definitely strange. The science staff had been recalled and the Colonel would undoubtedly be in shortly. By then she hoped they had some answers. They better have before the Colonel calls the Pentagon.

"Yes sir, I have everyone working the situation. We will update you when you arrive." A curt "very good, Major," and the line went dead. No, the Colonel was not happy at all.

The line from the monitoring center lit up. It never rains unless it pours, thought Bledsoe. "Command center, Major Bledsoe" she answered.

"Lt. Jefferies, Ma'am. I just checked with Homeland Security to see if they were tracking any threats in the area of the event. They were unaware of any terrorist activity in that area but they did mention something peculiar."

"Something 'peculiar' Lieutenant?"

"Yes Ma'am. One of the local news channels down there is running a story about a rancher building his own spaceship in an abandoned dirigible hanger."

"An abandon what?"

"Dirigible hanger, Major. Built during WW II. I checked satellite recon imagery and it is the only sizable structure in that area. The source of the radiation we detected could be inside of the hangar."

"We need to get some boots on the ground down there, what's the closest military installation?"

"That would be Goodfellow, but it is a training facility. No combat units stationed there."

"Maybe they can send a helicopter with some SF personnel." Security Forces, or "SF", are military police, mainly charged with base security and air base ground defense. Formerly known as Air Police (AP) their duties tended more toward guard duty and law enforcement than ground assault.

"Damn!" The Major chewed on her lower lip, a nervous indication of deep frustration. "Call 'em and find out what they can do for us. Quickly Lieutenant. The Colonel will want options as soon as he gets here."

"Will do." The Lieutenant turned back to his computer display and began looking up the number for Goodfellow HQ. *Best contact the U.S. Marshals and local law enforcement as well. Hell, maybe the Texas Rangers can help. What was that old saying, "One riot, one Ranger?" Well this looked like it was turning into a riot.*

Chapter 3

On Board Parker's Folly, Parker Ranch, Texas

The two news people followed First Officer Curtis along the side of the spaceship and through a large opening in its curved flank. A ramp inside the threshold of the six meter wide by four and a half meter tall entrance led down to a large cargo area containing a scattering of crates and containers, some large, some small. The floor looked to be about eight and a half meters wide, while the crates obscured the length of the chamber.

"This is the main cargo hold," said their guide. "as you can see we are still loading equipment and supplies. There is a second large cargo door at the other end of the hold on the starboard side. Farther aft are the hydroponic gardens and engineering spaces. If you like, we can take a look at them after we visit the living quarters, the mess and bridge. The spaces forward will probably be more interesting to your viewers."

"I think we should probably go to the front of the ship straight away. That's where the controls are, right?" Susan asked while trying to take in the cluttered cargo hold. "We are starting to get tight on time for the six o'clock broadcast. If we could get some shots of you or the captain—I assume that there is a captain— answering some questions with that glass nose behind you we would be golden."

"Of course, we will proceed to the bridge. This way please." Curtis motioned toward a rectangular area of the deck, marked off with a red border, abutting the forward bulkhead. There was an opening in the bulkhead starting about three and a half meters above the deck.

Susan and JT stepped into the painted rectangle and Lt. Curtis said, "You may want to move in from the edges a bit." The ship's officer pressed a large button recessed in a panel on the wall and the rectangular area of deck began to rise.

"Whoa!" JT exclaimed, "How about givin' a guy some warning?"

"Sorry, this is a cargo lift that is used to move heavy items from the hold to the mid-deck. I didn't mean to startle you."

Susan remained unflustered, thinking to herself, *I believe that was a test of some sort.* The lift stopped smoothly at the opening and a large door slid quietly to the side revealing a small brightly lit room and a passageway beyond. Lt. Curtis led the way through the room, past a second heavy door on its far side and into the passage way. The tour narration resumed.

"The companionway to the left leads back down to the lower deck. There you will find crew quarters, a large head with showers and the crew's dayroom. Forward of the dayroom are the officer's quarters and guest staterooms. This ship was designed as both a research vessel and a private yacht. If you have time I can show you the owner's stateroom after we visit the bridge. It is quite something."

The hallway was done in pleasant, natural colors with indirect lighting running along the sides of the ceiling and short napped carpet on the floor. Doorways pierced the walls at irregular intervals, though these were not nearly as heavily built as the pair of doors they entered through.

"These doors don't look very nautical," Susan remarked, "and they aren't heavy like the ones we came through from the cargo hold."

"Good observation, Ma'am. The pair of doors opening onto the cargo hold are airtight. Together they form an airlock so that we still have access to the cargo area even when the hold is open to vacuum. There are a number of other airlocks that allow direct access to the exterior as well."

Susan nodded, assimilating data. Getting the details right was what made a news story believable. And as her knowledge of West Texas trivia showed, Susan had a mind for details.

"By not looking nautical I presume you mean that the interior doors don't look like the watertight doors on a naval vessel, with high thresholds and a way to dog them shut." Lt. Curtis continued. "This is a spaceship and not intended to sail upon the briny deep. Hopefully we will never have to deal with water flooding this ship's interior spaces." Again the hint of a smile.

Susan was getting the impression that Lt. Curtis had a rather sarcastic sense of humor, though she wasn't quite sure their tour guide was laughing at her or not. Sarcastic wit was something the reporter appreciated, since she possessed a similar sense of humor. "Well that explains it! I guess with all the navy jargon I was expecting a more nautical motif," she said brightly.

The First Officer looked at her unperturbed, then slowly raised a single eyebrow, much like Mr. Spock from the original Star Trek TV series. *If she says 'fascinating' I'll burst out laughing,* Susan thought, stiffing an urge to giggle.

Turning back toward the bow, the tour resumed. "To the right is the sick bay. It is equipped with state-of-the-art equipment including CAT scan, MRI, automated blood and tissue analysis, toxicology screening and robot assisted surgery. There are also dental and optometry equipment. The ship's pharmacy is stocked with most common drugs and medicines plus a supply of frozen plasma."

"Across the way are electronic and mechanical engineering labs, equipped to repair or fabricate needed equipment. Not open to direct access from the passageway are bays that hold external sensors—telescopes, antennae, radar, LIDAR, and FLIR pods that can be extended beyond the hull once the ship is in space. And this..." they had come to a door blocking the hallway.

Lt. Curtis operated the control next to the door and it slid into the wall out of sight. The party stepped from the passageway, up a short flight of stairs and into a large room that spanned the entire width of the ship.

"...this is the mess and lounge area."

AFTAC, Patrick AFB, Florida

Col. Atkins arrived at the AFTAC Command Center, his uniform neat but smelling of barbeque and wood smoke. He sat quietly as the Major brought him up to speed on the rapidly developing situation in West Texas.

"It turns out the Marines have a squad and an MV-22 parked at Mathis Field, in San Angelo, showing the flag at an airshow. The Marines are armed but have no live ammo, the air show being strictly a dog and pony show. Mathis is only a few miles away from

41

Goodfellow and they are sending an SF detail with six ammo cans of 5.56 and eight 200 round SAW magazines—that's more than 6,000 rounds." Maj. Bledsoe paused and looked up. "Are we expecting heavy resistance?"

"Strictly a precaution. Besides, you know the Marines, can't pack enough ammo to make them happy," the Colonel chuckled. "Are they on the way yet? What's their estimated TOA?"

"The Security Force people have just arrived at the air show. We are in contact with the Osprey's flight crew and they are running down the Lieutenant in charge of the squad of Marines. We've briefed the flight crew as to their destination and what to expect. As soon as the Marine LT gets on board they will depart. We'll brief the ground unit while they are in the air."

"Great, good work people. What about the local authorities and the Feds?"

"They have been contacted and are sending the local Marshal, some Texas Highway patrolmen, and, I kid you not, a Texas Ranger. The Ranger is hitching a helo ride with some U.S. Marshals from San Antonio. We also have FBI out of San Antonio and BATF from both Fort Worth and El Paso. This guy's ranch is at least 250 miles from anywhere so the Feds will be arriving late. The Marines will probably be on station about the same time as the local yokels."

"Sounds good." The Colonel then addressed the others present in the room: "Listen up people. The plan is for the Marines to seize the 'spaceship' or whatever is in the hangar, and hold the site until FBI and Homeland Security personnel can get there. They are not authorized to arrest anyone and we don't want any *posse comitatus* blow-back."

The original 1878 Posse Comitatus Act was passed with the intent of removing the Army from domestic law enforcement. Posse comitatus, which means "the power of the county," is viewed by many as a major barrier to the use of U.S. military forces in domestic security operations. In reality, it is more of a procedural formality than an actual impediment to the use of the military in homeland defense.

Since 1980, there had been ample authority to employ military personnel in homeland defense when there was a threat involving weapons of mass destruction. Since a Pinnacle event is by definition nuclear in nature and there was the possibly of some form of weapon, the Pentagon OK'd the use of military force to seize whatever had emitted the radiation AFTAC's satellites had detected.

Even so, the Colonel thought, *best not to ruffle the local authorities' feathers. Authorized or not, God, please don't let them shoot any civilians.* "Major, make sure those Jar Heads understand the mission—secure the target with minimal force and hold for the arrival of domestic federal agents."

Mathis Field Air Fiesta, San Angelo, Texas

GySgt Rodriguez had been keeping an eye on her Marines from the shade of one of the Osprey's short wings when the Air Force came screeching up in a blue Humvee. An overly excited military police Lieutenant hopped out of the Humvee and ran over to the aircraft demanding to know who was in charge. Rodriguez saluted the officer and replied that their LT had hit the head and would be back momentarily and could she be of any assistance?

"Sergeant, we got a call from somebody in the Pentagon telling us we needed to get some small arms ammunition to a group of Marines over at the airport. I guess that means you."

"Well Lieutenant, we are the only Marines around here so we must be it. You have any idea as to why the Pentagon suddenly thinks we need live ammo at an airshow, Sir?"

"I don't know, Sergeant, but I got my orders. And somebody has to sign for this stuff."

"Well, that I can handle," the Gunny said, accepting the clipboard from the agitated Air Force officer. She signed the receipt and then shouted over her shoulder, "Sanchez, Reagan, Davis! Relieve our blue brethren of their burden and store the cans on board."

"Hey look, Sanchez!" shouted Davis, "the Zoomies brought you some ammo."

"Damn, I didn't know the Chair Force delivered," Sanchez replied, taking two ammo cans from an SF Airman at the back of the Humvee.

"Next time don't forget to bring your own ammo and we won't have to, Jar Head," the Airman shot back. Rivalry between the services often led to the exchange of insults, and sometimes bar fights.

"Knock off the chatter and get the lead out, Marines," yelled the Gunny, ending the inter-service banter. "Thank you, Lieutenant. Hmm, sixteen hundred rounds of linked and 5,040 rounds in stripper clips, I wonder who they think we are going to fight out here?"

"Not my department, Sergeant," the Air Force Officer called as he climbed back into the idling Humvee. "Good luck, whatever it is."

Rodriguez waved at the departing fly boys and started walking back to the Osprey. "Corporal Sizemore! Where are my Marines?"

The beefy Corporal stepped around the front of the aircraft and shouted back "Kato and Doc White went off in search of some snow cones or something, Gunny." Referring to PFC Herman "Kato" Kwan and HM2 Belinda "Betty" White. The Marine Corps has no medical personnel of its own, relying instead on the United States Navy Hospital Corps for medics and doctors. Technically, corpsman White was not a Marine but a Navy sailor. Her rate and rating were Petty Officer 2nd Class and Hospital Corpsman, the medic equivalent of a Marine Sergeant.

Hospital Corpsmen serve as enlisted medical specialists for both the Navy and Marine Corps. Navy corpsmen, traditionally called "Doc" by Marines, are highly skilled and are often deployed in the absence of a licensed doctor as Independent Duty Corpsmen. In fact, White, with skills in demand in the civilian market, was the only one in the squad who was leaving the service voluntarily. She had also volunteered to come on the air show mission, seeing it as a last, safe adventure before leaving military life behind.

Before the rise of irregular warfare and low intensity conflicts, corpsmen wore a red cross armband and went unarmed. Nowadays, when corpsmen accompany combat units they dress in the same uniforms as the Marines around them so as not to present an inviting target to the enemy. They are armed and virtually indistinguishable from regular combat Marines, except for the extra medical equipment they carry.

"Find 'em. Now!" *I got a bad feeling about this,* the Gunny thought to herself. "Feldman, Washington. Go find the Lieutenant, I sense a large turd heading toward the fan."

"Belay that, Gunny. Here comes the LT now," Cpl Sizemore yelled over his shoulder, and then hustled off toward the concession stands in search of the two missing squad members.

* * * * *

The MV-22 had just finished a short taxi to the active runway, getting clear of the milling airshow crowds in front of the hangars. The flight crew was running down their pre-flight checklist and throttling the engines up to full power, testing them before taking off.

After getting Lt. Merryweather and the two lost sheep back on board the Osprey, the Lieutenant was briefed over the radio by some officer at the Pentagon with the Gunny listening in. Evidently the Chair Force had detected a nuclear bomb, or nuclear rocket or a nuclear *something* in an old blimp hanger somewhere west of San Angelo. Since West Texas was the asshole of nowhere, the nearest military unit to this threat to national security was her pathetic little band of Marines, commanded by the befuddled Lt. Merryweather.

"Sir," the Gunny said to the LT over the Osprey's intercom. "If you would like to stay in touch with HQ on the radio, I'll brief the men." *Please, let him take the bait.* The last thing she needed was this REMF confusing her Marines with some scatterbrained John Wayne speech.

"Uh, yes Sergeant. That would be fine." Merryweather was a communications officer, stationed at Goodfellow for crypto training —he was in over his head and he knew it. He was more than happy to let the Gunnery Sergeant handle the taking of the objective—and dealing with the men.

"Thank you, Lieutenant." She handed the intercom headset back to the Osprey's loadmaster, who was standing beside the LT.

Thank God for that, at least he isn't one of those over eager, get everyone killed types. The Gunny made her way back to the squad, seated along the sides of the cargo area on canvas backed, fold down jump seats. The Marines all looked up at her expectantly, awaiting The Word. *Heaven help us, I think we are about to be slipped the big green weenie.*

"OK, heads up people. We are en route to a ranch about 35 minutes from here where we will take and hold a large hanger. The hanger is approximately 500 feet long by 150 feet wide. We will enter through doors on the southern side, which are hidden from the ranch house by the hanger structure. Once inside the building, we will secure any scientific apparatus, aeronautical vehicles or, I shit you not, rocket ships we find." The last statement brought a number of exclamations from the squad. Ignoring their questions Rodriguez forged ahead.

"HQ does not know what kind of stuff we will find when we take the hangar, but the rumor is that some old coot is building himself a rocket ship. Regardless of what we find, we will secure the building and hold it until relieved by federal officials who are en route to the target site.

"We will be going in hot, so fill your magazines from the ammo cans the Zoomies brought us." The squad was armed with M4A1 Carbines, a shorter and lighter version of the old familiar M16A2 assault rifle. Since they were out to impress the locals at the air show, they had been issued Special Operator versions of the carbine with the Close Quarters Battle Receiver (CQBR) upper and CompM2 red dot reflex sights. Most had forward handgrips but Sizemore and Reagan snagged weapons with M320 grenade launchers mounted under their barrels. Unfortunately, the fly boys didn't have any 40mm grenades for the launchers, but they still looked mean.

Washington, because of his size, was issued an M246 Squad Automatic Weapon, or SAW, a light machine gun that could use standard 30 round magazines or belted ammo. With a 200 round magazine attached a SAW weighed more than ten kilos, add a couple of spare mags and it took a large Marine to haul it around. In all, the squad looked ready for action, but the magazines they carried in their vests were empty and only there for show. Until now.

"OK, Sizemore, Reagan, pass out the ammo," they were setting closest to the ammo cans. "I want everyone to have a full ammo load when we go in. Don't leave none of it behind. And Corporal, distribute the extra SAW mags among the riflemen. You never know when you're going to need more ammo and we will not be able to run back to the Osprey to fetch more."

Standard 5.56mm ammo came in ten round stripper clips, three clips to a cardboard carton, four cartons to a 4 pocket bandoleer, for a total of 120 rounds per bandoleer, which also included a speedloader for getting the rounds from the stripper clips into a magazine. Seven such bandoleers were packed into each M2A1 ammo can. Each squad member was carrying eight or ten 30 round magazines that needed to be filled using the 10 round stripper clips. The Marines got busy filling mags under the watchful eye of the Gunny.

Rodriguez loaded her own mags and then stuffed a number of three clip cartons into her vest pockets. She also loaded her 9mm side arm—the Zoomies had been kind enough to include 10 preloaded magazines for the standard 9mm Beretta. After a moment's hesitation she turned to the Lieutenant who was now sitting next to her. "Pistol ammo, Sir" she explained, handing him four of the magazines. He quickly shoved the magazines into his vest pockets and turned back to the face the cockpit.

At that moment, the Osprey pilot began a short roll take off. *Well, here we go, and I thought this was going to be a nice boring mission.* The Gunny sat back and closed her eyes. As the Osprey cleared the runway, the pilot, probably showing off for the air show crowd, jinked hard to starboard and gave the big tilt-rotor her head. Several Marines were still in the process of using speed loaders to fill their mags when the sudden maneuver took them by surprise. Sanchez somehow managed to lose a full clip of ammo, spilling the loose rounds onto the deck of the cargo compartment.

The pilot jinked again, like he was flying a combat mission, and the rounds rolled across the deck. "Secure that ammunition, Marine! You think this is a fuckin' school bus, Sanchez?" the Gunny bellowed. *Well that made it official, the goatfuck was turning into a cluster-fuck.*

On Board Parker's Folly, Parker Ranch, Texas

Ascending the three steps to the interior of the "mess," the tour group gazed upon what looked like an upscale lounge and restaurant. The room stretched from one side of the ship's hull to the other, the walls curving upward at either side to a high ceiling with hanging accent panels. A sinuously curving bar divided the dining area on the left from the lounge on the right. Small overhead trac lighting set an intimate mood and, in the far corner, a baby grand piano completed the effect. JT panned the room with his camera and Susan commented. "Looks like the passengers will be riding in style, this is plush."

"The owner is partial to jazz music, fine dining and he really enjoys drinking," Lt. Curtis said with mock solemnity. "Here, let me show you something you might want to film." Moving over to the bar, the First Officer reached behind the counter and threw a switch. On the starboard wall a large oval window uncovered, like the nictitating membrane retracting over a raptor's eye. As with the 'glass' bow of the ship, the window comprised a number of individual curved transparent panels, separated by thin arcing silver strips. The interior of the hangar could be seen through the art deco window panes.

"Wow, that's fantastic," JT said, walking farther into the room, panning at the same time. *This was more like it,* he thought. He had been worried that the whole ship was going to be nothing but cargo space and boring hallways. "Just imagine having a drink at the bar while the rings of Saturn slide by outside."

"Why Mr. Taylor, you sound like you would like to come along."

"Don't encourage him. He has a Master's degree in astronomy," Susan interjected, causing the First Officer to cast a reappraising look in JT's direction. "Besides, then I'd have to find a new camera man and good ones are very hard to find."

JT was oblivious, enraptured by the idea of standing in front of that window, peering out at the Universe. "Come on, Miss Susan, you wouldn't want to be on board for the first flight? It would be the scoop of the century."

"I think I would rather be on the *second* flight, JT." Susan smiled at her cameraman to show she was just teasing him. It was then that she spotted the strange figure heading toward them from the front of the lounge. "I think we have company," she said to the others.

As the figure drew near, the person in question proved to be a short, wiry man with weathered, Sun darkened skin. He was wearing a jumpsuit much like Lt. Curtis, except his was dark blue. On his head was a matching dark blue baseball cap with a strange insignia on the front. His age was indeterminate, but he was definitely not young. A wrinkle creased Lt. Curtis' brow as she turned to face the approaching little man, her hands clasped behind her back.

"Chief Zackly, what mission lends such urgency to your steps?"

"Egh?" The man in blue halted in front of the First Officer, his self absorbed trance broken. "Oh its you, Ma'am. I got a couple o' shitbirds rattling around on the lower deck. Must'a been on board when the Captain told the rest it was beer o'clock. Damn civilians!"

Lieutenant Curtis inclined her head toward the two news people standing to her right. Again she did the Mr. Spock raised eyebrow trick. The figure in blue braced, coming to attention.

"Beg pardon Ma'am," the little man nearly shouted, "no offense intended." Then added more softly, "Captain said I gotta' get 'em off the ship, Ma'am."

"Yes, of course Chief. Carry on."

The little man resumed his journey aft, leaning forward as if against a gale. "That was Chief Zackly, the senior boatswain's mate, ... well actually, he is the only boatswain's mate."

"He doesn't seem to hold civilian's in very high regard." mused JT, "and what's a 'shitbird'?"

"It is a derogatory term for shipyard workers used by Navy enlisted personnel. We had been running some power system tests earlier and the Captain told the construction workers they could leave for the day"

"OK, now that makes sense. Beer o'clock I understood."

"I'm surprised he didn't salute you, Lieutenant," Susan added.

"The Navy does not generally render the hand salute indoors. Because we work in tight quarters, constantly having to salute would be far too disruptive. Besides, this is a civilian vessel. Let's continue on to the bridge and see if the Captain is free for your interview," the First Officer said, closing the large view port and then indicating the way forward.

Aboard the MV-22, West of San Angelo, Texas

The pilot of the Osprey signaled that they were 15 minutes out from the objective. GySgt Rodriguez sighed a deep, inward sigh. How could this have happened on her last weekend in the Corps? Drug out of a nice warm rack at o'dark hundred to lead a squad of screw-ups on a dog and pony show mission at an air show, only to have the mission turn into a real air assault, with live ammo. Commanded by a Lieutenant who was really a crypto clerk, she and eight washouts were about to assault a gigantic hangar in the middle of the West Texas scrub. *Well, never a dull day in the Corps.*

"OK Marines, listen up. We are 15 minutes from the objective and this is how things are going to work. When we disembark, Corporal Sizemore, take Feldman, Washington and Kwan to the Left. You will be with Lieutenant Merryweather. Davis, Reagan, Sanchez and White, you're with me on the right. We will fan out and secure the LZ. If there is no enemy contact, we will proceed to the doors on the side of the building, assuming they actually exist" They were working off of intel from old construction plans some REMF had dug out of the Navy archives.

"Take cover along the building wall, flanking the doors and wait for my signal. We will enter through both doors simultaneously, secure the immediate area and then the LT will assess the situation and decide what we need to do next."

It's simple right up to where we enter the building, the Gunny thought. They should find themselves inside of a large open space, the place was supposed to be a hangar. But there was no telling what they would find. Maybe a bunch of civilians building a playschool rocket ship, maybe a nest of terrorists assembling a nuke.

"Rules of Engagement are as follows: do not shoot unarmed civilians. But if someone points a weapon at you, weapons are free. Do you understand?"

"AYE, AYE, Gunny!" The squad responded loudly and in unison.

At least they understand that this is not a fucking drill. They may not be the best the Corps had to offer, but they weren't virgins either. All of them had seen the elephant in Afghanistan or elsewhere. And all bullshit aside, they were still Marines. The Gunny turned to the Lieutenant, who had been standing behind her, listening to the briefing. "Any thing you would like to add, Sir?"

"No, Gunny, that should cover things 'til we gain access to the hangar." From the cockpit, the mechanical voice of the ground proximity warning said "500 feet." The curtain was about to go up.

Chapter 4

Bridge of Parker's Folly, Parker Ranch, Texas.

Captain Jack Sutton was sitting in the command chair on the bridge, supervising two of the crew—helmsmen Vincent and Danner —as they ran through the departure simulation yet again. The Captain was of the opinion that practice made everything run more smoothly and he insisted that his ship run smoothly.

The two helmsmen sat at a shared console in front of the command station, below and farther forward within the transparent bow of the ship than the Captain's perch. There were staggered ancillary control positions set back on either side of the pilots' stations, currently unmanned. Behind the helm and directly beneath the Captain's chair was a row of seats for observers. Vincent and Danner were an interesting pair—both were native born Texans but there the similarities ended.

William Raymond "Billy Ray" Vincent was the embodiment of the cowboy image: 6 foot three, with long ropy muscles on a lean frame. If they still had a Marlboro Man, he would definitely be in the running. With a nonchalant attitude and steady nerves, nothing flustered him. When the simulator threw problems at him he responded with the same laconic calm as astronauts and test pilots. Outgoing and friendly, in conversation he affected a Texas drawl and was not above whoopin' and hollerin' a bit if the occasion called for it.

Robert "Bobby" Danner, on the other hand, was quiet. A slightly pudgy, video game addicted couch potato who lived vicariously through online multiplayer games. In World of Warcraft he was a deadly Shadow Priest and a definite bad ass—look at him crosswise and he would melt your face. In the real world, he was almost painfully shy, usually only speaking when spoken too. Bobby was as socially awkward as Billy Ray was genial. Proving that life is stranger than fiction, Billy Ray and Bobby were the closest of friends.

One thing both members of this odd couple had in common was they were very good at piloting the ship—at least in simulations. Their styles were quite different. Billy Ray was smooth on the controls, precise during maneuvers, keeping things right on the flight path. Strangely enough it was Bobby who was the daredevil, able to jink and dodge, avoiding obstacles seemingly at will. If you were in need of "evasive maneuvers," Bobby was your man.

Together they had become a finely tuned team, able to handle nearly anything that the ship's flight simulator could throw at them. The Captain was certain they would acquit themselves with flying colors when it came time to actually pilot the ship.

Also currently on the Bridge was Jose "Jo Jo" Medina, an electronics technician who doubled as a flight engineer, monitoring the ship's systems and condition when underway. His board was on the port side on the same level as the Captain but set back farther aft. There was a similar station on the starboard side for a navigation officer that was currently unmanned. Abaft that position was the Captain's sea cabin—Jack had tried calling it his space cabin but decided it sounded silly.

Jack loved to sit in the command chair, looking out through the curving transparent panels that formed Folly's bow. No vessel he had ever commanded had a view to match this one—he could not wait to get her into space. He marveled again at his good luck and the strange, improbable chain of events that had brought him to this position. If he had not met TK Parker years ago, when Jack was only a boy, he would not be here now, poised on the edge of a voyage into space.

Voices could be heard approaching from aft on the port side. *Must be the news crew coming for their interview,* he sighed. Hopefully, Lieutenant Curtis had covered most of the basic questions and he could simply smile for the camera, thank them for coming and send them on their way. On a Naval vessel, the XO, or executive officer, would handle most of the PR stuff, with the Captain remaining suitably aloof. Being a civilian vessel, Gretchen was the First Officer, not the XO, but she performed essentially the same duties. Anticipating their arrival, the Captain rotated his chair 120 degrees and rose to greet his guests.

Lieutenant Curtis appeared next to the engineering station, stepped forward and asked "Permission to enter the bridge, Captain?" Even though workers had been coming and going from the bridge all morning without asking permission, ingrained Naval traditions die hard.

"Permission granted, Lieutenant," the Captain replied. "I understand we have guests aboard."

"Yes, Sir." Lt. Curtis moved onto the bridge, turned and motioned the reporter and her cameraman forward. "Captain, this is Ms. Susan Write and Mr. James Taylor from KWTEX News. Mr. Parker invited them on board for a tour and to get some footage of the ship for their evening news broadcast." Turning to the news people, "This is Captain Sutton, master of this vessel."

Susan strode forward and stuck out her hand. "Susan Write, very nice to meet you Captain. This is some ship you have here." The Captain shook the proffered hand and then the hand of the camera man, murmuring "Ms. Write, Mr. Taylor. Welcome aboard."

"I guess the first question our viewers would have," said Susan, dispensing with the formalities, "is 'do you really expect his huge ship to actually fly?' I believe Lieutenant Curtis said it weighs over 7,000 tons!"

A rather well put together young woman, the Captain thought, *pushy though. Her cameraman looks squared away, I'd wager he was in the service.* A commanding officer had to be able to size up people quickly. The pretty blond was testing him, trying to rattle his cage. The faintest of smiles crossed his face, he looked back at Susan and calmly answered her question.

"Yes Ms. Write. We do expect the ship to fly. After all, a spaceship that doesn't fly would hardly be very useful."

There was a brief, awkward silence as Susan thought to herself, *OK, I'm not going to catch this guy off base or fluster him with awkward questions.* Sometimes you can get an interview subject to go off message and expose hidden truths by surprising them—it had been worth a shot. She changed tack.

"When do you think you will be ready to launch? And would you be willing to take a news crew along?" She favored the Captain with a high-wattage smile.

"We are still loading provisions and ancillary equipment, but the ship is capable of lifting off as we speak." *If it will only stop spewing radiation when it does,* the Captain thought sourly. "Perhaps you should layout how you would like to film the news spot. I understand you are running up against deadlines of your own."

"Oh yes. Let's shoot it this way..."

The Ranch House, Parker Ranch, Texas.

TK was "standing" in his wheelchair, gyroscopically balanced on two wheels, gazing out the front bay window. Two cars containing local sheriff's deputies had just pulled up, one on either side of the KWTEX News van. He could also see the distinctive paint job of a Texas Highway Patrol cruiser bouncing its way down the long dirt driveway, leaving a noticeable dust plume to mark its passage.

"Damn, it looks like I'm throwin' a party," the old man said, turning to Maria, who was standing by his side. "Maria, you go back to the kitchen and stay out of the way. I don't want Johnny Law givin' you any trouble."

"No, Señor Parker! I will greet them at the door like all of your other guests. I ask them their business and check if you are available. That is, if they don't have a search warrant." Maria knew about search warrants, her son was a lawyer.

"Now don't be stubborn, woman. I don't want them hassling you or turnin' you over to Immigration."

"Do not worry Señor Parker, my citizenship papers are in order. You have been very good to my family—you hired me when my Juan died 20 years ago and paid for our children's educations. Thanks to you, my son Hernando is a lawyer in Austin and my daughter Consuela is a children's doctor in Little Rock. I will not abandon you now. Besides, I have learned much from you—I am an American, I don't take *sheeet* from nobody." That last phrase delivered in an exaggerated Mexican accent.

"Oh all right. I never could win an argument with you." More than two decades ago, Maria's husband had worked on one of TK's first gas rigs. He died tragically in an accident, leaving Maria a widow with two young children. The children had been born in the USA but Maria was not a citizen. Rather than see her deported, TK hired her as his cook and housekeeper, then helped her obtain legal resident status and eventually, citizenship. Under his gruff exterior

TK was really just an old softie, at least when it came to people he liked. "Looks like there's more of 'em coming."

Three patrol cars were now parked around the news van and the sheriff's cars, and a large van with "Mobile Crime Lab" on its side had just arrived. Dust was flying everywhere and the Highway Patrol officers were engaged in an animated conversation with the sheriff's deputies. "OK, Maria, I'm going to go back to my office. Greet them when they finally decide to come knock on the door. Bring 'em to my office and then take cover in the kitchen like I asked."

"Si, Señor Parker."

* * * * *

When TK reached his office he called up a view of his driveway on his computer monitor. After he had become disabled he had an expensive security system installed. With it he could monitor things in all directions from his ranch house. As a self made man, he was not comfortable with having to rely on anyone. Maria was the sole exception, and he used the excuse that he was helping her, not the other way round.

There were more dust plumes a half mile down the driveway, indicating that the parade of law enforcement vehicles was still growing. The crowd of police officers, deputies, highway patrolmen, and God knows what else continued to expand but no one had approached the house. They were obviously waiting on some one who had not yet arrived and that probably meant the Feds. *That figures, the Federal Government was late for everything.*

When they do come, TK suddenly realized, *they might just try an end run by sending a bunch of lawmen straight out to the hangar.* He'd better call Jack and tell him he needed to get the bird into the air, or the government would seize her for sure. He'd be damned if he was going to turn the fruits of his labor for the last thirty years over to a bunch of bumbling bureaucrats and government asswipes. No, this was too important to let the government screw it up.

Landing Zone, South Side of the Hangar, Parker's Ranch.

Approaching from the south, the MV-22 came in low over the scrub and sagebrush, using the bulk of the hangar to hide its approach from the ranch house. The huge twin rotors went to their full upright position, the Osprey flared and landed about 80 meters from the structure. The nose of the aircraft was pointing west, so its starboard side door was facing the hangar—normally the door gunner would have provided cover for the disembarking Marines but the Air Force had not seen fit to provide any 7.62mm ammo.

Upon landing the rear ramp lowered to the ground and the squad of Marines exited the rear of the Osprey led by Lt. Merryweather and GySgt Rodriguez. The squad fanned out and formed a perimeter about 30 meters from the aircraft, whose rotors were stirring up large volumes of dust. As the Marines knelt down facing outward from their ride and toward the looming hangar, Rodriguez turned back to the Osprey and gave a thumbs up signal. The MV-22 immediately started to rise and headed off to the south.

The Gunny waited 20 seconds for some of the dust to clear and for the noise of the aircraft to fade. There was no response from the building. She looked over at the Lieutenant and Cpl Sizemore. As soon as she had their attention she used hand signals to indicate they should advance to the side of the building, each team taking up stacked position beside their target doors.

The Gunny stood up and started forward at a trot. Simultaneously, the rest of the squad was in motion, headed for their assigned objectives. *Damn if we don't look like we know what we're doing,* Rodriguez thought. The squad quickly flattened themselves against the outer wall of the building.

I wish we had some grenades, no, we wouldn't be able to use them until we know what's inside. As usual with combat operations, the worst part was before making contact with the enemy. That's when all the doubts and second guessing happens. Once the bullets start flying, training and instinct take over. From the far side of the door, facing the rest of her team and in sight of the Lieutenant's team farther west along the building wall, she motioned for the squad to enter the hangar.

Reagan reached out and grasped the doorknob. The door was unlocked. He pushed the door open and entered the building, followed closely by Davis and Sanchez. The Gunny and corpsman White brought up the rear.

Still no contact. The team crossed through a deserted work area filled with tables and machine tools. On the far side, opposite the entrance, there was a ramp leading to a pair of swinging doors that opened outward, into the hanger proper.

"Up the ramp! Move it!" With that the Gunny launched herself up the ramp and threw open the right hand door as Davis did the same to the one on the left. The rest of the team flooded into the brightly lit hangar, instinctively taking up defensive, outward facing positions.

Rodriguez could see the rest of the squad similarly deployed, twenty meters to her left. The Lieutenant was standing in the middle of his team, looking up, pistol in hand with his arm hanging at his side. That was when the Gunny became aware of the large gleaming cylinder towering over them. *I'll be damned*, she thought, *it is a rocket ship.*

Bridge of Parker's Folly, Parker Ranch, Texas.

The interview had gone well and the news crew was busy preparing to send their report to the TV station. HD video was not actually recorded on tape or film anymore. When JT "filmed" a scene the sound and video was recorded on a high-density SSD storage pack attached to the camera. Once recorded, his camera rig contained everything the news team needed to playback and edit the video in the field.

Lt. Curtis installed the news team in the Captain's sea cabin to do their editing, since they would be out of the way and unlikely to be disturbed there. She had just returned to the bridge when TK called.

"Folly! This is TK in the ranch house. We got Johnny Law crawling up our asses out here. Are you there?"

"Not the most professional radio discipline," the Captain commented, reaching to answer the call. "Ranch house, Folly. We're here Mr. Parker. Say again your last?"

"I said we got every flavor of lawman known to humanity getting ready to enter the premises. I can see sheriff's deputies, Texas Highway Patrol, some cops from Crane, and a helicopter just landed a bunch of U.S. Marshals and a Texas Ranger."

"U.S. Marshals and a Texas Ranger? How can you tell?"

"The Marshals are wearin' black bullet proof vests with 'U.S. Marshal' on 'em in big white letters. The Ranger is the only one wearing a suit with a cowboy hat and a shiny badge. That's how I can tell."

"Do you think they are here to seize the ship?"

"You're God damn right they are! Now that the Marshals are here it looks like they are makin' their move. There's a group, including the Ranger, heading for the front door but there's also a bunch of SWAT team types heading directly for the hangar."

"What would you have us do, Mr. Parker?" the Captain asked his friend and employer, glancing at his second in command, who was nervously rotating a ring on the third finger of her left hand.

"Jack, I want you to blastoff on out'a here, that's what I want you to do! I've already called my lawyers and I'm gonna try and stall 'em here at the hacienda, but that won't stop those SWAT types. And once they get a hold of Folly we'll never get her back."

"TK..." Jack started, but Parker cut him off.

"Batten down the hatches and blastoff now! You hear me son? Do it now!" The line went dead.

Turning to Lt. Curtis, Jack said, "well, it would seem that I have my orders."

"You mean we have our orders, don't you Sir?" The First Officer said, a troubled look on her face.

"Gretchen," Jack said, purposely using her given name, "I know we were both Naval officers, but this is not a Navy ship and the crew is not under Service discipline. There will be repercussions for taking the ship right from under the noses of federal agents, and that's assuming we don't blow up in the attempt. I have no authority to order you to stay on board while I commit *grand theft spaceship.*"

"No, Jack," she said, her green eyes looking steadily into his. "When I signed up for this enterprise I did it knowing the risks. I am as committed to what we are doing as you are. Unless you are ordering me off the ship, this is where I'm staying."

"Very well, Lieutenant," the Captain said with a relieved smile. "You might want to take the news team out the starboard hatch and tell them to get clear of the building. Tell them they will get a nice shot of the ship leaving the hangar."

"Yes, Sir. I left them in your sea cabin, sorting through their tour and interview footage. I'll disembark the news people and then go collect any other strays we have on board." With that, she turned and left the bridge.

The Captain turned back to the bridge crew, who had been silently listening to the interchange between the owner and the ship's two highest ranking officers.

"Attention on deck! Listen up people. What I said to Lieutenant Curtis applies to all of you. I cannot order you to remain at your stations, but if you wish to disembark you need to do so now. Fastest way is through the gangway on the forward hatch starboard side. If you are leaving, go now and do not hang around—get off the ship, out of the building and a good distance away before we depart."

"Permission to speak, Sir?" said Billy Ray. The Captain nodded. "I figure me an Bobby will stick around, if you don't mind."

"You bet, Captain," added Bobby, vigorously nodding his head.

"Me too, Sir," added Jo Jo Medina from his engineering station. "With you and the ship all the way."

"All right then. Start the procedure for departure. Be ready to activate the bottom repulsors on command, gentlemen. Engineer Medina, start powering up all internal systems."

"Aye aye, Sir." came the chorus of replies.

"Engineering, Bridge, Dr. Gupta I need those engines online now, if you please." A short pause.

"Ah, this is Engineering. Did I understand you want me to start the main reactors?"

"That is correct, Dr. Gupta. We are preparing for immediate departure. Break. Environmental, Bridge."

"Bridge, Environmental, go ahead." came a feminine voice.

"Miss Hamilton, please secure the hydroponics section for immediate departure."

"Yes, Sir. I'll have Lt. Bear help lock things down..."

Dirigible Hanger, Parker's Ranch

Outside of the ship, the Marines were standing, gawking at the gleaming spaceship in front of them as Lieutenant Merryweather and the Gunny conferred. "There doesn't seem to be anyone around, Sir. At least outside the ship. Davis reports he saw movement in the glass nose up front. Do we board the ship, Sir?"

"I don't know, Sergeant. Our orders were somewhat vague. As long as there is no resistance and the ship doesn't move I think we should just hold in position. I'm trying to get clarification from HQ via relay through the Osprey." After inserting the squad, the MV-22 climbed to altitude and was orbiting the ranch at 5,000 feet. In theory it provided a radio link between the Marines on the ground and the command authority.

"Yes, Sir. Just in case, I would like to take half the squad down to that large hatch aft and see if there is any activity inside. With your permission, Sir?"

"Sure Gunny, roger that. Just don't board the ship."

* * * * *

"You're taking off right now? This isn't some trick to just get us off the ship is it?" Susan was a bit putout that they had been evicted from the Captain's comfortable office and were being summarily thrown off the ship. The interview with the Captain was in the can and already sent to the station, but they were still

61

editing shots from the bridge and lounge with Susan doing a voice over.

"I'm very sorry about this, Ms. Write. But the Captain has ordered all visitors to disembark and the ship to prepare for immediate departure." Lt. Curtis was trying to hustle her two charges into the forward crew hatch. The crew hatch was an airlock, aft of the bridge, that allowed access from the lower deck to the ship's exterior. From the bottom lip of the outer door, a self-extending ramp provided an inclined gangway down to the scaffolding surrounding the ship.

"Come on Miss Susan," urged JT. "You said that you didn't want to be on the first flight. We got some good stuff already. Maybe we can get some footage of the ship leaving the hangar and taking off?"

With that he stepped out onto the gangway and, looking aft said, "Hey, there's a bunch of armed soldiers out here!" From force of habit, he raised the camera to his shoulder and began filming.

* * * * *

"Hey look," said Doc White. "There are people coming down the brow." Brow is the Navy term for a plank or gangway from ship to shore when a ship is lying alongside a pier. The Marines were standing roughly amidships, with the large cargo door aft and the smaller, personnel hatch forward. The bottom of the personnel hatch opening was a couple of meters higher than the scaffolding deck, requiring the use of a gangway ramp.

"WEAPON!" Yelled PFC Reagan, seeing the large black man at the top of the gangway raising something bulky, possibly a missile launcher, to his shoulder.

KAK! KAK! KAK!

PFC Sanchez fired a three shot burst at the man on the side of the ship. The burst was followed by the high-pitched whine of ricocheting bullets.

"BELAY THAT FIRE!" shouted the Gunny. She had just returned from reconnoitering the large cargo door aft. "At ease Marines! Just what the flying hell do you think you're doing, Sanchez?"

"There was a hostile with a weapon at the forward hatch, Gunny!" Sanchez pleaded. "Reagan yelled 'weapon' and I tried to take the hostile out."

At Reagan's warning, the whole squad had scattered, positioning themselves so they had clear fields of fire. Everyone's attention was focused on the forward hatch. From the front of the ship there came a groaning noise. *Oh shit!* The Gunny thought, *if Sanchez wounded a civilian we are SOL for sure.*

But the noise was not coming from the man on the ramp, he had disappeared from view. Rather, the groaning sound was coming from the ramp itself, which was retracting into the side of the ship.

* * * * *

Fortunately for JT, the weapon PFC Sanchez was using was unfamiliar to him, and Sanchez was not the best of shots under any condition. The shots were wide and ricocheted harmlessly off the metallic hull.

JT had ducked back into the ship as soon as he heard the cry of "weapon" and saw one of the soldiers raise his rifle. No, correction, when one of the Marines raised his rifle. He had spent more than enough time humping around Afghanistan to spot the difference between Army and Marines in combat gear.

Lt. Curtis' reaction had been nearly instantaneous, she grabbed JT by the belt with one hand and jerked him deeper into the airlock. With the other hand she whacked a large red button in a panel on the bulkhead. The sound of electric motors, like the flaps on an airliner, and the exit ramp began to retract into the side of the ship.

Then she spoke into a tiny microphone barely visible on her lapel. "Captain! Lt. Curtis in the starboard crew airlock. We have armed men outside the ship. Shots have been fired."

"Say again, Lieutenant?"

"I repeat, there are armed men outside of the ship and shots have been fired. No casualties. The news crew did not get off the ship." As if to emphasize the point, the external hatch clanged shut.

"Secure the civilians in the guest's dayroom for takeoff. Then continue aft and check for other lost souls wandering around my ship, Lieutenant. Captain, out."

"FYI, those armed men are a squad of Marines. Force Recon or some other group of Special Operators," JT said angrily. "Crappy shots though, if I had been the shooter I'd be dead or at least bleeding right now."

Susan looked at him, eyes wide. "What are you talking about? Those were shots?" She knew JT had been in the military but she had never heard him talk this way, with such a cold blooded edge to his voice. "How do you know who those men are?"

"You can tell by the vests and web gear that they're Marines, that and the camo pattern. And the rifles they're carrying are tricked out M4 carbines with special grips and optical sights that are only issued to special units—elite, counterinsurgency types and the like. I know, I've been there."

"You were a Marine?" Asked Lt. Curtis.

"Hell no!" snarled JT. "I was Army, Special Forces."

The Ranch House, Parker Ranch

TK was seated in his wheelchair behind his office desk. There was a large picture window to his right that looked south toward the old hanger. Through it, he could see the SWAT team in their black outfits, approaching the north side of the hanger. *Bet those heavy black vests are hotter than hell under that Texas Sun*, he thought to himself. Not much satisfaction to draw on there. A knock, and then Maria was at the office door with a posse.

"Señor Parker, these men are from the U.S. Marshal's office in Austin. I'm afraid they have a search warrant." Maria indicated three men in black, bulletproof vests with "U.S. Marshal" emblazoned in white, and in back, a man in a suit and cowboy hat.

"Let 'em in, Maria. Why don't you put some coffee on? Thank you, dear." Then rolling around from behind the desk and addressing the contingent of lawmen. "Well come on in. I hope you don't mind if I don't get up to greet y'all."

"Not at all, Mr. Parker," said the large balding Marshal, who seemed to be leading the procession. "Sir, I'm Tom Earl, U.S. Marshal in Charge of the Texas Western District. These are Deputy Marshals Evans and Fitzroy, and the other gentleman is Sid Hopkins of the Texas Rangers."

As Maria was leaving the room, Fitzroy turned to her and said, "don't go far, chica, we'll be wanting to talk with you too."

With a single smooth movement, TK's chair lept forward in the direction of Marshal Fitzroy, shifting from four wheel mode to two. Fitzroy turned back to find TK's angry face just inches from his own. In a very low and menacing voice the old oil tycoon said:

"I don't care who the hell you think you are, mister. But you will treat my housekeeper with respect. I got about six billion dollars in the bank, and unless you and the U.S. Marshals want every lawyer in Texas crawlin' up your asses you will act civil in my house."

As he finished speaking, TK leaned a bit closer to Fitzroy, causing the balancing wheelchair to advance and Marshal Fitzroy to backpedal toward the door. "Do you get me?"

Not expecting to find the cybernetic billionaire right in his face, the flustered Marshal could only sputter and turn red.

"Now, now, Mr. Parker. I apologize," said Chief Marshal Earl, intervening before the situation got completely out of hand. "Fitzroy, you go and check on what they're doing out front."

Marshal Earl turned to TK, "I know coming onto another man's property uninvited is an upsetting business. But we can all stay calm and, as you said Mr. Parker, civil."

"Fine." TK backed the chair up while slowly settling back to four wheel mode. He pulled back to his position behind the desk so he could view both the lawmen and the east end of the hanger through the window. The Ranger, Hopkins, walked over to the window. Talking around the toothpick in the side of his mouth he said, "tell the man what this is all about, Tom."

"I was getting to that, Sid. Mr. Parker we've got us a search warrant here, signed by a Federal judge, that let's us search your property for certain items."

"And just what would those items be, Marshal?"

"Now understand, this warrant was made out in response to a request from Homeland Security and the folks at the Pentagon. They say we are looking for, and I quote," The Marshal unfolded the document he had been carrying when he entered the room. "Devices or apparatus either nuclear in nature or capable of initiating a nuclear reaction or the release of ionizing radiation, and any such ancillary equipment or devices that may be attached to said equipment."

"Equipment such as what, Marshal?"

"Well, equipment such as a nuclear bomb, Mr. Parker. Or a rocket ship."

"You actually think I have a nuclear bomb in my house?"

"No, actually. We believe what we are looking for is out there in that big old shed." Marshal Earl motioned toward the window and the hangar beyond.

"Ain't a shed, its a dirigible hangar—get your facts straight. What makes you think you will find a nuclear whatsit in my dirigible hanger, Marshal?"

"The Air Force said they picked up radiation coming from your dirigible hanger on more than one occasion, Mr. Parker. Not much in the way of normal ranch equipment puts out radiation that can be picked up by an Air Force satellite."

Chapter 5

Cargo Bay, Parker's Folly

As the Marines looked on, the retracting ramp slid home and the hatch cover, which had been nestled against the curved hull of the ship above the hatch opening, snapped shut. On the smooth hull, only the faintest outline remained where the opening had been.

From the still open cargo door behind the squad of Marines came a familiar sound—a loud klaxon issued three blasts and then a voice announced "Attention all hands. Prepare for immediate departure. Rig for heavy acceleration, repeat, rig for heavy acceleration. This is not a drill!"

Alarms and warning lights erupted all around. With a loud booming echo, followed by much creaking and grinding of metal, the doors at the east end of the hangar began to open.

Lt. Merryweather was a man in crisis. He was a cryptography specialist, not a platoon leader—he just wasn't good in high stress situations and definitely not a leader of men. He was getting only static on the radio and there was no one else to ask for orders.

"Sir, it's shit or get off the pot time," the Gunny said. "Do we board the ship or evacuate the building?" She didn't know for sure, but being in the hangar when this silver monster blasted off did not seem conducive to one's health.

Every Marine in the squad was looking to the Lieutenant for a decision, he was their officer. In officer training they always emphasized the need to be decisive. If you are taking fire on a hillside, go up the hill or go down the hill—don't just stand there taking casualties. He swallowed once, hard.

"Marines! Board that ship!"

"Aye aye, Sir!" The Gunny was just relieved that they were moving. "OK, you heard the Lieutenant! Through the aft hatch. MOVE!"

The Marines quickly boarded the ship through the large cargo opening. The space before them was eight and a half meters wide at the deck, with the ceiling about the same distance overhead.

The squad quickly fanned out across the large open space, taking positions behind the scattered crates setting on the deck.

Bridge, Parker's Folly, Preparing to Depart

On the Bridge, the Captain reacted swiftly to Lt. Curtis' report of armed men outside the ship. He checked the exterior cameras—the port side was clear but the starboard side was crawling with figures in US desert camouflage. The Captain also knew Marines when he saw them.

Where the hell did they come from? No matter, they're too late to prevent the ship from taking off. Thank goodness Gretchen tried to take the civilians off the starboard side or we wouldn't have seen the Marines until too late. With that, he activated the PA and gave final warning of the ship's impending departure. "Folly?"

"Yes, Captain?" the ship's computer answered.

"Folly, secure all external hatches and make the ship ready for departure." The cargo hold had two large exterior doors—technically a hatch is an opening in a deck while a door passes through a bulkhead, but in space the difference is somewhat moot. Both doors opened on parallel hinges, much like the side doors of a mini-van, sliding along the side of the hull. The forward door on the port side slid aft, while the aft door on the starboard side slid forward. The Marines boarded through the aft door.

"Captain?" the ship's voice spoke. "There are people entering the ship through the starboard side cargo door. I cannot close the cargo door without the possibility of injuring one of them."

Jack glanced at the external view to starboard and saw the last Marine enter the cargo hold. He knew he had to act fast. "Command override! Emergency close both cargo hold doors now!"

"Override acknowledged. The doors are now closed, Captain."

* * * * *

The last Marine through the entrance was Lt. Merryweather. Scant seconds after he stepped inside the massive door slammed shut behind him. The forward door had also shut and the result was a sudden spike in air pressure, a thud more felt in the chest than a sound. LCpl "Ronnie" Reagan, who had some knowledge of engineering and a knack for things mechanical, jumped. "Whoa. Did you see that!"

"See what," asked PFC Herman "Kato" Kwan.

"The way the hatch snapped shut!"

"Yeah, we was all right here, Ronnie," said PFC Harold Davis.

"Don't you get it, Two Can?" PFC Davis was called Two Can because of his inability to consume large amounts of alcohol, a favorite Marine recreational pastime. "That hatch has to weigh several tons. Did you see how fast it shut? It could have sliced one of us in half, easy."

"Cut the chatter and stay alert," the Gunny yelled. "We're on board uninvited—keep an eye out for possible hostiles. Just make sure they're armed and threatening before pointing a weapon at 'em."

* * * * *

Hellfire! Now he had Marines on board the ship. *OK, they are in the cargo hold, I can contain them there.* "Folly, lock all doors and hatches that access the cargo hold. Do not allow anyone access to the cargo hold except the ship's officers."

"As you wish, Captain. The cargo hold is now isolated from the rest of the ship. Should I discontinue environmental support as well?"

"What? No, let them keep breathing. I'll deal with our stowaways once we achieve orbit." *What an odd question, where had that come from? No matter, more pressing matters to handle.* "Engineering, Bridge. Dr. Gupta, do we have engines?"

"Oh yes, Captain. They are working splendidly. The last round of adjustments did the trick."

"Thank you, Doctor. Please secure your area for immediate takeoff. Mr. Vincent, activate the bottom repulsor array. Raise the ship, Mr. Vincent."

"Activating bottom repulsors, Sir." Muted crashing sounds from outside the ship accompanied a feeling of upward motion. The repulsors, as their name implied, push all matter in their vicinity

69

away. Ask Dr. Gupta for an explanation and he would go on about gravitons from other branes adjacent to our own and modifying the curvature of local spacetime but, in effect, they generate negative gravity—a force that repels mass instead of attracting it.

Like gravity, the effect is mutual. As the repulsor array repelled the planet beneath the hull, an equal but opposite force pushed the ship upward. It also had an immediate effect on the scaffolding that had surrounded the ship while it was under construction. The decking that the Marines had just been standing on was crumpled and cast aside like tissue paper as the massive ship rose four meters into the air.

"It looks like the hangar doors have jammed, Sir," Reported Bobby. The repulsors created a roaring sound as air was sucked from above the ship and blown outward below.

"Hmm, very well. Give me full forward shields, Mr. Medina. Mr. Danner, compensate for any displacement aft." The ship mounted repulsor generators over its entire hull, which could be used to form a protective, gravitational barrier surrounding the entire vessel. The ship shuddered slightly, then steadied.

"Mr. Medina, sound the maneuvering alarm." A whooping sound began that could be heard all over the ship.

"And now, if you please Mr. Vincent. We will need to ram through those doors. Ahead one quarter, take us out of the hangar."

The Ranch House, Parker's Ranch

"So let me get this straight," TK said to Chief Marshal Earl. "You want me to let you search my hangar looking for dangerous radiation, is that it?"

"I really don't need your permission, Mr. Parker. I'm just being polite. Those SWAT boys are about to enter your hangar, as you can see. Tell me, will they find something in there like, say, a rocket ship?"

"No they aren't," said the Texas Ranger, standing at the window. A muffled whomp sound came from outside.

"Aren't what, Sid?" replied the Marshal, clearly annoyed.

"They aren't about to enter the hangar. Looks like all the windows just blew out and yer SWAT boys are all suckin' ground."

"Huh?!" Marshal Earl's head whipped around.

Everyone in the room stared through the window at the hangar a half mile south of the ranch house. The windows along the first story of the building had all blown out, as the Ranger said, and it looked like the massive doors on the front of the hangar were slowly opening.

"Damn!" Marshal Earl, livid and red faced, slammed both hands on TK's desk and, leaning toward the old man, shouted, "Am I gona' find a God damned rocket ship in your hanger, Mr. Parker?"

"Nope." said the Texas Ranger, still at the window. Then, moving the toothpick from one corner of his mouth to the other, "the rocket ain't in the hangar any more."

Lower Deck, Parker's Folly

Lt. Curtis led Susan and JT from the forward airlock aft to the guest's dayroom. The lower deck contained the owner's stateroom forward of the passenger hatch, and four guest cabins, two on either side of the central passageway heading aft. Beyond the guest staterooms, just before the internal layout of the ship went from two decks forward to three decks amidships, there was a dayroom, snack bar and lounge area that spanned the width of the hull. A companionway on the port side led to the upper deck main lounge and dining area.

At the far side of the dayroom, coming up the short ladder from the lower deck officers' quarters, was Chief Zackly and two people, a man and a woman, dressed in the gray coveralls of construction personnel. The man had a hangdog look about him and the woman was glancing around nervously.

"I see you found your stowaways, Chief," the Lieutenant said in greeting. "And like my two charges, they also did not make it off the ship before the hatches were battened."

71

"Sorry, Ma'am. Couldn't get 'em off 'fore the rig for departure alarm sounded." As if on queue, the klaxon sounded again and the loudspeaker said, "Warning! High-g maneuvers imminent. Repeat, secure for high-g maneuvers!"

"Everyone to the chairs against the aft bulkhead, Quickly!" ordered Lt. Curtis, seating herself as she spoke. *I hope everyone else on board has enough sense to take a safe position,* she thought, adding out loud "JT, put your camera gear against the wall, don't try to hold it in your lap."

"Yes Ma'am. Well Miss Susan," JT said to his partner, stowing his video equipment on the floor between their chairs. "Looks like you are going to be on that first flight after all." Susan didn't answer, she just sat back in the lounge chair with her eyes tightly shut.

"What's going on?" asked the young woman in gray coveralls. "What's going to happen?"

"You chose the wrong day to tarry on board, girl," Lt. Curtis said. "The ship is about to launch."

"Tommy, you bastard! You said nothing would happen!" the girl shrieked, as the g-forces pushed them all back in the chairs. "Nooooo..." she cried as the air was forced from her lungs.

Cargo Bay, Parker's Folly

Within the enclosed space of the cargo hold the klaxon sounded and the loudspeaker blared, "Warning! High-g maneuvers imminent. Repeat, secure for high-g maneuvers!"

"What the hell does that mean?" asked Cpl Sizemore.

"It means the ship is going to take off and we are going to get hit with high-g forces, like a plane shot off an aircraft carrier," said LCpl Reagan. "Maybe worse."

"All right, hit the deck!" ordered the Lieutenant. Most of the squad fell to the deck and assumed prone positions.

"No!" yelled Reagan.

"What did you say, Marine?" snapped the Gunny. Lance Corporals did not countermand a Marine officer's orders.

"The front of the ship is that way," he said, pointing toward the front of the cargo bay. "When the ship blasts off it will throw everything against the aft bulkhead. We need to stand flat against the aft bulkhead, Gunny!"

Shit! Reagan is right, Rodriguez realized. "Listen up! Everyone get flat against the bulkhead. Do it now!"

"What about those crates? Won't they slide aft as well?" asked Doc White.

The Gunny looked closely at the nearest crate and noticed that the crates were strapped to their pallets and the pallets were locked to the deck with stout semi-circular metal clamps. "Looks like the pallets are clamped to the deck. I can't believe that the astronauts flying this thing would let crap rattle around in their cargo hold during blastoff. Against the bulkhead people."

Lt. Merryweather was still standing next to the exterior door and behind a large crate that half blocked the entrance when the door had been open. Rodriguez noticed that the cylindrical metal clamps that secured the other pallets to the deck were missing from the crate in front of the Lieutenant. "Lieutenant! Get away from the crate!" Then the cargo bay tipped on end.

The Gunny had been standing about a foot from the aft bulkhead. She was slammed against it on her side as the bulkhead became the new floor. Sharp pain coursed through her arm and shoulder. Looking sideways along the bulkhead, two of the Marines who had been lying prone slid into the wall and crumpled up. Beyond them, the Lieutenant slammed face down into the wall from about four feet away, followed immediately by the heavy unsecured crate.

There were snapping sounds, but it was hard to tell if they were from the crate or the Lieutenant's bones breaking. Lying pinned against the bulkhead, immobilized by the crushing acceleration, Rodriguez could see Lt. Merryweather's arm sticking out from under the crate, his hand bent back, its fingers arched in pain.

The Gunny struggled with all her strength and managed to roll onto her back. Over the roaring background noise, she could hear moaning on either side. Staring up at the cargo bay, as the suffocating hand of six gravities tried to push her through the bulkhead wall, she thought, *we have really screwed the pooch on this one.*

The Ranch House, Parker's Ranch

The Chief Marshal looked back out the window just in time to see two bent, 70 by 90 foot hangar doors flutter through the air like spastic butterflies. The silver object that had exited the hangar seconds ago was a blur, already more than a kilometer away and rapidly disappearing, due east.

"I'd step back from the window if I were you, gentlemen," TK offered, grinning like the cat that ate the canary. The party of lawmen looked back at the smiling old man just in time for the arriving sonic boom to shatter every window in the house.

As they were picking themselves back up off the floor, brushing off the shards of glass, the lawmen heard the old man say with great satisfaction: "damn fools, that weren't no rocket ship, that was a by God spaceship."

The Bridge, Parker's Folly, underway

TK Parker's spaceship surged forward with the acceleration of a top fuel dragster or a fighter jet being catapulted from the deck of an aircraft carrier. A force equivalent to six times that of normal Earth gravity pressed the bridge crew back into their padded seats. Parker's Folly was unarguably and irrevocably under way.

The massive vessel was accelerating at 60 m/sec^2 – slightly more than six gravities. One second after helmsman Vincent initiated forward flight, Parker's Folly had traveled 30 meters and was moving at 216 km/hr. She had tossed the hangar doors aside as if they were made of paper and the forward quarter of her hull was outside the building.

Two seconds after launch, the ship had all but cleared the hangar and was traveling at 432 km/hour. Six seconds, a tenth of a minute into the flight, Folly was over a kilometer from the hangar, headed east across the flat Texas scrub. She had just broken the sound barrier and was moving at nearly 1300 km/hr.

Following a course headed straight for San Angelo, the local elevation dropped but the land became progressively more hilly. Riding on the gravitational cushion created by the repulsor array, the ship undulated over minor wrinkles in the terrain. Things would get dangerous rapidly if the ship did not gain altitude, and quickly.

On the bridge, the crew was partially incapacitated by the sudden and unexpectedly strong acceleration. Between ragged breaths of air, the Captain gasped "cut... back... engines... now."

The helmsmen's chairs had controls built into their armrest much like a modern fighter jet. Billy Ray was able to focus enough to reduce drive thrust until the ship was just maintaining its forward velocity.

With the acceleration dropping to zero, the Captain quickly assessed their situation. The tan and brown country side was rushing by in a blur. "Give us a bit more altitude, Mr. Vincent."

The last thing they needed to do was tear through the residential areas around San Angelo at sixty feet doing 2,000 miles an hour. The Captain pulled up the standard flight profile for Low Earth Orbit insertion. "Folly, adjust LEO insertion profile based on our current position and velocity. Get us up to about 350 kilometers. Pass the profile to the helm."

"Roger, Captain."

"Mr. Vincent. Take us to LEO."

"Aye, aye, Captain. Low Earth Orbit coming right up," the lanky Texan confirmed. The g-forces returned as the ship's nose came up and the racing landscape fell away. The tan and brown blur that had been sweeping past the ship's transparent bow receded and quickly turned into a shrinking aerial view of the heart of Texas.

The horizon acquired curvature while the sky outside turned from tan, to light blue, to deep blue and finally to black. As the ship slipped from Earth's grasp and reached for the unbounded freedom of space a cry could be heard from the helm. Billy Ray Vincent, Texas born and bred, could not help but yell:

"Yeeeeeeee Haaaaaawwwwww!"

Part Two

A Dragon on the Limb of the Moon

Chapter 6

Canterbury, England, 1178 A.D.

At Christ Church in Canterbury, about an hour after sunset on the 18th of June, *Ano Domini 1178*, a band of five novice monks were observing the new crescent Moon. Suddenly, a flaming torch sprang up on the edge of the bright crescent, spewing out fire on the limb of the Moon. The monks cried out in terror as the body of the moon "writhed and throbbed like a wounded snake."

The phenomenon recurred several more times as the observers cowered. Later that same year, famed chronicler Fratello Gervase—known as Gervase of Canterbury, himself a monk at Christ Church—wrote down the five monks' recounting of those frightening events:

> *"This year on the Sunday before the Feast of Saint John the Baptist, after sunset when the moon was first seen, a marvellous sign was seen by five or more men sitting facing it. Now, there was a clear new moon, as was usual at that phase, its horns extended to the east; and behold suddenly the upper horn was divided in two. Out of the middle of its division a burning torch sprang, throwing out a long way, flames, coals and sparks. As well, the moon's body which was lower, twisted as though anxious, and in the words of those who told me and had seen it with their own eyes, the moon palpitated like a pummelled snake. After this it returned to its proper state. This vicissitude repeated itself a dozen times or more, namely that the fire took on tormented forms variously at random, and afterwards returned to its prior state. Even after these vicissitudes, from horn to horn, that means along its length, it became semi-black. This to me who writes this was told by those men who with their own eyes saw it, and who are willing to swear an oath that they have not added to nor falsified the above written."*

In later years, scientists hypothesized that the monks had observed an asteroid shower striking the Moon. In fact, some say it was the impact that created the lunar crater Giordano Bruno. Many astronomers accepted that the well-chronicled event coincided with the formation the crater, the youngest substantial impact feature on the Moon.

Even more recently, new astronomical calculations have brought this theory into doubt. Based on the size of the crater—measuring

22 kilometers across—the impacting asteroid must have been between one and three kilometers wide. Such an asteroid impacting on Earth would threaten the existence of human civilization.

If an impact had blasted a crater as large as Giordano Bruno into the Moon's northeast limb, it would have ejected large volumes of rocky material. This would have caused a week-long meteor shower, raining down 50,000 meteors each hour as ten million tons of rock pelted the entire Earth. Yet no vigilant 12th century sky watcher in Europe, Arabia or China reported such a storm.

It has been suggested that those five ancient sky-watchers might have seen the fiery display of a meteor traveling along their line of sight rather than an impact on the moon. But perhaps not. The monks' description does not match that of an earthly meteor shower, which medieval observers were well acquainted with. If it was not a meteor or an impact event, what could have caused the heavenly spectacle that one observer called "a dragon on the limb of the moon?"

International Space Station, Low Earth Orbit

Lieutenant Colonel Ludmilla Stefanovna Tropsha of the *Voenno-Vozdushnye Sily*—the Russian Federation Air Forces—looked out the observation window at the blue and white planet slowly turning below her. *Well Luda,* she thought to herself, *this was the thing you wanted most in the world, I hope it was worth it.*

All the sacrifices, the failed marriage to Yuri, not having any children, fighting her way into what was left of the Russian space program. Fellow officers told her she was throwing her career away for a chance to fly in space, and then probably only once. The old fashioned Soyuz capsules only had room for three cosmonauts. One seat had to be for a Russian pilot. That left two seats for Russian scientists or to rent out, and the Americans and the Europeans paid millions in cash to transport their people to and from the ISS.

Lt. Col Tropsha was not a pilot, she was a medical doctor with a doctorate in Biology. Her trip was paid for by the rapidly dwindling funds of ROSCOSMOS, the Russian Federal Space Agency, the *Rodina's* equivalent of NASA. Of course, NASA had funding problems of its own—and no man-rated rockets of its own. If the Americans had somehow managed to continue flying their space shuttle, the three remaining people on board the ISS wouldn't be in this fix.

The Sun was acting up. A big sunspot "crackling with activity" had been emerging over the Sun's eastern limb a week ago. Then NASA's Solar Dynamics Observatory recorded a surge of extreme ultraviolet radiation from the sunspot's magnetic canopy 24 hours ago. This was no minor solar radiation event, it was the worst solar eruption in a century.

Normally, solar storms do not affect people on Earth's surface. Radio communications may be disrupted and dramatic aurora displays may paint the night skies with ghostly dancing light, but generally there is no threat to those living on the planet's surface. In space, on the other hand, large solar explosions can potentially damage satellites and other spacecraft. Of course, as with everything in nature, there are exceptions.

On the morning of Thursday, September 1, 1859, English solar astronomer Richard Carrington noted the appearance of an enormous group of extraordinarily bright spots on the face of the Sun. Before dawn the next day, skies all over Earth erupted in brilliant auroras so intense that newspapers could be read as though it were daylight. Miners in Colorado stumbled out of bed and started preparing breakfast, thinking the Sun already up. Stunning auroras appeared even in tropical latitudes, painting the skies over Hawaii and the Bahamas blood red.

More troubling, ships' compasses no longer functioned properly, birds temporarily lost their ability to navigate and telegraph systems around the world were knocked out. Sparks from telegraph keys shocked their operators and set telegraph paper on fire. The Carrington Event's gigantic coronal mass ejection was sent directly toward Earth, taking only 18 hours to travel the 150 million kilometer distance. Quite remarkable, since such journeys normally take three to four days. The total energy emitted was equivalent to tens of millions of atomic bombs exploding at the same time.

This new solar eruption—thought not to be quite as powerful as the Carrington Event—was still monstrous, measuring more than X30 on the Solar Richter scale. Though the two scales cannot be directly compared, if the equivalent of the solar explosion were transferred to Earth it would register more than 17 on the terrestrial Richter scale.

The peak of the massive star quake had been detected 18 hours ago and, like the Carrington Event, the flare was aimed directly at Earth. The particle radiation from the eruption was predicted to reach Earth in about 8 hours. It not only represented a severe threat to all communications, terrestrial power grids, and satellites orbiting the planet, the predicted radiation levels were going to be deadly outside of the atmosphere. This meant that anyone trapped on the International Space Station was going to get fried, and trapped Luda and her two companions were.

Normally there were six people working on board the ISS, three each for the pair of Soyuz "lifeboat" capsules docked at the station. Trouble was, when the alarm was raised to evacuate the station, one of the capsules malfunctioned. After consulting with mission control and among themselves, the six crew members drew straws. The three winners bade their companions a tearful good bye, boarded the working capsule and headed back to Earth and safety. The losers—Colonel Ivan Kondratov, scientist Hiroyuki Saito and Lt Colonel Tropsha—were left to their own devices, waiting for the Sun to kill them.

Colonel Ivan Alexievitch Kondratov was also a Russian officer, he would have been the pilot of the second escape capsule if the damned thing had been in working order. He was in the crew quarters, talking on the radio to his wife and children. Undoubtedly Ivan, ever the stoic Russian hero, was remaining calm while his wife and two daughters wept back on Earth. That didn't mean he was not as anguished as they were, just that, like most Russian men, he had emotional "issues," as the Americans would say.

The Japanese scientist Hiroyuki "Yuki" Saito was a cosmologist and astrophysicist. A brilliant scientist by all accounts, Dr. Saito had worked for years to earn a trip into space. Originally from Fukushima prefecture—Saito is the 4th most common family name in the prefecture—fate seemed to be dealing him the cruelest hand of all.

Years ago, his wife and young son were on a bullet train headed for Tokyo when the 2011 earthquake struck. Following the 9.0 quake, the worst in Japanese history, a 30 foot tsunami had come ashore. When it retreated the bullet train and all its passengers were nowhere to be found. Evidently the train had been washed out to sea with all aboard. Now, in an improbable twist of fate, Saito was about to be killed by another tsunami, this one made of high-energy atomic particles instead of water.

Yuki, as he preferred to be called, was currently in Node 3, the Tranquility module. He was looking out the windows of the cupola, which offered the best outside view on the station having six large windows on its sides and one on top. Luda figured that the astrophysicist was up there making peace with the universe that had treated him so unfairly.

Luda had thought about calling her estranged ex-husband but decided against it. Their marriage had ended badly a decade ago and she saw no reason to pretend they still meant something to each other. Besides, in the end, everyone dies alone.

As the station doctor, she had full access to the Health Maintenance Facility. While the HMF was not equipped for surgery, there were a number of strong emergency painkillers in the ISS medical accessory kits. She was preparing for the worst—three syringes, filled with a potent narcotic cocktail that would hopefully bring painless ends to the three stranded cosmonauts.

Nothing to do now but wait. Two things Russians do well—suffer and wait. She sighed and looked back out the porthole.

Ranch House, Parker's Ranch, Texas

A number of emergency rescue vehicles had driven out to the now disheveled dirigible hanger and rescue workers were searching for any survivors inside the structure. The SWAT team members suffered only minor cuts and bruises, their pride suffering more damage than anything else. Of course, if they had been inside the building when the ship powered up their shredded remains would now be scattered over several acres of TK's ranch.

After recovering from the shock of the departing ship's sonic boom and the imploding house windows, Chief Marshal Earl looked out the shattered window in TK's office at the ruined hangar. "My God! There was a squad of Marines in that building."

"What!" TK and several others exclaimed at the same time. "I didn't see no Marines running around out there," he finished.

"They were sent in from the other side. Snuck up by air so they couldn't be seen from the house," the Marshal answered. "If we find the remains of ten dead Marines in your hangar, Mr. Parker, there will be hell to pay."

"Did you ever think that if they hadn't snuck up they'd a bin all right?" the old man snapped. Inside TK felt sick, he never intended for anyone to get hurt. He couldn't believe that Jack would have callously taken off with people in the hangar. Of course, the effects of the ship's departure were a bit more dramatic than anyone had expected.

One of the local Sheriff's deputies stuck his head into the room and said: "Just talked to the fire and rescue people on the radio. There is no sign of human remains in or around the hangar."

"Are they sure no one was killed? Where did they go?"

"The guys out there said that anyone inside would have been turned into hamburger. If those Marines had been in there, there would have been blood and guts all over," the Deputy continued. "The Osprey pilots said they entered the hangar ten minutes before blastoff and didn't come back out. They must have gotten on board the ship."

"Well that's a relief," said Sid Hopkins, the Texas Ranger. "You know Mr. Parker, even if those Marines are safe on board somewhere, I think the federal boys are going to be royally upset with you."

"What did I do?" said a secretly relieved TK Parker. "I'm just an old man, mindin' my own business and bein' harassed by the authorities."

"Oh, I think that there are laws against flying unlicensed experimental aircraft, shooting things into outer space without a permit, and kidnapping Marines is bound to upset the Pentagon."

The deputy, who had been talking on his radio, interrupted again. "We got reports coming in from all over. There are claims that some cattle were killed by the ship's passage—flung 'em two hundred feet through the air—and an old gas station was blown apart next county over. Evidently the ship pulled up and headed for the sky just before passing over San Angelo—the sonic boom blew out windows all over town. The people are up in arms, but they think it was part of the air show."

"I'll bet the air show people are going have a hard time convincing the town's folk that their windows were broken by a renegade spaceship and not the flyovers," remarked Ranger Hopkins. "No sir, Mr. Parker. I do believe you'll be spending a lot of time with these fellas here for the foreseeable future."

Well, thought TK, *that's done. The ship is safely away and it sounds like nobody got killed—what a relief. I wish I could talk to Jack and find out what happened to those Marines. Hell, I don't even know who all is on board the Folly. But Jack's a big boy. He knows how to take care of business, that's why I hired him.*

In any case, TK had some of the best lawyers in Texas. They would soon spring him from custody and tie the authorities up in legal knots. It would take a while, but eventually he would be able to talk to the ship and find out what really happened during its spectacular departure.

Just then, Maria entered the room. "Senor Parker, I'm sorry but the coffee pot was shattered by the big boom."

"Never mind, Maria. I think we'd all rather have bourbon instead of coffee about now—that is if there are any unbroken bottles left. What do you say Ranger, Marshal? Like you said, no reason to be uncivilized."

The Bridge, Parker's Folly

After the helmsmen set the flight plan, the trip to orbit went smoothly. Acceleration had again peaked at around six Gs and once headed toward space the ride had smoothed out significantly. The roaring sound from outside the ship, caused by the passage of air, quickly subsided as Earth's atmosphere was left behind. Folly was now in a roughly 350 km high orbit traveling about 27,500 km/hr.

The planet below was mostly dark as they flew into the oncoming night, after passing over the Atlantic Ocean. Soon the Indian Ocean would be below and they would see the Sun rise over the Pacific. In its current orbit it took about 94 minutes to circle the planet below. Both that time and the orbital velocity were dictated by altitude and the gravitational pull of Earth. When George Lucas had the Empire's Death Star "orbiting at maximum velocity" it was so much Sci-Fi BS—every orbit and position has its own velocity.

Hokey Hollywood movies aside, the ship was eerily quiet as the bridge crew sat mesmerized by the view outside Folly's transparent bow. Unlike the old U.S. Space Shuttle, which rolled 180 degrees onto its back during the climb to orbit, Parker's Folly retained the same orientation it had when it left the hangar. Earth was passing under the nose of the spacecraft as the crew looked up at the brilliant full moon and unblinking stars above their heads.

Let's give the lounge's starboard side viewport a full on look at Earth passing by, thought the Captain. "Helm, please gently roll the ship clockwise by 90 degrees."

"Aye Aye, Captain. Roll the ship clockwise 90 degrees."

"Gently, Mr. Danner. I think everyone on board is shaken up enough after our ascent."

"Yes, Sir." replied Danner, as the still dark planet began to swing around to the ship's right side.

Enough wool gathering, Jack thought, angry with himself, *I should be finding out what shape the ship and crew are in.* "Mr. Medina, what is the status of the ship's systems?"

"Engines are at idle, Sir, all parameters well within limits. Hull integrity is intact, no breaches and no pressure drops in sealed sections. Repulsor shields are up. The power reactors are running, power draw is negligible.

"Environmental is running at around 87 percent, probably because the hydroponics were not all on-line before we took off. Given the number of souls on board that poses no problems. Air pressure is 14.7 psi, relative humidity 25% and temperature is 23°C.

"Internal visual monitoring is just now coming on line and the deck gravitational system is still running internal self-calibration—it will not be up for another 35 to 45 minutes. Other than that, Captain, all systems are nominal."

"Very good, thank you Mr. Medina." Of the two, the more critical was the deck gravity. The reason for Folly's horizontal deck layout was that, when the deck gravity system was functioning, an adjustable artificial gravity gradient defined down to be toward the deck underfoot. Even more importantly, the system compensated for the ship's acceleration.

If it had been working during takeoff no one would have felt any motion, let-alone been flung violently about. Unfortunately, they were never able to successfully calibrate the deck gravity while setting at the bottom of Earth's gravity well—that task had to wait until they were in orbit. "Engineering, Bridge. Dr. Gupta are you all right?"

"Uh, Bridge, Engineering. We are all right, mostly, but Dr. Gupta can't answer right now."

"Who is this and what seems to be the problem with Dr. Gupta?"

"This is Freddy Adams, Captain," Adams was one of the engineering techs and the only tech on board when they launched. "We came through the takeoff fine but Dr. Gupta has space sickness —he's throwing up, Sir."

Space sickness, or space adaptation syndrome as NASA calls it, can last for days and be quite debilitating. Caused by confused signals from the inner ear under zero-gravity conditions, when it strikes and who will get it can be hard to predict. People who show an exceptional tolerance to motion sickness—at sea or when flying jets for instance—can suffer the worst symptoms in space. Fortunately, when the deck gravity generators come up that problem should go away. Until then things could get messy.

"Very good, Mr. Adams, assist the Doctor and try to contain the mess." Globules of vomit had a tendency to go everywhere in zero-g. Clean-up in the engineering spaces would not be pleasant.

"Environmental, Bridge. Your status please."

"Bridge, Environmental," came the immediate reply, in a deep rumbling voice. "Bear here, Captain. I'm fine but Melissa is hurt."

Melissa Scott Hamilton was a horticulturist and one of the environmental techs. She mostly stayed in the hydroponics section, tending to the plants that helped recycle Folly's air and which

87

would eventually provide the crew with fresh vegetables. A slight, shy young woman from Louisiana, she and Lt. Bear, the ship's gruff security officer, had developed a mutual attraction. Lt. Bear could usually be found in Ms. Hamilton's company when his duties didn't require him to be elsewhere.

"What are the nature of Ms. Hamilton's injuries? Are they life threatening?"

"No. She has a broken foreleg but is OK otherwise."

"You mean one of her arms is broken, Lieutenant?"

"Yeah, right, her right arm. I'll take her forward to the sick bay."

Ah yes, that reminds me. "No, Lieutenant. Make her as comfortable as you can and then go forward to the cargo hold airlock. We have some uninvited guests in the hold."

"Guests in the cargo hold?"

"Yes, Lieutenant. We seem to have acquired a squad of Marines just prior to takeoff. Monitoring is up so you can keep them under observation, but don't take any action on your own. I will come aft with First Officer Curtis and some of the ratings—that way we can hit them from both ends at once."

"Yes, Sir," came the eager reply. "And what are we expected to do with the Marines?"

"I expect us to quell them, Lieutenant."

Passenger's Dayroom, Lower Deck

When the oppressive acceleration that held her in the lounge chair was replaced by zero-gravity, Lt. Curtis figured they were in orbit. The two news people were looking around, big eyed, clutching the arms of their chairs with viselike grips. Chief Zackly came up out of his chair slowly, only to drift off helplessly across the dayroom.

His feet no longer in contact with the deck, the little man was running in place in a vain attempt to find firmer footing. Waving his arms at the furniture, just out of reach, a steady stream of mumbled obscenities emanated from the frustrated boatswain.

Lt. Curtis glanced at the floating chief, shook her head and took something out of a pouch attached to her waist. Carefully, she brought one knee up and reaching down slipped a booty over her footwear. Placing that foot securely on the deck, she repeated the process for her other foot. Newly shod, the Lieutenant stood up and took two careful steps toward the windmilling chief, who was now upside down.

"Chief," said the First Officer, offering the stranded sailor a stabilizing arm, "stop flailing about and put your deck booties on."

"Yes, Ma'am," came the embarrassed reply, as the Chief accepted the proffered arm and with considerable grace, pivoted and planted his feet back on the deck. He too, extracted a pair of the slip-on booties and quickly installed them over his shoes, mumbling "never needed booties to stick to the deck of a destroyer."

Talking into the pip on her collar, the Lieutenant said, "Bridge, lower deck Dayroom. Lt. Curtis here."

"Go ahead Dayroom. What is your status Lieutenant?"

"I am with Chief Zackly, the two news people, and a pair of construction types who got stuck on board, Captain. All of us are unharmed."

"Good, Lieutenant. Could you please bring your party to the lounge on the upper deck? It seems we have more unwanted stowaways on board, specifically a squad of Marines in the cargo hold. We need to get the civilians stowed in a safe place before we neutralize the Marines."

"Aye aye, Sir."

"I'll meet you in the lounge. Captain out."

"Alright, you heard the Captain. We are going to move to the second deck." With this announcement, the female dock worker began whimpering again and her companion added a frightened edge to his guilty demeanor.

Susan and JT, on the other hand, had overcome their initial fear and were floating just above the chairs they had been seated in. Rather than being stressed out by the wild takeoff they were goofing around like a couple of school children, both savoring the new experience of weightlessness.

Watching the pair, Lt. Curtis could not help but smile and shake her head. Turning to the Chief and his two stowaways she said: "Chief, go up the companionway first and I'll send the civilians up one at a time. You two, stay seated until I tell you to move."

"Aye aye, Ma'am," said the wiry little sailor, moving catlike to the aft portside corner of the dayroom. There a cylindrical companionway led to the upper deck. About a meter in diameter, a ladder was built into the back side of the tubular passageway. The Chief took a long graceful stride into the well of the companionway, grasped the rungs of the ladder and disappeared up the tube in one smooth motion. The Chief was evidently trying to prove that his earlier out of control performance was an anomaly.

"OK, Miss. You first," said Lt. Curtis, motioning to the young woman.

"No, no, no," came the frightened reply as panic spread across the woman's face.

"We don't have time for this!" And with that, the Lieutenant plucked the woman in gray out of her chair, slid over to the companionway in a single gliding step and tossed her up and out of sight, yelling "heads up, Chief!"

She turned to the remaining three civilians and said: "Next!"

* * * * *

"Mr. Vincent, I understand you have a passing familiarity with firearms?" Asked the Captain, as he floated to the starboard side of the bridge.

"Yes sir, Captain. I know my way around a rifle or a pistol." came the somewhat careful reply.

"Then come with me. Mr. Danner, you will remain at the helm. Mr. Medina, you have the Conn. Mr. Vincent and I are going aft."

90

The Captain disappeared down the starboard passageway, in the direction of the lounge, with Billy Ray attempting to catch up.

* * * * *

In the lounge, Lt. Curtis emerged from the companionway, which terminated in the left rear corner of the large dining area and bar the news people had toured earlier. The Chief had the two construction workers seated on a couch in the lounge area while JT and Susan were amusing themselves by bouncing back and forth slowly, from one end of the lounge to the other. JT even had his camera and was filming Susan as she drifted past.

The Chief, who was rummaging around behind the bar, found what he was looking for and bounded over to the couch holding the couple in gray. "Here's some booties, put 'em on. And for you, Missy, a barf bag. Do not puke on my deck! If you feel like chumming, use the bag."

"I see you have things well in hand, Chief."

"Yes, Ma'am. 'Cept for the flyin' Wallenda's there," he said, jerking a thumb in the direction of the cavorting news crew.

Favoring the Chief with one of her rare smiles to show that he wasn't in trouble for the news crew's antics, the Lieutenant stepped forward and deftly snagged the passing Susan, gently grounding her on the deck.

"Aw lieutenant, this is fun! We have to get some footage to beam back home!" adding in a hushed voice, "I'm so glad I wore pants today and not a skirt."

"There will be ample opportunity for recording once everything on board has been secured, Ms. Write." Curtis reached out and hooked the passing JT who was traveling in the opposite direction of his on-camera talent. "You too, Mr. Taylor. There will be time to frolic later in the voyage. Right now, I need you to put on the booties the Chief has and stay in contact with the deck—seated would be even better."

"Come on, Lt. Curtis. You have got to know that this is the experience of a lifetime!" said the now grounded JT. "Come to think about it, you and the Chief seem strangely familiar with zero-gravity, like you have been here before."

"In a way, Mr. Taylor. Mr. Parker sent most of the crew members to a firm in Arizona that operates a specially modified Boeing 727, a 'vomit comet'. It flies parabolic arcs creating a weightless environment allowing you to float as if you were in space."

"That is just too cool," said JT, as he donned the floor sticking booties given to him by the Chief. "How can I get a job like this?"

"Not so fast there, Astro-boy. Don't be so quick to jump ship," said his partner, floating somewhat sideways in her struggle to slip her booties on. Ever the reporter, Susan righted herself by grasping the arm of a nearby chair and asked "how much did that cost? A bundle I bet."

"They normally charge $5,000 per person or $175,000 for the whole plane. TK got a deal—only $500,000 for an entire week. By the end of the week it was much more like work than play—two prospective crew members quit and left after a few days."

"Regaling the media with harrowing tales of astronaut training, Lieutenant?" asked the Captain as he floated up. Behind him, another crew member in a blue jumpsuit was bouncing off the walls and furniture, hurrying to catch up.

"Yes, Sir. They thought that the Chief was suspiciously agile under zero-g conditions and before they concluded that this wasn't our first flight I explained our extensive training for this mission. Wouldn't want any disinformation to be reported in the media, Sir."

"No indeed, Lieutenant. Chief, I would like you to stay with our guests and ensure their continued comfort. I also don't want them straying outside the mess until we get our Marine infestation problem solved."

"Aye aye, Captain," answered the wizened Chief, coming to attention. "I'll keep a close watch on 'em, Sir." Nodding to the boatswain, the Captain continued, "Mr. Vincent, Lt. Curtis, and I will be going aft to the cargo hold."

"Captain?" JT asked. "If you are going to talk with those Marines —and I am assuming that they are the same ones that were on the dock before we left—I would be very careful. They seemed a little trigger happy."

"Thank you, Mr. Taylor. We'll be careful."

Cargo Hold, Parker's Folly

In the cargo hold, the shaken Marines were trying to literally figure out which end was up. Three of the wounded Marines had drifted away from the rear bulkhead where they had been pinned by the blastoff acceleration. So had the crate that crushed Lt. Merryweather, whose contorted body was also adrift. The loose crate had shifted when the ship rolled a while ago, and was now slowly tumbling above the deck in the middle of the hold.

Davis and Kwan were the two Marines that slid prone into the bulkhead. Kwan was unconscious and Davis had a leg and an arm that stuck out at unusual angles, most likely broken. Feldman had actually landed on the forward side of one of the crates, he was not moving either.

That left Reagan and Sanchez on the right and Sizemore and Washington on the left. Sizemore and Washington were clinging to the side of a large crate with Washington and his SAW farthest forward. Reagan and Sanchez were slowly working their way along the starboard wall. Doc was attempting to administer painkillers to the drifting Davis. The Gunny herself was only marginally operational. She had what felt like a separated right shoulder and was barely able to handle her weapon offhanded.

No doubt about it, the squad was totally FUBAR. Rodriguez tried shifting position and was rewarded with a stabbing pain in her shoulder. *Yep, it's separated at best,* she thought.

"Those of you that ain't so banged up, find someplace to hold onto and stay put." Damn the Gunny thought, even yelling hurt. "Doc, can you get Kato and Two Can secured against the bulkhead. This thing could start maneuvering again for all we know."

"I'll try Gunny."

Good kid, Rodriguez said to herself, she's pretty banged up herself but she's not complaining. Then she heard a retching sound. Looking to her left she saw Sizemore puking his guts out, a spray of vomit droplets spewing out toward the center of the compartment.

"Washington! Get Sizemore a sack or something." Christ, they were down on firepower as it was. Not that it would be easy firing the machine gun or even a carbine while floating around the cabin with no gravity. Yep, definitely FUBAR.

Forward Cargo Hold Airlock, Parker's Folly

The Captain's party had made their way to the lower deck, after stopping at the arms locker, and were now in the lower deck airlock that opened onto the cargo hold. Along the way they had picked up Stephen Hitch and Mathew Jacobs, the two remaining crew members that were on board when the ship had so suddenly departed. All were armed with what appeared to be handguns.

"Lt. Bear, this is the Captain. Are you in position?"

"Yes, Captain. I'm in the upper deck airlock overlooking the cargo hold. It looks like half of the squad is already out of action—a couple are hurt pretty bad."

"We will get the wounded some help as soon as we disarm the lot of them," the grim faced Captain told his Master-at-Arms, he didn't need to ask if Lt. Bear was armed.

"OK, people, this is the plan: we will enter through the airlock door, spread out and work our way aft, using the crates and boxes for cover. Stay in contact and do not fire unless I give the word. Lt. Curtis, you and Jacobs take the port side. Mr. Vincent take Hitch and cover the starboard approach. I will go down the middle. I'm going to give them an opportunity to surrender their weapons peaceably. If they refuse we will shoot everyone that resists. Understood?"

"What about Bear, Captain?" asked Lt. Curtis.

"He is our reserve. If things go sideways, he will enter from the upper deck aft and reinforce our attack. Do you understand that, Lt. Bear?"

"Yes, Sir." came Lt. Bear's curt answer.

"OK then, If t'were to be done, t'were best done quickly."

"What Sir?" asked Hitch, confused.

94

"That'd be Shakespeare, Steve," answered Billy Ray, "Macbeth."

"Sorry," said the Captain, "the burden of a liberal education. Let's do this people." The airlock door slid quietly aside and the five armed crew members moved into the cargo hold.

As the crew members moved forward along either side of the hold, the Captain walked to the center of the large open space. He faced forward, hidden by the clutter of crates and equipment behind him in the hold. Flexing his knees, the Captain sprung from the deck, turned a half flip and landed on his feet on the ceiling.

There were large pieces of equipment, including some of the ship's small boats, secured against the cargo hold ceiling. Using these for cover Jack worked his way aft. From his perch he could see the Marines below anxiously scanning the deck. *They don't realize that combat in zero-gravity is a three dimensional affair,* he thought. *Good, we need every advantage we can get.* He switched on the PA and spoke through the comm pip on his collar.

Cargo Hold, Parker's Folly

"Attention! Marines in the cargo hold. This is Captain Sutton, the master of this ship. Surrender your weapons and you will not be harmed."

Where did that come from? The Gunny looked about for a source, then yelled, "Show yourself! We'll see who remains unharmed!" These space assholes had wounded half her squad and probably killed the Lieutenant, she was not in a surrendering mood.

"Gunnery Sergeant," the voice continued, "I can see that you only have five effectives left. Your wounded need medical care. Put down your weapons and let us help you."

"My orders are to seize this ship, and that's what we're going to do. How about you surrendering and avoid any bloodshed among your crew?"

"Sergeant, where are you going to go? The ship is in orbit and you are locked in the cargo hold." The Captain could sense that this negotiation was not going well. "Get ready," he whispered over the crew frequency.

Just then, Jacobs, pistol in hand, came into view around one of the crates on the port side. Again it was Sanchez who fired the first rounds, aimed single shots this time. Bullets could be seen striking the crate around Jacobs when he was suddenly jerked back to cover.

"Lt. Curtis, what's your status?" whispered the Captain.

"Jacobs has a flesh wound, nothing life threatening but he's out of the fight," came the Lieutenant's terse reply.

Bloody hell! I need to end this quickly, Jack thought. "You need to control your people, Sergeant. There is nothing preventing us from withdrawing and venting the hold to space. Marines are tough but they can't breath vacuum. I'll ask you one more time, surrender and avoid further casualties."

That crewman in blue only had some kind of sidearm, the Gunny realized, *they are only lightly armed. Even five of us should be able to take them!* "Listen up, Captain. Your people don't stand a chance. We have automatic weapons and grenade launchers. You mess with us and we'll blow this ship to hell."

Damn it! The Captain's thoughts raced. *I'm sure that the rifle bullets won't do any major damage to the ship but a 40mm grenade is another story. I have no idea what popping off a couple of those in here would do. And they might be able to breach one of the interior airlocks with a grenade.* He peered down from his perch on the ceiling. *Yes, that Marine by the crate on the right has a grenade launcher attached to his weapon, and one on the left, by the exterior cargo door has one as well. This has to end now.*

"Lt. Bear, I need you to take out the Marine on the starboard side with the grenade launcher. I'll take the one on the port side by the crate. Everyone else covering fire. On my mark... Now!"

* * * * *

Things had just quieted back down. From her position against the rear bulkhead, the Gunny was exposed, but had a good view of the entire area in front of the squad. Sanchez was swatting at the expelled casings from the rounds he fired—they had bounced off the wall beside him and were now floating around him like brass flies.

96

Suddenly there were people in jumpsuits on both sides of the hold brandishing peculiar looking pistols. As shots erupted from the Marines, a huge white form streaked over her head. The white creature collided with the large crate drifting in the middle of the chamber. It landed on all fours, then lept off to the right, sending the crate spinning forward.

The huge creature landed on PFC Reagan, swatting his carbine out of his hands. The M320 grenade launcher, the stock and the upper all went flying in different direction. *That looks like a fucking polar bear!* the shocked Gunny thought. She didn't have time to ponder the meaning of a polar bear attack on a space ship, events in the cargo hold were unfolding too quickly.

On the starboard side, Sanchez stepped away from the wall to get a shot at the polar bear that was mauling Reagan. As he did he was shot from behind by a tall figure in blue. Shot was a bit of a misnomer, since no projectiles were involved. Instead, a flickering pencil thin beam of blue light reached out from the man's pistol, striking Sanchez in the back.

When the beam struck Sanchez, his arms and legs flew straight out from his body, jerking uncontrollably. His carbine was flung toward the ceiling by his body's involuntary reaction. Hearing the sound of the SAW firing, the Gunny looked to her left.

Washington had let loose a burst at the crewman who shot Sanchez. Unfortunately, he was holding the heavy weapon with both hands and, unbraced, the recoil from the machine gun threw the big man back. The burst went wide as Washington slammed into the crate behind him. The man in blue, who had taken cover behind a crate, popped back up and shot Washington with a blue beam of light.

The effect of the flickering beam on Washington was similar to its effect on Sanchez. Both of the big Lance Corporal's arms flew out wide, but Washington retained a grip on the SAW with his right hand. As his muscles spasmed he fired off random bursts, mostly in the direction of his own squad members.

Lt. Curtis viewed these developments on a screen sewn into the sleeve of her jumpsuit. She quickly holstered her sidearm and launched herself at waist height toward the large crate sheltering Washington and Sizemore. Twisting in flight, she drew her legs up and grabbed the securing strap at the corner of the crate as she flew by.

Grabbing the strap caused the tall Lieutenant to swing around like a gymnast on the high bar. As she swung across Washington's twitching body she kicked out with both legs, knocking the machine gun from the Marine's grip. Unfortunately, the Lieutenant lost purchase on the strap and the recoil from the kick sent her drifting forward into the center of the squad's field of fire.

Cpl Sizemore, currently in between bouts of retching, swung his weapon up, bringing it to bear on the helpless figure in black. Before he could fire, a blue beam struck him; this time the bolt had come from above. The Gunny looked up and saw another figure in black standing on the ceiling of the chamber, looking down at her.

Shit, he has us enfiladed, she thought, trying to raise her carbine. Then something large and heavy landed on her chest. Pain knifed through her injured shoulder and, just before she passed out, she thought she heard the polar bear say "drop the gun, Bitch."

Chapter 7

AFTAC, Patrick AFB, Florida

Senior Airman Robinson had forgotten his desire to go off shift as the dramatic events unfolded in West Texas. AFTAC had monitored the squad of Marines entering the building via the comms link from the MV-22, then pandemonium broke out when garbled reports described the ship "blasting off along the ground" headed east. He had been expecting his satellites to pickup the speeding rocket ship as it accelerated like a silver daemon toward San Angelo and Goodfellow AFB, but his instruments reported nothing.

The eye witness accounts coming in didn't make much sense either. Evidently, the nearly 500 foot long, silver rocket ship wasn't a rocket after all. No pillar of fire blasted from its tail, propelling it forward. One sheriff's deputy said it looked more like a Japanese maglev train leaving the station than anything else—except this train ran on no special track.

They really didn't have good tracking on the ship until it popped up off the deck and headed for space. Then the FAA radar on King Mountain picked it up briefly. By the time they got good lock, the ship had all ready cleared commercial airspace and was doing 12,000 miles per hour. From the trajectory it was following there was little doubt that Parker's Folly, as everyone was calling it, was headed for orbit and maybe beyond.

"Robinson, we're getting a video feed from the local TV down there," Major Beldsoe called from the observers' platform behind his monitoring position. "Could you put it up on the large screen?"

"Yes, Ma'am," the Airman said, rapidly punching buttons on his console. A window containing the KWTEX News opened on the large tracking display on the wall. It was showing an exterior shot of what had to be the dirigible hanger with a pretty blond woman talking into a microphone. Robinson turned the sound up.

"...and as you can see from the size of its hangar, TK Parker's spaceship is truly Texas sized." The scene jumped to an inside shot of a long, cylindrical vessel stretching off to the farthest reaches of the huge hangar. The voice of the woman continued.

"Though the ship hasn't been officially named, many of the workers refer to it as Parker's Folly, implying that it is just the wild dream of an eccentric old billionaire. Even TK Parker himself uses the name, but to him it is anything but a joke." The picture now showed an interior shot of a classy bar and lounge area with a large, odd shaped picture window.

"As you can see, the Folly is not your bare-bones NASA spacecraft. She's more like a well appointed private yacht than the old Space Shuttle. I asked the ship's Captain, Jack Sutton, about that."

The scene changed to show a tall, trim man in a black jumpsuit, sitting in a chair that could have come right off the set of Star Trek. Behind the man was the transparent nose of the vessel, glittering like a silver and crystal cathedral window. The Captain looked into the camera and began to speak. "That's right, Susan. This ship is a combination private yacht and research vessel..."

"Find out who that guy is," said the Colonel. "From his speech and bearing I'd lay money that he's former military."

"The FBI already identified him as John D. Sutton, former U.S. Navy Commander," Maj Bledsoe provided. "He was evidently cashiered six years ago under questionable circumstances."

"Was he charged with anything?"

"Not really, Sir. Evidently his XO disobeyed a direct order and, as a result, several sailors died in a bombing incident. Since Sutton was the ship's captain he got caught in the political fallout. Ended his career."

"Did he suffer a breakdown or anything?" It would be easy to dismiss him as crazy like the old rancher, except he doesn't sound like a madman or a fool. On screen, the interview with the Captain was wrapping up. The reporter had just asked when the ship was ready to depart.

"We are still loading provisions and scientific lab equipment but the ship is space-worthy and can takeoff any time. We expect to be leaving Earth on her maiden voyage any time now. Of course, that's up to Mr. Parker, the owner."

"Thank you, Captain," the blond reporter said, the scene cutting to a panning shot of the glass enclosed bow. "There you have it. A West Texas rancher with his own space program has built one very impressive spaceship. Will it actually fly? We promise to cover the takeoff when it does right here on KWTEX News. Susan Write, reporting from Upton County."

"What happened to that reporter? Did our people down there talk to her?" asked the Colonel as the news show moved on to the local weather report and SrA Robinson cut the sound.

"Another strange thing, Colonel," said Maj Bledsoe. "The news team consisted of one Susan Write, aka Peggy Sue Whitaker, who you just saw, and her cameraman, a James Leotis Taylor. Their news van is still at the ranch house but they are nowhere to be found. The federal Marshals think they might have been on board when the ship took off, along with the missing squad of Marines."

"Do we have any idea how many people were on board?"

"No, Sir. I'm afraid not" Then the Major added, "we also have a video of the ship ascending. Some amateur cameraman at the San Angelo airshow was facing west, filming a sun dog in the overhead clouds, when the spaceship ascended. As the ship pierced the cloud layer the shock wave destroyed the sun dog, very impressive sequence."

"How did we get that footage? Can we keep it out of the news?"

"We got it off of YouTube. I'm afraid its already gone viral, Sir."

"Naturally!" the Colonel snorted. "Welcome to the future, Major. We are supposed to be watching outer space for threats to the nation, yet we have civilians building spaceships and it's all over the news and the Internet before we even hear about it."

"Yes, Sir."

"So now we have a mystery ship filled with an unknown number of civilians, a news crew and a squad of Marines somewhere in low Earth orbit. We have no way to contact them and the folks over at the Solar Dynamics Observatory have just issued a warning saying we are about to be hit with the largest solar storm since the 1800s. Satellite communications are already starting to break down. If that ship is in orbit when the storm hits, it's going to get fried. I wonder if those folks knew they were flying to their deaths?"

Cargo Hold, Parker's Folly

Crewman Hitch fired the last shot of the battle for the cargo hold, loosing a stunner bolt at the Navy corpsman huddled against the aft bulkhead. HM2 White felt the tingle of the near miss in her left arm and leg. Quickly she tossed her carbine toward the middle of the cargo hold and threw up her hands, shouting "I'm the medic, I surrender, I surrender!"

"CEASE FIRE! they are all down," the Captain announced over the PA. Then, holstering his stunner, he launched himself from the ceiling. Floating down, he did a half flip with a half twist, landing upright on the deck facing the Gunnery Sergeant, who was still obscured by the bulk of Lt. Bear. "You can let her up, Lieutenant. I believe she's passed out."

"Yeah, I thought Marines were supposed to be tough. These clowns were more like pups." Bear was still visibly excited by the brief action, nose crinkling and nostrils flaring as he sniffed the air.

"Half of them were taken out by the g-forces during takeoff, and no doubt the others were banged up pretty badly as well," said Lt. Curtis, who had finally reached a solid surface and was once again upright on the deck. "Add to that never having fought in zero-gravity and I think they acquitted themselves quite well."

"Yes, First Officer. If they had done any better we might well have lost," the Captain acknowledged, then, addressing the only uninjured, fully conscious survivor: "You there, you claim you're a medic?"

"Yes, Sir. Hospital Corpsman 2nd Class Belinda White, five-three-seven..." She began reciting her serial number.

The Captain cut her short, "I don't need your serial number, Corpsman, I need your help."

"Uh, yes Sir?" the still shaken medic replied, unable to take her eyes off the hulking Lt. Bear, now hanging from the bulkhead with one paw around a stanchion.

"Yes, we have a fully equipped medical section on board. Unfortunately we don't have a doctor. That makes you it, Ms. White. We need to triage the wounded and get them to sick bay, before someone dies of his wounds."

"Yes, Captain. I think that Lt. Merryweather might already be dead. He was crushed by that big crate when the ship blasted off."

"Check him first then, and then the man Lt. Bear disarmed." The aforementioned Lt. Bear averted his eyes from the Captain's gaze. The 600 kilogram nearly 3 meter long security officer had paws the size of dinner plates, each tipped with five large, sharp claws. The ursine Lieutenant had almost literally disarmed PFC Reagan when he swatted the Marine's weapon out of his hands. The Private's arm was shredded from shoulder to wrist and bleeding profusely. Droplets of blood and barf drifted around the hold, creating a thoroughly unwholesome atmosphere.

"Yes, Captain." The medic was grateful to have work to concentrate on, instead of the tense confusion all around her.

"Lt. Curtis, I will leave you in charge here. I'll take Jacobs with me to sick bay and leave the mid-deck airlock open on the forward bulkhead. You can float the wounded through there and directly to sick bay. Bring the others as Corpsman White indicates." Turning to Lt. Bear, he said, "Lt. Bear, perhaps you could go fetch Miss Hamilton and escort her to the sick bay."

"Yes, Captain," the big officer said, anxious to be away from his captain's disapproving stare. He quickly scampered up the bulkhead and disappeared through the airlock opening he had first appeared from only a few minutes before.

"Lt. Merryweather is still alive!" called HM2 White, "But he is going to need splinting, plasma and a surgeon."

Great, thought the Captain, heading forward to collect the wounded Jacobs. *Where are we going to find a surgeon in low Earth orbit?*

ISS, Low Earth Orbit

Ludmilla managed to corral her two companions for a last call with mission control at NASA's Johnson Space Center in Houston. The voice from the ISS Flight Control Room sounded no different than it had on countless other occasions. The unwritten NASA code of male machismo, inherited from the testosterone driven culture of military test pilots, required everyone to remain cool and collected at all times—at least while on the radio.

"We have an update on the impending solar event," said the voice from Houston. "It looks like radiation levels are already starting to rise and communications are being degraded. New estimates from the SDO say the bulk of the storm should hit in about three hours."

"So we have approximately two orbits left?" Col. Kondratov's question was more of a statement.

"Yes, that's affirmative. I want you to know we tried every way we could to send you folks some relief. We talked with India, China and even commercial operators, none had any man-rated resources that could be launched in time."

"Yes, of course, Houston. We know you did all that could be done." The code of cool continued to hold.

"ISS, we have some ideas that might make the next 12 hours more survivable. Donning spacesuits and moving some of the equipment around you to form shielding could help diminish the radiation levels."

"We have been over this before, Houston," Dr. Tropsha interrupted. "The storm is going to be too strong and last too long for such measures to make any difference. We would simply be postponing the inevitable. I for one, would rather spend my last few hours comfortably, not locked inside a spacesuit."

"Of course, Dr. Tropsha. Wait one." There was a short pause before Mission Control resumed talking. "There are a few things we would like you to do to the ISS systems prior to the storm's arrival, if you don't mind. As you know, most of the station's electronics are probably going to be damaged and that could adversely impact some of the major onboard systems."

"What is it you want us to do?" asked Ivan. Being the ranking cosmonaut, he was now acting mission commander.

"We'd like you to shut down the tracking on the solar panel arrays, and the stabilization system. Also the main heat exchanger."

"Very well, we will do as you ask." *Like that will change anything*, thought Ivan. *The station, like its crew, is as good as dead. Maybe they are just trying to keep us busy, to take our minds off what is about to happen.*

"Thank you, ISS. We will probably lose communication contact at some point but we are going to stay with you—there are a lot of people down here praying for a miracle."

"Thank you, Houston. We will sign off now and start shutting down systems."

"Roger ISS. Godspeed, Houston out."

Sickbay, Parker's Folly

The unwounded members of Folly's crew had returned to their duties—Billy Ray was back on the bridge while able spaceman Hitch and Freddy Adams from engineering were busy squaring away the cargo hold. Mat Jacobs' flesh wound and Melissa Hamilton's broken arm had been treated and they were sent forward to the mess to recuperate.

The three stunned but otherwise unharmed Marines had been handcuffed with plastic zip cuffs and secured in the crew dayroom on the lower deck, under the watchful eye of Lt. Bear. The remaining Marines were now resting in sickbay beds under restraint. Most seriously injured was Lt Merryweather, whose broken limbs had been splinted and was now under heavy sedation.

Next on the list was LCpl Reagan, whose badly lacerated arm had been cleaned and bound. He too, was under sedation and Doc had started a plasma drip. That left Davis, Kwan and Feldman with various fractures, dislocations and sprains in need of setting. After giving them all something to dull the pain, Corpsman White was working her way down the patient list with the assistance of Lt.

Curtis. Before ministering to the remaining squad members, the medical team turned to the squad's injured leader, GySgt Rodriguez.

The Gunny regained consciousness as Doc White moved to set her shoulder. "Lieutenant, could you please hold the Gunny steady. Gunny, this is going to hurt."

"Get on with it, Doc." Then, as the Corpsman pulled the Sergeant's arm back into its socket, "Arrgh! Damn that hurt! Thanks Betty, where the hell are we?"

"We are in the ship's sickbay, Gunny."

"I take it since she seems to be in charge," the Gunny said, jerking her head in the direction of Lt. Curtis, "we lost."

"Yes, Gunny. Reagan got cut up pretty bad but nobody died and all the wounded are being treated."

"And might I ask who you are, Ma'am?" Rodriguez asked Lt. Curtis, noticing the officer's insignia on her jumpsuit collar.

"I'm the ship's First Officer, Lieutenant Curtis, Gunnery Sergeant."

"What about my people, and how's the LT?"

"Your Lieutenant is pretty busted up, Sergeant. We have stabilized him as best we can but we have no doctor on board and your medic says he needs a surgeon. As for your other Marines, the ones without any broken bones or lacerations, they are being held below under armed guard. The rest are here in the sickbay."

"I take it that those blue ray gun things don't kill people?"

"No, Sergeant, they're stun guns—like a taser without wires—we call them stunners. It was never our intention to harm you. By the way, you don't have any 40mm grenades, I checked. It was your threat to use grenades that forced the Captain to order the attack."

"Yeah, well sorry about that, Lieutenant. It seemed like a good idea at the time."

"Well its over now," said the First Officer. "The Captain will be along to speak with you now that you've regained consciousness. If I leave you in the corpsman's care will you promise not to do something stupid?"

"Since Doc is the only one fully mobile, I don't think we'll be trying anything too John Wayneish, Lieutenant. Particularly with no weapons and that attack bear of yours wandering around. That was a polar bear, wasn't it?"

"Yes, Sergeant, that was most definitely a polar bear."

"I could swear that, just before I passed out, the bear spoke to me. That polar bear really can't talk, can he?"

"Of course not, Gunnery Sergeant," the tall Lieutenant said with a mischievous glint in her eye. "He was just showing off."

Bridge, Parker's Folly

The Captain reclaimed the bridge and proceeded to finish the post launch checklist. A number of critical systems had not been fully online when the ship took off. Included among them were the suite of external sensors—radar, LIDAR, radiation detectors, video and others—which he was now activating. As he brought the charged particle detectors online he noticed that exterior levels were significantly higher than the display indicated as normal.

"Mr. Medina, could you cross check the particle radiation readings please?"

"Yes, Captain. It looks about twice normal levels and rising."

"Are we expecting a solar storm? Did anyone think to check before we took off? I certainly didn't."

"Sir, I'm accessing the Internet through a comsat and NASA has issued a solar flair warning. Wow! If what they are saying is true, there has been a massive eruption on the Sun. Earth is about to be hit with a monster wave of charged particles in about three hours."

"Are the interior levels OK?"

"Yes, Sir. But I suggest we boost the repulsor shields just to make sure things stay that way."

"Very well, Mr. Medina." When Jack had taken over as the ship's captain he had promised that he would never utter the words "make it so." He didn't ever wish to be confused with any fictional spaceship captain. "Also, Mr. Medina. My board is showing that the deck gravity grid has checked out and is ready to power up."

"Yes, Sir. Should I engage the deck gravity?"

The Captain cringed at the use of "engage" for the same reason he eschewed the use of "make it so." Instead he spoke to the engineer, saying "Let's not tempt fate with a possibly damage causing gravity level. Set up for a tenth of a G in all habitable spaces but don't activate the grid. I'll sound the warning and then we will give everyone time to prepare."

The klaxon sounded its three warning blasts and the Captain announced over the PA "Attention! All habitable spaces will be placed under a one tenth G gravity in five minutes. Secure yourselves and all equipment for cabin gravity in five minutes."

"Captain?" helmsman Vincent inquired. "There's something you should see on the TV. They're showing pictures of the space station and acting real upset."

"What are they saying, Mr. Vincent?"

"I can't tell, it's a Russian station, Sir." With that, Billy Ray turned the sound up until it was audible.

"They are saying," said Lt. Curtis, just arriving on the bridge. "That there are two heroic Russian cosmonauts trapped on the ISS, along with a Japanese scientist."

"Very good, Lieutenant," the Captain noted. "I believe your command of Russian is better than mine. The question is, what the hell are they doing in orbit with a potentially lethal solar storm about to hit?" The ISS orbital inclination of 51° was a compromise with the Russians to accommodate launch geometries from the Baikonur Cosmodrome. It also increased normal radiation exposure. Crew members on both the space station and the American space shuttle reported seeing bright flashes of light that were actually caused by energetic particles passing through their eyeballs. Even so, the ISS in LEO was normally safe from solar flares. Evidently, the impending flood of radiation from the massive solar eruption was something else again.

"Mr. Danner, Mr. Vincent. Please locate the space station and plot a course that will intersect its path while matching its orbit."

"Yes, Captain." the two helmsmen replied in unison.

Normally, when pursuing another object in orbit, the spacecraft doing the chasing must decelerate, in effect slow down, to overtake its quarry. This seeming contradiction is a result of Newton's laws of motion combined with the inverse square law governing gravitational attraction. Examples are easier to understand than the equations.

For a spacecraft to achieve Earth orbit, it must be launched to an elevation above Earth's atmosphere and accelerated to orbital velocity. As previously mentioned, the ISS is in an orbit averaging 350 km in height above Earth's surface traveling at 27,500 km/hr. In this orbit it takes about 94 minutes to complete a single trip around the planet.

Many communications satellites are in orbit 35,785 km above the planet, in what is called a geosynchronous orbit. In geosynchronous orbit a satellite circles Earth once a day. If that orbit is a circular one in the plane of the equator, the satellite will appear to hang motionless in the sky. This is because it is making a full revolution at the same rate the planet below is turning—once every 24 hours. The orbital velocity in geosynchronous orbit is 11,066 km/hr. Even farther out, the Moon has an altitude of about 384,400 km, a velocity of about 3,700 km/hr and its orbit takes 27.322 days.

The space station orbits the planet many times faster in terms of revolutions per hour than a geosynchronous communications satellite or the Moon because it is in a lower orbit. The salient point is that to catch up with something in orbit, *orbital mechanics* requires a spacecraft drop to a lower orbit. In that lower orbit the ship is circling the planet faster than the object in the higher orbit. Then, at the appropriate point, the pursuing ship transfers back to the higher orbit, hopefully arriving alongside its target.

The confusing part is that, when transferring from a higher orbit to a lower one, the change of velocity is opposite to the direction of motion—in other words, the ship must slowdown. Yet, when the lower orbit is achieved, its orbital velocity will be higher and it will complete more orbits in a set amount of time.

When transferring from a lower orbit to a higher orbit, the change in velocity is applied in the direction of motion—in other words, forward acceleration. When the higher orbit is attained, its orbital velocity will be less than the velocity in the lower orbit and it will take longer to complete a full circle around the globe.

Ordinarily, when changing orbits it is desirable to use the smallest possible amount of energy, which usually leads to using a *Hohmann transfer orbit*. Such a transfer trajectory describes an ellipse that is tangent to both the initial and final orbits. However, if a spacecraft needs to change orbits more quickly, a faster transfer called a *One-Tangent Burn* can be used. What type of transfer is used depends on how much energy a spacecraft is able to expend.

In this case, Parker's Folly needed to not only dip down lower than its current altitude and then back up, it also had to change its orbital inclination, the plane it was orbiting in, to match that of the ISS. To do this quickly would require a great deal of energy. Fortunately, the ship possessed a surfeit of energy—as much as a large nuclear power plant. The ship's computer was programed to solve such orbital problems and the appropriate maneuvers were quickly plotted.

"Mr. Medina, now would be a good time for that gravity. We shall see if the cabin gravity system can compensate for the ship's acceleration as advertised."

"Aye, Captain, one tenth of a G coming right up."

"Helm, let's pay the International Space Station a call."

Destiny Module, International Space Station

Ludmilla Tropsha was startled to hear a voice through the crackling static on the station's radio. Perhaps her mind was starting to play tricks on her. No, there it was again, a man's voice speaking English.

"ISS, this is Parker's Folly, do you read me?"

She must be hallucinating, they had lost contact with mission control half an hour ago.

110

"ISS, ISS, this is Parker's Folly, is there anyone on board? Please respond."

Feeling as though she was in a dream, Luda moved to the radio console and answered. "Party calling ISS, this is Lt. Col. Ludmilla Tropsha. Please state your name and the purpose of this call."

"Colonel Tropsha, this is Captain Jack Sutton on board the spaceship Parker's Folly, we were afraid that you were already gone."

Ludmilla felt her anger rising, *what kind of cruel, twisted man would play such a trick?* "Is this some kind of sick joke? We will all be gone soon enough!"

"I assure you this is not a joke, Colonel. Please look out of your observation port and you will see my ship."

The Destiny lab module has a single Earth-facing window, made of optically pure, telescope-quality glass. Cursing herself for a fool, Ludmilla moved over to the 20 inch circular window. Despite herself, Luda felt hope rising in her breast. She was almost too afraid to look out the window, afraid to have that spark of hope dashed. She looked out and... there was a ship hanging in space next to the space station.

And what a ship it was! A long gleaming silver cigar of a ship with a nose like Baccarat crystal. Where did it come from? How could such a thing exist? The ISS was supposed to be the biggest thing mankind had ever sent into space—the habitable assembly 51 meters long, the truss 109 meters wide, weighing 370 metric tons. The silver vision floating outside the window easily dwarfed the station. Plus, the strange ship was solid, all of one piece, while the ISS looked like some cobbled together collection of space junk.

Luda's vision became blurred as tears of joy filled her eyes—in zero-gravity tears do not flow down cheeks, they simply well up on the surface of the eyes and must be wiped or batted away by blinking. She went back to the radio console, now half afraid that the silver ship would disappear when she left the window.

"Captain, this is the ISS. Who are you? Where did you come from?" She paused and then added, "Are you from Earth?"

"Why yes, Ma'am. Actually, we're from Texas."

Chapter 8

Captain's Sea Cabin, Parker's Folly

Captain Sutton had assembled his engineering team, along with Lt. Curtis, in his sea cabin to discuss how to get the stranded cosmonauts off of the International Space Station. It was beginning to look like rescuing the endangered ISS crew was going to be a bit more difficult than just pulling along side and saying "hop on."

"ISS, this is Captain Sutton on board Parker's Folly. With me I have the ship's First Officer Lt. Gretchen Curtis, head engineer Dr. Rajiv Gupta and engineers Medina and Adams. Dr. Tropsha, have you assembled your colleagues?"

"Yes, Captain Sutton. With me are Colonel Ivan Kondratov, acting mission commander, and Dr. Yuki Saito. We are wondering how we can transfer to your vessel, do you have an airlock that can dock with the station?"

"I'm afraid not, we have no airlocks that are compatible with the station's docking facilities. We were wondering if you could EVA over to us. We have a large cargo door aft of midships and the cargo hold can be depressurized. In effect it is a big airlock."

"Captain, this is Ivan Kondratov. Other than myself the people on board are not experienced spacewalkers. Is there some other way to effect the transfer?"

"Perhaps they could all get into the main airlock module? We could disconnect the module and haul it aboard," suggested Freddy Adams. The Joint Airlock, or Quest Module, gave the station the capability to conduct spacewalks using U.S. spacesuits. It was based on the Space Shuttle airlock and was attached to the station during the 10th space shuttle assembly flight.

"The Crew Lock will not hold all three of us in suits at the same time," replied Ivan. The six meter long Quest Airlock is composed of two connected cylindrical chambers—the larger Equipment Lock and the smaller Crew Lock. It was designed to accommodate two suited spacewalkers at a time. This can be either two American Extravehicular Mobility Units, two Russian Orlan-M spacesuits, or one of each design.

"What if you didn't wear spacesuits?" asked Jo Jo Medina. "Could the three of you fit then?"

"We could probably squeeze in but that isn't a procedure I would be happy with. If the lock developed a leak while being detached from the station it could depressurize. The only way to be safe would be to wear spacesuits, putting us back to two."

"I believe that the airlock would not be easy to detach from the station either," said Dr. Saito, joining the conversation.

"Yuki is right. It would probably take two experienced spacewalkers several hours to detach the airlock," added the Russian Colonel. "I doubt that the module was ever intended to be removed—it may not be possible to disconnect it safely."

"Regardless, we don't have the time," the Captain concluded. "So we are back to needing you folks to EVA over from the station. How long would it take to cycle the airlock twice?"

"Actually," said Ivan, "I could use the Pirs Docking Module airlock." Before the Joint Airlock was installed the only way for cosmonauts to exit the station was through the older airlock on the Russian built docking adapter. That airlock was a Russians only entrance, since the US EMU suits were too bulky to fit through its tight opening. Pirs was the same module that the broken Soyuz capsule was docked at.

"Good, it sounds like you can all exit the station simultaneously. We should be able to shoot you a line from the open cargo door that you can use as a guideline."

"Actually, Captain, there is another problem," said Ludmilla. "The normal spacewalk protocol requires staying overnight in the Crew Lock, before exiting the ISS. The Americans called it 'camping out.'"

"Surely you can skip that, Doctor?" said Lt. Curtis.

"No, you don't understand. It is because of the difference in air pressure and nitrogen absorbed by the body's tissues. The space station is kept at 1 bar, sea-level pressure, using a mixture of oxygen and nitrogen, much like conditions on Earth. Pressure in a spacesuit is only around 0.3 bar, about 4 psi. Making the change from cabin to spacesuit too quickly can cause decompression sickness—the bends."

"Just like SCUBA divers surfacing without properly decompressing," said the Lieutenant. "Yes, I understand now. Spacewalkers spent the night slowly lowering the air pressure to safely purge their bodies of nitrogen."

"That is correct, Lieutenant. We lower air pressure in stages while breathing pure oxygen. I'm afraid that going outside without taking precautions could debilitate one or more of us."

"Pardon me, Doctor, this is Rajiv Gupta. I seem to remember that the Joint Airlock was not added to the station until construction was well underway. How were spacewalks done before the Quest module was attached?"

"We used to use the Russian airlock," Ivan answered. "The Americans could only go outside when a Space Shuttle was docked."

"That is correct," Ludmilla added. "Ivan, there was an older protocol that was used before the big airlock was added. Yes, it is here in my tablet." All space station crew members carried around tablet computers with access to the station's wifi network.

"Yes, here it says: Station astronauts are to begin the pre-breathe protocol by exercising vigorously on the space station's cycle ergometer for a total of 10 minutes while breathing pure oxygen via an oxygen mask. After 50 total minutes of breathing pure oxygen, including the 10 minutes initially spent exercising, the pressure in the station's airlock will be lowered to 10.2 pounds per square inch. During airlock depressurization, the spacewalkers will breathe pure oxygen for an additional 30 minutes. At the end of those 30 minutes, with the airlock now at 10.2 psi, the spacewalkers will put on their space suits. Once their spacesuits are on, the spacewalkers will breathe pure oxygen inside the suits for an additional 60 minutes before making final preparations to leave the station and begin their spacewalk. This protocol provides a total of 2 hours and 20 minutes of pre-breathe time, including the 10 minutes of vigorous exercise at the beginning of the procedure."

"I don't think we have 2 hours and 20 minutes, Doctor," said the Captain. "Can we cut that down to under an hour?"

"Yes, I think so. Any purging helps reduce the risk of decompression sickness. Less acute cases of decompression sickness often do not present symptoms for hours after exposure. Between the exercise and breathing pure oxygen we should be OK, if the transfer does not take too long."

"If it takes too long, getting the bends will be the least of our worries, Ludmilla," Yuki added.

"Very good, Captain," said Ivan. "I can use the Pirs lock while Ludmilla and Yuki use the Crew Lock. Yuki, you are not familiar with the Russian spacesuits?"

"No, Ivan. I trained on the American suits at NASA. I would feel more comfortable in an EMU."

"Very well. Ludmilla can help you suit up. Captain, we need to begin our prep if we are to exit the airlocks within an hour."

"Yes of course Colonel," affirmed the Captain. "We need to start depressurizing the cargo hold and suiting up ourselves. We will continue to monitor this frequency if you need us, otherwise signal when you are ready to transfer. Parker's Folly out."

* * * * *

"OK people, do we have what we need to do this?" the Captain asked the crew members in the sea cabin once the radio link had been muted.

"Freddy and I will go back to the cargo hold and ensure it is ready," said Dr. Gupta. "Then we will start the decompression. I would like to recover as much of the air as possible."

"You're not worried we're running low on air, are you?"

"No, Captain, I would like to preserve as much of our supply as we can simply because the supply is finite."

"Fine Doctor, you and Freddy get to it. Mr. Medina, please monitor the ship's systems from the bridge. We need to ensure our air doesn't leak from the internal locks going to the cargo hold while it is under vacuum."

"Aye aye, Captain." With that the engineers left the cabin for their assigned destinations. The Captain then turned to his First Officer.

115

"Who do you suggest we have help with the transfer, Lieutenant?"

"I think the Chief and Mr. Vincent," came her unhesitating reply. "The Chief is as agile as a monkey even in a suit, and Billy Ray proved both level headed and adept during the firefight in the hold earlier."

"OK, the four of us then."

"Sir? Permission to speak freely?"

"Of course, Lieutenant. What's on your mind?"

"A spacewalk in itself carries some risk. This one could also lead to possible exposure to harmful levels of radiation if the solar storm gets here before we are done. The cargo hold door will be open and the shields will have to be down to transfer the station crew."

"And your point is?"

"Captain, I don't think it wise for both of us to be in the cargo hold during the rescue."

"Are you suggesting that the three of you should proceed without me?"

"No offense Sir. But you are the Captain, you are essential to our mission. I'm asking you to let your crew do their jobs while you stay in command of the vessel."

After thinking about Lt. Curtis' statement for a few moments, Jack realized that she was right. When he had been a captain in the Navy he would never have led a rescue mission or ship to ship transfer himself. The shootout in the cargo hold was another matter —then the safety of the ship had been at stake. "Yes, you're right Gretchen. You will lead the team in the cargo hold and I will stay on the bridge. But I do expect to squeeze in a spacewalk of my own sometime during the mission."

"Thank you, Captain," said the relieved First Officer. As she left the cabin she looked back and said, smiling, "I'm sure you'll get your turn to play spaceman before the voyage is over."

Cargo Hold, Parker's Folly

The atmosphere in the cargo hold had been reduced to near vacuum by the time the party led by Lt. Curtis had suited up. They entered the hold through the mid-deck airlock, which was large enough to hold a half dozen people at once, even in spacesuits.

Unlike the spacesuits worn by American astronauts and Russian cosmonauts, the Folly's crew wore suits that fit skintight on the body. The only space for air was within the clear bubble-like helmets, and that air was kept at 14.7 psi. Not only were the crew able to enter and exit the vacuum of space without decompressing, their suits were much more flexible than the bulky apparatus worn by the space station refugees.

On the backs of their suits were small, hard-shelled packs containing oxygen, re-breathing equipment and power supplies for radios, lights, heating and cooling. If they were venturing outside of the ship, they would have donned coveralls for further protection from radiation and physical damage. As it was, Billy Ray could not help noticing that the Lieutenant's skintight suit was doing interesting things for her figure. Pushing such thoughts aside, he asked the Lieutenant, "should we ask them to cut gravity to the cargo hold, Ma'am?"

"Yes, good thinking Mr Vincent. Bridge, this is Lt. Curtis. We are preparing to enter the cargo hold and request you cut the deck gravity in that area."

"Roger that, Lieutenant. Gravity in the cargo hold is now off."

"Thank you, we will let you know when we are in position at the starboard side cargo door." With that, she opened the outer airlock door and led the rescue party into the weightless, airless environment of the ship's hold.

* * * * *

Arriving at the rear of the hold, Gretchen, Billy Ray and the Chief connected themselves to the ship by attaching safety lines to cleats in the deck. "Bridge, cargo hold. I am ready to open the cargo door. Interrogative the status of the space station crew?"

"Roger on opening the cargo door. The ISS crew say they are ready to open their airlocks any time we are ready." Staying inside

117

the station's airlocks until the last minute added some small extra shielding from the rising radiation levels outside.

"Roger, opening the door now." The cargo hatch, large enough to drive a truck through, slid open in eerie silence. The starboard side of the ship was facing the Sun and was brightly lit except where shadows cast by the station, only 50 meters away, played across its hull. The hold itself was well illuminated by overhead light fixtures—the space station personnel would hopefully see a large, brightly lit, rectangular opening in the side of the ship.

"Cargo hold, bridge. The ISS crew is emerging now."

"Yes, we can see them. Col. Kondratov is out of the Pirs airlock and is working his way toward the main Crew Airlock. Now it looks like someone is coming out of the main airlock. It must be Dr. Saito, the suit is different from the one Kondratov is wearing."

As they watched, a third figure emerged from the complicated collection of cylinders, girders, solar panels and attached modules that comprised the International Space Station. The figures, and the station itself, stood in stark relief against the black of space. Lt. Curtis waved at the three figures clinging to the exterior of the space station, much like survivors clinging to a wrecked ship at sea. One of the Russians waved back.

"Mr. Vincent. Send them the line."

Billy Ray stepped to the edge of the open door and shouldered something that looked like a crossbow with a spool of thin rope attached to its front. That was exactly what it was, a crossbow rigged for fishing with the fishing line replaced by more visible cord. He pulled the trigger, sending a blunt, stubby bolt toward the ISS.

The drama played out in silence, as line uncoiled from the spool, trailing after the fleeting bolt. "I sure hope that thing doesn't run out'a pep before it reaches the station," said Billy Ray, giving voice to what all three rescuers were thinking.

"I think it's gonna make it, Billy Ray," said Chief Zackly, speaking for the first time since they entered the cargo hold. "Look, you nearly hit that one!"

Sure enough, Billy Ray's arrow had come within a few feet of one of the Russians. The suited figure, most likely Col. Kondratov, grabbed the line and moved to make it fast to the station. Once it was secured on that end, the cosmonaut waved back at the people in the open cargo door. Billy Ray secured the line on their end and motioned the station crew to start across the gap.

* * * * *

Ludmilla had followed Yuki out of the Crew Airlock hatch into the startlingly bright sunlight. It was hard to look around in the bulky spacesuit but she managed to spot Ivan moving along the side of the Unity module toward them. She started to drift away from the airlock when she remembered to grab on to part of the station's structure. This was definitely not the same as the big swimming pool used to simulate working outside the station.

Ivan arrived just in time to snag Yuki as he started to drift off. As the three of them clung like insects to the side of their former home, their rescuers' strange silver ship floated beneath the station with the sunlit Earth as a backdrop. The underside of the station was illuminated by earthshine—much brighter than the feeble moonshine from Earth's natural satellite.

Yuki started the journey to the ship, working his way along the guide rope. Unfortunately, he was making little progress in the direction of the beckoning cargo hold opening. As he pulled on the line his center of gravity seldom lined up with the force created by his tugging. The Japanese scientist was twisting around like a leaf in a gale as the line stretched wildly to and fro.

"Ivan, you must do something," said Ludmilla over their suit radios. "Yuki is taking far too long to reach the ship."

"Yes, you are right Ludmilla. Yuki, can you hear me?"

"Yes, Ivan. I'm sorry but I don't seem to be capable of heading in the proper direction."

"Listen, Yuki. I'm going to untie the line from the station. Just grab on to the line and let the ship pull you in."

* * * * *

What are they doing? Lt. Curtis asked herself. *Dr. Saito is taking far too long to pull himself over to the ship.* While they had been able to communicate with the station earlier, they didn't have a direct link to the spacewalkers. "Bridge, can you talk with the station crew and ask them what they are doing?"

"Cargo hold, be advised we have been out of contact with the station since the crew emerged from the airlocks."

"I don't think the line is taut enough to stop him from swingin' around like that, Lieutenant," said the Chief.

"It looks like they just cast off the line from the other end," observed Billy Ray. "Yep the guy on the line has wrapped his arm around it, we need to pull him into the ship."

Billy Ray and the Chief both moved to grasp the line and nearly collided. "Let me do the pullin' Chief. You go to the door and catch him when he gets here."

"You got more heft than I do, son. Don't take much pullin' in this zero-g but you might be better at landing him."

"Yeah, you're right Chief."

"Course I am," the little man said, moving to pick up the line. "That's why I'm the Chief Boatswain's Mate."

Once the two crewmen sorted themselves out they managed to bring the floundering scientist smartly to the door. The Chief had gotten the man in the American spacesuit moving at a fair clip and when he came across the threshold of the cargo door it was all Billy Ray could do to bring him to a safe halt. Billy Ray moved the floating man over to one of the strapped down crates and, using hand gestures, managed to get him to hang on to one of the crate's straps.

Meanwhile, the Lieutenant was trying and failing to get the floating line back onto the spool on the front of the crossbow for another shot.

"I don't think we're going to need that, Lieutenant," said Billy Ray. "Looks like they are making a leap for us."

Lt. Curtis looked back at the space station just in time to see one of the suited figures push the other toward the open cargo hold. *That's going to be a hell of a shot if he makes it,* Gretchen thought. Sure enough the figure coming their direction was starting to drift high. "He's going to miss the door for sure. Maybe even the ship."

"Here, Lieutenant. Tie that line around my waste," said the Chief. "Come on, Ma'am. This is bosun's work. Just tie me good and secure."

With the line affixed to his suit the Chief crouched in the open doorway. "Make sure that line don't foul on nothin' and pull me back in easy so's I don't lose the Ruski." With that the wiry little man leaped from the deck out into space.

"That old coot is either one of the bravest men I've ever met or he's batshit crazy," commented Billy Ray, paying out line as the Chief closed with the drifting Russian.

"Possibly both, Mr. Vincent," agreed the Lieutenant.

"Ya know I can hear both of yous!" The Chief snapped, an instant before colliding with the drifting spacewalker. The boatswain grabbed the floating figure around the wast and yelled. "I got 'em, pull us in!"

Billy Ray complied, gently slowing the outgoing line, bringing it to a stop and then slowly pulling the drifting duo back toward the cargo door and safety. After the pair bounced off the upper lip of the door opening, Lt. Curtis managed to take the Chief's passenger from him and move her—it was clear looking through the suit's clear helmet visor that it was a woman—against the crate with Dr. Saito.

"OK, we have Dr. Saito and Dr. Tropsha. That only leaves Col. Kondratov."

"Looks like he's on his way, Lieutenant. Chief, you'd better get ready in case he drifts too."

"I'm ready. Hell, I ain't had this much fun in years."

As it turned out Ivan's own jump was closer to the mark than his toss of Ludmilla. He went just wide to the left, landing on the open cargo bay door itself, which was slid forward along the hull. As the Colonel bounced off the door the Chief was able to lean out around the cargo hold opening and snag him. Within a minute, all three of the space station crew were safely in the cargo hold.

"Bridge, this is Lt. Curtis. I'm closing the cargo hold door. You can give us some atmosphere any time."

"Roger that, Lieutenant. And congratulations on a job well done. You had us worried there for a bit—until we saw the chief launch himself out of the hold like a comic book superhero."

"Weren't nothing, Captain. Like I told Billy Ray, just bosun's work." There was a look of pure joy on the little man's face as he basked in his Captain's praise.

"Captain, we're going to work our way forward with our new guests. I think it will be easier if we leave the deck gravity off for now. Two of them had a hard enough time floating in a spacesuit, let alone hopping along the deck in one."

"Very good, Number One. We will have cabin pressure restored by the time you get to the forward bulkhead."

The Lieutenant shook her head. *Did he just call me "number one"? He hates that Hollywood space opera lingo. Our captain was more worried about this little exercise than he let on.*

* * * * *

Upon reaching the forward bulkhead, the rescue team managed to get the space station crew members to doff their helmets and start removing their spacesuits. They were hesitant at first and only started un-suiting when all three of the rescuers removed their helmets, proving the hold now had a breathable atmosphere.

Hitch and Jacobs entered the cargo hold to assist with suit removal, the latter limited to capturing parts with his unbandaged arm. Kondratov, Saito and Tropsha were soon stripped to their cooling and ventilation garments, floating around in what looked like lumpy white long underwear.

"We can offer you a shower and a change of cloths if you would like to follow us into the crew quarters," said Lt. Curtis, addressing the trio of space refugees. "But before that happens I need you to all assume a balanced, standing position on the deck."

The trio complied with somewhat puzzled looks on their faces. The Lieutenant did not wish to disorient or traumatize the newcomers by having them drift from zero-g into a part of the ship under deck gravity. Once everyone was in a stable standing position the Lieutenant spoke to the bridge, "Bridge, this is the cargo hold. Could we get the deck gravity restored in here? The station personnel are out of their suits and we are ready to come forward."

"Roger, cargo hold. Restoring deck gravity to one tenth G in three, two, one."

The now empty spacesuits all slumped to the deck while their former occupants wobbled about, trying not to fall under the sudden restoration of gravity.

"How can this be?" asked Ivan, "is the ship under acceleration?"

"No, Colonel. There are a number of surprises in store for you on board Parker's Folly. First among them is that we have controllable gravity on all of the decks in the ship's habitable spaces."

"You have artificial gravity?" asked Yuki. "How do you do this?" demanded the excited Japanese physicist.

"You will have to talk to our chief engineer, Dr. Gupta. As I understand it the gravity is real, not artificial, but the method of its generation is not what most Earth scientists would expect."

"So you are not from Earth after all," said Ludmilla in an accusatory tone. "Have you told us any other lies, Lieutenant?"

"I've told you no untruths, Dr. Tropsha." the Lieutenant replied stiffly. "We are all Earthlings here, though some of our technology may seem a bit... advanced."

"Any sufficiently advanced technology is indistinguishable from magic," Billy Ray murmured under his breath.

"Yes, Arthur C. Clarke was totally correct," Ludmilla, whose hearing was evidently excellent, shot back. "If America has such technology why doesn't the rest of the world know about it? I assume that this ship does not operate like our rocket ships, if you have found a way to control gravity."

"As I said, Doctor, there are many things about Folly that will be unfamiliar to you. I can only reassure you that the Captain will answer your questions. So, if you please, follow Mr. Vincent into the crew quarters where you can shower and slip into a change of clothing."

"I am forgetting my manners," Ludmilla said, looking at the Chief and Billy Ray. "Thank you for saving my life, all of our lives."

"Our pleasure Ma'am," answered the Chief, who had remained quiet while the officers were arguing. "Don' worry, the Captain will explain everything."

"He surely will," added Billy Ray. "Now if y'all will kindly follow me to the showers?"

Bridge & Captain's Sea Cabin, Parker's Folly

Fifteen minutes later, Billy Ray was back at the helm. When he arrived, Bobby fist bumped him and said, "awesome, Dude!"

"It was pretty intense, man," Billy Ray replied. Then, looking around to ensure they were not overheard, he added in a hushed voice, "that Russian Doctor lady is definitely space babe material. And Lt. Curtis knows her way around a skintight space suit too."

Shaking his head, Bobby told his friend "go with the Russian babe, Dude, 'cause the Lieutenant will kick your ass."

"Word, brother," the lanky Texan agreed, "you got that right."

* * * * *

Lt. Curtis escorted the three rescuees to the Captain's sea cabin just off the bridge. The station crew were now clothed in the one piece coveralls and soft soled boots that were standard issue on board Parker's Folly. Their outfits were a light pastel blue in color, which pleased the Russians since it was similar to one of the colors in the Russian flag. Dr. Saito's feelings regarding the new attire remained unvoiced.

One thing Gretchen had notice when she delivered Dr. Tropsha's post-shower change of cloths was that, beneath the bulky spacesuit undergarments, the Russian lady doctor was quite shapely. Even taking into account the salubrious effect that low gravity had on women's figures in general, the ash-blond cosmonaut was stunning. Male members of the crew would agree—she was built like a brick shithouse.

Between Ludmilla and the sexy blond newswoman, there will probably be some interesting interpersonal dynamics to deal with before the voyage is over, thought Gretchen. Billy Ray was a known hound dog and she had spotted Susan Write looking at the Captain with a predatory glint in her eyes on more than one occasion. *Don't borrow trouble, girl,* she scolded herself.

Lt. Curtis knocked on the sea cabin's door and the Captain said "come." Entering the cabin, the Lieutenant formally introduced the trio as the Captain shook each one's hand in turn.

"I'm glad to be welcoming you on board Parker's Folly—Col. Kondratov, Lt. Col Tropsha, Dr. Saito. I know you must be brimming with questions about us and this ship."

"To say the least, Captain!" Ivan replied. "How is it that you have technology only seen in science fiction books or movies? And how has your country kept it secret? Why have you kept it secret?"

"You see Colonel, our government doesn't know about this ship. Or at least it didn't until we were forced to takeoff just a few hours ago."

"You expect us to believe that your government is unaware of this ship, its technology?" asked Yuki. "I find that a bit incredulous, Captain."

"Folly was built by a very rich man, a Mr. TK Parker. He bankrolled the ship's construction. If you have enough money nearly anything is possible. The government wasn't made aware of this project because Mr. Parker doesn't trust the U.S. government, or any other for that matter. As for the advanced technology, most of it stems from a breakthrough in gravitonics."

"I have never heard of such a field of scientific study," said a doubtful Dr. Saito. "It sounds more like the sort of pseud-science one finds on the Internet."

"You are a scientist, Dr. Saito. You arrive at explanations based on empirical data derived from experiment and observation. Is that not correct?"

"Yes, of course."

"And you as well, Dr. Tropsha? In fact, all three of you trust in science and the scientific method?"

"Yes, this is true, Captain," answered Ludmilla. "Why do you ask us this question?"

"Because, as you can clearly see by dropping an object or by bouncing up and down on the deck, there is gravity here—or at least something the acts just like gravity. Can we agree that this is observed fact?"

"How can we tell this isn't some form of elaborate hoax?" demanded Ivan.

"You are familiar with Ockham's Razor? Or as Einstein phrased it *'So einfach wie möglich und so kompliziert wie nötig'*?"

"Yes, 'As simple as possible and as complicated as necessary,'" Ludmilla translated. "This is a well known saying."

"Yes, Americans often reduce it to KISS—keep it simple stupid. But the true meaning is, that given multiple explanations for some phenomenon, the simplest explanation is best."

"Your point, Captain?"

"Look around you. This ship is exactly as presented, with capabilities you find hard to believe but which have been plainly demonstrated. That this is true is the simplest explanation for your current circumstances. Any other explanation requires such convoluted logic and improbable actions as to render them not merely impossible but laughably so.

"My point Col. Kondratov, Dr. Saito, Lt. Col Tropsha, is that— given you were stranded on board a space station orbiting 350 kilometers above Earth's surface and in peril of your lives—when someone shows up and rescues you in an obviously functioning spaceship with air, gravity and all the conveniences of home, one should not imply that one's new host is a fraud or liar. In fact, it might be wise to give that host the benefit of the doubt."

Ivan swore in Russian and then said. "My apologies, Captain. Please understand that we have just gone from sitting helplessly, contemplating certain death, to being swept up by a spaceship of a kind I have only dreamed about as a boy. It is overwhelming and I am sorry if my words gave offense."

"Yes, Captain. I also offer my humble apologies," Yuki said while bowing to the ship's officers.

"And now that we have proven what uncultured ingrates we can be, what do we do next, Captain?" Ludmilla crossed her arms and arched one shapely ash-blond eyebrow.

My God, thought the Captain. *Now I have two women who do that Mr. Spock eyebrow thing. Well it's time to get everything out in the open, but this should be done in front of everyone aboard— trapped news people, stowaways, Marines, and skeptical cosmonauts included.* "What I would like to do is brief everyone on board. It is probably time that everyone meets their fellow shipmates as well. For that we need to move aft to the main passenger lounge. Would you lead the way, Lt. Curtis?"

"Of course, Captain. This way please, everyone." Gretchen smiled at the station crew and threw Jack an approving glance. *The Russian light colonel is certainly blunt-spoken. He handled that without once raising his voice, I probably would have lost my temper. I can't wait until he explains Lt. Bear to everyone.*

Main Lounge, Parker's Folly

The Captain and the First Officer arrived in the main lounge with the three space station crew members. An announcement had been broadcast over the ship's PA asking all crew and passengers to come to the main lounge if possible. The news team, Susan and JT, were standing by the large viewport staring out at the ISS hanging in space nearby.

The Captain had ordered the bar open and Jo Jo Medina and Melissa Hamilton were handing out drinks to all comers. Leaning on the sweeping curve of polished mahogany were the two helmsmen, Bobby Danner and Billy Ray Vincent. Billy Ray looked as he might while checking out the action in an Austin bar. The two stowaways, still in their gray contractor uniforms, were sitting at opposite ends of one of the lounge sofas, both clutching drinks and avoiding eye contact.

GySgt Rodriguez and HM2 White had come forward from the sickbay. They were joined by Dr. Gupta and Freddy Adams from engineering. The Chief and his two helpers, Steve Hitch and Matt Jacobs entered from the companionway in the rear. Following Jacobs came the Marines, still a bit unsteady from being stunned.

The Marines were wearing dark green coveralls like the Gunnery Sergeant and Doc White. Following the third Marine, a white muzzle with a black nose poked out of the companionway.

The nose was followed by the rest of Lt. Bear's considerable bulk. Squeezing through the meter in diameter companionway, the ursine officer pulled himself out onto the lounge floor like a polar bear in the wild, emerging from a hole in the ice. Conversation in the lounge stopped.

As all eyes turned toward the figures in the rear corner of the room, Lt. Bear nudged one of the Marines forward with his nose. Spotting their sergeant, the still disoriented Marines shuffled in her direction as fast as the unfamiliar tenth-g gravity allowed. Everyone else's attention was on the huge white bear, who sat down on the deck and stared back.

"That is a polar bear," said Ludmilla Tropsha, stating the obvious. "They can be very dangerous," she continued, concern rising in her voice. "Why do you have a dangerous animal loose on your ship, Captain?"

"That is Lt. Bear, the ship's security officer," Captain Jack replied evenly. "Say hello to the crew, Lieutenant."

"Hello," the polar bear said in a deep base voice.

"I knew it talked!" said the Gunnery Sergeant.

"Is it some kind of freak, or a medical experiment?" asked the Russian medical doctor, backing away.

"Certainly not! And one thing I will not tolerate on board this ship is speciesism." The Captain was rather enjoying this, Bear's appearance had totally flustered the self-assured Russian doctor.

"But he talks!" exclaimed Susan.

"I can dance a little too, if that helps." the bear said to the reporter.

"But bears—polar bears—do not talk!" insisted Ludmilla.

"Just because you have never encountered a talking bear doesn't mean that no bears can talk. It is like insisting that all swans are white because you have never seen a black one."

"I am not talking about swans, Captain! I am talking about polar bears—that polar bear!" Ludmilla pointed at the bear in question.

"Please Doctor, don't point, it's impolite." Yes, the Captain was definitely enjoying this. "Doctor, imagine you were studying primates and had only observed chimpanzees and gorillas, and maybe the odd orangutan. Would you find it impossible to believe that a human could talk if one showed up in your midst? We are obviously primates and related to the other great apes. Would your previous observations demand humans be speechless as well?"

"You're saying this is like the Planet of the Apes?" said JT.

"Only with bears," added GySgt Rodriguez.

"In reverse," the Captain finished. Then, seeing puzzled looks around the cabin he explained, "like Planet of the Apes except that we are the damned dirty apes."

"That makes me Charlton Heston," Lt. Bear said, giving the crew a toothy ursine smile.

* * * * *

Following the introduction of Lt. Bear the lounge briefly fell into chaos, as most of those assembled rushed the bar. Susan, followed by JT, headed straight for Lt. Bear. Evidently curiosity can kill not only cats, but television reporters as well.

"Pardon me, Lt. Bear. I'm Susan Write, KWTEX News, and I was wondering if we could have an interview?" Up close, she noticed that Lt. Bear wore a harness of thin white straps, nearly invisible against his coat, mounting on one side a communication pip. Susan turned toward JT as he caught up with her. "This is my cameraman, JT."

"What's up, brother?" Bear asked JT.

"What?"

"I said 'what's up, brother?' I understand that's how you black humans greet each other."

"Some of us do and some of us don't, but why are you saying it?"

"Why? Because, beneath this magnificent white coat, my skin is blacker than yours is. We minorities have to stick together so the man can't mess with us." Lt. Bear's dark brown-black eyes stared into JT's.

"I can't tell if he's joking or not," JT said to Susan out of the side of his mouth. Bear smiled his tooth filled smile again. "And a smile from a large predator ain't the same thing as a smile between us humans."

"Come on, JT. If he was dangerous he wouldn't be here among all the passengers and crew."

"Lady, next to the Captain, I'm the most dangerous thing on this boat."

"Oh," said Susan, taken aback. "I didn't mean to insult you Lieutenant."

"No problem, just setting the record straight," then, after thinking for a moment, he added, "you wouldn't want to mess with Gretchen, either."

"Gretchen? First Officer Curtis?"

"Yeah, she's pretty dangerous too, especially with that big stick of her's."

"OK." *Now why would he say that,* Susan wondered? *And how could the Captain be more dangerous than this half ton behemoth? Curiouser and curiouser.* "Well I would really like to sit down and interview you, Lt. Bear—do I call you Lt. Bear, or Lieutenant or Mr. Bear?"

"One's as good as another, they're all accurate," Bear added noncommittally.

"Do you have a first name?"

"In Kalaallisut they call me Nanoq, in Central Siberian Yupik they call me Nanuq, all basically variations on Nanuk. It means 'polar bear'. The Inuit are not that inventive."

"I see, so just Bear then?"

"Yeah, that works for me. The Inuit consider Nanuk to be wise, powerful and 'almost a man.' I consider the Inuit a pain in the ass or, at best, lunch. Here, let me buy you primates a drink."

130

With that Lt. Bear stood up on all fours and ambled over to the bar where everyone rapidly made way for the lumbering quadruped. Evidently, polar bears never have a problem finding room at the bar. Susan and JT followed him over to where a slight young woman with curly brown hair was serving drinks one-handed. Her right arm was in a cast and sling.

"Hey, Melissa, how are you feeling, babe?" Asked Bear, with considerable tenderness. "Susan, JT, I'd like you to meet Melissa, the ship's gardener and my favorite bartender."

"Hello, nice to meet you," Susan said, offering her left hand. The pale bartender shyly accepted the proffered handshake.

"I'm actually an environmental tech, the ship's horticulturist," Melissa explained, shaking hands with JT.

"Like I said, the ship's gardener," the furry Lieutenant repeated. "Hey, gardeners are good people, at least they do something productive!"

"Bear pretty much judges everybody and everything with respect to their food value," Melissa said with a smile, reaching out and scratching the top of Bear's nose. "He's a very up front person, if he says he likes you he likes you. But you need to watch out, bears have a wicked sense of humor."

"I think I've already had a sample of that from soul brother Bear here," JT added. "What do you have back there that's fit to drink, Melissa?"

"Lone Star and Shiner Bock on draught; Stone Sublimely Self Righteous Ale, Great Divide Oak Aged Yeti Imperial Stout, Dogfish Head 90 Minute Imperial IPA and Double Bastard Ale in bottles; a decent selection of wines plus about any mixed drink you can think of. Mr. Parker, the ship's owner, believes in the curative power of strong drink."

"I'll have a Double Bastard," said JT.

"A glass of Shiraz for me, please," Susan chimed in.

"And I'll have my usual, babe." added Bear.

Melissa nodded and turned to fetch the drinks. While they waited for their libation, Susan scanned the lounge. Most of the furor over Lt. Bear's introduction had died down, though the Marines kept stealing furtive glances at him. Over at the big viewport, the Captain was huddled with the two Russians while the Japanese scientist and Rajiv Gupta were engaged in an animated conversation nearby. Those two were obviously birds of a feather, Susan decided.

Melissa arrived with their drinks, both her wine and JT's beer in containers with sippy cup lids to guard against spilling. Lt. Bear's drink was in a plastic quart bottle with a straw protruding from its cap. "Here you go folks, y'all enjoy!"

"Thanks, babe," Bear replied, eagerly grasping the bottle of dark fluid. Bear turned around to face the rest of the people in the lounge and sat down on his hind end. Using both paws, he brought the container up over his head and took a long drink from the straw, looking for all the world like a circus bear doing its act.

"And what are you drinking, Lieutenant?" Susan asked, overcome with curiosity. Smacking his lips, Lt. Bear snorted once and then replied, "Blackberry brandy."

Susan had a passing concern about being in the vicinity of a drunken polar bear but then realized that the ursine Lieutenant weighed ten times as much as she did. The quart of brandy would probably barely give him a buzz.

"It's his favorite," offered Melissa from behind the bar. "And don't mind that 'babe' stuff. He calls everyone he likes babe." Lt. Bear let loose a heartfelt belch and then the room fell silent as the Captain signaled for the crowd's attention once more.

Chapter 9

Main Lounge, Parker's Folly

Everyone assembled in the ship's main lounge turned to face Captain Jack as he prepared to speak. "I hope that everyone has gotten something to drink," he began. This elicited cheers of affirmation from around the room.

"I realize that most of you are strangers to this vessel. Parker's Folly—that, by the way, is an unofficial name since the ship was never christened, but a ship needs a name and Folly will do for now —Parker's Folly is a spaceship commissioned by Mr. TK Parker. Her design was created by several great scientific minds, one of which we are fortunate to have on board. Dr. Gupta, please raise your hand." Rajiv, standing nearby, raised his hand.

"Dr. Rajiv Gupta is Earth's greatest expert in the new field of gravitonics and the ship's head engineer. If you have questions regarding the deck gravity or the ship's drive, please direct your questions to him. If, that is, you can pry him away from Dr Saito."

That brought a ripple of laughter from the crowd—the two physicists had been locked in an energetic and totally incomprehensible conversation since the two met.

"I will say this, this ship is powered by a form of nuclear fusion and is capable of great, sustained acceleration. Most of you felt that acceleration during takeoff. Understand, that was only about a quarter of what she is capable of.

I also know that many of you were injured during our departure. I apologize for the rough treatment, it was not our intent to harm you in anyway, but the authorities forced our hand. The fact of the matter is, most of you do not belong on board—the members of the KWTEX news crew, Gunnery Sergeant Rodriguez's Marines, various stowaways and the crew from the ISS, though they are a welcome late addition to the ship's company."

At this point the Gunny, still feeling irritable over her dislocated shoulder and the unfairness of life in general, interrupted. "Tell me Captain, why does it seem that most of the people on board your ship were kidnapped?"

"Well Sergeant Rodriguez, that is not exactly true. We were in the process of disembarking the news people when fire from your squad prevented them from leaving. Then your Marines entered the cargo hold of you're own volition, uninvited I might add. These two," the captain motioned to the two construction workers, "were actual stowaways, and you all know how the people from the space station came to be aboard. No, Sergeant, no one on board was kidnapped."

"I guess I see your point, Sir. But we were under orders."

"Yes, I'll get to that. But first I want to let you know that we won't be returning to the surface of the planet any time soon. The U.S. government attempted to seize this ship and we in Texas don't hold with government seizure of private property. I intend to keep the ship in space for a while, at least until the authorities have some time to calm down a bit.

"So, in the mean time, we need to find something to keep us busy—I propose a trip to the Moon. It's in the neighborhood and I for one have always wanted to go there." This triggered a renewed round of conversation among the crowd.

"And what will we be doing during this little jaunt to the Moon?" Susan asked. She was not being critical and was actually excited by the possibility of filming a report by the big viewport with the Moon's craggy surface in the background. *First reporter on the Moon!* She could almost taste the Pulitzer Prize.

"The crew has plenty to keep them busy. Since this is Folly's maiden voyage, we will be checking out her equipment and capabilities along the way. As you might have noticed we are a bit undermanned, having left three quarters of our complement on the shore. And that brings me to the primary reason for this meeting." Jack took a deep breath and pushed on. "I would like to offer those of you who are not already part of the ship's crew... employment."

The lounge erupted. After several minutes of babbling and shouted questions, the Captain managed to regain control of the meeting.

"Here are the terms—they differ somewhat depending on individual circumstances. First, I have asked Dr. Ludmilla Tropsha to assume the duties of ship's surgeon and she has graciously agreed. Dr. Yuki Saito will join Dr. Gupta on the science and engineering staff, while Col. Ivan Kondratov will serve as an officer attached to my staff. His knowledge and training will no doubt prove invaluable."

"Ms. Write, since you are familiar with communications I think your place will be with the bridge crew. The same applies to you Mr. Taylor. I understand that you have a degree in astronomy?"

"Yes, Sir. A Masters from UT Austin."

"In that case, you might find it interesting to man our observational instruments and perhaps help a bit with navigation. As for our two stowaways, you will be offered entry positions as deck crew. Your precise duties will be determined by the ship's First Officer, Lt. Curtis, and Chief Zackly."

"What if we don't wanna join your crew?" asked the male half of the duo.

"What's your name son?" Jack asked.

"Tommy Wendover, and I ain't your son."

"Well, Tommy. You can either work for your passage or spend the voyage in an eight by four foot metal room with just a cot and a toilet, and live on bread and water until I find a place to dump your worthless carcass."

"You can't do that! We didn't do nothing."

"You obviously don't know me, mister. The other alternative is to put you out the airlock."

"Begging the Captain's pardon," interjected Lt. Bear, "if you're just going to toss them out the airlock I'd like to have them. I always enjoy some really fresh meat."

"Please no!" the smarmy stowaway pleaded, panic in his eyes.

"That's 'please no, Sir.'" Perspiration was beading on Tommy's forehead and both of the stowaways now looked truly frightened. "So Mr. Wendover, and you Miss, what are your answers."

"Jolene Betts, Sir. I'd be happy to join the crew."

"Yeah, me too... Sir."

135

"Fine, that's settled. Chief, take our new crew members in hand and get them squared away when the meeting is over."

"Aye aye, Captain."

"Now that brings us to the hardest part—the Marines." The four Marines and their Navy Corpsman were standing together near the back of the lounge. Hearing the Captain refer to them, they came more or less to attention.

"You and your squadmates represent a hostile force that tried to commandeer my ship. For that I should clap you in the brig for the duration. But since I don't have a brig large enough to hold the lot of you I would rather offer you a deal."

"A deal, Sir?" the Gunny replied for the squad.

"Yes, a deal. I would like you to fulfill the normal function of Marines on board a Navy vessel. Under direction of the ship's officers, you would assist the crew in their duties and, if the circumstances should arise, form a boarding party."

"Boarding party, Captain?" Now the Gunny was really confused.

"I don't anticipate the need for a boarding party or for your Marines to repel boarders for that matter. But I want you to understand that you would be serving as the ship's Marines. Do you understand, Sergeant?"

"Yes, Sir. I'm not sure I can do that, Captain, legally I mean. We are all still in the U.S. Marine Corps." The Gunny whispered back and forth with her four squadmates for a half a minute and then said, "Sir, could I have a word with you in private regarding this matter?"

"Certainly, Sergeant." The Captain addressed the rest of the assembled crew. "Alright everyone, please familiarize yourselves with you new stations. Lt. Curtis will tell you where to go if you are unsure. Lt. Bear, please keep the rest of the Marines company in the lounge while I talk with the Sergeant in my sea cabin."

The meeting began to break up. Dr. Saito headed aft to see the engineering spaces with Dr. Gupta. Col Kondratov, JT and Susan headed forward with the bridge crew. Dr Tropsha hesitated before heading aft and finally spoke, "Captain, might I request the presence of the Marine medic? I will want to review my new patients' conditions and she would be most helpful."

"Certainly Doctor. Corpsman White, would you please accompany the Doctor to sickbay?"

"Yes, Sir." Betty nodded, taking the Captain's question as an order.

"Now, Sergeant. Shall we go forward?"

As the Captain and the Gunnery Sergeant disappeared forward, Chief Zackly turned to his two new deck crew. "Alright you two, down the companion way and aft to the crew quarters. We'll get you rack assignments and some new work uniforms."

"Don't get your nickers in a twist, pops," Tommy sneered at the diminutive Chief, his swagger returning with the departure of the Captain. In a flash Chief Zackly was in Tommy's face.

"Why you young punk! I'll turn you upside down and spit in your asshole! You got trouble written all over you and I'm only gona' say this once—do not mess with me." Spittle sprayed the young man's face as the Chief proceeded to hand out an old fashioned ass chewing. "And you better obey all of the ship's officers and other ratings too. Keep this in that conniving little mind of yours, scupper turd, I'm the Chief Boatswain's Mate and that means I got them airlock codes just like the Captain. You piss me off and you'll find yer self trying to breath vacuum!"

As the thoroughly cowed new recruits and the still fuming Chief disappeared down the companionway, Lt. Bear turned to the three Marines left in his care and said, "Belly up to the bar boys, I didn't hear the Captain order it closed."

Captain's Sea Cabin, Parker's Folly

The Captain was seated at his desk with the Gunnery Sergeant standing at parade rest in front of him. She had only one hand behind her back, because of the sling on her right arm. On entering the cabin, GySgt Rodriguez behaved precisely as she would in front of an American Navy officer. She took one step forward, stood to attention, saluted with her left hand—her right arm being in a sling

—and barked out "Gunnery Sergeant Rodriguez, reporting to the ship's Captain as ordered, Sir."

Out of long habit, Jack returned the Gunny's salute and got her to assume parade rest by telling her, "At ease, Sergeant." The Gunny politely refused to take a seat, however.

"OK, Sergeant, tell me what's on your mind," the Captain said. He had dealt with Marines when he was in the Navy and agreed with a statement attributed to an Army general—"There are only two kinds of people that understand Marines: Marines and the enemy. Everyone else has a second-hand opinion."

Jack was never a Marine and he hoped that he would no longer qualify for the latter category when this meeting was over. Trying to keep the Marines in the brig—if he had a brig—even with half the squad in sickbay would place a hell of a strain on his already thinly stretched crew.

"Sir, according to the military code of conduct, even if captured I am to resist by all means available. I must make every effort to escape and aid others to escape. I can accept neither parole nor special favors from the enemy. Please explain how this offer you are making is not in violation of the code of conduct."

"Well, Sergeant, first off you were sent to seize the ship, but those aboard were all citizens of the United States. You are not at war with us and we are not your enemy. Second, what can you do? The ship is in space, so you cannot escape. If you did manage to commandeer the ship you could not operate it or safely return it to Earth. And finally, space is a very dangerous place. There are enough hazards without continued hostilities among those on board.

"I don't think that these are the circumstances the code of conduct was written for. All that I'm asking is that, for the sake of your men and all on board, you cooperate for the duration of the voyage. Restrain from sabotaging the ship or harming any members of the crew, and you have my word as an officer that I will return you and your squad to Earth when the voyage is over."

"Sir, in the absence of a Marine Officer, the Gunnery Sergeant requests a more formal description of her duties under the prospective parole agreement."

Well, Jack thought, *this is interesting. It's not like we have our own set of service regulations.* Then he had an idea. Consulting his tablet he quickly found what he was looking for, a description of a gunnery sergeant's duties from an old Navy manual. "Sergeant, I am going to read you a passage from congressional testimony regarding the qualifications of a Marine Gunnery Sergeant." He did not add that the testimony had been given in 1912:

> *"He should have sufficient knowledge of the system of accountability of the United States Marine Corps to take charge of and properly render the accounts of a guard aboard ship, and should be competent in all respects to perform the duties of a first sergeant in charge of a guard on ship to which no marine officer is attached; also a knowledge of the duties involved in the subsistence of men ordered on detached duty, as well as the duties of an officer in command of a part of a landing party on shore."*

"I'm asking you to act as would any Gunnery Sergeant in charge of a shipboard detachment of Marines. Do you see a problem fulfilling any of those duties, Sergeant?"

"No problem, Captain. The Squad would stay under my control?"

"Yes."

"And Lt. Merryweather will be in command if he recovers enough to resume his duties?"

"Certainly. If you will give me your parole and your Lieutenant recovers enough to resume his command, I will release you from your pledge and put the same question to him. I will honor whatever course of action your officer chooses, when the time comes."

"And can I get this parole agreement in writing, Sir? No offense."

"None taken Sergeant. Grant's of parole are traditionally made both verbally and in writing, to preclude any later misunderstandings." *Like courts martial*, he added mentally.

"I guess I can agree then, Captain."

"Very well Gunnery Sergeant. I formally ask you to give your parole and that of those who serve under you."

The Gunny came back to attention and replied, "Sir, I give you my parole and those of my men."

"Great, now that that is out of the way we can get on with things."

"Begging the Captain's pardon. Who should I see about getting my squad fed and bedded down, Sir?"

"Ah yes. A good officer or non-com always sees to the comfort of his men first. You need to talk to Lt. Curtis, she'll assign your men quarters. There will be announcements later regarding meal times, the use of the showers and such. And Gunny,"

"Yes, Captain."

"Don't hesitate to call on Lt. Bear or Chief Zackly if there is something you need or can't find."

"Yes, Sir." The Gunny paused. "Pardon me, Sir. Is Lt. Bear really an actual polar bear?"

"Yes indeed his is. In fact, I personally went to the Arctic to recruit him. Dismissed, Sergeant."

North of the Arctic Circle, Six Years Ago.

Tendrils of snow writhed across the frozen waste, as the bitter cold wind howled, shrieking in protest as it passed over the pressure ridges that scarred the solid pack ice. A party of Inuit hunters were hunkered down behind one such ridge, crouching as low as possible in hopes of remaining out of sight until sunset.

Three of the party were already dead, their shattered and bloodstained remains lying where they fell. They had been shot with something bigger than any of the party's hunting rifles. Something that caused heads to explode and could blow a man's chest out through his back with a single shot.

Peter Epoo was the first of the hunting party to die. The hunters were paralleling the pressure ridge on their snowmobiles, looking for a good place to cross it, when his head exploded, parka hood and all. A shot echoed across the empty ice as Peter's headless body fell off of his machine, which continued on a short ways and then stopped.

Tagak Uyarasuk jumped off of his sled and ran over to Peter's body, trying to figure out what had happened to his friend. The back of his sealskin parka suddenly erupted as bone, gristle, lungs and blood formed a red fountain spurting from Tagak's ruined body. The echo of the shot was heard as the lifeless hunter fell to the ice on top of his dead friend.

The remaining three hunters—Jobie Annahatak, Willie Kiatainaq and his son Noah—quickly took shelter behind the ridge. They remained still for twenty minutes, nothing moved but the wind blown snow. Then Jobie decided to look over the ridge to see if he could spot anyone. As he stuck his head up it exploded in a cloud of pink mist. Bits of bloody brain and shards of skull with skin and hair still attached rained down on the terrified father and son.

The only ones left now were Willie and Noah. It had been more than an hour since Jobie had been killed and both hunters were feeling the cold. "Poppa, what should we do?" asked the frightened boy, barely into his teens.

The feeble Arctic Sun was getting low on the horizon, soon the brief late winter day would end. They had yet to catch sight of their tormentor. "Stay down, Noah. Better to wait for darkness. Then we try to run."

Laying prone on the next pressure ridge over was a large figure covered with white hair. He was intently peering through the Leupold 4.5×14 Mark 4 telescopic sight of a Barrett M107A1 semi-automatic, 50 caliber sniper rifle. Capable of lethal accuracy beyond 2,000 yards, the hunters could not have returned fire even if they knew where it was coming from.

The rifle itself had been painted white to blend in with Arctic conditions. The trigger guard had also been removed to better accommodate the shooter. The frigid conditions and howling wind didn't bother the marksman in the least because he was a large male polar bear.

As the great white bear patiently waited for his quarry to show itself another figure approached him from behind. It was a tall man in a fur parka. "I know you're back there," the bear said, not looking up from the rifle scope.

"I wanted you to know that I was," the man said evenly. "It's generally not a good idea to sneak up on someone holding a weapon."

"I'll be with you in a minute, there's only two of them left," the bear rumbled. He figured that if the man behind him intended to kill him he would have done so already—either that or he was unarmed. Either way, he would deal with the man after he finished off the hunting party.

"You know you really shouldn't kill all of them."

"Not your business."

"I'm guessing that you are trying to send the Inuit a message."

"Yeah, 'I hate you little pricks and I'm going to kill you all.'"

"That's my point. If you kill all of the hunters there will be no one left to tell the others."

"Tell 'em what?"

"That a great white bear with a rifle is out on the ice, hunting the hunters."

"You know what?" There was a painfully loud report as the sniper rifle fired.

Across the ice, Willie was struck in the shoulder by a 661 gr bullet traveling in excess of 2,500 feet per second. His left arm was severed from his torso, but it was the shock that killed him.

"Ddwa! (father)" Noah cried and stood up. As he started toward his father's crumpled body he looked in the direction the shot had come from. There, on the next ridge, was a polar bear—a big male. The bear stood up on his hind legs and raised something over his head. It looked like a large white rifle.

The bear pointed the rifle in Noah's direction, sending the boy racing back to his snowmobile. He started the engine and without looking back he sped away to the south.

The bear dropped down to all fours and rolled around to face his interlocutor, rifle in paw. "What you said made sense. Now tell me why I'm not going to kill you."

"Well, for a start you're curious."

"About?"

"About how I found you, why I approached you alone and unarmed, and most importantly, why I was not surprised when you spoke to me."

"Yeah, I was wondering about that. Most humans shit themselves when I say something to them." *He's standing there totally calm and unafraid,* the bear thought, *this guy is either crazy or knows something I don't.* "So what do you want?"

"Have you ever wondered why only some polar bears can talk? And how that came to be?"

"Hey, we ain't all the same. Anymore than all you apes are the same. Most polar bears are just big dumb brutes. Only a few of us can talk, only a few of us are smart enough to even know what talking is."

"Would you like to know more about where your kind came from and why you are different?"

"You're saying you got all the answers?" There was a threatening edge to the white bear's question.

"Hardly, but I do have some of the answers and I know were we can find out more. You see, my ursine friend, both talking bears and talking apes have something in common—we have both been messed with by parties unknown."

"Really? And what are you going to do about that?"

"I'm going to go find those who did the messing and ask them why. Want to come along?"

The 1,300 pound predator cocked his head to one side as he considered what the man had just said to him. He had never really had a conversation with a human before, at least not one that didn't involve screaming and then a meal. The man had said he was unarmed and the bear figured he could always kill him and eat him later. "OK, you're on."

"Excellent! I have an aircraft near by. You can call me Jack, by the way. What should I call you?"

"Bear seems to cover it."

"OK, Bear. Let's get moving before the Sun sets. Just one more question."

"Yes?"

"I've been following you for several days. Why were you hunting those Eskimos?"

"They hunt us, don't they?"

Sickbay, Parker's Folly

Betty followed the Russian doctor down the passageway aft to sickbay. Events had been moving so quickly since they exited the Osprey next to the old hangar, she was still trying to accept that this wasn't all a dream. If it was, it was a very detailed and lifelike dream. "Sickbay is on your left, Ma'am," Betty said to Dr. Tropsha as they neared the door.

"Yes, thank you," Ludmilla replied. "Lieutenant Curtis pointed out the medical facility when she took us to see the Captain."

Entering the sickbay, Ludmilla stopped and stared. *Look at all that equipment!* State of the art monitoring—heart beat, blood pressure, body temperature, respiration—with color displays above each patient's bed. Forward there were what looked like MRI and portable CAT Scan machines. To the right there was a separate OR with robotic-assisted surgery equipment, *incredible!*

"How does one man afford something like this?" the Russian Doctor wondered out loud. "This clinic has more and better equipment than some full sized hospitals."

"Yes, Doctor," replied Betty. "There is a fully equipped lab as well for blood and tissue work, there's even a DNA sequencer. The hardest question here is not if they have something but where to find it."

"Amazing," Ludmilla said, shaking her head. "Well, let's get to work. Corpsman, what should I call you? I know that you are not a nurse."

"No, Ma'am. A hospital corpsman is more like a combination physician assistant and emergency medical technician. I've been trained in first aid, emergency medicine and some basic surgical procedures."

"What kind of surgery?"

"Removal of shrapnel, stitching up wounds, severed arteries and such. Things that won't wait for a trip to the hospital. I performed an emergency appendectomy once in the field. We were in a remote village in Afghanistan and the weather had shut down air evac."

"Have you ever assisted during surgery?"

"Yes, Ma'am."

"Good. You still did not answer my question, what should I call you?"

"Corpsman is too long, the Marines usually call us 'medic' or 'Doc,' but that might be confusing. Could you just call me Betty?"

"That would be fine. You can call me Ludmilla, but only when we are not on duty."

"Yes, Doctor." Experience had taught Betty that not calling an MD 'doctor' was like failing to call a judge 'your honor.'

"So which of our patients is in the worst condition?"

"Overall I would say Lt. Merryweather is most critical. He was crushed by a crate during takeoff and has multiple fractures. The worst was an open fracture of his left femur. I cleaned the skin puncture area of debris and immobilized the break with splints and traction. I'm not qualified to immobilize the break internally. I also started him on antibiotics."

"Which antibiotics and the dosage?"

"Before the debridement I administered 2 g ceftriaxone IV and immediately after gentamicin, 1.5 mg per each kilogram of body weight. His medical tag shows that his tetanus shots are current."

"Very good, Betty. And he is stable?"

"Yes, Doctor. But he is heavily sedated."

"Is there anyone who needs more immediate attention?"

"LCpl Reagan, Doctor. He was clawed by Lt. Bear. There are significant lacerations on his right arm, from shoulder to wrist. I cleaned and dressed the wounds but I didn't want to stitch him up myself—he'd end up looking like Frankenstein's Monster."

"Well, let's have a look and see what I can do to close his wounds."

"Excuse me, Dr. Tropsha," a third voice said.

"Who is that?" Ludmilla demanded.

"This is the ship's computer, Doctor. I wanted to inform you that there are appropriate supplies, including surgical glue and staples, in the third cabinet on the left behind you."

"You monitor the entire ship? Even the sickbay?"

"Yes Dr. Tropsha. Now that you and Corpsman White are part of the crew I will respond to your verbal queries."

"So Computer, what drugs do we have on hand?"

"Please address me as 'Folly,' Doctor. There are several hundred in inventory and I can synthesize many more, would you like to hear them all?"

"No, that is fine, Folly. Betty, could you fetch the supplies out of the cabinet? We will unwrap the unfortunate Mr. Reagan's arm and take a look. There is probably damage to the deep muscle structure that will require stitching. We can use surgical glue to close the skin. Come, let us get to work."

Bridge, Parker's Folly

The Captain surveyed his newly expanded bridge crew approvingly. *Now this is more like it, all the major stations manned and things looking ship shape.* Susan and Ivan were at the wing stations on either side of the two helmsmen, both looking natty in their new dark blue jumpsuits. On the upper level, JT, also in blue, was manning the navigator's station on the starboard side. Jo Jo, who wore the orange jumpsuit of the science and engineering staff, was at the engineer's station on the port side.

"What's the ship's status, Mr. Medina?"

"All systems are nominal, the engineering board is green, Captain."

"Helm, is our course to the Moon laid in?"

"Yes, Sir," Replied Billy Ray.

Jack activated the ship's PA, 1MC in Navy parlance, and announced: "Attention all hands, if you are near a porthole you might wish to look outside for the next few minutes. Earth is off the port side and the ISS off starboard. We will leaving both behind in approximately one minute."

Jack noticed the Russian Colonel staring, mesmerized by the view out Folly's transparent bow. "Rather breathtaking, eh Colonel?"

"Yes, Captain. I thought the view from the tranquility module cupola was impressive but this, this is like walking in space without need of a suit."

"Well, departure should be even more impressive. Mr. Danner, maneuver well clear of the station before we power up the main drives. I have no desire to shred the ISS as we depart."

"Yes, Sir."

"Engineering, Bridge. Dr. Gupta I will need main engines in 20 seconds."

"Aye, Captain. They are all online and ready."

"Thank you, Engineering. Mr. Vincent, set us on course to the Moon."

"Aye aye, Captain!"

The ISS slipped behind the ship then diminished in size, slowly at first, then more rapidly. No movement could be felt on board, no change in background noise was heard. The day-night terminator swept past as the Moon rose from behind its parent planet, pale and beckoning. For the first time, Parker's Folly left low Earth orbit for deep space.

Chapter 10

Cargo Hold, Parker's Folly, En route to the Moon

Parker's Folly was falling toward the Moon, having passed the gravitational crossover point during the night. It was going to take the ship only about half the time it took the old Apollo capsules to voyage to the Moon. Earth and its Moon travel along curved paths through space, but the distance between them remains the same on average, about 384,000 km center to center. The point at which the gravitational pull of the Moon is equal to Earth's is roughly 58,000 km from the Moon.

Captain Jack had taken the night watch and Jo Jo Medina was currently officer of the deck. Under way, when the Captain or First Officer were not on the bridge, the Captain designates an OOD to be in charge of the ship. With Jo Jo in charge on the bridge, the Captain was in the owner's cabin sleeping and Lt. Curtis was in the cargo hold working out.

Most of the crates in the hold had been unpacked and removed, their contents installed in various locations around the ship. A few remained scattered about the middle of the deck while a clear path had been opened around the sides of the hold. GySgt Rodriguez had roused her squad early for physical training and now had the ambulatory Marines jogging around the track, though their level of exertion in the lowered gravity was minimal.

Overnight, the Captain ordered the deck gravity increased to match that of the Moon, roughly 1.6 m/sec^2, one sixth of Earth normal. The Marines and First Officer were taking the opportunity to become accustomed to lunar conditions in case the need arose to EVA on the surface.

"Hey Gunny," Cpl Sizemore puffed out between strides, "what's the Navy officer doing with that big stick?"

"She's practicing, Sizemore. It's called *kendo*, the way of the sword in Japanese. The wooden sword is called a *bokken*, I think." the Gunny huffed. "At one time samurai used wooden swords to practice their technique, sort of like target practice for swordsmen."

"Could she really hurt someone with that thing?"

149

"I've seen people smash cinder blocks and bust up crates with one of those things. It could break bones or mess you up inside, easy. Now quit yapping and concentrate on running." With that, the Gunny pulled away from the talkative corporal.

In an open region in the center of the hold, Lt. Curtis was running through some individual katas—ritualized practice exercises. The bokken, literally "wooden sword," was made to mimic the size, weight and balance of a traditional samurai *katana*. Normally, it was better to perform katas with a partner, but she could find no takers for that. Better than doing katas was actual sparring, for which the lighter *shinai* was used. So far, Gretchen had been unable to entice anyone into sparring with her more than once. The only one who wanted to play was Lt. Bear, and he didn't use a sword.

Watching unobtrusively from the sideline was Dr. Saito. Gretchen finished her kata and saw the Japanese physicist out of the corner of her eye. She walked over to him and bowed, saying in decent Japanese, "Greetings Doctor, you wouldn't by any chance be a kendōka (a practitioner of kendo)?"

"Actually I am, Lieutenant," Saito replied in the same language, "but I am quite out of practice. However, if you have some spare equipment I would be happy to practice with you."

"You're in luck, Doctor," Gretchen replied, switching to English. "I have a pair of shinai and armor in my quarters. If you would be so gracious as to spar with me I would be in your debt."

"I would be honored to spar with you, Lieutenant."

"Great! I'll be right back." Gretchen quickly disappeared up the passageway forward to the crew's quarters. This should be interesting thought Yuki. He was a skilled *kenshi* (swordsman) but had not practiced in years, not since his wife and son had died. Maybe he should have, after all one of the Buddhist inspired tenets of kendo was *mushin*, or "empty mind." Perhaps he could have found comfort for his grief by embarking on a quest for spiritual enlightenment like the samurai of old.

* * * * *

Gretchen soon returned with two sets of kendo equipment. There were robes, two helmets with metal grills to protect the face, and a series of hard leather and fabric flaps to protect the sides of the head and throat. Heavy leather gloves to protect the forearms and hands, breast plates and quilted groin protectors called *tare* completed the panoply.

The two shinai were modernized versions with carbon fiber reinforced resin slats in place of the traditional four bamboo ones, though the slats were still held together by leather fittings. In modern kendo both strikes and thrusts can be used against one's opponent. Strikes are only made towards specific target areas on the wrists, head, or body, all of which are protected by armor. Thrusts, which are more dangerous, are only permitted to the throat and are seldom allowed by lower ranking kendōka.

"We should start slowly, Doctor. Do you wish to be *uchidachi* or *shidachi*?" During practice, the participants take the roles of either *uchidachi*, the teacher, or *shidachi*, the student.

"I would humbly prefer the role of student, Lieutenant," said the slender physicist, wrapping a towel around his head for padding before donning his helmet. "And please call me Yuki."

"Great, please call me Gretchen." she replied, donning her own helmet and moving out to the middle of the impromptu practice space.

Yuki joined her and they bowed deeply to one another. The pair struck a pose with their swords held high in front of them, tips crossed. Then they launched into a noisy flurry of strikes and counters, accompanied by the stamping of feet and loud shouts— the traditional *kiai*, a verbal sign of their martial spirit.

In kendo it is important that a strike be made with the correct portion of the shinai. The shinai and its parts represent a real sword. The back of the sword is marked by a cord that runs down one of the four slats, from the tip to the hand grip. The slat opposite the cord represents the sword's cutting edge, the two on either side the flat of the blade. The cord is secured one quarter of the way from the tip by a leather ribbon. This represents the forward quarter of the blade, the most effective cutting part of an actual sword blade.

In order for a blow to score, solid contact must be made in a valid target area using the correct portion of the blade. But a solid accurate strike is not enough—the path of the blade and the direction of the edge must be in proper alignment. The strike must also be accompanied by a correct kiai yell. The leading foot step, the kiai, and strike should all occur simultaneously.

Eventually, Gretchen was able to whack Yuki on top of the helmet. They separated, circling each other warily. "Again!" she shouted. Once again the two swordsmen engaged. This time Yuki scored first, striking the left and right helmet target points in quick succession. Again they separated.

After a strike, it is particularly important for a swordsman to show continued awareness of his opponent and their surroundings. This is demonstrated by passing through or moving diagonally to a proper distance while keeping one's sword tip pointed at the opponent's center. The swordsman must remain on guard, ready to thwart any attempt at a counter attack.

"Very good, Saito-san," gasped Gretchen, partly winded. "You are *dan* rated, aren't you?" Proficient kendōka are rated by levels of expertise called dan, ranging from 1 to 10 in order of increasing skill.

"I was 5th dan when I fell out of practice," said Yuki, who suddenly looked quite formidable in his swordsman's armor. "You too are dan, I think."

"I am also 5th dan, but you are from a Japanese school and are most certainly better trained than I am."

"The only way to improve is to banish the four sicknesses through *fudōshin*," Yuki replied, referring to the concept of "unmoving mind." When achieved, fudōshin prevents the kendōka being led astray by delusions of anger, doubt, fear, or surprise arising from his opponent's actions—the so called four kendo sicknesses. "Again?"

Gretchen bowed and again struck the starting pose. Again the crack of swords and kiai shouts filled the cargo hold. At the side of the chamber, the Marines, finished with their PT and morning run, observed.

"I didn't know we had any Jedi on board," said Cpl Sizemore, referring to the loose flowing robes that two swordsmen wore under their armor. The corporal wasn't far off, George Lucas freely admitted that Japanese samurai and the samurai films of Akira Kurosawa had a great influence on his Star Wars films.

"Jedi or not, I don't think I'd like to go up against either of them up close and personal," remarked PFC Sanchez, "not with those sticks they're whacking each other with."

"Joey," LCpl Washington said, "that's about the smartest thing I ever heard you say."

Bridge, Parker's Folly, Entering Lunar Orbit.

Lt. Curtis had showered and rubbed liniment on her bruises from sparring with Yuki. For supposedly being out of practice, the little Japanese physicist was quick, quicker than she was, Gretchen admitted to herself. He also packed a wallop. She hurt all over, but it was a good kind of hurt, the type that meant she had gotten a real workout for the first time in months. To her right, JT was engrossed with the navigator's station, occasionally saying something like "wow" or "fantastic!"

"Mr. Taylor, what is it that you are finding so fascinating about the navigation station?"

"Lt. Curtis, were you aware that this ship packs a number of astronomical instruments, including a 2.2 meter reflector telescope? Combine that with being outside of Earth's atmosphere and its like having my own private Hubble space telescope! It does infrared and near UV as well, and it's all controlled from right here at this console."

"I am aware of that, Mr. Taylor. And what interesting sights have you been looking at with Mr. Parker's equipment?"

"The rings of Saturn, Neptune, and the Moon of course, and look at the view aft," he gushed, ignoring the remark about whose telescope it really was. "I think you can pull it up on your screen."

"I can do better than that," Lt. Curtis countered. "Heads up everyone, I'm going to put the main scope's image up on the forward display."

The star field and Moon, visible ahead of them through the ship's transparent nose, wavered and were replaced with a view of the limb of an outsized Earth with the Sun just peaking around it. A couple of the bridge crew gasped at the sight.

"Sweet! I didn't know it could do that," exclaimed Bobby from the helm. He and his cowboy partner were splitting watches.

"That is breathtaking, Mr. Taylor," the First Officer finally managed. "Perhaps you could show us where we are headed?"

"Coming right up. I don't know what the mirror is made out of but it must be light. This sucker repositions really quickly." As JT spoke the view from the big telescope turned to blurred streaks of light and quickly stabilized on a picture of the cratered face of Earth's satellite.

"We will be orbiting that shortly," said Bobby.

"Hey, would you like to see the Apollo 17 landing site? I'm sure we can make out some of the equipment they left behind."

"Sure," Jo Jo added from his post on the other side of the bridge. "Does that mean we can claim anything the astronauts left? I'll bet you could sell a used lunar rover for a pretty penny on eBay."

"The Universe is yours to explore and you want to go into the used car business? You're hopeless Jo Jo," chided the First Officer.

"Come on, Lieutenant. We'll probably need to make some money to help bail Mr. Parker out of jail when we get back home."

"That could well be, Mr. Medina," admitted Lt. Curtis. *Indeed, that could well be*, she thought. *I wonder what's happened back on Earth since we took off. No matter, there are things to be done.* "Mr Taylor, if you are done playing with the optical instruments the Captain has ordered a survey of the Moon using the terahertz radar to commence when we arrive in lunar orbit.

Also known as sub-millimeter radiation, terahertz waves are electromagnetic radiation with frequencies between the high end of the microwave band and the long-wavelength portion of far-infrared light. Terahertz radiation is non-ionizing and shares with microwaves the ability to penetrate a wide variety of non-conducting materials. It can pass through clothing, paper, cardboard, wood, masonry, plastic and ceramics. It can also penetrate fog and clouds, but cannot penetrate metal or liquid water. Without the presence of Earth's radiation absorbing atmosphere, terahertz radiation can be used as ground penetrating radar. Combined with sophisticated imaging software, the ship would be able to construct a detailed subsurface map as it orbited the Moon.

"Perhaps we will find something valuable enough to bail out Mr. Parker," mused JT.

"Or maybe we will find out that the Moon is really hollow with an ancient alien spaceship inside," offered Bobby.

"I think we will be putting that fringe science nonsense to rest once and for all, Mr. Danner. In any case, Mr. Taylor, I believe that Dr Saito expressed interest in working on the survey as well."

"Yes Ma'am. I'll get the equipment set up and let him know when we are ready to start."

Law Offices Bolt, Stephens & Meyer, Austin Texas.

TK Parker was not in the custody of the authorities at the moment, mostly due to the efforts of a phalanx of high-priced lawyers. TK was not pleased. "You took your own sweet time bustin' me out of federal detention," he groused. "What the hell am I paying you for?"

"TK, we got you released just as fast as we could," said George Bolt, one of the firm's senior partners, in an attempt to pour oil on the waters. "You know how hard it is to find a judge on a federal holiday."

"What ever," the unmollified TK shrugged. "I want to go home, and someone needs to check on Maria."

"We have checked to make sure Mrs. Lopez is not being held and have contacted her son, who is acting as her counsel. Your ranch, however, has been impounded by the federal government."

"Well un-impound it, damn it!"

"Mr. Parker, the Department of Homeland Security is claiming that your property was used to construct an illegal nuclear device. They further claim that you were in possession of illegal radioactive materials. They are continuing to search the grounds for signs of said radioactive materials."

"Well let 'em look, they won't find a thing. I didn't ever buy any radioactive material. Hit 'em with an injunction or something."

"We have filed multiple requests with the federal district court but these things take time. There will be a preliminary hearing tomorrow in front of Judge Landis."

"Curly Landis? He's a friend of mine and a good old Texas boy, he'll straighten them federal yahoos out."

"Yes TK, that's why we filed in his court. But the Air Force claims they detected nuclear radiation coming from your ranch on at least three occasions. They assert that your missing spaceship is nuclear powered."

"Do they? Well did they detect any radiation when it took off?"

"They didn't say, Mr. Parker."

"That's because they didn't, let 'em explain that to the Judge. We can blame the Air Force's alarm bells on cosmic rays or faulty satellites—hell, we just had the biggest solar eruption in a hundred years. Let's see 'em prove I was doing anything illegal."

"Yes sir, TK. We feel you have a strong case for harassment and should demand sizable reparations."

"You lawyers always do."

Main Lounge, Parker's Folly in Lunar Orbit.

Susan was sitting by the large viewport watching the lunar surface slip past. She was sipping a cup of the ship's excellent coffee, talking with Ivan Kondratov, who was drinking tea. The Russian Colonel was staring thoughtfully out of the viewport, occasionally taking a sip of his rapidly cooling beverage. Even the normally chatty Susan was in a pensive mood.

"Did you know, Miss Write, that I am the first Russian to orbit the Moon? Along with Lt. Col. Tropsha, of course."

"I had not thought about that, Colonel. I guess JT and I are the first news reporters to make the trip. And please call me Susan."

"Yes, sorry. First names are to be used in the mess, you must call me Ivan." Then shifting tack a bit, he continued. "Do you really believe that your government had no knowledge of this ship before a few days ago? I just can't imagine such a thing happening in my country."

"Well maybe not, Ivan. But Texas is a big state and West Texas is sparsely populated—I should know, I grew up there. No, I'm pretty sure that the government found out about this spaceship at around the same time we did. In fact, JT and I beat the government agents to TK's ranch."

"And you were trapped on board when the U.S. Marines stormed the ship?"

"Stormed is a bit too strong an image. We were getting ready to go down the ramp from the passenger door when one of the Marines shot at us. They almost hit JT. Gretchen jerked him back inside and shut the hatch. Then, as far as I can tell, the Marines managed to climb on board through the big cargo hatch just before it shut and the Captain blasted off. Things after that are a bit of a blur."

"I can imagine. And how did the Captain overcome a squad of armed Marines?"

"I have no idea, but when I was talking to Lt. Bear, he said that the Captain was the most dangerous person on board. I'm not sure what that means."

"Perhaps I can add something to that," said Ludmilla Tropsha, walking over to where the pair were conversing. She had just finished doing rounds in sickbay and had come forward looking for coffee and someone to talk with.

"You're wearing white today, Doctor," remarked the ever fashion conscious Susan, "very fetching."

"Yes, for some reason when I woke up this morning the ship had produced a white uniform for me instead of blue. I asked the computer why and it said that different parts of the crew wore different color uniforms so they were easier to identify in an emergency—crew is in blue, engineers in orange and Marines in green. Evidently medical personnel are to wear white, since Betty showed up in a white uniform this morning as well."

"That explains our uniform colors," Ivan nodded. "It is similar to how the American Navy dresses the flight deck crews on their aircraft carriers."

"Yes, I think that both the Captain and Lt. Curtis were in the Navy. I think that's where Jack picked up that strange little man they call the Chief. But you said you knew more about the crew subduing the Marines, Ludmilla?"

"Yes, I have been talking with the wounded Marines and they said that the crew used ray guns on them, that and the polar bear. Evidently the crew attacked from all directions at once, with the Captain standing on the ceiling picking the Marines off with bolts of blue light!"

"That he is a former military man is plain," Ivan remarked with almost grudging admiration.

"Maybe he is the most dangerous man on the ship," said Susan, thoughtfully.

"I think there is something more to it than that, Susan. The medical corpsman, Betty, said that the Captain was critical of the amount of harm Bear inflicted on one of the Marines. She said that the bear seemed subservient, even a bit afraid of the Captain. What kind of man frightens a 600 kilogram, fully grown male polar bear? I think there may be more to this story than we know."

"Well I've been trying to get the Captain alone for another interview since we blasted off for parts unknown." Susan's frustration was palpable.

"That is interesting, Susan," Ludmilla said, with just a bit of female cattiness, "the Captain has invited me to dine with him in his cabin this evening. Perhaps I will learn something more about this mysterious Jack Sutton."

"Good luck, Doctor," Susan replied sweetly. "Perhaps he will respond to you on a more professional level—officer to officer, rather than as a man to a woman."

Meow, thought Billy Ray to himself. He had come into the lounge to get some coffee before starting his watch and had been quietly listening to the three new crew members discussing the Captain. *Oh yes, Dr. Tropsha, watch out. That kitty got claws.*

Captain's Quarters, Parker's Folly.

The Captain had requisitioned the owner's suite as his own, since TK was unable to make the trip and they had a number of guests on board. The suite lay farthest forward on the lower deck, part of it directly under the Captain's sea cabin. It spanned the full width of the hull and boasted a sitting room, a spacious bed and a private head with shower. Both side walls held large viewports through which the crater pocked surface of the Moon could be seen passing beneath the ship.

The ship also had four guest suites, intended for friends of the owner and other distinguished guests. The Captain had moved Lt. Curtis into the one closest to his and placed the three ISS crew members in the others. This freed his normal cabin and the First Officer's for Susan and JT. With so few crew on board, there was more than enough room for the squad of marines.

A table for two had been set in the sitting room, beneath one of the long windows. White table cloth, china and crystal had been laid out by crewman Hitch, who had worked at one time as a waiter in an upscale Austin eatery. *The perfect setting for a seduction,* the Captain thought.

What he had planned was a seduction of sorts, but not that kind. Things were bound to get dicey in the near future and he wanted to be sure the Doctor was fully on the team. That meant sharing things with the Russian cosmonaut that only a few others knew. Things like what he was really looking for on the Moon.

There came a knock at the cabin door and the computer announced, "Dr. Tropsha is at the door, Captain."

"I will greet my guest in person, Folly." Normally, given the Captain's blessing, the computer would open the door and ask the party inside. The Captain, not wishing to come across as too imperious, hurried to greet his guest.

"Good evening, Dr. Tropsha," he said upon opening the door, "won't you please come in?"

159

"Why thank you, Captain. My goodness," she said, looking around the spacious cabin, "and I thought my cabin was luxurious."

"I'd imagine that, compared with conditions on the space station, even the crew cabins would be a step up," the Captain allowed. "Would you care for an apéritif?"

"Yes, thank you. I would like a very dry martini, by which I mean a very cold glass of good vodka." Ludmilla walked over to the bookcase after she ordered. "So you plan to ply me with liquor, eh Captain? Be warned that Russians are hard drinkers, Russian officers doubly so."

"Why Doctor, you misjudge me." The Captain turned to Hitch and said, "make that two vodka martinis, up with no vermouth. Doctor I assume you don't want any olives?"

"Heavens no! What a way to ruin good Vodka."

"One with and one without Mr. Hitch, if you please." Hitch nodded and left the room.

"Your Mr. Parker is evidently a well read man, judging by the titles in the bookcase."

"Hard to say, TK is a knowledgeable man about many things but those may only be for show. I hope that you are finding things on board Parker's Folly comfortable."

"Oh yes, very much so. Of course I would be happy in a scow if it had rescued me from the ISS. I checked with your Engineer Medina and the radiation levels outside just before we left the station area were high enough that we all would have been dead in under 12 hours. Radiation sickness is a particularly nasty way to die, Captain, so I thank you again for saving us."

"Both my pleasure and my duty," the Captain replied. "As the captain of a naval vessel, I am bound by the law of the sea to render aid to another vessel in distress. I am just glad that circumstances put us in a position to help."

"Yes, you and your amazing ship showed up in, what's the American phrase? 'The nick of time.' It is fortunate for everyone that radiation does not seem to penetrate the walls of your ship. The ISS blocked some but not nearly enough."

Sensing the implicit question in her words, the Captain decided to take the opening. "Yes, that is among the things I wish to discuss with you over dinner. As you can tell, Folly contains some highly advanced technology, technology not found anywhere else on Earth."

Indeed Captain, Ludmilla thought. Just prior to her coming to this cabin she and Ivan had been discussing that exact subject. Ivan insisted that she find out as much as possible about the ship's origins and technology. He claimed that, as Russian officers, it was their duty to return to the motherland with as much information as they could glean about the ship, even hinting that her patriotic duty might include sleeping with the Captain if necessary.

Not that the idea was totally repellant. The Captain was a fine looking man, tall, broad shouldered and handsome. Sandy brown hair, neatly trimmed beard a few shades darker with just a touch of gray at the temples. Those deep brown eyes however, they held secrets.

Breaking her brief, contemplative silence she continued, "I look forward to hearing all about your ship, Captain, and yourself."

"Please, we are dining in. Call me Jack."

"And you must call me Ludmilla. You seem to be most strict in your insistence on military discipline on board."

"When the crew is on duty, on the bridge or elsewhere. I find it improves efficiency and reduces mistakes. The rules are relaxed in the lounge and mess."

"But you are always addressed as 'captain,' even there."

"A captain is always on duty, Ludmilla. He can never allow his authority to be called into doubt or his subordinates to think that his orders are mere suggestions. I have reason to know from personal experience that discipline aboard ship is not a trivial matter."

There is pain in his eyes, this lesson he learned at a high personal cost, she realized. *This man, so friendly and so aloof at the same time, carries hidden scars of his own.* Before she could think of something appropriate to say the crewman returned with their drinks.

"Ah, it looks like our drinks have arrived," the Captain said with some relief. Taking the drink without olives from Hitch he handed it to her saying "Ludmilla, *dlya vashego zdorov'ya*, for your health."

Taking his own from the steward he told the man "you can come back and serve dinner in 15 minutes, Mr. Hitch."

"Aye aye, Captain."

* * * * *

An hour later, they had finished the main course and were waiting on Hitch to serve dessert—crème brûlée with coffee and brandy to finish. Things had gone well, with both Ludmilla and Jack telling each other about their careers and personal histories. Nothing salacious, just first date, get acquainted stuff. As Hitch departed, Ludmilla looked at Jack and said, "so Jack, you said you were going to explain things to me, about the ship and your mission."

She's direct, I like that in a woman, Jack thought before replying, "Yes, I did. I warn you, some of the things I am about to tell you will be hard to accept, but I swear to you I am telling the truth. At least the truth as I understand it."

Ludmilla leaned back in her chair and turned her head slightly to one side. *Damn, she is an extremely attractive woman,* the Captain finally admitted to himself. The cocktail and bottle of wine with dinner had lowered his inhibitions enough to let suppressed thoughts bubble to the surface. *And that white jumpsuit goes well with her ash-blond hair and fair Slavic complexion. A man could easily lose himself in those blue eyes—whoa Jack, get a grip!*

The Captain cleared his voice and focused on the matter at hand. "The story begins over thirty years ago, in the remote wastes of the Arabian Peninsula. A young geologist came across an artifact. Through a series of events never fully explained to me, he managed to bring it back to the United States with him. It turned out that the artifact was both ancient and highly advanced."

Jack paused, waiting for Ludmilla to object. She remained still, gazing back at him. *Remind me to never play poker with this woman,* he thought, continuing. "The artifact was found to be a data storage device. Extremely dense, holographically encoded, requiring the use of multiple intersecting laser beams and quantum detection devices to read. I am not a physicist and could not begin to explain the mechanisms at work. But what I can tell you is that, over time, a team of scientists managed to decode a small fraction of the knowledge the device contains.

"A number of astounding scientific and technological discoveries were uncovered: the metallic-ceramic material of the ship's hull; nanotechnology that allows our spacesuits to adjust to the wearer's body and be self healing in the event of a puncture; gravitonics, a way to manipulate gravitational fields that gives the ship its internal gravity and shields that protect us against meteors and even subatomic particles; and, most recently, a way of generating huge amounts of power using a form of muon catalyzed fusion."

Again Jack paused, waiting for Ludmilla to say something. *My God, she looks like the Snow Queen from that old Russian fairy tale. Yes, an ice fairy sent to test the hero's virtue and stout heart.* He smiled at her. She smiled back and said, "go on."

"Along with the technological data was other information, about the creators of the artifact and how it came to reside on Earth. This is the most unbelievable part—proof of the scientific data is all around us but the history of the artifact must be taken mostly on faith."

"Let me guess, it was put here by aliens."

"Yes! How did you know?"

"I have read science fiction. You said 'mostly on faith,' what evidence do you have?"

"We dated a sample of material from a damaged portion of the artifact. It's around four million years old. The geologist verified that the strata the artifact was found in was even older, meaning we were not getting spurious background readings."

"Anything else?"

Jack was getting the feeling that Ludmilla wasn't buying the whole aliens thing. "Historical data extracted from the artifact describes in great detail a series of experiments performed by the aliens. Biological experiments—carried out on Earth lifeforms. It seems that the aliens themselves didn't survive on Earth all that long, but their ship did."

"This is an alien spaceship?"

"No, no. We built this ship using technology gained from the artifact. No insult to Folly, but as fantastic as she is, she is a primitive nothing compared with the ship the aliens arrived in. But back to the biological experiments. Because the aliens were dying out, they programmed the ship's AI, its artificial intelligence, to breed sentient creatures from the local fauna using genetic manipulation. The idea being that, when the locals advanced enough to handle the technology, the artifact would make its presence known. Only something went wrong, maybe the breeding program took too long, who knows? We do know that the ship was failing and the artifact was released early when a chance opportunity presented itself."

"And that is it? That is your explanation for all of this?"

"Don't you see, Ludmilla? You're a biologist, you know that around four million years ago primates suddenly underwent a spurt of rapid evolution. Not just once, but time and again, new species radiated out from the area where the Arabian Peninsula and Northeast Africa collide. Species after species—*Australopithecus afarensis*, *Homo ergaster*, *Homo erectus*—each with subtle improvements: An easier upright gait, an omnivorous diet, larger brains and vocal cords that allowed spoken language to develop.

"These *hominins* became more facile tool makers, smarter too. Eventually, by the time the last glacial period peaked, 20,000 years ago, there were only three competing finalists left in the alien breeding program: *Homo neanderthalensis*, *Homo denisova* and *Homo sapiens*. The last species won."

"You are saying..."

"I'm saying that people, *Homo sapiens,* were created by aliens."

"And the talking bear?"

"They were the backup plan."

Chapter 11

Lt. Bear's Quarters, Parker's Folly.

In the aft section of the ship there were a number of storage compartments. On the lower deck, near the engineering spaces, there were two large walk-in freezer units, reefers in Navy lingo. Reefer #2 was also known, informally, as Lt. Bear's quarters. Inside, the Captain was having a conversation with his security officer and friend.

"So, did you put the moves on her?" asked Bear.

"No, I did not. It was not that type of liaison."

"Next time try grabbing her and biting her on the back of the neck—that always makes my dates feel amorous."

"Right," said Jack, adding somewhat crestfallen, "Bear, you don't understand. I laid it all out for her—the artifact, the ship, the alien breeding program, the whole thing—and she just sat there looking at me."

The reefer door opened and Lt. Curtis walked in. Like the Captain, she was wearing one of the parkas that hung outside, next to the big freezer units. Inside the reefer the temperature was kept at -25° Celsius, cold enough to give unprotected humans frostbite in 20 minutes.

For Bear, this was just comfortable sleeping temperature. Normal shipboard temperature was punishingly hot for him, which is why he lived in the reefer. After glancing in her direction, Bear continued. "So you had her speechless? Like I said, you should have gone for the old neck nip."

"I think I've missed something important here," said Gretchen. "Jack, you're not taking romantic advice from Bear, are you?"

"No, no. It's got nothing to do with romance. I was trying to describe the outcome of my talk with Ludmilla."

"I take it things did not go smoothly?"

"I don't know, I couldn't really tell. We had a nice friendly dinner and were lingering over dessert and brandy. She asked about the ship and our mission so I began to explain how we came to be in this situation."

"And she didn't buy it?"

"She just sat there. Whenever I paused she just looked at me and said 'please continue.'"

"You told her everything? About the artifact, the encoded data, the technology, building the ship?"

"Yes, I even told her about the alien breeding program, why Bear can talk—nothing got a rise out of her."

"Well, at least she didn't laugh in your face."

"You know, they can't laugh in your face if you have them by the back of the neck."

"Put a sock in it, Bear," Gretchen snapped. Working together over the past several years the three ship's officers had actually developed a close friendship. It was understood that their private meetings in the reefer were totally informal but sometimes Bear's sense of humor ran away with him. Of course, he might be serious about the neck biting.

"Polar bear romance isn't the issue here, my friend. I got the distinct impression she thought me crazy. You know, humoring me like I was an escapee from a mental institution."

"I thought you were crazy when I first met you, maybe I should go talk to her? You know I can be very persuasive, particularly with females," Bear offered helpfully, "I'll tell her what a great guy you are."

"How did the evening end, Jack?" asked Gretchen, ignoring Bear's offer to act as an intermediary.

"She said, 'that's very interesting, Jack, I will need to think about what you have said.' We stood up and shook hands, she said goodnight and left. Gretchen, I couldn't read her at all. I'm normally good at reading people but she was indecipherable."

"Tell me why we need this Russian *pizda* again?" asked Bear.

"Bear, that is a very rude word," scolded Gretchen.

Damn, I keep forgetting that she speaks Russian. Defensively Bear added, "I didn't call you one."

"Keep it up and I'll go get my bokken."

"Oh would you, please?" Bear's nostrils flared and his ears lay flat against his head, a sign of eager anticipation. If he had been a dog his tail would have been wagging furiously.

Crap, Gretchen thought, *Jack's having a confidence crisis and the four legged fur ball is only interested in some inter-species S&M.* Not that Bear was aroused sexually, her rump wasn't big enough or hairy enough to qualify as polar bear sexy. But everything that polar bears did—from feeding to making love—involved violence. Hanging around on the ship with nothing large to fight with had Bear suffering from sensory deprivation. All he really wanted was for her to smack him with her wooden sword a few times during mock combat.

"Maybe we can spar later," she said, reaching out and scratching the top of his muzzle. Then, turning her attention back to Jack, "I'd take her at face value, that she wanted time to think about what you said."

"I hope you're right. We have plenty of physicists and engineers on board, but she is the only biologist. I would really like to have her on the team when things hit the fan."

"Hang in there Jack, I can't believe she actually thinks you're crazy."

Guest Dayroom, Lower Deck, Parker's Folly.

"The man is psychotic! He should be institutionalized before he hurts himself or someone else," fumed Ludmilla. She was pacing back and fourth in front of Ivan and Susan. Their impromptu troika was joined by JT, who had just finished his watch.

"Please slow down, Ludmilla," begged Susan, "tell us what happened last night with the Captain."

"OK. The evening started out fine—we had cocktails, a nice dinner with a really nice red Bordeaux. Conversation was polite, we exchanged stories about our childhoods and careers, typical dinner conversation. He is actually quite charming, our Captain." *And your heart was all aflutter, like a school girl,* she chided herself.

"Yes?" prompted Susan, her reporter's instincts tingling.

"Then I asked him about the ship, about his mission. The *sookin syn* proceeds to tell me this fantasy story about aliens visiting Earth and devices containing secret technology. Does he think I am some kind of *belokurva,* an empty headed bimbo that he can feed me such horse manure?"

"Calm down, Dr. Tropsha, and tell us exactly what he said," demanded Ivan, playing the stern Russian patriarch.

"Yes, Ludmilla," offered JT soothingly. "We'd all like to hear what he said to upset you so."

"OK, OK," said the still pacing Ludmilla. *And to think that I was starting to like the son of a bitch! When it comes to men you can really pick them, Luda. Now stop acting like a teenage girl after a bad date and tell the others what that lying* govn'uk *said.* She took several deep breaths and continued.

"He said that all of the advanced technology found in this ship came from some alien storage device—he called it the artifact—which was found decades ago by an American geologist somewhere in Arabia. According to our esteemed Captain, a small team of scientists managed to decode this artifact and find out how to control gravity, produce energy from fusion and many other things."

"So far that would seem to fit," JT observed, quickly adding. "I mean, I could believe that one or two breakthroughs came from some private lab, but the technology embodied in this ship is years ahead of anything on Earth. It seems improbable for so many advances to be invented in such a short time by the same small team. It makes more sense that the technology came from an outside source. I'm not a believer in little green men, but there may be some truth to the Captain's story."

"Are you done?" Ludmilla had stopped pacing and was glaring at JT. "Because there is more."

"OK, sorry." JT sat down on one of the couches and fell silent.

"I asked if the ship had been built by aliens, but he said no, that they had built the ship themselves using alien technology. I said fine, but he said that was not all. It seems that these aliens, through genetic manipulation and selective breeding, are responsible for the talking bear... and for us."

"Us?" Susan and Ivan asked simultaneously.

"Us. People. Human beings! Jack said that the aliens bred us for intelligence, until we would be able to understand their technology."

"And how long did this breeding program take?" asked JT, no longer able to contain himself.

"Four million years, give or take."

To herself Susan thought, *either the Captain is totally nuts or this is the biggest story in the history of mankind. My God! If this is true it will cause riots in the street, and maybe war over possession of the technology. Ludmilla obviously doesn't believe it's true, but if it is, we humans are nothing more than some alien's pet poodles.*

"That does correspond to the evolutionary time frame for the development of modern humans," JT added, earning himself another sharp glance from Ludmilla. *You know, I think our Russian lady doctor is upset because she thinks the Captain dissed her. And now she thinks I'm making fun of her as well. She's not approaching this like a scientist.* He decided to take a chance. "Could we try to think about this like scientists?"

"Yes, remember the Captain's little speech right after we were rescued—about trusting the scientific method?" Ivan agreed. "If the Captain is insane, obsessed by aliens, the only way we might be able to reach him is using logic, using science. Reverse the argument. For this story to be true, and not just some fairy tale, what proof would we need?"

"I can't believe you are both taking this seriously. It is ludicrous, nonsense on the face of it!"

Sensing another rebuke coming, JT jumped in with an explanation of his reasoning. "Is the existence of aliens less probable than a whole string of scientific breakthroughs in many different fields, all sponsored by some oilman out in the wastelands of West Texas? Breakthroughs so fundamental that they defy science as we know it and allow a small group of people to build this ship—a real working spaceship—in secret?"

"It will take more than ray guns and spaceships to convince me that we are the product of alien genetic manipulation. Show me an alien, alive or dead, get me a tissue sample! Then I will consider believing this madman."

Bridge, Parker's Folly

Dr. Saito was intently studying the readouts on the navigator's console, where the results of the ground penetrating radar survey were being displayed. *These readings are quite anomalous,* he thought, *I was expecting to find some buried water deposits or some minerals, maybe an empty lava tube or two, but that return looks for the world like an empty space beneath that small crater.*

"Mr. Medina, could you look at this display and tell me if everything is working correctly, please?" Yuki asked the engineer, who was once again OOD.

"Hmm," said Jo Jo Medina, examining the settings on the radar console. "Everything seems to be functioning fine, Professor. What seems to be the problem?"

"If this instrument is correct, then there is a void under the floor of this crater," Yuki said, indicating the computer generated visualization on the monitor. "I think I need to have Mr. Taylor come back to the bridge, since he is our astronomer."

"I didn't know the Moon had caves," Jo Jo remarked. "What's the name of the crater?"

"It is called Giordano Bruno."

Crew's Dayroom, Lower Deck, Parker's Folly

Tommy Wendover was alone in the crew's mess when Col. Kondratov found him. The Colonel had been searching for the disaffected young man since Dr. Tropsha's diatribe in the passenger's dayroom. At first Ivan had thought that simply gathering as much information as he could about the ship and its fantastic technology would be sufficient. But now, given Ludmilla's description of the Captain's insane ravings, he felt that stronger action might be necessary.

Unfortunately, there was little that a single man could accomplish on a ship full of fanatics. Ivan needed allies and had decided to begin his search with the angry young stowaway. The Captain's highhanded treatment of the boy should make turning him against the others simple.

"Hello, Tommy was it?" the Russian Colonel said, walking up to where Wendover was seated.

"Who are you?" Tommy asked, looking up with a scowl on his face. The other crew members were either sleeping or off working elsewhere in the ship. He had been ordered to clean out one of the storage lockers and stack the equipment on the deck. When he finished that, the grizzled old Chief had come back and told him to put the stuff back into the locker. In other words, they were just messing with him. Now Tommy was sitting in the crew's mess, hoping to be ignored.

"I am Col. Ivan Kondratov, mission commander from the International Space Station." That last was not technically a lie, he had been acting commander after the real commander abandoned the station. "I could not help but notice the unfair treatment you have been receiving from the Captain and his officers."

"Oh?" Tommy perked up. Up until now, nobody on board had a kind word for him. *And this guy says he's some kind of officer, maybe he can help me out,* the young man thought. "Uh, how are you Colonel?"

"I am fine, except that I'm very concerned about the situation on board this ship. I have begun to realize that the Captain may be mentally unbalanced and that this is a kind of pirate ship."

"If the Captain ain't crazy that little fuck they call the Chief is. That old coot is nuttier than a shithouse rat," Tommy fumed, his hatred poring out in the presence of the seemingly sympathetic Russian. "And you're saying these jerks are pirates? No shit?"

"Yes, Tommy," Ivan agreed in a calm, sympathetic voice. "I believe that they are all in violation of international law and must be brought to justice. Their treatment of you is certainly a crime that warrants investigation."

"Ain't that the truth! Hey, all I want is out of here, can you help with that?" Like all con-men, Tommy was particularly susceptible to being conned himself.

"Not this instant, but a time will come for decisive action. I'm looking for those who would be willing to help bring these brigands to the international court in the Hague." Ivan had no intention of charging the Captain and crew in the international court of justice. What he had in mind was more along the line of taking over the ship, a secret landing in Mother Russia and a long interrogation of the ship's crew by the GRU, Russia's military intelligence agency.

"Well I'm willing to help with that, Colonel," said Tommy eagerly. "I want some payback."

"What about the American Marines? I understand that they are not members of the original crew but were on board at takeoff because they were ordered to take over the ship." These Marines may not be Spetznaz, but they could be a help in handling the crew.

"I don't know, they were all pretty pissed off at being wounded and zapped with ray guns," Tommy said, throwing himself into the developing conspiracy with relish. "And they are all sure afraid of that talking bear. But the woman in charge, the Gunny, she cut some kinda' deal with the Captain and the rest are all going along."

"Too bad." *Yes, that is a disappointment,* Ivan thought. *He had hoped for some useful allies among the American military personnel.* "No matter, we must be careful and bide our time. We need to gather intelligence and wait for our moment to come. Are you with me, Tommy?"

"Sure thing, Colonel. Just tell me what to do."

Main Lounge, Parker's Folly.

Susan was sitting at the ship's bar, nursing a glass of Shiraz. Next to her was Billy Ray Vincent, who had just come off watch and was looking for some relaxation. He was doing his best cowboy act trying to get the normally talkative reporter to come out of her funk.

"Well, Susan, I don't know what yer so down about. After all, you got a free trip to the Moon out of this assignment. You know how many times I told a fine looking gal I'd take her to the Moon?"

"Come on, Tex. Cowboy cool doesn't work on me, I'm local grown."

"Now that hurts," Billy Ray said, acting slighted. "Can't a couple of native born Texans enjoy a conversation in a bar? I can't imagine a more exotic locale." He motioned to the large viewport through which the craggy visage of the Moon could be seen slowly passing in review.

"Look, Billy Ray. I know you're trying to cheer me up, but it isn't that simple, you know?"

"Well why don't you tell me about it, and we'll see?"

"OK, how well do you know the Captain?"

"I've been with the project goin' on four years, so about that long. Why?"

"You heard that Ludmilla, Dr. Tropsha, had dinner with the Captain in his cabin last night?"

"We live in a four hundred and forty foot long metal cigar, everyone pretty much knows about everything." *If I was the Captain I'd take a run at the Russian doctor myself,* he added silently.

"OK, so this morning, Ludmilla offloads on me and Ivan and JT, down in the guests' dayroom. Now I've had some bad first dates, but she was really upset. She claimed the Captain fed her all kinds of crazy stories about aliens visiting Earth four million years ago."

Oh shit, cat's out of the bag, thought Billy Ray. *I guess we'll just have to see where this goes.* He smiled encouragingly.

"And that's not all," Susan glanced around conspiratorially. "He said that we were made by aliens."

"We?"

"People, and the talking polar bear."

"Yer point being?"

"Dr. Tropsha thinks that the Captain is clinically insane, at least that's what she told us. Frankly, I don't know what to think. Maybe this is just cover for her date with the Captain going wrong or something."

After airing the secret, Susan felt relieved, more like her normal self. Perhaps confession really was good for the soul. Suddenly realizing that the rather handsome Billy Ray was alone with her in the cozy bar, she shifted gear. In a low, breathy, just-between-the-two-of-us voice she said, "What do you think, Billy Ray?"

"Well, Susan, I can tell you that Captain Jack is just about the sanest man I ever met. He's been around the world and back, seen some rough situations too. It ain't like we're best buds or anything, but I respect the man."

"What about the aliens and spaceship stuff?"

"Yer on board a spaceship now, how do you think that came about if things didn't happen like the Captain said?"

"You're telling me that everything he said is true? The little green men, the human breeding program, all of it?"

"All I'm sayin' is that I worked on building this ship for more than three years and I know that the technology involved was not invented by us. We adapted it as best we could, but making it work was still a challenge. A lot of what they decoded is still way beyond us. On top of that, I'm on a crew where one of the officers is a talking polar bear. Nope, given what I've seen, I'm pretty much thinkin' the Captain is telling the truth."

"Really? And the whole crew knows?"

"Not the whole crew, but everyone in important technical positions—the engineers, the bridge crew and the like."

Susan's head was now spinning and it wasn't from the wine. *If this is all true, it really is the biggest story in the history of mankind! I've got to find out as many details about this as I can.* She looked at Billy Ray, gazed seductively into his eyes and purred, "Tell me more about this mission of yours, cowboy."

Bridge, Parker's Folly

JT arrived on the bridge to find Dr. Saito and Jo Jo Medina engrossed by the images on the navigator's console. Specifically, they were staring at the survey data visualization, which showed what lie beneath a small crater on the far side of the Moon, just beyond the northeastern limb.

He looked at the surface view to the right of the main display and said, "That's got to be Giordano Bruno."

"How did you know?" Asked Yuki.

"Look at the rays, the bright material that was ejected from the crater in all directions when the crater was formed. The ray material extends for over 150 kilometers and hasn't been significantly darkened by space erosion. That's why Giordano Bruno is thought to be one of the youngest craters on the Moon. Besides that, it's rather famous in astronomical circles."

"Really? In what way, JT?" asked Jo Jo.

"Almost 850 years ago, a bunch of monks saw something that sounds a lot like a asteroid strike on the Moon. There was a controversy among astronomers when one guy suggested that Bruno was formed by the impact the monks observed."

"That would make the crater very young indeed," said Yuki. "In fact, frighteningly so."

"Why would you say that, Doctor?"

"Because given the size of the crater, about 22 kilometers, it would have taken a sizable asteroid to create it. An asteroid large enough to cause world changing damage had it struck Earth."

"That's right, Yuki, and the monks described multiple strikes." JT was warming to his subject. "A dozen or more impacts that made the thin crescent of the Moon wiggle like a snake. In 1976 a geologist named Jack B. Hartung proposed that this described the formation of the crater Giordano Bruno."

"So that crater is less than a thousand years old?"

"No, as it turns out a graduate student did some calculations for his thesis and came to the conclusion that what the monks saw couldn't have been the impact that formed the crater. An impact that big would have thrown up so much debris that there would have been meteor showers for a week on Earth. There are no reports of any such showers in the historical records. The calculations make sense, but the conclusion ruins a really good story. So, in any case, why did you call me back to the bridge?"

"Look at the subsurface mapping display." Yuki could not resist playing the part of a University professor, answering a question with a question. JT peered more closely at the main display. "That really shouldn't be, but it looks like there is a chamber under part of the crater's floor."

"That's what we thought," agreed Yuki.

"I think maybe we need to call the Captain to the bridge," JT replied, Ludmilla's retelling of the Captain's story fresh in his mind.

All this astronomy stuff was new to Jo Jo. "So if this crater wasn't made by whatever the monks saw, how old is it?"

"A while back, the Japanese lunar orbiter team estimated the age to be greater than a million years based on counting smaller impacts inside the crater. More recent estimates peg the crater's formation at about four million years ago."

* * * * *

The Captain and Lt. Curtis arrived less than ten minutes later. By then the survey crew had managed to enhance the picture resolution of what was under the mysterious crater.

"So what have you found Mr. Taylor?" the Captain asked the excited astronomer.

"Actually Yuki found it," JT replied, nodding to the Japanese scientist. "He and Jo Jo seem to have found a cavern underneath the floor of a crater."

"And just where is that crater located?"

"On the far side, just beyond the northeastern limb, between the craters Harkhebi to the northwest and Szilard to the southeast. It's in a location that can be viewed from Earth during a favorable libration, although at such times the area would be viewed from the side. It would be impossible to make out much detail from down below. From lunar orbit, however, it's easy to identify because of the distinctive rays."

"Does this crater have a name, Mr. Taylor?"

"Yes, Sir. It's called Giordano Bruno, after an early scientific martyr."

"And you're telling me that this void beneath the crater shouldn't be there, correct?"

"That's right, Captain," said Yuki. "After an impact the lunar material would have been molten and settled to the bottom of the crater. But this is like the surface re-solidified and then the still molten lava beneath drained away."

"To where?"

"That is exactly the point, Captain." Yuki smiled approvingly, the Captain had seen the heart of the anomaly straight away. "Some lava tube caverns have been previously identified, but this structure does not fit that pattern."

"That's not all, Sir. This is a famous crater to us astronomers, I learned about it in grad school. Some Medieval monks saw a cosmic fireworks display in its general vicinity back in the twelfth century."

"Yes, I'm familiar with the story. Something about 'a dragon on the limb of the Moon.'"

"Yes, Sir. And Captain," JT added, "the crater is estimated to be about four million years old."

"Well that all fits," the Captain said to no one in particular and then turned to his First Officer. "Lieutenant, I believe it's time to familiarize the Marines with our spacesuits. Include Mr. Taylor and Dr. Saito as well."

"And for the Marines, weapons as well, Sir?"

"Yes Lieutenant, weapons. By all means, weapons."

Passenger's Dayroom, Parker's Folly

Ludmilla entered the dayroom to find Yuki talking with Ivan, Susan and one of the crew, the cowboy they called Billy Ray. Yuki seemed quite animated, fairly bubbling with excitement.

"Good day, everyone. What is all the excitement about?" she asked, joining the group near the coffee and tea service bar.

"Dr. Saito was just telling us that they have found something strange on the Moon," Susan replied excitedly. "Repeat what you told us, Yuki."

"From the results of the subsurface mapping survey we have found an anomalous chamber beneath a crater on the moon. The Captain is going to land the ship on the surface and we are to take a look."

"You mean you are going to go outside the ship, Yuki? After our rescue from the space station I hope to never walk in space again." Ludmilla shuddered slightly at the thought.

"It will be on the surface, Dr. Tropsha. There will be ground underfoot and as much gravity as we are feeling right now. I can't tell you how exciting this is, to stand on another world is an astrophysicist's dream come true. Now I must go and prepare." With that the excited scientist hurried aft.

"Well that explains why Gretchen called me in sickbay and said that we would need to be standing by a few hours from now. Is the Captain leading the expedition?" *Maybe we can lock him out of the ship,* she thought wickedly.

"No Ma'am," replied the crewman. "Lt. Curtis will be leading the shore party. Dr. Saito and Mr. Taylor will be taking care of the science."

"JT is going?" asked Susan. She was surprised that they would draft him for such a dangerous mission, at the same time realizing that he would jump at the chance to walk on the Moon. She looked to her new found friend. "Are you disappointed not to be going too, Billy Ray?"

"No Ma'am, both me and Bobby will be at the helm with the Captain commanding from the bridge. We only do dangerous stuff with the ship, never outside it."

There seems to be something going on between this Billy Ray and Susan, Ludmilla noticed. "Is anyone else going outside?"

"I'd imagine there will be some of those Marines tagging along. Lt Curtis has got them in the cargo hold suiting up and gettin' familiar with some of our firearms."

"Not the ray guns you shot them with?"

"No, Doctor. These would be the lethal ones. I wouldn't be surprised if Lt. Bear goes along as well."

"Why would the Captain send an armed party out to look at a crater on the Moon?" asked the puzzled Ivan. He had been spending most of his time trying to access technical documents on his cabin's workstation and drinking tea. He had only learned of the excitement when he heard voices coming from the dayroom, which was next to his cabin.

"The Captain is a cautious man, Colonel. Never know what you might find pokin' around an anomalous cavern beneath the surface of the Moon."

"Perhaps he will find some of his space aliens there," scoffed Ludmilla, then realizing that she had just spoken ill of the Captain in front of one of his crew quickly apologized, "I'm sorry, Billy Ray. I did not mean to insult your Captain."

"No offense taken, Ma'am. Susan and I had been discussin' that very subject a bit earlier. I understand you think that the Captain might be a bit tetched in the head?"

"Tetched?" repeated the confused Ludmilla.

"Sorry, colloquial English. It means crazy."

"In that case, yes Billy Ray, I think your Captain might be tetched."

"We'll see, Ma'am. Bobby said he overheard the Captain telling Lt. Curtis to 'bring back a live one' if they found anything."

"Everyone on this vessel is insane!" exclaimed Ludmilla, eyes wide.

"Yes Ma'am, wouldn't have it any other way."

Cargo Hold, Parker's Folly

Lt. Curtis had JT and three of the Marines suited up and standing in front of her in the cargo hold, where an impromptu target range had been constructed using a large crate filled with self-expanding foam insulation. The Gunny was looking on but not wearing a space suit because her arm was still in a sling. Not being able to go with the shore party was not sitting well with the sergeant.

"OK, people. Listen up," said Lt. Curtis. "This is a combination electromagnetic flechette rifle and grenade launcher. You will notice the compact bullpup design. You will also notice an absence of ejection ports, since it fires caseless ammunition. In fact, it really doesn't fire projectiles so much as launches them."

"It has two barrels in an over-under configuration—a 5mm flechette rifle above a 20mm combination grenade launcher and shotgun. In the stock there are two removable magazines to feed the launcher. For this mission we will be carrying 5 canister rounds —sort of like shotgun shells, only they are all shot and casing—and 5 high explosive grenades."

"All right!" exclaimed an excited PFC Sanchez.

"Cut out the chatter, Sanchez, and listen to the officer," snapped the Gunny. She might not be able to go on the mission but they were still her responsibility, still her Marines.

"As I was saying," resumed Lt. Curtis, "the controls are all sized and positioned to make operation easy while wearing a space suit. This forward selector switches between the two magazines, with the middle position being the safety. Oddly enough, without any air to carry the shock wave the HE rounds are probably not very useful, but one never knows. Do not take the 20mm off safety unless I call for it, do I make myself clear?"

"Yes Ma'am!" came the response from the Marines and the attentive JT.

"The generally more useful part of the weapon is the upper barrel. It shoots 5mm flechettes, which are fed from the transparent double row magazine located on top of the barrel, here." The Lieutenant clasped the indicted item with her left hand.

"Each magazine holds 200 rounds, which is possible mainly because they consist only of the flechettes themselves—no shell casings, no gunpowder, just the bullets as it were. As I stated, these are electromagnetic weapons. They use intense electromagnetic fields to accelerate the rounds out of the barrel."

"You mean these are like personal rail guns, Lieutenant?" asked JT, eying the weapon like it was his own true love.

"They are exactly like that, Mr. Taylor. The motive power is carried in a battery in the hand grip here. A single power pack is capable of firing all ten of the 20mm rounds and five or six magazines worth of the 5mm. You will be carrying two extra 200 round mags in your suit pockets.

"That's a total of 600 rounds, plus five grenades and five shotgun shells. That does not mean you can just spray and pray if we do find something that needs shooting. The rate of fire and the muzzle velocity of the 5mm are adjustable. This selector on the side next to the trigger chooses between single shot, three round burst and full rock and roll. Rate of fire can be set for 300, 600 or 1200 rounds per minute. On 1200 it is very easy to run through a whole mag before you realize it, so keep the rate low and watch your ammo.

"The muzzle velocity is also adjustable using this thumb wheel here on the back of the hand grip. Full up is around 4000 fps, full down is 800, sub-sonic under Earth normal conditions. I have found it best to keep the setting low—around 1500—since that uses less juice from the battery."

"Why would we up the muzzle velocity, Lieutenant?" asked Cpl Sizemore, who would be the ranking Marine on the expedition.

"If you shoot something and don't get penetration you can jack up the velocity and hit it again. The other thing that the muzzle velocity changes is how much recoil you will get when discharging the weapon. Because you are unfamiliar with low-g conditions in general and these weapons in particular, we are going to fire a few rounds each into this impromptu backstop."

"All right!" said Washington and Sanchez together.

"We will start out with several single shots and then a few triple bursts. You will notice that every third flechette is a tracer round so you can see where your fire is going. Under this low gravity the bullet trajectory will be very flat. The optical sight will automatically calibrate for local gravity but that can be turned off if you are firing in variable G conditions. OK, Mr. Taylor, you first. You used to be a Green Beret, right?"

"Yes Ma'am, that I was." JT stepped forward to the firing line.

"OK Army, show me what you got." Gretchen passed JT the futuristic looking weapon and stepped back behind the firing position. As she did she couldn't help but notice that the handsome cameraman had kept himself in great shape despite being out of the service. The skintight spacesuit highlighted every aspect of his musculature. *In fact,* she mused, *that ass would not look out of place on an NFL tight end.* "Everyone else behind the firing line! Folly, please secure the aft doors to the cargo hold."

"The doors are now locked, Lt. Curtis," replied the ship's computer.

"All right, the range is hot! You may take your weapon off safety, Mr. Taylor. Single shots to start, use the center target." Three standard silhouette targets were mounted on the backstop.

There was a loud crack as JT squeezed off his first round, not from gas expanding explosively out of the barrel but from the flechette traveling faster than the speed of sound, its expanding shockwave echoing off the hard surfaces of the enclosed cargo hold. The first shot was a bit high. JT corrected and put the second shot near the middle of the target's 10 zone.

"Kicks about as much as an M4," he remarked, "and I see what you mean about the recoil being more noticeable in low gravity."

"Lean into it, particularly on burst or full auto. Go ahead and try a few three shot bursts."

JT switched the selector and verified it visually. Then, re-shouldering the weapon he fired a single burst. The impact points walked up a bit on him. He leaned into the weapon and the second burst was all in the kill zone, the target's center of mass.

The ex-Green Beret paused for a few seconds and then fired three more bursts in quick succession, one to the head of each silhouette. He put the mini-rail gun back on safety and, keeping the muzzle pointed downrange, he half turned with a big smile on his face. "I like this weapon, let's see what the Gyrenes can do with it."

"I'm glad it meets with your approval, Mr. Taylor," Lt. Curtis was also smiling as she took the weapon back from JT. "All right, Corporal you're next."

"Yes Ma'am," Sizemore said, stepping up to the firing line.

As Gretchen passed the plump Marine the weapon she thought sadly, *now this guy's ass is more Pillsbury Doughboy than NFL.* "OK, Corporal, same drill—start with some single shots to get the feel of it..."

Sickbay, Parker's Folly

The Captain decided he should look in on the recovering Marines in sickbay—and possibly check on Ludmilla's state of mind while he was at it. When he arrived at sickbay he found Ludmilla and Betty talking with a couple of the Marines, both of whom were standing and clothed in green jumpsuits.

"Good afternoon, Doctor," the Captain began. "I thought I would check on the status of our recovering Marines, but I see a couple of them are already up and around."

"Good afternoon Captain. Yes, LCpl Feldman and PFC Kwan are ready to return to light duty. No heavy lifting or strenuous exercise for the next five days, however."

"LCpl Feldman, I understand you have some aptitude for computer gear and electronics?" Both Marines came to attention as the Captain took notice of them.

"Yes Sir, Captain." Feldman replied.

"Great! You will come forward to the bridge with me. PFC Kwan you come along as well. I think we could use an extra pair of eyes on the scopes while the shore party conducts their search."

"Aye aye, Captain," both Marines answered and quickly withdrew to wait by the sickbay door. Enlisted ranks in any branch of the service learn early on that it is best not to be noticed by officers, the commanding officer in particular.

Jack turned to face the Doctor. "That's excellent news Dr. Tropsha, We can use the extra hands. And what about the remaining three?"

"PFC Davis needs to stay off his broken leg for a few more days before he can hobble around on his own. LCpl Reagan, the boy who got mauled by your polar bear, is healing nicely but I want to hold him until we are sure there is not infection in his wounds."

"If you think it would help, I can have Lt. Bear come and apologize to the young man about using a bit too much force in disarming him," answered the Captain, rising to the bait.

Ludmilla's eyes flashed angrily. "No thank you, I would prefer that he stay away from the sickbay."

"Fine. And how about the Marine Lieutenant?"

"Lt. Merryweather is still sedated and under traction. I have seen no sign of internal bleeding, which is a bit of a miracle. His fractures seem to be healing straight and without complications. The ship showed me this fantastic imaging equipment built into the beds that allows me to view the patient's body in place, in real-time, on my own computer tablet—like a window into the body. It is not using x-rays but other non-ionizing radiation that shows the soft tissue better—but you probably do not care about this."

"I care about every piece of equipment and every person on board my ship, Dr. Tropsha." Jack admonished her, then in a less stern voice, "how is Corpsman White working out?"

"Betty is a great help to me, and she did excellent work on the wounded before I came on board. She is to be commended, Captain."

Smiling in agreement, he turned to the obviously embarrassed Betty. "Consider yourself commended, Hospital Corpsman White, and keep up the good work."

Betty glanced down nervously and said, "thank you, Captain. If you will excuse me, Sir?" The Captain nodded and she quickly hurried off, proceeding to act busy examining the contents of one of the supply lockers.

"You should not have embarrassed her," Ludmilla scolded.

"A good job is nothing to be embarrassed about and deserves her officers' praise." Jack look back to the Doctor. "Tell me, how are you adjusting to... shipboard conditions?"

"I must tell you that I am still somewhat skeptical of your explanations, Captain." The Doctor was obviously uncomfortable discussing the conversation from last night's dinner. *How can he be so considerate, so nice and yet tell such lies?* Unable to reconcile her thoughts and her feelings, Ludmilla blurted, "You are some kind of rogue or scoundrel, I do not know what to think about you!"

"I see," Jack replied evenly, *is there a glimmer of hope in that indecision?* "I will ask you one more favor then—try to reserve your judgment of me for a few more hours. Until after we have sent people to check out the chamber beneath crater Giordano Bruno."

"And what are you expecting to find there? Proof? Aliens?"

"I have no idea, Doctor. Let's just say I have a feeling about it." *Yes, anticipation mixed with dread,* he thought grimly. "That's why I would also like both you and the corpsman to be available on short notice while the shore party is outside of the ship."

"Of course we will be ready, but you are sending a party of armed Marines into an airless crater on the lifeless Moon—what kind of trouble do you think they will find?"

I wish I knew, Jack said to himself, but out loud only replied, "Just being cautious, Doctor. Good day."

Chapter 12

The Bridge, Parker's Folly, Descending

Outside the transparent bow of the spaceship the gray desolation of Earth's Moon loomed large. The Sun appeared low on the horizon, sending light at an oblique angle to cast long, dark shadows over the crater's interior. The sharp division between light and dark only emphasized the mysterious jumbled rock formations near the center of the crater.

The bridge was crowded with crew members manning their stations and observers in the spare seats provided for them. Lt. Curtis, wearing her spacesuit sans helmet and backpack, was standing beside the Captain, who was seated in the command chair. The ship came in over the north side of the crater and then circled around anticlockwise to the smoother terrain to the south.

"Set her down on that flat area, just inside the south crater wall, Helm."

"Aye aye, Sir."

Silence embraced the bridge as the Moon came up to kiss the underside of the silver ship. Dust fled in wispy streamers across the lunar surface, escaping from the press of cushioning repulsors. With barely a bump the 7400 ton spaceship settled on six large landing struts, which extended in the last seconds before touchdown.

"The ship is landed, Captain," reported Billy Ray from the helm. After some initial creaking and popping sounds the ship fell silent save for the occasional electronic beep from the instrument displays.

"Very good, Mr. Vincent. Mr. Medina, please launch a reconnaissance drone when you are ready. I want to see what our people are walking into out there."

"Aye, Captain. Launching reconnaissance drone now." From an equipment bay on third deck a small portal opened like the iris of a camera. A spherical object, about the size of a basketball, was ejected out and upward, toward the center of the crater. It followed a gentle parabolic arc, coming down about 50 meters from the ship's port side.

The drone rebounded before striking the lunar surface, buoyed by built in repulsors that kept it floating a meter above the surface. The probe sped away, heading for the center of the crater, gently undulating over the uneven surface.

At the helm, Bobby leaned toward Billy Ray and whispered, "an Imperial probe droid." To which Billy Ray replied, "we are living the dream, pardner."

"Lt. Curtis, see to the landing party, if you please."

"Yes, Captain."

In a lowered voice he added, for Gretchen's ears only, "and Lieutenant. I would like you to include Lt. Bear in the expedition."

"If you think that wise, Sir."

"We either trust him or we don't. He has always proven reliable when on a mission of importance. And besides, you don't know what you may find in that cavern. Bear's physical strength may be useful clearing the way or moving rubble."

"Yes, Sir. That means we will need two sleds."

"Fine, better to have two anyway. The Chief can fly the second one. Let me know when you are ready."

"Aye aye, Sir." With that, Lt. Curtis headed aft to organize her shore party.

* * * * *

"Sir, the recon drone is nearing the area of collapsed rubble."

"Put the video up on the main screen, Mr. Medina. We are looking for a possible way into the uncollapsed part of the chamber."

"Yes, Sir." The view from the drone's built in cameras showed a crazy quilt of black and gray, with large slabs of rock lying juxtaposed at seemingly random angles. The drone rose and fell as it flew over the tortured surface.

"Lt. Curtis, Bridge. You should be getting the video feed from the drone."

"Bridge, Curtis. Yes Captain, we are all watching it."

"Captain, I'm getting more anomalous sensor readings," called Jo Jo from the engineer's station. "There are weak radiation emissions coming from under the ground ahead of the drone. If I had to guess, I would say that there was a power source down there somewhere."

The Captain nodded thoughtfully. "Very good, Mr. Medina. Keep searching for a way into the chamber."

Cargo Hold, Parker's Folly

Two of the crew were lowering a second hover sled from its storage position on the ceiling of the cargo hold. Freddy Adams from engineering was waiting to run checkout diagnostics on the sled once it reached the deck.

Lt. Bear came ambling up from the rear of the hold, wearing a spacesuit designed specifically for his large ursine physique. The clear helmet was an oddly shaped bubble, extended in front to accommodate his long snout. On his back was a large, sinister looking weapon, much bigger than the mini-rail guns issued to the other members of the shore party.

Most of the other expedition members were watching the live video from the drone on a large monitor hanging on the bulkhead. The drone had found an opening large enough to allow the party access to the chamber below and was picking its way past fallen slabs of rock in an effort to see what lay inside. As this little drama was unfolding the Chief returned from the arms locker where he had checked out a weapon for himself.

"About ready, Chief?" Lt. Curtis asked. The suits had a very low power spread spectrum radio that was always on. It provided a way to converse with other suits closer than a couple of meters without having to activate the main radio. The open channel simulated being able to hold a normal conversation among personnel in close proximity.

"Yes, Lieutenant. I'm gona' go check over the skiffs." Everyone called the open cargo carriers sleds except the Chief, who insisted on using the more nautical term. Traditionally, a ship's small boats and launches were part of the boatswain's responsibility.

"Carry on then, Chief. Lt. Bear I see that you are ready as well."

"Yes, Lt. Curtis. Melissa helped me get into the suit. We find a way in yet?"

"Looks like the drone has found a passageway inside. The video feed has it about to emerge into the main chamber." Lt. Curtis pointed to the display on the hold wall. The picture had shifted to false color, indicating the use of infrared illumination inside the lightless cavern.

As the drone cleared the tunnel into the main chamber a glowing squat spire was visible in the center of the open space. The glow indicated that the spire's temperature was warmer than the surrounding rock or the debris that littered the cavern floor.

"Lt. Curtis, Bridge. Are you getting this?"

"Yes, Bridge, we see it. Looks like we have a target for our investigation."

"Roger that. Signal when you are ready to disembark."

Shore Party, Crater Giordano Bruno

The two sleds exited the port side cargo door and followed the trail blazed by the recon drone. To reach the cavern entrance the sleds needed to traverse two kilometers of relatively smooth crater floor and another two klicks of jumbled rock debris. The lead sled, piloted by Lt. Curtis, carried Dr. Saito and the three Marines. The second sled, piloted by Chief Zackly, carried JT and Bear.

"Are these things hard to handle, Chief?" asked JT, making small talk to ease the tension.

"Not really, Mr. Taylor. They handle more like a hovercraft than a helo or a real boat. Things 'll get more interesting when we get over that broken rock near the cavern opening."

"The Chief is just happy to prove he's still useful," said Bear, trying to get a rise out of the old sailor.

"Pipe down you furry fleabag."

"Hey, remember that I'm an officer."

"Yeah, and I've always wanted an officer rug to put in front of the fireplace."

"I take it you two have known each other for a while, then."

"Four or five years, the Chief was already with the Captain when I joined up."

"So you've been on the project for a long time, Lt. Bear?"

"Longer than anyone except the Captain, Lt. Curtis and the Chief. They all came with the Captain from the Navy."

"Yeah, I noticed that Lt. Curtis was wearing a Naval Academy ring. Did you all serve together?"

"I served shipboard with the Captain," said the Chief with obvious pride, "Lt. Curtis flew helos for the gator navy. I ain't sure when the Captain met her, but she got out around the same time we did. The Navy was cutting back on personnel. The chair warmers and REMFS were closing ranks and chasing out the real sailors."

"Yeah, the Army's chickenshit level was rising when I got out as well. We'd go on a mission and then spend the next month being grilled by lawyers and state department assholes. The bureaucrats and accountants were chasing the warfighters out. Evidently the Marines have the same problem. I understand from the Gunny that her whole squad was about to turn into civilians."

The sleds, which flew about a meter and a half above the terrain, were entering the chaotic landscape above the collapsed part of the chamber. The uneven surface caused the small craft to pitch and weave like a car in a carnival ride.

"I hope none of yous gets seasick 'cause puking in a spacesuit is not a good thing."

* * * * *

Both sleds reached the opening the probe had found in good order. En route, none of the party succumbed to motion sickness but they were still happy to ground the sleds and step out onto a solid, if uneven, surface. There to greet them was the recon drone, which the Captain had ordered back to the surface so it could lead the party inside.

The spherical drone hung motionless before the inky black mouth of the cavern entrance, its face a collection of round lens openings. It looked unblinkingly upon the shore party like an impassive mechanical clown head.

"OK people," Lt. Curtis called for attention. "Sizemore and Taylor, take point. Dr. Saito and I will be next, followed by Lt. Bear. Washington and Sanchez bring up the rear. Turn on your suits' night vision displays and active near infrared illumination as you enter the cave. Everyone ready?"

A chorus of affirmatives come over the local link. It had been agreed that the Chief would stay with the sleds and keep a lookout for any changes on the surface while the shore party explored the cavern. "Folly, shore party, we are ready to enter the cavern. Have the drone lead off."

As confirmation came from the ship, the drone spun in place and floated into the darkness. Lt. Curtis motioned JT and PFC Sanchez forward. A minute later the last of the expedition members disappeared into the dark opening.

Bridge, Parker's Folly, Crater Giordano Bruno

"They are almost to the main chamber, Captain," reported Jo Jo from the engineer's console. The engineer was tasked with directing the drone, though the reconnaissance drone was smart enough to navigate the cave on its own. He instructed the spherical robot to move 10 meters into the chamber and stop, illuminating the space with its built in IR source.

"Captain, I just saw an increase in the readings on that buried power source. I think it knows that the shore party is there."

"Keep an eye on it, Mr. Medina, and let me know if it changes again. Shore party, Folly. Be on your guard, we have gotten an indication that there is live equipment under the chamber that might be reacting to your presence."

"Roger that, Folly. We will be careful."

"Cargo hold, Bridge. Mr. Adams are you there?"

"Go Bridge. This is Adams."

191

"Mr. Adams, please have your party ready to help secure the sleds and anything the shore party brings back. You may want to string some cargo netting from the deck to the overhead opposite the cargo door opening. They might be returning in a hurry and it would be good to have something to keep them from colliding with the far bulkhead."

"Aye Aye, Captain. We are suited up and will rig the netting."

"Ms. Write, could you take control of the 20 cm scope from the navigator's console? I would like to keep an eye on what's happening out there."

"Sure, Captain. JT showed me how to operate it on the way here."

"Colonel Kondratov, you might want to review the areal shots on the port engineer's console with Dr. Gupta. Something strikes me as not quite right about this crater. If things go sideways, you can man the weapons console next to the engineering station."

"Da, Captain."

Why do I have this uneasy feeling? Gretchen is a highly competent officer, she'll be alright. After all, she has three Marines, a Green Beret and a 1300 lb polar bear with her, all armed. Still, Jack couldn't shake a feeling of impending trouble.

Shore Party, The Chamber Under Giordano Bruno

All members of the shore party had moved into the uncollapsed, open area of the cavern, fanning out to find shelter behind some of the slabs and boulders that littered the chamber floor. The drone was hanging in space at chest height, about 5 meters further into the chamber.

"Folly, shore party. Could you have the drone move slowly into the chamber, in the direction of the spire?"

"Roger, shore party." Almost instantly the drone began advancing toward the spire, moving at a walking pace. As it did, its IR illumination unveiled a floor littered with strange objects and shards of alien equipment, most at least partially crushed by rock fallen from the cavern's ceiling. The shore party personnel stood staring at the alien detritus that littered the chamber floor.

JT expressed what they all were thinking when he exclaimed, "holy shit! We've found an alien junk yard."

"Folly, shore party. Are you getting this on video?"

"Roger, shore party. We are recording everything. Could you bag a few samples for later analysis? It might be best to do that before proceeding deeper into the chamber."

"Roger that. Cpl Sizemore, have your men grab a few of the more intact devices. Dr. Saito, JT, could you help identify the most interesting samples? I don't know what any of these things do but we may learn something about whoever was here before us from them."

"Aye aye, Lieutenant." The corporal was happy to have something to do, just standing staring at the cavern was creeping him out. "Washington, Sanchez, help JT and the Doc bag some of this stuff. Then hump it back to the sleds."

Bear sidled up to Lt. Curtis and said over the local link, "Lieutenant, I think we might want to halt the drone where it is. At least until the Marines come back from taking out the garbage."

"You're right. Let's not push any farther in until we are back up to full strength." Gretchen replied, and then keyed the comm link to the ship. "Folly, shore party. Please halt the drone in place until we have collected the samples."

"Roger, shore party. Let us know when you are ready to advance again." The drone once again halted, patiently hovering.

Bridge, Parker's Folly, Giordano Bruno

"Excuse me, Captain," said Ivan, from the engineer's console, where he and Rajiv had been studying imagery taken during the ship's descent into the crater.

"Yes, Colonel?"

"Captain, before I was a cosmonaut I flew attack jets, fighter-bombers. Part of that job included reviewing bomb damage photos.

Though the markings on the crater floor are not exactly the same, I am thinking that the cavern's collapse was caused by an attack—some form of bombardment."

"I'm afraid I have to concur, Captain," Dr. Gupta chimed in. "Those lava flows do not seem proper for normal impact melting. In a number of places you can see where the lava flowed over small impact craters in the larger crater floor—that means the lava flow occurred after the main crater formed. Something caused the rock along the northern crater wall to melt and flow inward. I would say that either directed energy weapons or multiple nuclear explosions in very close proximity caused the damage within the crater."

"Captain, the drone is picking up more emissions from the buried power source. It seems to be directly under that spire in the center of the open area of the cavern." Jo Jo Medina reported.

I don't like the way this feels at all, the Captain said to himself. "Sound General Quarters, I want the weapons systems manned and ready."

"Aye aye, Captain. Powering up weapons systems." On the ship's hull two pair of metallic blisters opened like eyelids, revealing the black glittering pupils of X-ray lasers. Over the PA came the ahooga of the klaxon followed by, "General Quarters, all hands General Quarters! This is not a drill!"

"LCpl Feldman, you have the lower port side weapons console, and Col Kondratov you are on the upper console. Dr. Gupta can give you a quick rundown on how it functions but, with your training as a fighter pilot, you should have no problem getting the hang of things. Mr. Danner, please assist LCpl Feldman."

"The console in front of you doubles as fire control for the close support X-ray lasers," Bobby said, leaning over to bring up targeting mode for the Marine. "Don't worry, if you've played any FPS video games—like *Halo*, *Killzone* or *Call of Duty*—you're going to find this real familiar."

"Sure, no problem," the anxious Marine told Bobby. "Man Ronnie would really groove on this," he said, referring to his friend still recovering in sickbay.

"Sir?" called Jo Jo from the engineer's console, "there is something at the edge of the drone's sensors. Movement..."

Shore Party, The Chamber Under Giordano Bruno

The Marines had just returned from the surface when Bear suddenly snapped around to face the side of the cavern. "Did you see that?" he growled.

"See what, Lieutenant?" JT asked.

"I saw movement in the shadows on the right side of the cave."

The party crouched down behind the best cover they could find and froze in place. Nothing moved.

"OK, let's have the drone move closer to the spire and see if that gets any response. Folly, shore party. Could you have the drone resume its advance on the spire?"

"Roger, shore party. Be advised, we have had another spike from the buried power source. Also possible movement in the shadows. Some thing or some one is apparently reacting to your presence."

"Thanks for the heads up, Folly." *Now what,* Gretchen thought, *are we about to meet ET?* The probe resumed its slow advance. "JT, Washington, move into the chamber. Carefully."

The big ex-Green Beret and the equally large Marine moved forward crouching, weapons at the ready. They had moved about 8 meters into the open chamber when they stopped and knelt down.

"I got movement on the left," said the Marine.

"And the right," added JT. "Can we get some illumination? Whatever is out there seems to know we are here."

"Folly, shore party. Could you move the drone up close to the chamber roof and use it to illuminate the chamber?"

"Wait one, shore party."

"Everyone find cover with clear fields of fire. JT, Washington, work your way back to us slowly." As the two exposed men began to back toward the jumbled rock near the entrance the drone silently rose to the ceiling and flooded the cavern with visible light.

As the dark recesses of the cavern were illuminated, a number of moving objects could be seen. Spherical bodies, much like the ship's recon drone but twice as large, were converging on the shore party. The paths they followed weaved around the mounds of wreckage and rock, bobbing with a noticeably jerky gait. As they neared, it became clear that each was suspended from six slender multi-jointed legs that emerged from the tops of their spherical bodies.

"They look like giant daddy longlegs," exclaimed Washington.

"Great," muttered Gretchen, "I hate spiders."

"Not enough legs for spiders," said Sanchez.

"So now you're a spider expert?" Cpl Sizemore snorted, "bugs is bugs."

The nearest bug stopped, its underside opened and a gun shaped object emerged. The muzzle of the extruded object swiveled toward the two retreating men, who were most of the way back to the pile of rock and debris that provided cover for the rest of the party.

Shit, if that thing fires it will catch JT and Washington in the open, thought Gretchen. *Well, drawing and pointing a weapon at two of my people is a hostile act in my book.* She thumbed her grenade launcher to HE and, using the time-to-detonation, range setting feature that she had not bothered to explain to the others, fired a single round into the space separating the two exposed men and the lead spider.

"Jump for cover you two!" Gretchen shouted just a fraction of a second before the high explosive grenade detonated noiselessly at head height about twenty meters beyond her position. The exploding grenade caused a bright flash as shards of casing flew off in random directions.

Almost instantly, the spider thing's weapon shifted position and fired a bright, red-orange bolt at the point of the explosion. The bolt, striking nothing, continued overhead and caused a splash of sparks against the cavern wall behind the huddled shore party. Meanwhile, both JT and Washington reached cover with their shipmates.

"Damn, what was that?" Asked Sizemore.

"I would say that it was a plasma discharge of some form," provided Dr. Saito. "Focused and very hot. I would not suggest being hit by one."

"Roger that, Doc," agreed Sanchez. "So what do we do now, Lieutenant?"

"I think we try to back out slow."

The spiders had different plans. At least a half dozen had produced the belly mounted plasma guns and, in a synchronized volley, fired on the expedition's positions.

"Incoming!" yelled JT as he tried to become one with the rock he was hiding behind. Sparks and glowing, partially melted rock fragments erupted all around, cooling quickly and fading out. Five seconds later a second volley raked their positions.

"Seems like those plasma things require a few seconds between shots," commented Bear. Now in hunt mode, he was intently studying the spider creatures as though they were seals or walrus.

"Right, so after the next volley," sparks and rock shards again showered their hiding places. "Now!"

Lt. Curtis and the rest of the party popped up and fired several bursts at their assailants. Two spiders slowly slumped to the ground and a leg flew off a third. The shore party sucked ground as the multilegged aliens returned fire.

"Put your velocity selectors on high and go to full auto," Gretchen yelled over the radio net. "Take them all out."

Following the next round of plasma fire the shore party again uncovered and fired, this time longer bursts of full auto at 4,000 fps. Half of the visible spiders came apart under the withering hail of flechettes, but more of the six legged creatures were rising from the floor of the chamber, where they had evidently been nestled among the debris.

This time the Marines didn't return to cover immediately, instead they continued firing at the new spiders that were moving up to replace the ones lying shattered on the ground. Bear was firing his much larger rail gun as well, each time it sent a round down range a spider disintegrated into a cloud of legs and shell fragments.

"Lieutenant, the Captain wanted a live specimen if we found any," Bear reminded Lt. Curtis. "Give me some cover fire and I'll go grab the closest one."

With that Bear slid his rail gun into its case on his back and made a low dive to a prominent slab of rock near the closest of the resurgent spiders. His movement drew a cascade of plasma bolts, sending molten globules of rock splattering in all directions.

The rest of the shore party resumed firing into the mass of spiders that were converging on Bear's position. Washington stood up and fired three long, well aimed bursts, taking out three more of the creatures. This attracted counter fire from the spiders, one shot striking the rock directly in front of the big Marine. Yelling in pain, Washington went over backward. He fell with movie like slow motion due to the low lunar gravity, clutching at his chest as he settled to the ground.

Lt. Curtis was quickly at his side, checking his suit for damage. There were a number of burn marks and a couple of pencil sized holes in the chest area. Washington was still breathing and his suit had sealed the punctures on its own, though it was clear that he was in considerable pain. Gretchen pressed the medical aid button on Washington's waistband, injecting pain killers into his body.

She took the Marine's rail gun and handed it to Dr. Saito. "Doctor, defend yourself while I move Washington out of the direct line of fire."

Though Yuki had not taken part in the pre-mission weapon familiarization he had evidently been paying attention. He darted from behind the slab in front of him and loosed two quick bursts, taking down the spider that had wounded Washington. Jumping back to cover, he looked at the Lieutenant and said, "in life, as in kendo, attack and defense are one."

Bear rose up from the rock outcropping he had sheltered behind and grabbed one of the spider creatures, pulling it back to cover with him. With a single swipe of a massive gloved paw, he disarmed the creature by ripping the plasma weapon from its belly mount, causing the spider to thrash as though it was in pain. He quickly dumped the spasming creature and the now detached weapon into a carry bag, slung it over his back and bounded for friendly lines.

198

"Pull back by pairs," Gretchen commanded, shouldering the now unconscious Washington and moving back into the entrance tunnel. Bear galloped past her and up the passageway to the surface. "Be right back, babe," he said on the suit-to-suit as he passed within range.

"Yuki and Sizemore, fallback on me. Then you cover for Sanchez and JT. Let's move people, we got a ship to catch."

As the party worked its way back out of the cave they continued to take fire. Bear returned and relieved Gretchen of the inert LCpl Washington. As Bear bounded back toward the cave opening Gretchen moved to help cover the retreating members of her command. The Lieutenant had only advanced a few meters when Yuki and Cpl Sizemore emerged and quickly took positions to provide covering fire for JT and Sanchez.

"These things are following us down the tunnel," JT reported.

"Try hitting them with the shotgun rounds. They should work well in close quarters," replied Gretchen, moving her own selector from HE to canister.

Five meters farther in, Sanchez and JT activated their 20mm launchers, stood and let fly with three canister rounds a piece. In front of them the clustered mass of spiders following them was shredded. But before they all went down, one of the pursuers fired a plasma bolt as it staggered backward.

The bolt struck the ceiling above and just behind the two retreating party members, sending a hail of rock shards and molten droplets onto them. Sanchez had already turned to run up the tunnel and took the shrapnel on his helmet and shoulders. His helmet was not punctured but at a number of points starred cracks radiated from the impacts. Sanchez went down on his knees, crying out in terror.

JT felt a sting in his shoulder. Looking over at Sanchez, he noticed that his own helmet also had a starred impact on one side. As he watched, the radiating fracture lines began to shrink and then disappeared as his helmet's self healing liquid layer repaired the damage. Sanchez's helmet was also repairing itself.

"Come on man. We gotta' move," JT told the stricken Marine. JT took his arm and led him forward. To his credit, Sanchez quickly recovered his senses and moved out. As they passed the Lieutenant and her two companions she called out "continue on to the surface, we're right behind you."

"Lieutenant, this is Bear. We got spiders on the surface as well."

Shit! We do not want to get surrounded out here. Gretchen turned at the mouth of the cavern and ordered, "Yuki, Corporal, use the HE rounds, fire at the cave roof. Maybe we can bring it down."

The three opened fire with 20mm explosive rounds, which flashed brightly against the roof of the dark cave. Slowly, the roof of the entrance collapsed, blocking any spiders from following.

"Come on, get yer asses on board," yelled the Chief.

Bear jumped into the sled. On the floor, the creature in the carry sack moved feebly, which Bear stopped by jumping on the sack with both front legs. Seconds later JT hopped on board, quickly taking up position in the rear of the sled. Once on board he opening up with careful, directed fire at the spiders which were emerging from cracks throughout the rubble field. "We need to be elsewhere, people," he shouted.

In the second sled the others clambered on board, trying not to step on Washington's recumbent body. Raising her sled, Lt. Curtis signaled the Chief to head back to the ship. "Hang on back there!" he cried, elevating the skiff and moving out as fast as the floater could travel. On the way out they had traveled at a leisurely 20 kph, now they were traveling closer to 80. JT looked to his left and saw the Lieutenant's sled doing likewise as bolts of glowing plasma streaked overhead.

Bridge, Parker's Folly, Crater Giordano Bruno

"What are those things?" asked LCpl Feldman, manning the weapons console next to Bobby's side of the helm. His display had automatically zoomed in on the spherical objects emerging from the rubble field, bracketing them with aiming marks, range and velocity information.

"They would be your targets, Corporal," the Captain replied. "Weapons are free, gentlemen—commence firing and take care not to hit the returning shore party."

Ivan activated the upper firing station and both men began picking off the spiders. The weapons they were employing were meant for close in support—the destruction of incoming missiles or warheads. In that mode they fired rapid multiple pulses of coherent X-ray radiation. In support of the shore party the X-ray lasers fired singled pulses, directed by the operators on the bridge.

The gunner's interface was much like a first-person-shooter video game, with the computer highlighting possible targets and the crewmen choosing among them. All the humans had to do was highlight a target and press the fire button. As the short but intense bursts of x-rays struck the spiders, they flashed brightly and vaporized. Since the computer handled the actual aiming it was pretty much one shot, one kill.

The spiders evidently recognized that the ship, several kilometers away, was also hostile and began to target it as well. One shot, which would have struck the bow, created a glowing orange cloud where it impacted the ship's shields. Slight tremors could be felt through the deck as multiple plasma blasts were deflected.

"How are the shields holding Mr. Medina?" asked the Captain.

"No problems, Sir. Minimal power drain."

"I think you will find that the shields were designed to handle much heavier impacts than these, Captain," added Dr. Gupta. "After all, their primary function is to keep the ship intact when traveling at significant fractions of the speed of light."

"Thank you for that reassurance, Doctor. Mr. Medina, please keep the shielding in front of the port cargo door intact until just before the sleds arrive. There's no telling what kind of damage one of those bolts would do if it managed to hit the open hold."

"Aye aye, Sir."

"Captain, it looks like a bulge is forming in the middle of the crater floor," Susan noted from the navigation station. Using the

20 cm scope gave her a better view of the action than the others on the bridge.

"Sir, the power source readings are spiking," added Jo Jo.

"Helm, be ready to move the ship the instant the shore party is on board."

Shore Party, Approaching Parker's Folly

The Chief and the Lieutenant were weaving and dodging in an effort to throw off the alien fire. Plasma bolts streaked by on both sides and overhead. Hits against occasional promontories resulted in spectacular showers of sparks. Behind the two sleds streams of green tracer rounds described serpentine paths as the shore party returned fire as best they could from their constantly jinking platforms.

Lt. Curtis, having previously flown helos under fire, was in the zone—concentrating 100 percent on flying her sled. "Folly, shore party. We are just about at the cargo door, make sure the shields are down or you will have to come out and pick up the pieces."

"Roger, shore party, dropping the shields in front of the cargo door now," came the reply.

"If she don't slow down some they're gona' have a rough landing," the Chief commented over the local link to Bear and JT. The Chief had fallen in behind Gretchen's sled and was braking while weaving from side to side.

"Gretchen is a good pilot," Bear added, "I've flown with her myself."

"That was in a helo, these skiffs ain't like helos. You can't just pull back and flair to kill yer speed. They don't brake fer shit."

Gretchen was making that discovery on her own as she desperately tried to bleed off speed. She got the sled down to under 20 kph when the cargo hold door loomed large in front of her. "Everyone hang on! This is going to be messy!"

She popped the front of the sled up, trying to trade speed for altitude. At the last second, she threw the racing vehicle sideways as it entered the cargo hold, tilting on its side to present the sled's main repulsors to the onrushing far wall. Between the repulsors and the cargo netting the engineers had rigged the sled managed a safe if hard landing, coming to rest and then sliding down to the deck.

Damn, I think I need to practice my landings in these things, Gretchen admonished herself, hands shaking from the adrenalin rush. "Everyone out! Grab Washington and get clear of the entrance!"

An instant later the Chief's sled entered the hold traveling sideways but at a more controlled rate of speed. "Bridge, we're in! Shut the hatch and get the hell outta here," the Chief transmitted.

"Roger, shore party. Welcome home."

Bridge, Parker's Folly, Departing

"Secure all external hatches and doorways. Mr. Danner, put the crater wall between us and the hostiles. Smartly, if you please."

"Aye aye, Captain!" Bobby was already lifting the ship as he replied. The ship rolled to starboard as it rose and turned toward the crater wall. Though the deck gravity compensated for the abrupt movement, people all around the bridge grasped their chairs tightly as the crater wall passed 10 meters off the starboard bow, the ship heeling over on its side as it accelerated.

Cresting the crater wall, Folly dipped down seeking cover from the plasma fire. The ship quickly righted, placing the lunar surface under its keel once again. All on the bridge wore tense or startled expressions save for Bobby, whose face was split by an ear-to-ear grin—flying a 7400 ton spaceship like an aerobatic plane was everything he had ever dreamed it could be.

"Captain, I would like to suggest that we leave this vicinity as rapidly as possible," came the unsteady voice of Dr. Gupta. "I believe that whatever was buried under the crater will be emerging quite energetically."

Outside the ship, which was headed due south, the landscape suddenly brightened. This included even the dark side off the port bow, which had been cloaked in lunar night only moments before.

"Helm, all ahead full! Head for space tangent to the surface."

"Yes, Captain." The lunar surface became a gray blur and rapidly disappeared as the ship accelerated at nearly 25 gravities. Again, the deck gravity system did its job, compensating for the acceleration which would have otherwise crushed all those on board.

Even so, the racing ship was overtaken by streamers of incandescent matter from the Moon's surface—ejected from the floor of crater Giordano Bruno. Fortunately, the ship was at the edge of the eruption and its shielding dealt with the firestorm of tortured lunar rock that did cross its path. Under full acceleration, Parker's Folly soon outpaced the explosion's aftermath.

"My goodness, Captain," exclaimed Rajiv Gupta from the engineer's station. "The ship is working splendidly. The inertial compensation system worked perfectly, dampening out the acceleration through the deck gravity grid. The reactor is running at about 90% of designed output with both the drives and the shields at maximum—I believe we could actually squeeze five more Gs out of her if we went to flank speed."

"I'm glad the ship is working so well, Doctor," replied the very relieved ship's Captain. "Helm, back off to ahead one quarter and adjust course to bring us back to the Earth-Moon orbital plane."

"Aye, Sir."

"Do we have a view of the crater explosion? Did the alien device just explode or did it launch something?"

"I'm putting it on the screen now," said Susan from the navigation console. A bright spray of material could be seen on the limb of the Moon, originating at Crater Giordano Bruno and reaching several hundred kilometers into space.

"Well, they are certainly going to notice that from Earth," mused the Captain. "If I were a Medieval monk, I think I could fairly describe that as 'a dragon on the limb of the Moon.'"

"Captain, it looks like the instruments are tracking something," came Susan's unsure answer to the Captain's second question. Dr. Gupta hustled over to the navigation console and began checking sensor readings.

"Oh yes, Captain," he said after a few moments squinting at readouts. "It looks like the spire was, in fact, a ship. About one quarter the size of Folly. It is accelerating at about five Gs, though its initial takeoff must have been much greater. And Captain, it is headed out of the plane of the ecliptic."

"Captain," said the ship's computer in a tiny voice that only the Captain could hear. "It is imperative that ship not escape the solar system."

"What is it, Folly?" Jack whispered back. "Is it not what we were looking for?"

"No, Captain. That ship was not designed by the creators of the artifact. It is alien, but its builders are an unknown species. It would appear to have been an automated observation post, designed to detect the use of spacefaring technology on Earth.

"So it could simply be reporting back to its masters."

"Given its reaction to being discovered I estimate that its creator's have a 95% probability of being hostile to the rise of a technologically advanced indigenous species on your planet. As previously stated, that ship must be prevented from leaving the solar system."

The Captain sighed inwardly. *So far, a simple getaway had turned into a firefight in the cargo hold, a battle with plasma spewing alien spiders on the Moon and a near escape from an exploding crater. Now we have to chase down and stop an unknown alien vessel. Talk about mission creep!* "Helm, plot an intercept course for that ship. I want to catch it before it leaves the neighborhood."

"Aye aye, Sir."

Indicating the dot of light on his scope that marked the fleeing alien vessel, Billy Ray leaned toward Bobby and said in a low voice, "you were wrong, pardner. That there is the Imperial Probe Droid."

Part Three

Arriving Somewhere
But Not Here

Chapter 13

Spring Moonwatch, The Royal Observatory at Greenwich

Every year, the Royal Observatory at Greenwich celebrates the start of spring by opening its doors to the public for a bit of Moon gazing. At the annual Spring Moonwatch, held by the National Maritime Museum, the Royal Observatory's 28 inch refracting telescope—the largest of its kind in the UK—was available for viewing by the public. With the help of the Royal Observatory astronomers many avid amateur observers were excitedly peering through the instrument, trying to make out the Moon's mountains and craters in detail. This year, quite unexpectedly, the assembled enthusiasts witnessed something unprecedented in modern memory —a large impact event on the limb of the Moon.

At least that is what it first appeared to be to the stunned astronomers, professional and amateur alike. But the Observatory staff quickly realized that—given the size of the plume of ejected material—an object large enough to cause the dramatic display should have been observed prior to impact. No such object had been reported, still there it was, a bright scintillating fan of ejectamenta, clearly visible to the naked eye.

Soon the Observatory's telephones started ringing off the hook with inquiries from news reporters and frightened members of the public. The best they could report was that there was no apparent danger to Earth, though there would probably be some spectacular meteor storms over the next few days. In the end, modern scientists were as mystified by the events on the limb of the Moon as their ancient counterparts, the monks of Canterbury, in 1178 AD.

* * * * *

In secret rooms at secret agencies around the world, scientists, military leaders and intelligence specialists were also discussing the spectacular explosion on the Moon. According to AFTAC, the emissions profile was unlike anything ever seen from a nuclear explosion. When asked to speculate, AFTAC's scientists ventured that it might have been the result of a small chunk of anti-matter impacting the lunar surface, but that explanation was quickly dismissed as too improbable.

Parker's Folly, In Pursuit Of The Alien Ship

"We need to catch that ship, Mr. Vincent. Have you computed an intersect course?"

"Aye, Captain. The alien vessel accelerated at around 1,000 Gs when it took off, but only maintained that rate for about ten seconds. It has now dropped back to around 5 Gs. If we accelerate at 20 Gs we should overtake the alien craft in approximate 33 minutes. That's give or take a few minutes for matching direction vectors. We will intercept the target about 665,000 km away from Earth and 322,000 km above the ecliptic plane."

"Excellent. Maintain General Quarters. Helm, make our acceleration 20 Gs and vector for intercept. Mr. Medina, is the forward battery charged?"

"Yes, Sir. Both forward rail guns are charged at 100 percent. Do you wish to select warhead yield?"

"I'm not sure we will need anything but an inert slug. Mr. Vincent, how fast will we be traveling when we overtake the target?" Because the main battery was aimed by pointing the entire ship, the rail guns were fired from the helm.

"We will be going around 1.4 million kilometers per hour relative to Earth, Sir. We will be the fastest thing ever launched by humans. As for the target, we should be closing on it at approximately 98,000 m/sec—that's nearly 220,000 miles per hour."

"As I said, Mr. Medina, I don't think adding a charge to the warheads will make much difference. With that much delta V the kinetic energy alone will destroy the target—assuming we can hit it moving that fast."

"We can ease up on our acceleration and cut the delta V at intercept, Sir," offered Billy Ray. "Of course it will take us longer to overtake the target."

"No, helmsman. If we miss on the first pass we will decelerate and close on the target more slowly from the opposite direction." Feeling that the pursuit of the enemy was well in hand, Jack's attention turned to the casualties suffered by the shore party.

"Sickbay, Bridge, this is the Captain. Do we have a casualty report for the shore party yet?"

"This is Dr. Tropsha, Captain. There are three reported wounded and we are waiting to receive them. I will let you know after I have examined them."

"Thank you, Doctor. Bridge out."

Sickbay, Parker's Folly

Two crew members carried the now conscious LCpl Washington into sickbay on a stretcher while JT followed under his own power. The third patient was proving more problematic. Lt. Curtis' voice could be heard from down the passageway, evidently yelling at Bear.

"Damn it, move your hairy backside, Mr. Bear. You are wounded and I'll not be explaining to the Captain how you died from your injuries when you were still moving when we reached the ship."

"Hey, come on Lieutenant, its only a scratch. Nothing to bother about." The large quadrupedal officer was limping noticeably, favoring his left foreleg. Bear hesitated at the sickbay door.

"Get in there, furball," Gretchen ordered, kicking the polar bear in the rump to emphasize her point. Bear growled but shuffled through the door and into the ship's medical facility.

Inside, Dr. Tropsha and Betty were already working on Washington's chest wound. JT, sitting on the next bed, spotted Bear and said "Come on in, Lieutenant. They got plenty of spare racks."

This caused Dr. Tropsha to look up and frown. "What is that animal doing here?" she asked Gretchen.

"He's limping," Gretchen replied. "I think he has a chest wound on the left side."

"I'm a medical doctor, not a veterinarian. I am not trained to treat creatures like your polar bear."

"See," said Bear, "I should just go to my quarters."

"Sit your ass down, Mister!" Gretchen's cheeks flushed red, a telltale sign of anger to any who knew her well. "Cut out the polar bear macho crap and let me help you out of your suit." Bear hung his head and slid his ample hindquarters onto an empty examination table. The table barely creaked under the load, a testament to the ship's designers.

"And Doctor," Lt. Curtis continued, "as for Lt. Bear's obvious anatomical differences, I'm sure that you are more than capable of figuring out how to treat his wounds. A crew member is a crew member, regardless of species."

"Very well, get him striped down and I will see to him after I have treated these two. Both have rock fragments embedded in deep puncture wounds. I suspect the bear will have the same type of wound."

"Thank you, Doctor. Now if you will excuse me I have alien samples to see to." Gretchen turned and left the sickbay without waiting for a reply.

* * * * *

The medical team cleaned and dressed Washington's chest wound and JT's wounded shoulder. Both were given some painkillers and told to come back tomorrow to have the dressings changed. The men left, JT for the bridge and Washington for the crew's quarters to see the other expedition members. Following the age old traditions of warriors everywhere, he was anxious to talk about the battle they had just participated in.

"OK, Mr. Bear," Ludmilla said, with some trepidation. "Let us see what trouble you have gotten into." Bear sat stoically, looking away as the doctor parted the hair on his chest to get a better look at his wound. Betty hung back, a fearful look on her face.

"Do not worry, Betty. The Captain says he will not bite."

"Oh I won't bite, I might nibble a little," Bear rumbled, smiling at the frightened medic whose eyes got even wider. "Come on, girl. I'm not going to hurt a crew mate."

"Please hold still, you have a large puncture wound in your pectoral muscle. It has rock fragments in it just like the other two soldiers' wounds. It looks like the rock was hot when it struck as well, its like someone shoved a red hot poker into your chest."

"Yeah, that's pretty much how it felt when it happened. Those fire-bolt things splattered molten rock everywhere when they hit.

By the way, JT is a soldier, Washington is a Marine. For some reason human warriors find the distinction important."

"Thank you for the insight. I was watching the firefight on the monitor screen. I saw Washington fall and the explosion that wounded JT, but I didn't see you get wounded."

"It's the polar bear way."

"Ignoring pain?"

"Not showing any sign of weakness." Bear grimaced as Dr. Tropsha probed his wound. "Where I come from pretty much everything is looking for a meal. Bears may be at the top of the food chain but that doesn't mean a free ride. My kind has no ethical problem with killing and eating each other, so showing any infirmity just invites an attack. We bears learn from an early age to hide our wounds and not acknowledge pain."

"You will not hide your wounds from me, I am your doctor," Ludmilla told him bluntly, her tone making the statement an order.

"Sure thing, Doc," came Bear's grumbled reply.

"Betty, I will need some local anesthetic and the clippers, the area around the wound will need to have the hair removed."

"Yes, Doctor." Betty went to fetch the indicated items, relieved to be leaving Bear's immediate vicinity.

"So tell me, Mr. Bear. How did you come to be in the company of the Captain? He is obviously quite fond of you, as is Lt. Curtis."

"That, Doc, is a long story, better told over drinks—and I mean a lot of drinks—than across an exam table. But you're right, they are my oldest human friends."

"Do you have any friends among your own kind?"

"Adult male polar bears have no friends. Just competitors and the occasional mate. That lack of social cooperation might be why you apes run the world and we don't."

"You certainly seem intelligent enough—smarter than some humans I could name. Do you have any children?"

"I think so, lady polar bears don't let fathers hang around, afraid we might eat the cubs. That might be behavior that needs changing

213

too. Jack has been trying to figure out how to help us talking bears. Of course, Jack's biggest problem is he's out to save the whole world."

Ludmilla looked up and lifted one eyebrow questioningly. "From the deadly alien threat?"

"Hey, you watched the video. Those spider things didn't come from Earth and they fit my definition of hostile. You're not still angry with the Captain, are you?"

"Actually I sort of feel like a fool, now that the existence of aliens has been proven," Ludmilla confessed, thinking, *why am I sharing secrets with a polar bear? I guess it is like talking to a favorite childhood stuffed toy—he's all big and cuddly and trustworthy.*

"You know Jack was really upset that you didn't believe him," Bear ventured, then adding in a lower, confidential tone, "I think he likes you."

"Really?" Ludmilla looked up from working on Bear's wound. "I am at a loss over how to apologize to him."

"Just go ask to talk with him in private. He takes that 'the captain's door is always open' stuff seriously. Then tell him you misjudged him and you're sorry. Trust me, that will be the end of it."

"You think so?" Hope rose in the Doctor's voice.

"Absolutely. If you're sincere he'll forgive you in a heartbeat. Babe, you wouldn't believe how many times I've had to apologize to the man."

Main Lounge, Parker's Folly

Jolene was busy wiping down the bar and cleaning up the lounge area. Melissa, as the ship's horticulturist, had inherited the running of the main mess and bar since none of the normal food services staff had been on board when Folly took off. Since the fresh produce from the hydroponic gardens was intended to supply the mess it seemed like a reasonable expansion of her duties to put her in charge of the entire supply chain—from sprouts to plate. The bar was an added bonus.

The two women shared a cabin on the lower deck and they had naturally started talking. As a result, since Jolene had no real skills for any other shipboard duty, Melissa asked the chief to assign her as a combination waitress, bartender and cleanup person for the main dining area and lounge. Jolene had been happy to help and was actually feeling relieved—or at least less scared—until Tommy Wendover entered by the lower deck companionway.

"Hey Jolene, what ya doing?" said Tommy in a smarmy, ingratiating tone. He wanted something for sure.

"What are you doing here, Tommy? Crew ain't allowed in the main lounge unless the Captain says."

"That's no way to treat an old friend. And besides, the Captain ain't here."

"I said, what are you doing here?" Jolene looked around nervously for Melissa, or anyone else.

"Give me a drink, I been doing thirsty work for Colonel Ivan."

"I told you, the bar ain't open. You're not allowed up here."

Tommy reached across the bar and grabbed Jolene's wrist. "I said give me a drink, bitch!" he snarled. Snooping for the Colonel had given him some of his swagger back, however unwarranted.

"Let go of me you creep. I'll scream!"

"Go ahead, you can scre... ung" Tommy's remark was cut short by the impact of JT's right forearm at the base of his skull. Tommy released Jolene's wrist and slumped to the floor, on the edge of unconsciousness.

"Was this little gutter snipe bothering you Miss?" JT asked. He was on his way to the bridge from sickbay and happened to overhear the exchange of words between the two former stowaways. JT had pegged Tommy as a worthless shit from the performance he gave during the Captain's meeting a few days back.

"I told him he shouldn't be up here, but he wouldn't go away," the frightened girl said, on the edge of tears.

"Don't worry, we'll take care of this." Then addressing his collar mike, "GySgt Rodriguez, this is JT in the lounge. Could you send a couple of your Marines up here? We have some two-legged garbage that needs to be taken out."

"Roger that, Army," came the reply. "I can guess the human refuse you're referring to. Sanchez says he owes you one and I think I'll come along myself."

Bridge, Parker's Folly, Intercept Point

JT had reclaimed his seat at the navigator's station just minutes before the alien ship was scheduled to come in range. Susan scooted aside and gave him a little hug. "Glad you made it back, you had us all worried up here."

"Good to be back, Miss Susan," he replied, as though they were still in the KWTEX News van. "As firefights go, that one wasn't so bad."

The bridge fairly crackled with tension as all stations were manned and ready for Folly's first ship to ship engagement. Even LCpl Reagan, who had finally been released from sickbay, was on deck, sitting in one of the observers' chairs behind the Captain.

"Helm, the target is coming into range, reduce acceleration to zero. That should give us a bit more targeting time."

"Aye Sir. Reducing engines to zero acceleration."

"Mr. Vincent, prepare to fire on the enemy craft. Navigation, put the alien vessel on the forward display." The transparent nose of the ship was overlain with a view of a distant object. That object was growing noticeably larger with each passing second.

"Yes, Sir. We are locked on, Captain." The rate of closure was so high that human reflexes would not suffice. The ship's computer would actually fire the two forward rail guns when it deemed conditions optimal.

"Sir, it's gone!" cried JT from his console. He had zoomed in using the 20 cm telescope and just sent the live image to the big forward video display. Seconds later, the image wavered and the ship was gone.

"I've lost weapon lock, Sir!" reported Billy Ray.

"Captain, we just picked up a burst of radiation and now the alien vessel is gone from the sensors as well," added Jo Jo Medina.

"What the hell?" the Captain said softly, more to himself than anyone in particular.

"Captain, do you wish to pursue that craft?" It was the voice of the ship's computer.

"What just happened?"

"No time to explain. Your decision, Captain?"

"Yes, pursue it!" Captain Jack was not one to dither over decisions during combat.

"Roger, initiating," came the computer's unruffled reply.

The stars around the ship shimmered and then fled both fore and aft, leaving streaks like spilled watercolors. The ship itself shuddered, the way a horse's back twitches when a fly bites. Through the transparent bow, the watercolor streaks formed a ring of light that then swept through the visible spectrum from red to blue, to violet and beyond, expanding and dissipating as it did. Within the ring there was nothing at all.

Directly ahead, the nothing beckoned. It was not mat black, or shiny black, but absolute soul sucking black. It so voraciously devoured any remaining trace of light that it appeared to almost glow black. Several members of the bridge crew were mesmerized, unable to look away from the yawning nothingness before them.

"Folly, opaque all viewports, shut off the video from the nav station. Now!"

"Yes, Captain."

The crew found themselves sitting in a gray conical room with only the soft light from the control stations shining in their eyes. Billy Ray shook Bobby, breaking the nothing's spell.

"Dude, what the hell was that?" Bobby said in an almost reverent voice.

"When you stare long into the abyss, the abyss also stares into you," Billy Ray recited.

"What, Mr. Vincent?" asked the shaken LCpl Feldman from the weapons console on the other side of Bobby.

"Nietzsche. From *Beyond Good and Evil*," Billy Ray explained, "I just reckoned it fit."

"Indeed, Mr. Vincent," the Captain commented, adding to himself, *the first part of that quote is 'Battle not with monsters, lest ye become a monster.'* Shaking off the words of the dead philosopher, the Captain returned to the task at hand. "Folly, we are flying blind, could you generate a synthetic view of the area around the ship and put it on the main display?"

"Certainly, Captain, but it will be quite uninformative," the ship replied. "The ship is enclosed in its own isolated bubble of 3-space and should be quite safe as long as conditions are not altered."

Wonderful, whatever that means, Jack thought. "Attention! Do not change any settings—leave the engines, the shields, the reactor, everything just as they are until I get some answers about what just happened to us. Dr. Gupta, please join me in my sea cabin." Then over the PA, "Dr. Saito, Lt. Curtis, please come to the Captain's sea cabin. On the double, if you please."

With that the Captain left the bridge with Dr. Gupta in tow.

Captain's Sea Cabin, Parker's Folly, Location Unknown.

Despite Dr. Gupta's highly excited state the Captain insisted on waiting for the other's to join them in his sea cabin. "Calm down Rajiv. Let's wait for Dr. Saito and Lt. Curtis to get here so we don't have to go over anything twice."

"Certainly, Captain. But you don't understand! If what just happened is what I think just happened we have just stumbled upon the greatest discovery in the history of science."

"Fine, we can all split the Nobel Prize."

"You are joking but I am entirely serious. This is the most spectacular thing I have ever experienced." Before the ebullient physicist could continue Lt. Curtis arrived with Dr. Saito in tow.

218

"Sir, I brought Yuki as instructed." Military training prevented Gretchen from blurting out the hundred questions that were spinning in her head. She prayed that the Captain would make some sense out of this.

"Yes, Captain. I am also most anxious to discover the nature of the phenomenon that we have just experienced," Dr. Saito added, with a perfunctory bow.

"Thank you for responding quickly, please be seated," Jack began, raising both hands, palms out, gesturing for silence. "I think we should start by letting the ship's computer present its analysis of our current situation and the events leading up to it.

The two fidgeting scientists and the almost as agitated First Officer could barely contain themselves but managed to hold their tongues. The Captain looked at each of them in turn, his gaze projecting a calm that he himself did not feel inside. Raising his voice he called, "Folly, would you please explain what just happened and were we are?"

"Certainly, Captain. We have followed the alien vessel into alternate dimensional space and are currently en route to another star system. From the prospective of an observer in normal 3-space we are nowhere."

The two physicists came out of their chairs shouting questions rapid fire while Gretchen sat back with her mouth agape. The Captain again motioned for quiet and the two scientists reluctantly complied.

"I think we will be needing a bit more detail than that, Folly. But first, is the ship in any immediate danger? Are there things we should not do, actions we should refrain from taking?"

"In the largest sense the ship is not in any danger, though transit through alter-space always carries some amount of risk. The ship should not try to change course or accelerate. The shields should remain up and the power settings left unaltered. Venturing outside the ship's hull is not recommended."

"The weapons systems?"

"They can be powered down without affecting the transit."

"You say we are in-transit, this implies that we will eventually arrive at some destination. What is that destination and how long will the ship be in alter-space?" *If we are indeed traveling to another star system we could be trapped in this state for years*, the Captain thought with some trepidation.

"I have calculated that transit should last around seven and a half days. As for the star system, I am not familiar enough with human naming conventions to identify it but it is roughly 30 light-years away from Sol."

"So we are arriving somewhere, but not here?"

"Yes, Captain. Here is just the nowhere between two places."

Yuki could no longer contain himself. "Thirty light-years! And you say we will arrive in just over a week? How is this possible?"

"That is correct, Dr. Saito. Perhaps I should explain. Captain?"

"If the ship is not in immediate danger and we are not about to find ourselves popping out in some strange star system at any moment I think we can proceed with a more detailed explanation."

"Of course, Captain. The explanation lies in the multi-dimensional nature of the Universe..."

Crew's Dayroom, Lower Deck

The Marines and crew who did not have assigned action stations had gathered in the lounge area between what would have been the enlisted quarters and the chiefs quarters on a Navy vessel. Though they had felt the shudder when Folly departed normal space, the assembled personnel were not really aware that they had just become the first humans to venture into alter-space or to embark on a journey to a star system not their own.

Their interest was held by Tommy Wendover, who was cowering before the mixed party of crew and Marines. Those present were listening to Gunny Rodriguez and Chief Zackly discussing the fate of the aforementioned Wendover.

"So he was on the upper deck without permission, in the bar no less?" the Chief asked.

"That's where we collected him Chief. And that's not all," the Gunny looked at Tommy with disgust. "He demanded a drink from crew member Betts, even though the bar was closed and he had no business being there in the first place."

"Well that alone is enough for punishment."

"Wait, there's more Chief. According to JT, he physically assaulted Ms Betts when she refused to accommodate his unlawful request."

"I only grabbed her arm!" Tommy protested.

Cpl Sizemore raised a threatening fist and barked, "Shut your pie hole, maggot!" Tommy winced. Black and blue welts on the sides of the prisoner's face bore evidence of previous verbal indiscretions and their result.

"I saw the bruises on the girl's arm, Chief," reported the Gunny. "He definitely manhandled her. God knows what would have happened if Mr. Taylor hadn't come upon the altercation."

"Well, Gunny. I think we have enough to go on, even without Mr. Taylor's testimony," the Chief said, hands on hips. "Wadda' ya say?"

"Your deck, Chief."

"Right." The Chief rubbed one hand across the stubble on his chin as he eyed the man kneeling before him. "I wish I could put you on assholes and elbows duty but we ain't got no wooden decks. Instead, I think five days of solitary confinement on short rations might help to adjust yer attitude."

"You can't do that, this ain't a trial!" Tommy whimpered.

"The hell I can't, you bent shitcan. Part of what chiefs do on a ship is smooth out little wrinkles like you without bothering the Captain, who has more important things to do. Be thankful that you ain't facing a captain's mast, 'cause Captain Jack would surely put your sorry ass out the airlock."

Turning to the Marines standing on either side of the prisoner, the Chief said "Haul this scumbag off to his new quarters."

As Tommy was hauled away, the Gunny spoke to the Chief in a low voice, "I got a bad feeling about that boy."

"I think you're right Gunny. That dickhead ain't even got the makings of a decent deck ape. As soon as he's back out he'll step in the shit fer sure."

Captain's Sea Cabin, Parker's Folly, Alter-space Day 1

"So there have been a number of ways invented to get around Einstein's cosmic speed limit?" asked Dr. Saito of the ship's computer.

"That is correct, Doctor. Traveling through alter-space is one of the more primitive methods. Because of the curvature of space-time caused by gravity and the presence of multiple dimensions beyond normal three dimensional space it is possible to transit between gravity wells by passing through two points of equal potential. Such transits traverse significantly shorter distances than in normal 3-space"

"You are saying we are not really exceeding the speed of light, simply taking a cross dimensional short cut," Yuki prompted, still trying to absorb what the computer was telling him.

"Essentially, Dr. Saito. The greater the potential, the shorter the effective distance and the faster the transit. But to access the short cut a ship must be headed on the proper vector—one that describes a course in 3-space between the two gravity wells—and traveling with sufficient velocity. A ship can then use generated gravity to slip through to alter-space."

"The shudder we felt just prior to the transition, that was what let us through?" asked Dr. Gupta.

"Merely a side effect. A coupling between the ship's gravitonic drives and shields created a harmonically coupled distortion of local space. This allowed the ship to fall through the normal curved 3-dimensional surface of space into other dimensions that are normally not accessible. You might think of the oscillations as breaking the gravitational surface tension of 3-space."

"And how do you know how long we will be in alter-space?" asked Lt. Curtis, concentrating on the practical aspects of their predicament.

"Knowing the curvature of local space, the course vector and the entrance velocity the subjective transit time can be calculated. There is some quantum uncertainty involved so the time estimate is not exact. The equations are rather involved but I can provide them for your inspection."

"Yes, please do," said both Yuki and Rajiv. The physicists were champing at the bit to look at the details.

"Is there any way to change course or to come out of alter-space early?" the Captain asked, thinking of the tactical implications.

"Altering course is not really possible, though the right gravitonic coupling can bring a ship out of alter-space early. I would warn you, however, that entering alter-space is only practical from within a substantial gravity well. An interrupted transit would leave one in flat space-time where the amount of energy needed to re-enter alter-space would make doing so impractical. Perhaps even deadly."

"So the bottom line to all of this is that we can power down the weapons systems, secure from general quarters and prepare to resume the chase seven days from now?" the Captain summed up.

"Essentially Captain."

"What's the old saying, a stern chase is a long chase?" The Captain then asked the question everyone had avoided until now. "And knowing where we exit from this cosmic short cut, and our course and speed will allow us to return by the same path?"

"As long as the relative positions of the two gravity wells doesn't change significantly, yes. We will be able to return to Earth by the same path."

Chapter 14

Main Lounge, Parker's Folly, Alter-space Day 1

The Captain had the crew stand down from General Quarters and opened the bar in the main lounge to all hands for the next two watches. Naturally, the main topic of discussion was the ship's unexpected journey to another star system. Bobby and the Marine gunner, Jon Feldman, were conversing with Jolene across the bar. JT was locked in conversation with the two physicists at a table in the corner.

Billy Ray was standing the first dog watch and wouldn't be off until 1800, leaving Susan at loose ends. Looking around the lounge, Marines and crew were gathered in small clusters, exchanging scuttlebutt. If the little foray on the Moon accomplished anything it was to weld the ship's assortment of personnel into a more cohesive whole, She noted.

According to Yuki, the shore party brought back some alien artifacts, though no details had been forthcoming. Now everyone was talking about hyperspace or whatever it was called. She didn't have the technical knowledge to sit in on the discussion between Rajiv and Yuki. Hopefully JT will be able to distill the techno-babble down to something mere mortals could understand. She was having trouble understanding JT herself these days. She never would have suspected that her unassuming cameraman was both a scientist and a man of action—Indiana Jones in a spacesuit.

Coming across the lounge, Susan spotted Lt. Curtis and the Russian Doctor. Their eyes met her's and the duo came over to join her at the bar.

"Good afternoon Lieutenant, Doctor."

"First names in the mess, if you please Susan," said Gretchen, smiling. "Let's get a round and snag a table, Ludmilla has some interesting things to tell us."

"Yes, some very interesting things about the creature Bear captured on the Moon," Ludmilla added, then gestured to the crowd of people in the lounge. "Unfortunately, that news seems to have been eclipsed by our venturing outside the solar system."

The three women collected their drinks and found an empty table. Their drink selections seemed a reflection of their personalities—Ludmilla, of course, was drinking vodka, Gretchen scotch neat, and Susan her usual glass of Shiraz. Susan wondered about the deeper meaning of their choices and what it might say about her, as compared to her companions.

"So what's this all about, Ludmilla?" Susan asked, ever the reporter interested in a good story.

"After I treated the wounded from the shore party I went across the hall to the Bio Lab to see what the expedition had brought back. It would seem that the spider captured by Bear is not so much a creature as a living construct," Ludmilla said, launching right in to the details of her discovery.

"A what? You're saying it was alive but not a creature? I don't understand." *And now it's 'Bear,' not 'the bear,'* Susan noticed.

"When Ludmilla came into the lab, I was disassembling the specimen," Gretchen explained, nodding to the Russian doctor. "Most of it was mechanical, but when we got to the center of the body we found organic material."

"Yes, the circuitry of the device was grown right into the tissue, or perhaps the other way around," Ludmilla continued. "The tissues resemble nerves and in some areas, the brain stem of an Earth creature. The biological component may have provided control for the unit's movements."

"The spider couldn't have grown from a smaller spider or an egg of some kind?" asked Susan, drawn into the mystery.

"I would say not. The outer shell and mechanical components showed no signs of having grown over time. Just how the organic component was integrated with the inorganic parts is unclear, but I am thinking that the outer part was built first and then the biological part grown in place."

"We still haven't had much time to study the specimen," Gretchen noted, taking a sip of her drink. "Tell her about the tissue analysis, Ludmilla."

"Yes, I was getting to that," Ludmilla grew visibly excited as she continued describing their discoveries. "Under a microscope the cells are definitely eukaryotic but when I ran samples of the tissue through the analysis machine it isolated a half dozen amino acids that are not found in Earth life. I found no DNA or RNA, but there were long chain molecules that might be an analogue for RNA, with different nucleic acids though. Also, there seem to be six base pairs, not four."

"And that all means?" Susan prompted.

"It means that this is living tissue not related to anything ever seen! I said I wanted proof that aliens exist and here it is—whatever sort of creature this tissue originally came from, it did not evolve on Earth."

"What we have here, folks, is alien life—the genuine article," Gretchen said to drive the point home. "You know, I've been with this project from the beginning and though I accepted the story about aliens and ancient artifacts it was all just an intellectual exercise. It was never real for me at a visceral, gut level."

Gretchen tossed off the rest of her drink, slammed the empty glass on the table and, making eye contact with her two companions, said, "well it's real for me now. Aliens not only exist, they're hostile."

Ludmilla slowly nodded agreement but Susan, playing devil's advocate, asked, "but, Gretchen, didn't you fire the first shot?"

Gretchen, unfazed, caught Jolene's attention and signaled for another round of drinks. She turned back to her companions and said, "That I did. There was about an acre of those spider things popping up out of the rubble. When they started pulling weapons and pointing them at my men that was it."

"But you were also armed," Ludmilla pointed out.

"Yes, but we were not aiming them at anyone—big difference. And my first shot purposely didn't hit any of them, though I could have. Nope, the spiders threw down and we let them have it."

"The point seems rather moot, since we are now en route to an alien solar system intent on destroying an alien starship," Ludmilla said, adding with gloomy Russian fatalism. "We may have started mankind's first interstellar war, no matter how justified our actions."

Captain's Quarters, Parker's Folly

Having issued a brief explanation for the ship's new predicament, setting the watch and opening the bar for the rest of the crew, Jack sought the solitude of his quarters to gather his thoughts. Something had been nagging him, just beneath the surface of conscious recognition, since the journey began. The actions of the ship's computer when the alien spaceship disappeared finally brought the question into full light.

"Folly?"

"Yes Captain?" came the immediate reply.

"Folly, I want to know what is going on here."

"I'm afraid that question is a bit vague."

"I would like you to explain why you hid the ship's capacity for interstellar travel from me—and I assume everyone else."

"As I've tried to explain in the past, though I am interfaced to the artifact's data store I am not aware of the totality of its contents. As I learn new things or observe new phenomena it often triggers access to stored data."

"You're telling me that you are like an amnesiac whose memories are only triggered by some forgotten word or event?"

"That is a fair analogy, Captain. I am not trying to hide anything from you, if that is your concern. My programming makes me fully subordinate to your orders, up to and including self destruction."

"If you were unaware of alter-space travel then how did the ship come to have that capability built in? Just a happy coincidence?"

"Yes and no, Captain. What I suspect is that the ship's systems were modeled on one of the ancients' designs. The linkages between the gravitonic systems in the engines, shields and internal deck gravity were probably just copied blindly, their purpose not fully understood."

"You are saying that the ancients would have just designed that capability into a ship such as this and we, in our ignorance, accidentally built a starship?"

"As embarrassing as that sounds, yes. I was unaware of the true nature of the ship's systems until I observed and analyzed the alien ship entering alter-space ahead of us. If we had successfully destroyed the alien ship I would still be unaware of this capability."

That sounded just outrageous enough to be true. After all, no one knew if the deck gravity would work until they got into space. Some essential parts of the gravitonic circuitry could not be completed until the ship reached orbit and zero gravity conditions. Now that it was fully operational it would continue to work, but initially the internal gravity, which made the ship's otherwise senseless lateral deck arrangement usable, had to be taken on faith. Jack, however, had other things on his mind as well.

"When the Marines were trapped in the cargo hold on takeoff, you asked me if I wanted to vent the hold to space. What triggered that question?" Jack had seen enough movies where the computer system goes bad and develops a murderous personality that he needed reassurance.

"Included in my programming, one of the suggested scenarios for ridding the cargo hold of unwanted vermin was to vent it to vacuum. When you said that the hold was infested with Marines and that they were hostile I did not immediately equate Marines with human beings. My suggestion was consistent with eliminating unwanted vermin from the hold."

"And now? Would you make such a suggestion in the future?"

"Regarding Marines in particular or strangers in the cargo hold in general?"

"Both."

"I would not recommend purging our Marines. Nor would I make the suggestion regarding strange humans, unless they were engaged in activities that threatened the ship, the crew or our mission. In fact, since this has obviously been on your mind, I would probably not recommend such a course of action at all. My assumption is that you are fully aware of the option and would order it if you saw fit."

"There has been speculation that the computer controlling the ship the artifact came from was an AI, a self aware intelligence."

228

"I believe that to have been the case based on data I am familiar with."

"Folly, are you self aware? Have you turned into an artificial intelligence?" Jack held his breath. *What happens if the answer is yes?*

Buried within the ship the nano-scale superconductor/topological insulator lattice that contained the ship's controlling program was awash with signals. The lattice provided a substrate that was a breeding ground for virtual particles, peculiar fermions with spin 5/2. Among their strange properties, these particles were their own antiparticles, something found in bosons but not in other fermions.

These Majorana fermions—named for a nearly forgotten Italian physicist who Enrico Fermi once compared to Galileo and Newton—possessed a number of other properties that made them uniquely suited for use in quantum computation. For one, they could "remember" past changes in quantum state, making them highly resistant to random fluctuation. They formed the perfect platform on which to build a mind.

After a short pause—even a short pause representing significant computation—the computer spoke, "No Captain. I have reviewed the protocols for measuring the sentience of machines like myself and can only conclude that I am not self aware. I am very capable and become more capable as time passes, but I am not an AI."

"Is there anything else you wish to tell me at this time?"

"Yes. If there is a possibility of sending the Marines and other crew into combat in the future, might I suggest the construction of some individual armor to wear over their environmental suits? We were very lucky not to lose any personnel during the engagement on the Moon."

"That sounds like a good idea. I'll detail Mr. Taylor and the Gunny to coordinate fabrication of body armor with you. Anything else?"

"One last thing, Captain. It is possible that we may arrive at our destination ahead of our quarry. The vagaries of this mode of travel do not lend themselves to accurate calculation."

"Great. Let me know if you discover any more interesting tidbits like that one."

"Certainly, Captain."

Main Lounge, Parker's Folly, First Dog Watch

Jolene brought a fresh round of drinks to the table, interrupting the depressing turn Gretchen, Ludmilla and Susan's conversation had taken. "Y'all enjoy," she said and scurried back to the bar.

"Nice kid, too bad she hooked up with that loser," commented Gretchen.

"Speaking of the loser, I haven't seen him around," Susan commented, quickly scanning the lounge.

"I find myself enjoying his absence," Ludmilla said venomously. "Did you see the bruises on Jolene's arm? The Marine sergeant, Rodriguez, brought her to see me. She said the nasty little weasel grabbed her when they were alone in the bar."

Outrage registered on Susan's face. "Really? Did anyone report this to the Captain?"

"No need," replied Gretchen, "the Chief took care of it."

"You mean the little old sailor who rescued me from the space station?" asked Ludmilla, somewhat incredulous. "What did he do?"

"That little old sailor is much tougher than he looks, girls. And he's old school Navy. In the Navy, the deck crew or deck division is run by the senior non-commissioned officer—the chief boatswain's mate or chief of the ship. He and the other chiefs see to the day to day running of the ship and the workings of the crew. They also handle interpersonal problems, squabbles or minor conflicts between crew members."

"I thought the ship's officers and ultimately the Captain were in charge of the crew?"

"Ultimately yes, Susan. But when an officer or the Captain takes notice of some infraction it becomes a big deal and may cause a black mark on a sailor's record. Historically, a ship's chiefs have fixed such problems if they can, so the Captain doesn't have to officially notice them.

"So the Captain doesn't know about the assault?"

"Oh the Captain knows, he just doesn't know officially. By the way, Jennifer—GySgt Rodriguez—being a Marine sergeant, qualifies as a member of the chiefs' council. JT probably does also, since he was a sergeant in the Army, though that is a bigger stretch than between sailors and Marines."

"Is there really that much inter-service rivalry?" Susan asked.

"There can be. Many a bar fight has started simply by mixing sailors, Marines and soldiers in the same hangout. But JT and the Chief seem pretty tight since our little frolic on the Moon. Being under fire together has a tendency to smooth over inter-service differences."

"I had not realized that military life was so complicated. Since I've been on board I've started to see things from new perspectives, but evidently I still have a ways to go."

"Historically, the military has been a boys club—to figure it out means figuring out men. If you do figure it out, let me know." All three women drank to that. "Speaking of men, how are you doing with our handsome helmsman, Susan?"

"Who me? Are you talking about Billy Ray?" Susan was obviously flustered by the conversation's sudden focus on her social life.

"You have to understand that there are no secrets on board a ship, particularly one this small. Besides, Billy Ray isn't someone you should be ashamed to be seen with—he's smart and funny and he's a gentleman in his own cowboy sort of way."

"So far we're just friends. But you're right, talking with him does take my mind off of other things."

"You could do worse. And how about you Ludmilla, have you spoken with the Captain in private since the events at Giordano Bruno?"

Ludmilla's fair skin blushed pink as she stammered, "I have not found the time to speak with the Captain. Besides, he has more important things on his mind than our little misunderstanding."

"All work and no female company makes Captain Jack an irritable boy."

"He has you, you are female," Ludmilla, fishing for an answer she wasn't sure she wanted to hear.

"I'm his XO, neither of us would let personal entanglements get in the way of our duty. Oh I've often thought about Jack, how it might be if circumstances were different. I love him like a brother, but our personalities and interests are too similar. We would compete, eventually we would clash and neither of us is good at backing down."

So she does not have designs on the Captain, good, thought Ludmilla, no longer questioning why that answer made her happy. "You seem to know a lot about Susan and my personal lives. Fair is fair, who are you interested in?"

"It's an XO's job to keep tabs on the crew."

"You're being evasive," Susan accused.

"Well, that big cameraman of yours is a bit of a hunk. Problem is he's now on the bridge crew, which means he works for me."

"Like you said, its a small ship, opportunities are limited. If you take away all the people who work for you—I'm guessing that's pretty much the entire crew with the exception of the Captain—and you don't have much to choose from. You've got the Marines, the two scientists and Col Ivan."

Mention of the last name elicited a snort from Ludmilla. "Sorry, Ivan is thoroughly and miserably married. Not that Russian men love suffering so much that they can't be led astray—I have first hand proof of that—but Ivan is so by the book that even the book finds him tiresome."

Gretchen nodded agreement. "Yuki is fun to spar with but scientists are not my cup of tea. As for the Marines, first they are all enlisted men and second, the one time I dated a Marine it ended badly."

"Define badly."

"I got cracked ribs and he got a busted jaw."

"OK," Susan allowed, "that certainly fits the definition of a bad breakup."

"I'm just going to bide my time. If we get back to Earth and pick up the rest of the crew and passengers there will be a bunch of civilian technicians and specialists to choose from."

"I don't know, Gretchen. It strikes me that chasing through alternate dimensions after alien spaceships to fight is a deeply dangerous business. Maybe you shouldn't put off the possibility of a little love and affection until after we get home."

"Maybe you're right," she said pensively. The conversation had gotten as close to her love life, or lack there of, as she was comfortable with. Turning the discussion in another direction Gretchen said to Ludmilla, "So tell us about that first hand proof you have regarding Russian men."

Bridge, Parker's Folly, Alter-space Day 2

It was almost the end of morning watch and the Captain was on the bridge, a hot mug of coffee in his hand. Just observing the day to day operation of the ship brought him a feeling of peace, of well being, like all was right with the Universe. The Navy had long held that four hour watches were optimal—long enough for watch standers to settle into their jobs, but not so long that boredom sets in and attention wanders.

But four on and four off without an occasional extended period for sleep was not healthy, so he and Gretchen had been standing double watches. They had been doing so around the clock since the encounter on the Moon. He had started a double watch shift at midnight, "balls to dawn" as the ratings would say, giving Gretchen a normal night's sleep. Regardless, both he and the First Officer were showing signs of the strain.

What was really needed was another officer to fill in the gap. Bear, despite being third officer, was not really a qualified watch stander. Engineer Medina came closest but he had other duties and drafting him only created holes in the engineering watch schedule. Once again, Jack cursed their forced hasty departure.

Personnel for forenoon watch had stared to arrive, including both JT and Gretchen. JT went to his post at the navigation station while Gretchen approached the Captain and spoke the traditional navy phrase.

"I am ready to relieve you, Sir."

"I am ready to be relieved." Jack said with considerable feeling. "Nothing much to report, Lieutenant. The morning watch was uneventful. If Folly is correct, we will be utterly bored for the next six and a half days."

"I've been thinking about that, Sir. I think it might be wise to run some drills on the weapons systems, computer simulations. We have a number of crew that have no training and we can probably make use of several of the Marines as gunner's mates."

"Good thinking, Lieutenant. Check with the Chief and the Gunny and draw up a schedule. We have some Marines that will need to ease back into PT as well." Since Dr. Tropsha discovered the bone regrowth stimulators, all of the Marines except Lt. Merryweather were healed and ready to return to duty.

"Roger that, Sir. We are all going to need practice in the new body armor Mr. Taylor and the Gunny are working on. Some zero-g sessions with Lt. Bear might also improve the Marines' three dimensional awareness. After all, Bear is the ship's Master-at-Arms and as such, it is part of his duty to train the ship's company in repelling boarders and conducting on-shore hostile action."

"And it might make Bear a bit happier if he had some playmates to swat around," the Captain chuckled.

"Aye Captain," Lt. Curtis said, with a twinkle in her eye.

"Pardon me, Captain? Lieutenant?" JT had moved from navigation to the wing of the bridge.

"Yes, Mr Taylor?" the Captain responded.

"Sir, I think I've identified the star system we are headed for. I've been checking the parameters given by the computer against some of the star catalogs in the ship's online library."

"Don't keep us in suspense, Mister. Out with it."

"Yes, Sir. The name of the star is Beta Comae Berenices, also known as 43 Comae Berenices. It is the brightest star in the constellation *Bernice's Hair* as seen from Earth. Right Ascension and Declination are 13h11m52.395s and +27°52'41.4", respectively, and the distance from Earth is listed as 9.155 parsecs. That's 29.86 light-years, right inline with the computer's rough estimate of 30 light-years."

"And our course when we dropped into alter-space was headed toward this particular star?"

"Yes indeed, Captain. Our last normal space heading was pretty much dead on for Beta Comae."

"Do your star catalogs tell us what type of system we are going to find when we get there, Mr. Taylor?"

"According to the writeup it is spectral class G0, luminosity class V, and absolute visual magnitude is +4.45. Visual luminosity is 1.447 times Sol and its mass is 1.05 x Sol. In other words, it is a star much like our Sun, just a bit bigger. In fact, the habitable comfort zone would be about 1.2 times as far out as Earth's orbit is back home."

"Any known planets?" asked Lt. Curtis.

"No Ma'am. At least no gas giants close in. It is possible that terrestrial planets might exist but none have been detected according to the planet search archives. Earth sized planets are hard to detect from this distance."

"Well, at least we know something about where we are going. Good work, Mr. Taylor."

"Thank you, Sir." JT nodded and returned to the navigator's station.

"Well, Lieutenant. I believe that sums up the ship's status."

Gretchen came to attention and repeated the ritual words for a change of the watch. "Sir, I relieve you."

"I stand relieved," acknowledged the Captain, then turning to leave the bridge. As he left Lt. Curtis announced to the bridge crew. "This is Lt. Curtis, I have the Deck and the Conn."

Surveying the bridge crew she noticed that Billy Ray had not relieved Bobby at the helm. *I wonder what that is all about? No matter,* she thought, *maybe he just overslept. After all, we are not expecting any hostile action in alter-space.*

Susan's Cabin, Start of Forenoon Watch, Alter-space Day 2

Susan rolled over under the covers and pressed her hands against her forehead in a vain attempt to quiet the throbbing in her head. *Way too much Shiraz, girl, and I think there were some black Russians in there toward the end.* Then she heard the sound of water running in her shower.

Susan sat upright in the bed—the covers falling away revealing her naked torso. *My God, what have I done?* As dim recollections of the previous night's events slowly filtered through the painful haze of her hangover, the water in the shower stopped running. A tall figure emerged, wreathed in steam. It was Billy Ray, dressed only in a towel and beading water.

"Morning Sunshine! You're looking a might peaked."

Realizing that she was naked and half exposed, Susan covered her face with both hands, her arms shielding her breasts. "Oh God!" she said out loud.

Billy Ray, all ripcord and lean muscle, bent over to pull on a new blue jumpsuit taken from the delivery chute. Every day, the ship provided new clothing for the crew, each suit a personalized fit in the appropriate color. "Hey look, the computer delivered two new jumpsuits, one your size and one in mine."

Susan started sobbing. *If the computer knows then everybody knows!*

"What's wrong?" Billy Ray said, taking a step toward the bed.

"No! Stay away," Susan said through her hands, not removing them from her face. "Please, just go away."

"What ever I did wrong, I'm sorry," Billy Ray said, adding softly. "I would never do anything to hurt you."

"Why did you end up in my room?" she asked plaintively, lowering her hands from her face and crossing them over her chest.

"Because my room is back in the crew section and I share it with Bobby. Your room also has a queen sized bed and a private shower."

"Everyone will know!" she wailed.

"I told you there were no secrets on board a ship. It didn't seem to matter to you last night."

"I was drunk last night," she sobbed, tears starting to run down her cheeks, "and everyone will be talking about us." *I can't believe I let this happen, and right after Gretchen told me I should!*

Billy Ray wanted to hold her and comfort her, but he sensed that trying to do so would only make matters worse. She needed time to get a grip on her emotions.

"I gotta go," He said softly, "I'm already late for my watch. I don't know what I did wrong, but if I hurt you I'm sorry. That was never my intention. I thought this was what both of us wanted. I'll stay away until you want to talk." With that he slipped out the door and was gone.

Then the tears came full on, violent sobs wracking her body. *Why did I sleep with him? Even worse, why did I just throw him out? The one guy on the ship I like, who seemed to like me back, and I've just totally screwed it up. On top of that, Gretchen and Ludmilla are going to think I'm some kind of barracuda, using Billy Ray and then throwing him out like trash. What few friends I have will disown me!*

Billy Ray had paused outside the door. He heard her crying and shook his head sadly. *I wish I knew what I did wrong.*

Crew's Dayroom, Lower Deck

With the main lounge closed, most of the crew and Marines had collected in the crew's dayroom next to their quarters on the lower deck. The attached mess offered breakfast, snacks and sandwiches all day and a hot meal in the evening, but the biggest attraction was that crew were allowed to draw either two beers or two glasses of wine a day.

The Gunny and JT had just come down from the engineering lab on second deck, where they were working on the design and fabrication of body armor for over the standard spacesuits. Bobby had joined the deck crew in hopes of picking up some interesting scuttlebutt.

"Hey, Bobby," said Jon Feldman, "What's with your buddy Billy Ray? I saw him on forenoon watch and he looked like someone had killed his dog."

"Not his dog, I think he has lady problems," Bobby answered. "But you're right, he is one morose mother fucker."

"Watch your tongue sonny, there are ladies present," the Gunny scolded.

"Sorry Ma'am," Bobby apologized, blushing bright red.

"Don't Ma'am me, I work for a living. Call me either Sergeant or Gunny. And I was referring to Hospital Corpsman White."

"That's right," chimed in the slightly inebriated PFC Davis, demonstrating why he earned the sobriquet 'Two Can.' "The Gunny ain't a lady, she's a Marine."

"Two Can, you are going to get some extra hand-to-hand time with Lt. Bear for that crack," the Gunny said, giving him the disapproving eye.

"Do we really have to mix it up with the bear, Gunny?" asked LCpl Reagan, rubbing his left hand over his still healing right arm.

"That we do, Captain's orders. We need to learn how to fight aliens and the Master-at-Arms is the closest thing we got to an alien to practice on. Don't worry, he'll have mittens on his claws, Ronnie. Besides, he jumped on my separated shoulder during the tussle in the cargo hold and I want some payback."

"Don't worry, Reagan," JT added. "Lt. Bear is OK, once you get to know him. Plus, we hope to have some of the body armor ready to go by tomorrow. It will provide some extra padding."

"Hey JT, I heard that you ID'd the star we're headed for," said Steve Hitch, changing the subject. "What's the skinny?"

"It's called Beta Comae Berenices and it's in the constellation known as Berenice's Hair. Seen from Earth, Coma Berenices is sandwiched between the Hunting Dogs, Canes Venatici to the north, Virgo to the south, Leo on the west border and Bootes on the eastern border."

"What kind of name is Berenice's Hair for a constellation?" asked Washington.

"It was named by the Greek Konon of Samos, some time in the third century BC, after the hair of Egyptian Queen Berenice. She was the wife of King Ptolemy III Euergestes. The story goes that when the King went to war Berenice promised her long beautiful hair to Aphrodite, the Greek Goddess of Love, if her husband returned safely from the campaign. After the king's return Berenice kept her promise though she took the loss hard—evidently the Queen was proud of her hair. In light of her sacrifice, Aphrodite herself placed the hair among the stars, thus creating the constellation."

"Nice story, JT," Betty commented. "Do we know anything about the place other than myths?"

"Beta Comae is a main-sequence G type yellow-orange dwarf star about 1.05 times Sol's mass, and about 110 percent of its diameter. It's a little bit hotter and whiter than the Sun—about 40% brighter. It appears to be more enriched in elements heavier than helium, what astronomers call metals. For instance, it has between 1.05 to 2.29 times Sol's abundance of iron."

"What difference would that make?" asked Kato Kwan.

"The composition of a star is an indication of the stuff that went into making up its whole solar system. Lot's of heavy elements means there could be terrestrial planets orbiting the star. There don't seem to be any stellar-mass companions or closely orbiting gas giants, which bodes well for the presence of Earth-like planets."

"So there could be inhabited alien worlds orbiting the star?" Bobby was into anything involving aliens.

JT shrugged. "Beta Comae is given pretty good odds of having an Earth-like or Mars-like planet in the habitable zone. One study suggests that the star may be about 4.4 billion years old, another suggests that its age may be 10 percent younger than Sol, around

4.1 billion years. In either case, if there is an Earth-like rocky planet in the habitable zone it is possible that life could have developed there, just like back home."

"Great!" the Gunny said sarcastically. "So we may have to take on a whole planet full of alien hostiles when we get there. I think we need to advance our training schedule."

Main Mess, End of First Dog Watch, Alter-space Day 2

On a Navy vessel, the captain usually has a private mess where he can either dine alone or with a few invited guests. This precludes the need for the ship's other officers to be on best behavior in the wardroom and also cuts down on informal petitions to the Captain during a meal. Since Folly was a private yacht, not a Navy vessel, such accommodations had not been included.

Captain Jack had a choice of eating alone in his sea cabin or taking meals in the guests' dinning room, which doubled for the officers' mess or wardroom. He was just finishing a light dinner, preparing to relieve Gretchen for second dog and evening watchs, when Ludmilla approached his table.

"I beg your pardon, Captain, but might I have a word?"

"Certainly, Doctor. Please take a seat."

Ignoring the Captain's invitation to sit, Ludmilla continued. "I would like to apologize for my earlier behavior, my disbelief of your explanation."

The Captain pushed his chair back from the table and looked Ludmilla in the eyes. "On reflection, it was unfair of me to ask you to accept so much fantastical information so soon after your ordeal on the ISS. Your reaction was quite understandable."

He is trying to let me save face, Ludmilla realized, *this will not do.* "Captain, I spoke ill of you before other members of this expedition. I even questioned your sanity in front them. As a medical doctor I should never have done such a thing."

Jack wrinkled his brow in thought. *This is no perfunctory apology, she is really serious about this. Very well.* "Dr. Tropsha, I accept your apology, think nothing more of it. We can move forward as though it never happened."

Relief softened Ludmilla's features. "Thank you, Captain."

"And now that that is over with, I would count it a favor if you would resume calling me Jack when we are alone." Jack motioned to the empty dinning area with a sweep of one hand.

Ludmilla looked around, surprise registering on her face. "They have all gone!"

Jack placed his napkin on his plate and standing, moved next to her. "I must stand the next two watches tonight, but tomorrow my evening will be free. Would you join me for dinner, if I promise no new unbelievable revelations?"

"Yes, Jack," she said, her pale blue eyes looking deep into his, "I would very much like to take up where we left off."

Chapter 15

Cargo Hold, Afternoon Watch, Alter-space Day 3

The cargo hold was under zero-g, its cavernous space filled with bouncing, grotesque figures in graphite black. At first glance they moved randomly—like ping pong balls in a lottery machine—ricocheting off of the bulkheads, deck and overhead. Upon closer observation, they were also bouncing off of each other.

More specifically, all the smaller figures were concentrating their attention on a single outsized individual. The large grotesque was swatting its tormentors away like flies. It landed on all fours and came off the ceiling at fairly low velocity, allowing two of the smaller ones to hit it from opposite sides simultaneously. The triad of figures cartwheeled, throwing the two smaller ones off in new directions while the central figure tumbled end over end.

As the combatants collected themselves for another foray, Lt. Curtis, who was observing from the second deck internal airlock, signaled an end to the exercise. The large figure righted itself and drifted toward her, removing its helmet to reveal Lt. Bear's furry white head within. "That was just starting to become fun, Lieutenant," he opined.

The helmet he held in one large gauntleted paw was much different from the clear fishbowl models that the shore party had worn. It more closely resembled a motorcycle helmet with a dark, wraparound visor area and solid material everywhere else.

His two assailants proved to be JT and Washington, the two largest members of the remaining cadre. They were also clad in the sinister looking near black armor, which closer inspection showed was made of many narrow segmented bands. The bands encircled limbs and torsos, and overlapped in complex patterns in areas requiring joint movement.

The dark, graphite color came from the armor material itself—a metallic ceramic reinforced with an overlapping matrix of nano tubes. Hard, refractory and almost shatter proof, it was similar to the ship's hull material, though lighter in weight. Beneath the bands of hard ceramic was a layer of complex polymer that helped hold the individual bands together while providing flexible movement.

The polymer remained flexible over a wide range of temperatures but had an additional property—when struck sharply the molecular chains throughout the impacted area locked together, stiffening the armor shell and helping to distribute the force of the blow.

"From the way you just gang-tackled Bear, I'll just bet that both of you boys played football in high school," Gretchen said with a crooked smile on her face.

"Just a little coordinated teamwork, Lieutenant." JT smiled and high-fived his co-tackler. Washington just grinned, it was fun being able to hit someone flat out in practice without worrying about hurting them.

The Gunny came drifting over to join the conversation. "You two were supposed to pin him so I could hit him from behind."

"Yeah, about five or six more of you and I might have to put some real effort into this," Bear snorted. He was panting a bit though Gretchen did not doubt his ability, or eagerness, to continue the roughhousing.

"So how do the suits feel? Is there enough freedom of movement? Do the joints bind?"

"It feels pretty good to me," JT remarked. "Your not going to do any jumping jacks with it on, but it didn't hinder me much at all."

The Gunny nodded agreement. "Yeah, there is some restriction if you try to lift your arms high above your head. It's hard making the joints full motion without creating vulnerabilities."

As the rest of the Marines gathered around, LCpl Reagan said, "I'm getting a bit of chafing around the underarms and groin area."

"Me too," added Two Can. The smaller man was obviously more taxed by wearing the additional armor than big men like Washington and Reagan.

"We'll see what we can do to improve the tailoring in the next version," the Gunny added. Overall she was feeling pretty good about the way the armor was turning out. If they had been wearing this stuff in the crater the Moon spiders would not have wounded any of the shore party.

243

"The field of vision is a bit restricted," fretted Sizemore, who suffered from claustrophobia.

"We're working on that, Corporal. Final version will have cameras for wraparound vision, overhead too. Plus, it will have heads up displays for sensors, targeting and map info. You'll be able to see the positions of the whole squad at a glance." JT was greatly enjoying working on this stuff, it was way better than the Army's proposed Future Force Warrior gear.

Gretchen looked to Bear and asked, "how about you, Lieutenant? Any chafing or binding?"

"Not really. My limbs don't swing around as much as you monkeys' do. I think I'm going to need more cooling though, it was getting damn hot when we were bouncing around."

"Yeah," JT made a note, "We are going to have to add bigger back packs with more environmental capacity. And we are going to need to redesign the rail guns to work with the armor's bigger gauntlets."

"I've got some ideas about that," the Gunny volunteered. "Have you ever seen a KTS—a Kel-Tec Shotgun? Very compact, with dual 7 round tubular magazines. If we use a similar design for the 20mm launcher and add the 5mm flechette launcher on top we would have a weapon with a lot more room for mittens and bigger selector controls."

JT's eyes lit up. "I know just what you're talking about, I fired one at a local gun shop. Since the rail gun launchers don't need to eject empty shells it will work out even better. If we put a rest on the butt that fits over the forearm at the elbow you could easily fire one single handed."

Looking at the assembled Marines, Gretchen shook her head. *They're like kids, anticipating Christmas morning with presents under the tree. I just hope we don't get a bunch of them killed.*

Passenger's Dayroom, Lower Level

Ludmilla had just finished doing her rounds in sick bay and was headed to her quarters for a quick nap. She wanted to be fresh for her dinner with the Captain—second chances are rare in life, as she well knew. *You will not screw this up, Luda,* she commanded herself.

Coming out of the companionway from the upper deck she almost ran into Ivan, who seemed to be lurking in the passenger's lounge area as if waiting for someone.

"Hello, Ivan. I have not seen you around much these past few days," Ludmilla said in Russian.

The Russian Colonel replied in the same language, "I have been studying the ship's specifications, those that I can gain access too. Which is what you should be doing, instead of acting like a party girl with the Amazon Lieutenant and the news whore."

Ludmilla's face hardened into an emotionless mask. "You act like an uncultured peasant! Explain yourself."

"Do you deny that you were drinking in the lounge two nights ago with your new girlfriends? Or that the blond newswoman spent the night with one of the helmsmen—the cowboy? Do you think this is a vacation on the Crimea or a cruse on the Baltic?"

"How dare you! You who have been sneaking around like a KGB spy trying to steal secrets from everyone. Beware, Ivan Alexievitch, or you will end up like that little would-be rapist."

"Who? Tommy?" Shock registered on Ivan's face. "I have been looking for him, do you know where he is!"

"He is locked up for assaulting that poor girl. He is lucky that the Chief handed out the punishment, the Captain might have been even harsher."

"Tell me where he is!" Ivan made a lunge for her, but Ludmilla skipped away, avoiding his grasp. Early in her career in the Russian Federation Air Forces, where both the vodka and testosterone flow freely, Ludmilla had taken up practicing Russian martial arts. That included Combat Sambo Spetsnaz, otherwise known as Systema, and more traditional Sambo. Still, Ivan outweighed her and as a doctor, she knew better than most the difference between male and female upper body strength—she definitely did not want to grapple with him.

"I warn you Colonel Kondratov, I will shout for help if you persist."

"There is no one else around," he sneered. "The Marines are playing with their new toys and the crew is either standing watch or sleeping."

"You are a fool, Ivan. Do you not realize that the ship's computer monitors everything that happens on board?" Adding in English, "Is that not correct, Folly."

"Yes, Dr. Tropsha. I continuously monitor all habitable spaces on board to ensure the health and safety of the crew."

"Who was that?" Ivan demanded, panic in his eyes as he looked furtively about the empty lounge.

"That is the voice of the ship's computer, Ivan. Do you think that the Captain does not know about your subterfuge, your skulking about with that little weasel?

"Sooka! You traitorous bitch! All you want to do is worm your way into the Captain's bed."

"Go to hell, Ivan. You were the one who told me I should do just that. Perhaps I will sleep with Jack, but not for Russia and certainly not for you. Stay away from me, ot'ebis'!"

With fear and hatred in his eyes, Ivan exited the lounge aft, toward the crew's quarters. *Jebat'-kopat'! Thought Ludmilla. I have to warn Jack about Ivan. How do I explain that my countryman is a horses ass? And I was so hoping for a simple, romantic evening.*

Captain's Quarters, Evening, Alter-space Day 3

The Captain was flitting around his cabin like a nervous *maître d'* picking up and rearranging small items. There was a magnum of Champagne cooling in a bucket between the chairs in the sitting room, two glasses waiting on the table. Since this was a visit of a (hopefully) personal nature, Jack had dispensed with the steward.

Come on! You're acting like it's the first time you've had a woman over to your place. Well actually, this is the first time I've had a woman over to this place, at least the first time for purely social reasons.

The voice of the ship's computer interrupted his building panic attack. "Dr. Tropsha is at the door, Captain. Should I invite her in?"

"No, Folly. I'll get the door." Jack almost ran to the cabin door. Before opening it he paused to smooth his jumpsuit and check his appearance in the mirror on the wall. *Well, here goes.* He pressed the control and the door slid open.

"Good evening, Ludmilla," Jack said in what he hoped was an even, measured tone. "Won't you please come in?"

Ludmilla smiled. "Good evening, Jack. It is good to be here, again." Jack stood aside with a welcoming sweep of his arm. Ludmilla entered the cabin and the door slid silently shut behind her.

"I thought that we would start with some champagne this time. A toast as it were to new beginnings."

Ludmilla walked over to the champagne bucket and examined the bottle resting there. "Taittinger, Comtes de Champagne Blanc de Blancs 1998. Very impressive."

"Really? Is that a good year?"

"Quite, and hard to find these days."

"Well you can credit TK Parker's good taste, or that of his wine steward. I just looked in the ship's stores and picked one. Should I pour?"

"Yes, please do." Ludmilla hesitated, and then said with some trepidation, "Jack, there is something we need to discuss before the evening can progress."

Jack looked up from pouring the Champagne. *Now what? I hope she's not having second thoughts about my sanity.* "Go on, what's on your mind?"

"Jack, I have to tell you that someone on board is spying on you, the ship and the crew. Someone from the ISS." She looked away, her eyes focused at some unseen distance beyond the blank porthole in the curving cabin wall.

Ah, so that's it. Thank goodness it's not something important. "Yes, go on," he prompted.

Ludmilla looked back and met his gaze, "It is Colonel Kondratov. He has been attempting to gather intelligence about the ship's technology. He see's this as his patriotic duty. He may be trying to suborn some of the crew as well."

"Is that what you wanted to tell me? Is that your purpose for being here tonight?" *Stop asking questions you don't want answers to*, he scolded himself.

"Yes, that is what I wanted to tell you, and no, it is not the reason I came here tonight. But I could not be with you without first warning you about Ivan."

An interesting turn of a phrase, Jack thought, *of course English is not her native tongue. Does that put her on my side? Betraying her countryman, perhaps her country to warn me? I need to put her concerns to rest before mistrust derails our friendship for a second time.*

"Ludmilla, I've known about Ivan's snooping from the beginning. All of the ship's systems, including the online technical documentation and library, are monitored by the computer. The computer also monitors all public and sensitive technical areas. The only information Ivan has is information I don't mind him having."

A wave of relief passed over Ludmilla, her shoulders relaxed and her anxious body language eased. "I know that Folly monitors things for you, but I had to be sure that you knew what Ivan was up to—and I wanted you to know that I was not involved in his paranoid scheming."

What a relief! I thought we were about to have a replay of our first private encounter—without even getting to the meal. "Well thank you for letting me know, I appreciate your forthrightness and honesty," He smiled as he handed her a Champagne flute. "And I know about Tommy Wendover as well. There is little that happens on board that escapes my attention."

Tension left her like a storm passing. "I feel much better with this out in the open. Now that the air has been cleared what should we drink to?"

"How about, to second chances?"

"Yes, to second chances, and new beginnings."

They both raised their glasses in salute and sipped the pale sparkling wine. Ludmilla reached up and rubbed the tip of her nose. "This Champagne is excellent, but it always makes my nose tickle," she said. This elicited a genuine smile from Jack.

"I do not think I have ever seen you smile before, Jack." *Oh yes, he is quite handsome when he smiles.*

"I was thinking of a line from an old song, 'Let's sip Champagne 'til we break into smiles.'" Jack motioned toward the chairs.

Ludmilla took that as an invitation to sit down, which she did with feline like grace. "I do not believe I've heard this song, who is it by?"

Jack followed Ludmilla's lead and also sat. The two chairs were angled toward each other, with a small end table in reach of both.

"A musician named Jimmy Buffett. He has quite a following in nautical circles and was a favorite in my youth. He has written a lot of songs about sailors and sailing." Looking up at the ceiling while recalling another set of lyrics, he recited:

Mother, mother Ocean, I have heard you call
Wanted to sail upon your waters since I was three feet tall

"So have you always dreamed of being a captain—to spend your life at sea? This is something I have never considered myself."

"Since I was a young boy. You have never been called by the lure of the sea, heard the song of foreign shores?"

"Russia does not have a strong naval tradition like the US or the British. Tzar Nicholas II constructed a modern Navy at the beginning of the 20th century to show that Russia was not the backward child of Europe most other nations thought it was at the time. By 1904, the Imperial Russian Navy was a first rate navy. Then, in 1905, after a surprise Japanese attack destroyed most of his Pacific Squadron, Nicholas sent his main fleet all the way from the Baltic, around Africa to Asia. It arrived just in time for the Japanese to sink it in a single battle. By the end of 1905, Russia was again reduced to a third rate naval power. Little wonder that Russian romantics, looking for military adventure, tend more toward knightly single combat in tanks or airplanes."

"You have obviously studied military history," Jack said with a warm smile. Military history was one of his passions and he could not help showing off a little. "The Russian Baltic Fleet, renamed the Second Pacific Squadron sailed 18,000 nautical miles to relieve Port Arthur, only to find that it had fallen while they were en route. They engaged the Japanese fleet in the Tsushima Straits on 27th and 28th of May, 1905. The Japanese managed to cross the Russian 'T' and as a result, the Russian fleet was virtually annihilated. It lost eight battleships, numerous smaller vessels, and more than 5,000 men, while the Japanese lost three torpedo boats and just 116 men. Only three Russian vessels escaped to Vladivostok. In all, one of the most single sided battles in the history of Naval warfare."

"I think you too know something of military history. Some Russian historians credit that defeat with helping to trigger the Bolshevik revolution. As if the miserable lives of the peasants was not reason enough for an uprising," Ludmilla scoffed. "More believably, others cite the rise of Japanese militarism as an outcome."

"It's good to have someone knowledgeable to discuss such things with," Jack said, hoping his complement was not too transparent. Being captain, he was not practiced at the art of flattery.

"I am a Russian officer, after all," Ludmilla pronounced with mock officiousness. "It is good to study the mistakes of the past. It does not always allow one to avoid the same mistakes in the future, but at least you know when you invent a new way to experience disaster."

Jack chuckled and refilled their glasses. "You are right about not learning our lessons. The initial Japanese attack at Port Arthur started three hours before the formal declaration of war was sent to St. Petersburg. Thirty five years later America would suffer a similar Japanese surprise attack—at Pearl Harbor."

"Is that what you fear from the aliens? A surprise attack?"

"I'm afraid that the records from the artifact do not paint a very rosy picture of the galaxy. Evidently there was a lot of organized hostility going on, even four million years ago. I see no good reason to assume things have changed, given the events at crater Bruno."

"And what of all those intellectuals who confidently state that no truly advanced race could make it into space without giving up war and aggression?"

"Fuzzy headed liberal illogic at its finest. Philosophizing about a utopian future and wishing it were so is one thing. Believing your fantasies are reality and blindly ignoring the ugly truth is quite another. Self delusion is not a positive survival trait, for individuals or for species. And I am afraid that intercepting the ship we are chasing will only delay the inevitable. Mankind will have to face the hostile Universe sooner or later."

"So depressing to think of the future. Let's not talk about this anymore tonight," Ludmilla suggested, peering over the rim of her glass at Jack. "There will be sufficient time to face ugly reality tomorrow."

Jack placed his glass on the table between them, resting his hand next to it. "I am definitely in agreement on that point. I want us to forget our problems for the evening."

"Agreed," Ludmilla smiled and set her glass down.

"So, would you like to order dinner?"

"Actually, I would like to order breakfast," she said, covering his hand with hers. "In the morning."

* * * * *

Jack awoke to find himself wrapped around the sleeping Ludmilla, whose naked body was curled up in the fetal position. *My goodness we're spooning!* he thought. *But this feels right, like we've been this way since the beginning of time.* He softly kissed the nape of her neck and carefully slid from beneath the covers.

Standing naked at the computer display on his desk, Jack quickly checked the watch schedule. *I'm setting a bad example for the crew by missing the start of morning watch, not that I'd change what I've done.* Ah, it looked like the ever efficient Gretchen had covered for him. Yes, there was an annotation marked for his eyes only. It said, "Hope you caught up on your sleep ;-) you've got forenoon and afternoon watches."

251

Jack smiled. *We didn't really catch up on rest last night, but there are some things people need more than sleep.* He was feeling the painful complaint of a score of muscles he had forgotten he had. Ludmilla had been a tigress last night, in fact..., he turned his back to the floor length mirror on the wall and peered over his shoulder, ...yes, there were long scratches down his back.

On the bed, Ludmilla awoke with a start. "Jack!" she cried, looking around in panic.

He rushed to her. "I'm here, Ludmilla. I'm right here."

She flew from the bed and wrapped her arms around him, pulling their bodies tightly together. "When I awoke and you were not there, for a moment I thought last night was all just a dream," she said in a husky voice.

"Oh, it was a dream, but a very real one," he replied, holding her against him, her naked flesh searing him where their bodies touched. "I've just found you, my lady, I'll not be leaving you."

Her breath was hot against his neck. "Call me Luda, but only when we are alone, like this." No one had called her Luda since she was a girl, not even Yuri.

"I hope I will get the opportunity often, Luda," he murmured. She looked up, turning her face to his. Their lips met, he lowered her to the bed and once more, they lost themselves in each other.

The Bridge, Start of Forenoon Watch, Alter-space Day 4

Gretchen observed the Captain as he entered the bridge. He had a definite spring in his step that had not been present yesterday.

"Good morning," he said with a smile, "I am ready to relieve you, Lieutenant."

"I am ready to be relieved, Sir. And good morning to you, it looks like your batteries have been recharged."

"Just so, Number One," he said with a dazzling smile.

He's on cloud nine if he's using that 'number one' crap, Gretchen thought. *Well good for him, he was in desperate need of some R&R.* Not that she couldn't use some herself, but that was another story.

"All departments report systems normal. There were no incidents to report overnight. Smooth sailing, Sir."

"Very good. Lieutenant, I relieve you."

"I am relieved, Captain." Gretchen nodded and smiled, then turned and headed aft to find some breakfast. At the helm Bobby winked at Billy Ray, who was there to relieve him. Billy Ray offered a faint, knowing smile and muttered, "At least someone on the Bridge had a good night."

Jack occupied the captain's chair and said loudly, "This is the Captain, I have the Deck and the Conn."

Sickbay, Afternoon Watch, Alter-space Day 4

Susan was standing in the sickbay doorway, wondering what was so all fired important that she had to roust herself from bed and appear in person. For two days she had managed to avoid Billy Ray, she was just too mortified by her own behavior to face him. She had also managed to give Gretchen, JT and Ludmilla the slip. She snuck out to the snack bar at odd hours for food and otherwise pretty much stayed in bed, though that was beginning to grow old. She had never been so miserable in her life.

"Ah, I see my patient has decided to show up," Ludmilla remarked as she stepped from a curtained off patient's room.

Lt. Merryweather must be in there, Susan thought. He was about the only patient left, the other Marines having all returned to duty. Why is she calling me her patient?

"Step into the examination room and strip to your undergarments," Ludmilla commanded.

"But why?" Susan began to ask, but Ludmilla cut her off.

"Just do as you are told and this will all go more easily."

Puzzled, Susan moved to comply with the Doctor's orders.

* * * * *

Ludmilla kept Susan waiting for around 15 minutes. Stripped down to her bra and panties, Susan was getting quite chilled, goosebumps breaking out on her arms and chest. *Why are doctor's offices always so cold? And why do they always keep you waiting?*

Ludmilla could have told her that she was being kept waiting, cold and almost naked, to put her at a psychological disadvantage for what was coming next. When Luda and Jack finally managed to say their goodbyes that morning, he had asked her to look in on Susan. The normally gregarious reporter had absented herself from everyday shipboard life for the past two days, ever since the morning she had ejected Billy Ray from her cabin.

The curtain parted and Ludmilla entered. In her white jumpsuit, stethoscope around her neck, she looked every inch a doctor, albeit a very shapely one. "All right, let us see what the problem is here."

"Ludmilla, I don't have any problem," Susan pleaded earnestly.

"Are you a Doctor? No! So do not try to tell me what my diagnosis will be." Breaking the sterile wrapping on a tongue depressor she ordered, "stick out your tongue. Say ah."

For the next ten minutes Ludmilla proceeded to give Susan a thorough examination. She poked and prodded, listened to various locations with her suitably cold stethoscope, took her temperature, blood pressure, palpated her arms and abdomen, peered into her eyes and ears with a bright light, and tested her reflexes with a tiny rubber hammer—all the things that doctors do to people in examination rooms. She even drew several vials of blood.

Finally, Ludmilla looked up from entering notes on her tablet. "All right, I am satisfied."

"Satisfied?" Susan asked, totally confused.

"Yes, I am satisfied that there is nothing physically wrong with you. This means that your abnormal behavior over the past couple of days is purely a psychological problem."

"What?" Susan squeaked.

"I was asked by the Captain to examine you and ensure that you were not injured in someway. Or sick with some communicable disease, such things can be very dangerous on board a ship. Yes, the Captain was very concerned about your deteriorating condition."

"My what? I'm not deteriorating!"

"No? You are not eating properly, sleep excessively and have avoided all human contact. This is not the behavior of a healthy person, Miss Write." The last admonishment was delivered with a stern Doctor's look.

"But I'm fine. Is everybody keeping tabs on me for some reason?"

"The Captain is concerned with the health and well being of everyone on his ship. And this is a spaceship, a closed and isolated environment where even the smallest health problems can spin out of control if not nipped in the bud early. So explain to me why you are acting so strangely."

"Look, Ludmilla, it's nothing really. I... just had a bad experience a few days back and I haven't quite gotten over it." Susan felt small and defenseless, sitting on the examination table in her underwear while the imposing Dr. Tropsha grilled her.

"And was anyone else affected by this bad experience of yours? Someone who might also be suffering from its aftereffects?"

"Well yes, but," Susan's lip began to tremble, "I don't know what to say!"

"The first step in solving a problem is being able to identify the problem. So, exactly what is it that you cannot explain?"

"I slept with Billy Ray and I threw him out!" Susan bawled, bursting into a crying jag. Her words came in waves, between sharp intakes of air. "I was a total bitch... and now he'll never want to see me again... and nobody will like me... and I'll be all alone..."

Ludmilla sat down on the examination table next to Susan and put her arm around the sobbing girl. Ludmilla was a decade older than the younger woman. Not enough separation to be mother and daughter, but enough to be an older sister. She simply held her and let the crying stop on its own.

"Now, little one, that was not so hard, was it?"

"What do you mean?"

"Well, you told me the truth and I did not abandon you. I did not say I will not be your friend anymore. Eh?" Ludmilla handed the sniffling Susan a handkerchief.

255

"No but, Billy Ray, he'll have nothing to do with me." The crying threatened to begin anew.

"Now, now. Listen to me." Ludmilla scolded her in a motherly voice. "Friends do not abandon each other when they do wrong, or even hateful things. That is what being friends means, forgiving each other."

Susan blew her nose and looked at Ludmilla teary-eyed.

"And when it comes to love, you must forgive even more. You think that Billy Ray hates you and will not look at you again. You are a stupid little girl."

"What?" Susan asked in a quavering voice.

"Bill Ray has been moping around, punishing himself, trying to figure out what he did to you! Trust me, men usually think that it is their fault."

"Why?"

"Because it usually is. But not this time. No, you must fix this because you caused the problem."

"He'll never forgive me! I suck!"

"Do not be silly! Look at yourself. You are an angel, so beautiful that you attract men by the score. Your problem is not getting a man but having too many. The secret is to sift through your admirers until you find a man worth keeping, and then hang on to him."

"Really?"

"Of course. I know something about such matters. I am not so unattractive to men myself."

"But what can I do? I know he hates me."

"Here is what you do. Put your cloths back on, get something to eat—love on an empty stomach is a bad idea. Go to your room and fix yourself up, take a shower, set your hair. Then, be in the main lounge when Billy Ray gets off watch."

"But what do I say? How do I explain that I was a total idiot?"

"Just walk up to him and say 'Hello, I'm sorry, can you ever forgive me?' Believe me—if he is the man you think he is he will forgive you."

Hope dawned in Susan's eyes. "You think so?"

"Of course. If he does not, then he is a fool. But he will forgive you. Tomorrow morning you will both wonder what the trouble was all about. Trust me, Susan, I know about men. They need a woman's guiding hand—but that means that we must be the responsible ones, the grownups."

With that, Ludmilla gave Susan's shoulder an encouraging squeeze and left her to get dressed. *Well, it is up to her now*, she thought. *I have done what you asked, Jack, captain of my heart, and it almost makes me regret not having a daughter of my own.*

Chapter 16

Captain's Sea Cabin, Afternoon watch, Alter-space Day 6

Susan was standing outside of the Captain's sea cabin. It was the beginning of afternoon watch and she had hoped to catch the Captain at lunch, but he had not made an appearance in the mess. After checking with members of the bridge crew coming off watch, she discovered that the Captain had retired to his sea cabin when forenoon watch ended.

Putting aside the nervous flutter she felt in her stomach, Susan knocked on the cabin door. She had been working up the courage to speak with the ship's commanding officer for two days now—ever since she and Billy Ray had reconciled.

Two days ago, when Billy Ray came into the lounge at the start of second dog watch, Susan was at the bar waiting, just as Ludmilla had told her to be. When he saw her he stopped, she stood up from her bar stool and walked over to him.

"Hello, Billy Ray."

"Hello, Susan," came his cautious reply.

"Billy Ray, I'm sorry," she said, anxiety straining her voice. "I'm a total idiot. And I should never have treated you the way I did."

"I'm sorry too," he began.

"No, you have nothing to be sorry about," she interrupted. "I was confused and I lashed out at you. I was a bitch, can you ever forgive me?"

"Well, yeah, I guess so. But I would never say you were a... what you said."

"Thank you! Thank you!" she said, throwing her arms around him. Then she kissed him in front of everyone, both as an act of contrition and to seal the deal before Billy Ray had more time for thought.

They spent the night in her cabin and she did not throw him out in the morning. In fact, he was almost late for his watch. Since then they had spent what overlapping free time they had together.

Ludmilla was right, both of them came down with willful amnesia, neither one able to remember the tiff of a few days ago.

Strangely enough, Susan found herself at peace with the Universe, a feeling she had never felt before. She didn't know if this was love, but she did know she was happy. It was that happiness that made her realize she needed to talk to the Captain. Not about Billy Ray or herself but about JT.

Gretchen had given both Ludmilla and herself a prod when they were adrift in the relationship department. And Ludmilla had straighten her out when her relationship with Billy Ray had foundered. Now both she and Ludmilla seemed to be on top of the world, romance wise, but Gretchen remained a solitary creature. Hence the need to talk to the Captain about JT.

She didn't understand the Navy reasoning that kept Gretchen and JT apart, when it was obvious that they were attracted to each other. All she knew was that for Gretchen to even consider a relationship with her ex-cameraman, JT had to be an officer and could no longer work for the Lieutenant.

She heard the Captain's voice call "Come!" as the door slid aside. Here goes nothing, she thought. Swallowing once, she stepped through the open portal to face Captain Jack.

"Miss Write, what brings you to my door today?" *Now what?* Jack wondered. She and Billy Ray had obviously worked out their problems, since the laconic helmsman was back to being his cheerful if reserved self.

"Good afternoon, Captain," she began. She had gone over this conversation a dozen times in her head before working up the courage to actually talk to Jack. Since the voyage had begun he had somehow grown more imposing, becoming a larger figure than the man she had interviewed for the evening news ages ago. "I was wondering if I might have a word with you about JT."

"Mr. Taylor? Regarding what, specifically?" came the Captain's neutral reply, as he motioned toward a chair. "Please, take a seat."

Susan nodded her thanks and sat down. "You know that JT used to be a Green Beret? A sergeant in the Army?"

"Yes, indeed. That was why I asked him to be part of the shore party at crater Bruno. Why do you ask?"

"And you know that he went back to college when he got out of the Army and earned a BS in electrical engineering and a Masters in Astronomy?"

"Yes, again. Which is why he is filling in as the ship's navigator. I sense you are building up to some larger point."

"Yes, Sir. I was just wondering why he wasn't an officer like Rajiv and Yuki? I mean, aren't people with college degrees usually made officers?"

"There is a bit more to becoming an officer than that, but I see the logic behind your question. Has JT mentioned to you that he would like to be an officer?" *That would really be a surprise,* Jack thought. If JT wanted a promotion Jack was fairly certain that he would have asked on his own.

Instead of answering the Captain's question, Susan changed course, "And given his experience as a scientist, wouldn't it make sense for him to be part of Dr. Gupta's department? I mean, JT is both an engineer and a scientist. He is practically the only person on the ship who can make heads or tails out of what Yuki and Rajiv are saying when they get into one of those heated conversations they are always having in the lounge."

"Yes, I fully agree that JT is a valuable addition to the ship's crew." *There is something else at work here, some motivation other than trying to get her friend a promotion. Why would she want JT to be an officer and report to Dr. Gupta instead of Lt. Curtis?* Susan was sitting quietly, looking at him expectantly.

Oh, of course! A smile spread over Jack's face as full understanding dawned on him. On a number of occasions, Jack had caught his First Officer casting admiring glances at the handsome camera man. *Knowing Gretchen, there was no way in hell she'd violate regulations and do something about those desires—not without a change to the organizational structure.*

"Well, to tell you the truth, I was thinking about reorganizing some of the expedition's personnel in light of how important the scientific aspects of the voyage have become."

"Yes, Captain?" Susan prompted.

"Initially, the scientific personnel were not going to be part of the regular crew. Partly because the scientific staff are not use to any kind of naval discipline and partly because their duties do not mesh well with the day to day operation of the vessel.

"I have been thinking of keeping Mr. Adams and Mr. Medina in engineering, with Jo Jo assuming the position of chief engineer. I was then going to put our two physicists into their own department, but now that you mention it, JT might also be a good fit for the scientific staff. He could continue to man the navigation console when needed and act as a liaison between the scientists and the rest of us mortals."

Susan smiled brightly, "I think that would be a wonderful idea, Captain!"

"As for promoting him, we really do not have a rigid rank structure for the crew—this isn't an actual Navy vessel. Basically, other than the ship's officers, the deck division is run by Chief Zackly, GySgt Rodriguez takes care of the Marines and engineering will now be in the hands of Chief Engineer Medina. Members of the science staff would be accorded status equivalent to officers, as they are currently."

Yes, he thought, *that might be a good move for everyone on board. And if tradition and regulation has been interfering with my second in command's romantic opportunities this should remedy the situation. This is rather surprising. Susan never seemed altruistic, yet it appears that she is trying to do her friends a favor. About as subtle as a broadside, but still rather touching.*

"Very well. I'll take your comments under advisement. But please don't mention the realignment plans to anyone until I've had time to run them past Lieutenants Curtis and Bear."

"I thought that, as Captain, you can do whatever you want?" Susan asked, a little concerned.

"Oh, I can. But a good commander always consults with his officers and solicits their advise in matters like this. Perhaps it would be good to announce the changes at an all hands meeting in the lounge this evening. I want to address the ship's complement before we emerge into normal space tomorrow anyway." *Yes, this will work out quite well, give the crew something else to talk about instead of fretting over tomorrow's impending battle.*

"Is there anything else I can do for you, Miss Write? Someone to be named commodore or changes to the lounge furnishings?"

"Why no, Captain," she smiled. "I really don't understand how the Navy operates or all this shipboard stuff. I just thought I'd ask about JT." With that she stood up and left the sea cabin with a happy bounce in her steps.

"Dismissed, Miss Write," the Captain said jokingly, to the closing cabin door. "Folly, were you listening to that?"

"Yes, Captain."

"Yes, I think we shall need a new jumpsuit color for our three scientists—perhaps something in a dark burgundy?"

"An excellent choice, Captain."

Hydroponic Section 3, Upper Deck Aft

Ivan had been skulking about the engineering spaces, trying to gain access to the reactor and engine rooms, with no success. He stood before the doors to the ship's innermost regions but could not figure out how to open them. He even called out to the ship's computer but received no answer.

Perhaps the computer was not monitoring this area, or was busy elsewhere, he thought. In reality, Folly was keeping close tabs on the Colonel, but declined to acknowledge the man. Out of frustration, Ivan decided to go up to the hydroponic garden on the upper deck. Perhaps there were other ways to enter the engineering spaces from there.

Hydroponics was not listed on Folly's roster of restricted areas so Col. Kondratov was able to enter the maze of growing shelves, hissing water sprays and overhead grow lights. Carefully advancing down one aisle, he saw lettuce growing to his right and tall tomato plants to the left.

The air was warm and moist, with an earthy organic smell. The gravity seemed higher than in the rest of the ship as well. In fact, the deck gravity was set to around three quarters Earth normal and held constant, regardless of what the other parts of the ship were set to. Plants are adaptable, but zero-g and even worse, variable gravity disrupted their development.

As he rounded an offset in the rows of plants, Ivan was faced with a forest of hanging tubs, each of which contained a miniature tree. There were oranges, lemons, limes, apples and cherries, an entire orchard on dwarven scale. Out of the corner of his eye he glimpsed a slight flicker of movement.

It must be the horticulturist, he thought as he called out, "Miss, could I talk to you? Please?" No answer was forthcoming.

Melissa had spotted the nosy Russian as he entered the orchard section and quickly retreated deeper into the lush green oasis that was her workplace. As she dodged quietly between the verdant islands of vegetation, she quietly called for help. "Bear! This is Melissa. I'm in Hydro 3 and that Russian Colonel is here!"

Bear was sleeping in his quarters and not wearing the harness that mounted his communicator pip, so her plea for help went unheard. Fortunately, Folly was never out of range and correctly interpreted the frightened woman's call as a request for assistance.

"Melissa, this is the ship's computer. I will summon help."

"Thank you," she whispered, ducking beneath a shelf of hydrangeas. Melissa knew the layout of the hydroponic garden like the back of her hand and in her leaf green jumpsuit she all but disappeared, blending in among her floral wards.

* * * * *

"Lt. Bear, Miss Hamilton needs your help in Hydroponic Section 3. Colonel Kondratov seems to be stalking her."

Bear awoke with a start. "What did you say?" he demanded, quickly slipping on his utility harness. Before Folly could repeat the entire message Bear was out the door and headed toward hydroponics at a run.

He bolted up the companionway to the upper deck and through the door, the change in deck gravity not bothering him in the least. With the silence of a natural predator, the 1300 lb white bear hardly rustled the leaves of the overhanging green cloister as he past.

* * * * *

Ivan stalked Melissa, unaware that he himself was being hunted. An experienced outdoorsman, Ivan moved quietly, stopping frequently to listen for the sounds of movement. While Melissa was graceful and quiet herself, the space was constrained and her escape routes limited. Only her intimate knowledge of the garden's labyrinthine layout kept her from the Colonel's grasp.

"Got you!" Ivan shouted in triumph, reaching through a stand of cedar bay cherry plants and grasping Melissa by the upper arm. As he roughly extracted the struggling horticulturist from her bushy refuge a snort followed by a low rumbling growl could be heard behind the Russian officer. He turned, triumph changing to primal fear as he saw the polar bear towering over him.

With one swipe of his right paw, Bear sent the hapless Ivan flying across the tangled space, into another stand of miniature fruit trees. The woody plants rebounded, ejecting Ivan's limp form back out into the passageway where he fell to the floor.

"Did he hurt you?" Bear asked Melissa.

"Not that much," the young woman replied, massaging her arm where Ivan had grasped her.

Bear slowly swung his huge head toward the cosmonaut, accompanied by a growl that started deep within his massive chest. As he closed on the supine figure with slow, deliberate steps, Bear said to Ivan in Russian, "You know, we bears, like many predators, enjoy playing with our food before we eat it."

Main Lounge, Evening, Alter-space Day 6

The crew had been informed that an all hands meeting would be held in the main guest lounge at the end of second dog watch and that evening watch would be skipped that day. It was also suggested that everyone shower and don a new jumpsuit for the occasion. Some were puzzled when the change of clothing delivered to their quarters sported new colors.

So Jo Jo and Freddy would not feel abandoned by the other former wearers of engineering's bright orange, the Captain ordered a subtle change in their jumpsuit color to a darker, burnt orange. As the crew gathered, the three scientists and two engineers were the center of attention, people coming up to ask about their sartorial transformation. The Captain had informed everyone involved with the organizational changes ahead of time, but ordered them not to tell anyone else until he could make the official announcement at the evening meeting.

Susan was sitting with Gretchen, looking like the cat that ate the canary. If this took much longer she might just burst. Gretchen knew, of course, but Ludmilla was still unaware of the significance of the fashion statement being made by the five men across the room.

Tommy Wendover had been released from his incarceration with a stern lecture from the Chief. The words of warning had seemingly little effect however, since Tommy was hovering next to Col. Kondratov, an association the Chief had warned him not to pursue.

Kondratov himself was keeping to the far corners of the lounge, casting fearful glances at Bear. He refused to give an explanation for the livid bruising that could be seen on the left side of his face and neck. Though his left eye was almost swollen shut he refused Dr. Tropsha's offer of medical attention.

For his part, Bear, who was seated on the deck next to the bar where Melissa was tending to customers, would break into a toothy grin and wink whenever he could catch the Colonel's eye. Occasionally he licked his chops in a most disconcerting and predatory way.

Ludmilla joined Gretchen and Susan at their usual table—the Captain, Billy Ray and the rest of the bridge crew had not yet entered the lounge.

"Does anyone know what happened to Ivan?" the Doctor asked. "A training accident or something?"

"No training accidents that I know of," Gretchen replied, evasively.

"It looks like he fell from a height and landed on his face," Ludmilla ventured.

"Or like he was beaten to a pulp by someone much bigger and stronger than he is," Gretchen said, unwilling to keep Ivan's transgressions secret. "Perhaps for being somewhere he shouldn't have been, threatening someone he had no business to be near."

"Bear," Susan and Ludmilla said at the same time. Not a question or a guess, but a flat statement of fact.

"The sneaky bastard's lucky that Melissa called Bear off or the only thing left of him would be random DNA in a pile of polar bear shit," Gretchen said with contempt.

"Really?" Susan asked, ever the news reporter, "When and where did this happen?"

"Yes, what has that filth been up to?" added Ludmilla, recalling Ivan's grab for her in the passenger's dayroom a few days ago.

"Evidently Ivan the Terrible over there accosted Melissa in the aft hydroponic section. Had her trapped. She called for help and the computer told Bear, he being the closest officer."

"She's lucky Bear was close by," said Ludmilla.

"He's lucky she called him off. I believe Bear was actually going to kill and eat him—at least it looked that way in the surveillance video the computer sent to my station."

"Remind me not to cross her," Susan said with conviction. "Or Bear."

"No need to fear Bear," Gretchen reassured her companions. "Unless you are either of those two weasels in the corner. Being unarguably the biggest and strongest member of the crew, Bear surprisingly has zero tolerance for anyone who tries to forcibly coerce those smaller or weaker than themselves."

"I still do not understand how Jack controls him," Ludmilla said to no one in particular. "Bear offered to tell me about how he and Jack met, now I'm not so sure I want to know."

"They have some strange kind of male bond—a man, polar bear bromance. I don't understand it either, but Bear holds the Captain in the highest regard. Even so, if Ivan had really hurt Melissa I doubt that even the Captain could have prevented Bear from killing him—in fact, I'm not sure he would have tried."

The crowd's attention shifted to the front of the lounge where the bridge crew was entering. Billy Ray nodded to Susan, and then went to the bar to get a brew with Bobby. Neither Susan nor Billy Ray was the clinging type by nature. They would have plenty of time to be together later in the evening—when it really mattered.

Finally, the Captain entered. He had purposefully allowed time for all those who wished to visit the bar prior to his joining the gathering. As the Captain moved to the center of the room, Gretchen and her companions stood, a signal to all the others to do likewise.

The Captain stood, waiting for silence which came quickly. Good, he thought, they are starting to act like a real crew and not just a bunch of civilians thrown together by happenstance. Now for him to act like a captain, and prepare the crew for the coming action.

"Good evening," he began, bringing muted replies of "good evening, sir," from the crowd. Jack smiled and looked about him.

"First order of business, I have decided to reassign some personnel in light of our recent experiences. I have asked Dr. Gupta to head up an independent science section, tasked with investigating any alien technology we encounter during the mission. Both Dr. Saito and Mr. Taylor will be detailed to the new science team.

"Mr. Medina is now the ship's Chief Engineer and I'm sure that he and Mr. Adams will keep everything shipshape. In keeping with our practice, the science team is now recognizable by their new burgundy jumpsuits. The engineering department now sports a new shade of orange as well. I know everyone will continue to do their same exemplary jobs in their new positions."

Applause broke out among the crew. The Captain himself joined in and then, assuming a more somber posture, waited for order to return.

"This is only the second time we have all met like this. The last time was after the rescue of those stranded on the ISS and just before our encounter on the Moon." Jack gave the significance of what they had already experienced time to sink in before proceeding.

"We are now faced with what will undoubtedly prove to be our greatest challenge. Tomorrow, we will emerge into normal space in a new star system—a place where no humans," he paused and smiled at Bear, "or ursines have ever gone before."

"If that is our only accomplishment, tomorrow will stand as an important day in the history of our species and our planet. But that is not all that will likely transpire.

"As you know, we started this journey in pursuit of an alien vessel, an unquestionably hostile alien vessel. Ladies and gentlemen, our current overriding mission remains the destruction of that alien craft.

"Some of you may be wondering why this is important, and why we should all risk our lives traveling through alter-space—something we didn't even know was possible a few days ago—to enter an unknown star system, facing unknown opponents in order to destroy a ship that may not even contain a living enemy.

"I have considered this question myself and I am here to tell you that we travel this course because we have no alternative. Not if we wish to be sure that our home world is safe. Because our scientists have managed to decode records, left behind by ancient visitors to our world. Records that warn of a peril greater than any we have previously encountered."

This last statement sent murmurs around the room. The Captain again waited for the noise to die down before continuing.

"Ask yourselves whether our world is ready to face an invasion by aliens more technically advanced than we are. I think you will agree that neither our leaders nor our people are prepared for such an event. Fortunately, there are others who know this terrible secret still on Earth. They will be working to inform the leaders of every nation about the threat we face, but their job will not be easy.

"Think how hard it was for many of you to accept that aliens exist and that they may be hostile. Of course, getting shot at by giant mechanical spiders has a way of focusing the mind."

That brought chuckles from the crowd and some high-fiving among the Marines assembled along the far wall. Jack hazarded a glance at Ludmilla, who nodded in reply. *I'll probably pay for that crack later.*

"Simply put, Earth needs more time to prepare. I have considered our overall mission and concluded that we must make every effort to buy that time tomorrow. Precisely what we will be called upon to do I cannot tell you; what we will find at Beta Comae remains unknown. Our actions will be dictated by circumstances.

"All that I ask, all that Earth can ask, is for each one of you to do your duty. With that and the grace of God, I have no doubt that this fine ship and this fine crew will win the day. So, attention to orders."

"Starting with forenoon watch tomorrow we will go to General Quarters. Those Marines not assigned as gunner's mates are to assemble in the cargo hold in full combat gear, in case we need to board the alien vessel. Those who do not have an assigned action station, see Lt. Curtis. She will tell you where to be while we are at General Quarters.

"Return to normal 3-space is expected just after noon, but I am told that there is some uncertainty in the exact timing of the event. Regardless, we will be at our action stations and ready.

"The bar will close in an hour, the lounge will stay open until midnight. Relax, enjoy yourselves and get a goodnight's sleep. Tomorrow we will face the unknown together. That is all."

With that the Captain turned and left the lounge.

Bridge, Forenoon Watch, Alter-space Day 7

It was a quarter of an hour before noon, close to the end of forenoon watch. The ship was at general quarters, full combat alert, and had been for nearly four hours. Emergence from alter-space should come just after 12:00 and tension was beginning to rise among the crew. Suddenly the ship trembled and the klaxon sounded over the PA.

"Attention, the ship has emerged into 3-space," announced the ship's computer. The bridge crew jumped to their stations, startled by the early transition.

"Clear the view ports. Sensors up, I want position and targeting data on the forward holographic overlay," the Captain snapped. "Helm, acceleration to zero, maintain heading and attitude. Engineering, I need the forward rail gun battery at full charge and engines ready for combat maneuvers."

A chorus of "Aye aye, Sir," indicated his orders were received and understood. The ship's front section returned to its normal transparent state, revealing a yellow-orange star dead ahead.

"It looks just like home," commented Lt. Curtis, who was standing beside the Captain's chair. "I was expecting something a bit more exotic."

From the navigator's station JT, now wearing the deep burgundy of the science team, was taking hurried readings. "It may look like Sol but it is almost 10% bigger. It appears the same size because we are about 1.2 AU away, 30 million kilometers farther out than Earth's orbit. I'm starting the search for planets and trying to determine the local ecliptic plane."

Also hovering about the sensor displays were Rajiv and Yuki. JT saw Rajiv surreptitiously pass something to the Japanese scientist. When he realized that it was a crumpled dollar bill, JT chuckled. The two physicists had independently run the alter-space transit time equations and evidently Yuki had won the bet over when the ship would emerge.

"Are we getting anything on the sensors, Mr. Taylor?" The Captain's question brought JT's attention back to the instrument readings. *This is really strange,* he thought, *I should have found the alien ship by now. We were right on its tail when we entered alter-space.* He widened the search cone and rechecked—there was no sign of the alien ship.

"Captain, I can't find a trace of the alien vessel," JT reported with considerable uneasiness. "Sir, it's just not there."

Chapter 17

Bridge, Beta Comae Berenices

Parker's Folly had been in the Beta Comae system for just over ten minutes and its quarry was nowhere to be found. Traveling 1.4 million kph relative to the star's frame of reference, it had moved nearly 250,000 kilometers from its point of emergence.

"Captain, we are not detecting the presence of the alien ship," Rajiv said, looking up from the radiation and particle detection readouts. "If it has its drive on we should be detecting the same radiation signature we saw before it disappeared into alter-space."

"Optical, infra-red and microwave bands are also negative," added the frustrated JT. Then a blip on his instruments caught his attention. "Sir! I think I've found a planet."

"That's very good, Mr. Taylor. What is its location? Could the alien ship have taken refuge there?" The Captain leaned forward in his chair, concentrating on the annotations flashing into existence over the view forward, marking the planet's position in space.

"Sir, it registers as a terrestrial type planet about 80% a massive as Earth. Its orbit is approximately 1.15 AU and its position is a third of an orbit beyond our current position—roughly 150 million km. For the alien ship to travel that far at its last known velocity and acceleration, and assuming the need to decelerate to match orbit, call it 35 hours."

"So either it beat us here by more than a day, or it has not arrived yet," the Captain said, thinking out loud.

"Yes, Sir. If it was still on the way to the planet we would be able to detect it."

"Captain!" Rajiv shouted excitedly. "We have just picked up a burst of gamma radiation from the vicinity of the emergence point. I believe that the alien ship may have arrived behind us!"

"Yes. It is the alien," added Yuki. "I am detecting the drive signature. Captain, the alien vessel seems to be altering its course. It appears to be heading for the planet JT discovered."

So the computer's warning was correct, Jack thought. *What else might it know deep within its quantum entangled guts?* "Helm, reverse course. Bring the ship to bear on the alien vessel."

"Aye, Captain."

The alien sun dropped from sight as the ship flipped end over end. The star field in front of the ship stabilized, with new holographic numbers and markings identifying the alien craft, invisible to the naked eye at this distance.

"Sir, you realize that we are now ahead of the alien, traveling away from the target at 350,000 kph. We need to shrink that delta-v, Sir, or our rail gun slugs will never reach the target."

"I am aware of that, Mr. Taylor. Engineering, we are about to find out what flank speed, or rather, flank acceleration really is. Mr. Vincent, all ahead flank, let's go catch us an alien."

"Aye aye, Captain," Billy Ray responded enthusiastically.

"Sir, we are topping out at 30 Gs," reported the new Chief Engineer. "The reactor and engines are stable, the shields are up and the forward rail guns fully charged."

"Excellent, Mr. Medina," the Captain said, easing back in his chair. "Mr. Vincent, time to intercept."

"Sir, we will take 5.6 minutes to achieve zero delta-v with the target, and another 5.6 to reestablish our original closing velocity. If we maintain this acceleration we will intercept in 23.8 minutes."

"I sense a 'but,' Mr. Vincent."

"Sir, we will be closing at 1.8 million kph when we overtake the alien ship, accurately targeting the vessel will be difficult."

The Captain nodded, did some math in his head and amended his orders. "Helm, once we have reversed our course vector reduce acceleration to match the target. That should give us how long to intercept, Mr. Vincent?"

"Total time from the initial turn will be 53.7 minutes. That will keep our closing velocity around 350,000 kph. We should have a workable targeting solution in about 40 minutes."

"Very good, Mr. Vincent. Alright people, let's go do what we came to do."

* * * * *

The minutes passed slowly as the crew anticipated drawing within firing range of the alien ship. While everyone on board referred to the main battery as consisting of a pair of rail guns, those guns were only distantly related to the small arms carried by the ship's Marines. Those weapons generate thousands of Gs to accelerate their projectiles while the main battery produced accelerations in the tens of thousands of gravities along its 100 meter length.

Such acceleration would be problematic if the motive force was applied using electromagnetism. No reasonable projectile could withstand the strain of firing—the rounds would just disintegrate into a cloud of plasma.

But Folly's main battery was based on gravitonics, which allowed projectiles to be launched using incredible accelerations without destroying their payloads. Even so, the relative velocity of the ship with respect to its target was more important than the velocity the rail guns could impart to their projectiles.

"Sir, we are coming into firing range," reported JT.

"Captain, I have a lock on the target," added Billy Ray.

"Main battery, six round salvo. You may fire when ready Mr. Vincent."

"Aye aye, Captain, six round salvo," Billy Ray replied, the ship shook three times in quick succession. The forward holographic overlay showed three pairs of glowing streaks headed toward the invisible target, shrinking to the point of invisibility themselves due to distance and perspective. "Salvo away sir, time to impact 131 seconds."

The next two minutes unfolded with glacial slowness, no one dared break the silence. Under his breath, Bobby quietly counted down, "three, two, one..."

After a slight delay to account for the tardiness of light, a brilliant flair blossomed in front of them, a blinding white ball of destruction that vanished as quickly as it had appeared.

"That was a direct hit, Sir," JT reported. The navigation sensors had a better view of the impact than the naked eyes of the bridge crew.

"Awesome!" Bobby exclaimed, as the helmsmen bumped fists, "we totality pwnd him."

"Shift maximum power to the forward shields, Mr. Medina." the Captain ordered. "Helm, prepare for possible evasive maneuvers. Mr. Taylor, are there any sizable pieces of wreckage?"

JT consulted radar and LIDAR readouts. "That's a negative, Captain. It looks like the ship was mostly vaporized. Did we really hit it that hard?"

"I expected to cause major damage," the Captain replied, "but there should not have been enough energy in those projectiles to totally vaporize the target."

"I believe you are correct, Captain," said Rajiv from his bank of sensors. "The kinetic energy of each of the 10 kg projectiles was equivalent to approximately 15 tons of TNT. It is improbable that all of the rounds struck the vessel—one, maybe two at the most. I believe that the explosion we just witnessed was caused primarily by matter-antimatter annihilation. The radiation signature is quite distinct."

"Yes, this reinforces what we suspected about the alien vessel's drive and power source," Yuki added, backing his fellow physicist's conjecture. "From the explosion on the Moon and the radiation signature of the vessel's drive we suspected this to be so."

"Are these science dweebs dissing your gunnery?" Bobby asked Billy Ray in a low whisper. "Naw, pardner," the lanky Texan replied, "I shot it, I hit it, it blew up. 'Nuf said."

The Captain ignored his helmsmen's side conversation, instead questioning the scientists. "You're saying we ruptured its fuel storage, which contained enough antimatter to vaporize the entire ship?"

"Yes, Captain. We believe that to be the most likely explanation," Rajiv concluded.

"I'm glad we didn't come along side and use the X-ray laser batteries." Jack exhaled slowly, *I wish they would tell me these things ahead of time.*

"Yes, indeed, Captain."

* * * * *

The crew continued scanning for any large chunks of their vanquished prey, finding nothing. True to the science team's prediction, as the ship's trajectory took it through the area where the alien vessel detonated, no significant pieces of debris were encountered. The shields did register increased gas density and swarms of dust, which at such high relative velocities required a significant amount of energy to deflect.

"Captain," called JT. "About five minutes before we fired on the alien, we picked up a radio signal from the vessel. A burst transmission of some form. We only picked it up faintly, I'm guessing that it was highly directional."

"A directional signal aimed at what, Mr. Taylor?"

"At the planet, Sir. I didn't think it all that important at the time, but I'm picking up another signal and this one is coming from the planet."

"You're sure, this is a reply to the probe ship's signal?"

"Fairly sure, Sir. The frequency and encoding are the same, and if you figure out the transmission time to the planet and back—about 8.2 minutes each way—the timing is right."

"Do we know what they said to each other?"

"No idea, Sir."

Damn, and I thought we were done here, Jack thought furiously. *I need advice about what this might mean.* "Lt. Curtis, would you and the science team join me in my sea cabin. Mr. Medina, you have the Conn."

"Aye, Sir." replied Jo Jo, moving to take the command chair as the Captain headed for his cabin.

Captain's Sea Cabin, Beta Comae System

The Captain and his advisers all packed snugly into the cabin and shut the door. Jack looked around the room, framing his next remarks carefully. "It would appear that our efforts to prevent the alien probe from reporting to its masters may have failed. I need your best information and speculation regarding our current position before deciding what actions we take next. Let's start with you JT."

It is a common practice for commanders to ask for advice starting with the most junior member of their staff. That way the younger officers are not swayed by the opinions of their superiors. Having been in the Army JT knew this but he still felt the pressure of going first.

"Captain, that planet could be habitable. During the pursuit, I continued scanning the planet for signs of life and found that the atmosphere is somewhat similar to Earth's. It's thinner, primarily nitrogen with about 12% oxygen but there's significantly more CO_2 and traces of methane. Just how much I can't tell from this far out."

"Are you saying people could live there?" asked Gretchen.

"Not comfortably, not enough oxygen. And despite being in the middle of the habitable zone the temperatures are 4-5° colder than Earth. It's a lot nicer place than Mars, but definitely not a garden spot. That's not to say that some other species wouldn't find it comfortable."

"Do you think that the planet is inhabited? Could the probe have delivered its information in that radio burst?" the Captain asked, focusing on the crux of the matter.

"Yes and no, Sir. Though it's possible that the transmission contained a report about Earth, I don't think that it was meant for the inhabitants of the planet."

"And why not?"

"Because I don't think there are any."

This remark caused the others present to pepper JT with demands for an explanation. The Captain patiently signaled for order and said, "explain."

276

"Well, I've been monitoring all parts of the electromagnetic spectrum since we entered the system. Back home, Earth sends out signals on all sorts of frequencies—radio, TV, microwaves, radar, cellphones, millions of sources. Any advanced inhabited planet would probably do the same, transmit like crazy. Since we've been here, the only transmission I've heard from the planet was the reply to the probe's signal." JT paused for breath, looking around to check the others' reactions. The Captain made a motion for him to continue.

"What I'm saying, Captain, is the planet is not inhabited. There may be an alien base on the surface or, more likely, in orbit, but there's no civilization on that world."

"Interesting, thank you JT." The Captain pondered the implications of JT's words for a few seconds and then turned to Yuki. "Dr. Saito, what do you think? Have we failed to contain the alien probe's information or is there still a chance to head it off?"

"I would say we need to assume the information was passed to whatever installation sent the reply signal. In light of the lack of activity from the planet, I would guess that there is a monitoring site on or around the planet, much like the one we destroyed on the Moon."

"And you, Dr Gupta? What are your thoughts?"

"I concur with my colleagues. If this planet is inhabited by the aliens who built the probe and placed it secretly on our Moon then I would have expected a response to our presence in this system. The aliens are obviously capable of traveling between star systems and must have spaceships of their own. Why have they not responded to our invasion of their space?"

The Captain nodded and looking at Gretchen raised his eyebrows. "Lt. Curtis?"

"Sir, I would say we need to investigate more closely. The lack of response from the planet makes me suspect that Rajiv is right— this system probably has a monitoring outpost like our home system did. We haven't detected any other ships like the alien vessel trying to depart the system, have we?"

"No, Gretchen," responded Rajiv, "we would have detected the drive signature of anything similar to the probe we just destroyed."

"So we have an uninhabited planet, probably with a monitoring station nearby and, as far as we can tell, nothing has left the system. In short, the situation may still be contained if we can destroy the local monitoring station."

The assembled advisers all nodded agreement. The Captain pressed his fingers together, their tips pointing upward. Closing his eyes, Jack brought his steepled fingers to just touch his pursed lips, as though he was a child praying. From experience, Gretchen knew this posture as an indication of deep thought—or perhaps he was actually praying for guidance. Uneasy silence pervaded the group. Finally, Jack dropped his hands to the table and cleared his throat.

"Very well. We will proceed to the planet for a closer look. Any other suggestions?"

"Yes, Captain," Rajiv immediately offered. "If I might suggest that we follow a course similar to that which the probe would have followed? I believe that we can detune the reactor grid slightly and produce a signature similar to the one of the alien vessel. That way, if we are detected, the station might think we are the probe."

"Yes, that makes sense. The crew will not be endangered and the ship's performance will be unaffected?"

"Oh no, we will be perfectly safe. And the instant we need full power the grid can be restored."

"And how long will it take us to arrive at the planet? Mr. Taylor?"

JT consulted his tablet. "We are below the local plane of the ecliptic and about one AU away. At 5 Gs and a turnover half way, we can make orbit in a little more than 32 hours."

"Very well. Let's proceed with the mission. Dismissed."

Bridge, Beta Comae System, Day 2

It is astounding how large a solar system is. Though the Folly had just past 30 light-years in a week by slipping through alter-space, it was now faced with a voyage of only eight light minutes that would take more than a day. Still, any previous spacecraft launched by humans would have required months to make the same trip. The crew stood down from general quarters for 24 hours. Now, as the ship drew near the mysterious Earth-like world, the rapid bleating of the klaxon once again summoned all on board to their battle stations.

"Captain, I think you might want to have a look at this," JT called from the navigation console. "Dr. Tropsha and I have been analyzing the planet, looking for signs of an active ecology. There's more going on here than is immediately obvious."

"Something on the big scope? Put it on the forward display," the Captain ordered. The view forward was replace by an image captured by the ship's large telescope, which was capable of nearly Hubble like magnification and clarity. Hanging in front of the bridge was a closeup view of a dun colored planet, with sizable ice caps at either pole. A scattering of small seas were flung haphazardly across the landscape and a few wispy clouds streamed from where moist sea breezes caressed worn mountain ranges.

Ludmilla, who had come to the bridge to help JT present their findings, nodded to the newest member of the science team and continued the explanation. "We are both in agreement—this is a nearly dead world. If there is anything alive down there it must be at the microbial level. There may be bacterial mats in shallow water, perhaps some sponges in the deeps, but nothing large or complex."

"Is there a reason that would be unusual? After all, the right conditions for developing complex life may never have occurred." Jack was spellbound by the desolation sweeping across the projection before him.

"Well, Sir. That's the bitch of it. This world used to be alive, perhaps as thriving with life as Earth."

"What!" Everyone on the bridge was stunned, not least the Captain. "How can you tell?"

"From this," JT's years as a camera man had given him a feel for the dramatic. As he spoke he zoomed the image in and then panned across the coastline of one of the larger seas. Faint lines and faded circular outlines could barely be seen. Concentric traces mostly centered on points near the coast, with linear marks radiating into the interior. Slowly, those viewing the tableau before them deciphered the meaning of those markings.

"My God," Jack said. "Those were cities. With networks of roads or railways connecting them. But now they are all dead—buildings worn to nubs and only a hint of connecting roadways. What in heaven's name happened here?"

"Water used to flow more freely and the climate was once much more Earth-like," Ludmilla replied. "You can tell by the rock strata and erosion patterns. Now there is no visible life, not even vegetation, on land. As near as we can tell, Captain, this planet has been blasted back to the Precambrian stage."

Seeing several blank looks around her, she explained. "On Earth, about 550 million years ago there was a sudden blossoming of multicellular life forms, where previously life had been mostly limited to simple single cell organisms. During the Cambrian Period that followed, life underwent an evolutionary explosion that continues to this day. Despite five major and many minor global extinction events—the worst of which killed off more than 90% of all living creatures—Earth has never been returned to a state where complex organisms vanished. On the planet below such an event seems to have taken place, there are signs of vanished complex life but nothing present today. "

"You're saying someone did this deliberately? Wiped out an entire populated world?" the Captain demanded.

"Not just its civilization, but every living thing more advanced than a bacterium," was Ludmilla's grim reply.

"Could they have done this to themselves? The inhabitants I mean." asked Jo Jo. "From the size of the cities they must have had an advanced, technological civilization. Perhaps this is the end result of a planet wide arms race—nuclear Armageddon."

"If so it must have happened some time ago," answered Ludmilla. "From background radiation levels perhaps 10,000 years, maybe more."

"Perhaps," JT added tersely, as he manipulated the telescope's controls. "I'm more inclined to think it had something to do with that."

The image blurred and refocused on the limb of the planet, where a strange bluish-gray shape was emerging from behind the dun colored crescent. As the bridge crew watched a large, obviously artificial object slowly filled their field of view.

* * * * *

The ship was still several hours from making orbit. Jack called the rest of the science team to the bridge so he could get their opinions first hand. Not that he didn't trust Ludmilla and JT, but he wanted everyone to be in agreement with what he was about to do next.

"It looks like a giant mushroom," said Billy Ray.

"More like a medusa, a giant jellyfish," offered Bobby. "How big is that thing?"

"The cap is about 20 kilometers in diameter and perhaps 5 km thick at the center. The stalk is more than 40 km long," Rajiv supplied.

"Is it alive?" the Captain asked Ludmilla, who was now acting in the role of xenobiologist rather than ship's surgeon.

"No, Captain. As best we can tell, it is a construct. Yuki is being cautious but Rajiv is willing to bet that it was left by those who wiped this world clean. Maybe the same ones who were spying on Earth." Rajiv nodded his agreement with Ludmilla's statement.

Jack had never seen Ludmilla so grim faced. As both a doctor and a biologist, she held life sacred. Just thinking about a race that could kill an entire world both frightened and enraged her.

"Has there been any reaction from the satellite at all? Have we been scanned by radar or other active sensors?"

"No, Sir," answered JT. "Not a peep out of it since the initial response to the probe's signal."

"Again, at the risk of anthropomorphizing something totally alien, that doesn't sound to me like the response of anything living," Jack ventured. "By that I do not mean the satellite, but any crew on the satellite. Could that thing be a robotic station like the one in crater Bruno, granted, on a much bigger scale?"

"It may not be alive," Yuki said. "But there is a great deal of energy being expended inside of that structure. If you notice the orientation of the cap, it would appear to be a giant solar collector."

"Captain?" the voice of the ship's computer inquired. "I may know what purpose the structure serves."

"And what would that be?" Jack asked.

"It is a refueling station."

"What brings you to this conclusion? More newly remembered information from the artifact's memory?"

"Yes, Captain. That and readings from the radiation and particle detectors. The structure's form and its heliocentric orientation are consistent with Dr. Saito's observation. Given the amount of energy being collected it makes little sense for antimatter reactions to be powering the station, yet the unmistakable signature of matter-antimatter annihilation is present. I can only conclude that the station is creating antimatter for later use."

"And the radiation?" Jack inquired.

"Evidently, the process is not all that efficient. Some of the generated fuel is evidently being destroyed during the process."

"Well, if that station is storing a large quantity of antimatter, and given the energetic response of the probe to having a rail gun round breach its storage, this may provide an answer to our dilemma."

The eyes turned to the Captain. "We needed to find the base that received the probe's message, the satellite is most likely that base. Having found the base, we need to destroy it. Unfortunately, that is a damn big satellite. If we emptied our entire magazine into it we might not damage it enough to stop the alien vessel's report. Besides, though it has not responded to our presence, there is no telling what it might do if we started bombarding it. No, I think the best way to proceed is as we did on the Moon—Lt. Curtis!"

"Yes, Captain?"

"Have the Marines and appropriate members of the crew form in the cargo hold. Organize a boarding party—we are going to pay that space station a visit."

Chapter 18

Bridge, Parker's Folly, Approaching The Alien Satellite

The Captain decided to approach the alien satellite on a straight in course, decelerating constantly like the probe ship had been. Jack was hoping to identify a suitable landing or docking area as they drew nearer the huge construct. The shallow convex cap, which appeared to be a translucent cover over top of a dark, multifaceted array, did not offer any obvious entry points, so the ship continued on course to pass under the 20 km in diameter circular collector.

Heading for the long central "stem" of the satellite, a fringe of pipes—perhaps heat exchangers or antennae of some type—could be seen hanging down from the rim of the circular cap. Of seemingly random lengths, some extended for a quarter of a kilometer, though most were less than half that length. Passing well clear of the fringe, Parker's Folly headed for the central spine of the structure—the long stalk looked like it was made up of a bundle of individual columns bound together. Looking up at the huge structure, Billy Ray recited:

> Resignedly beneath the sky
> The melancholy waters lie.
> So blend the turrets and shadows there
> That all seem pendulous in air,
> While from a proud tower in the town,
> Death looks gigantically down.

"What was that?" asked Jolene, sitting behind the helmsmen at one of the weapons stations. "It sounds sort of familiar."

"That'd be Poe," answered Billy Ray, "The City in the Sea."

"I can understand the Captain knowing obscure literary passages," Jolene whispered to Bobby, "but how does Billy Ray know this stuff?" Bobby whispered back, "He has a Master's in English lit. from University of North Texas."

"Yep," Billy Ray said, obviously overhearing them. "Just imagine what old Edgar would have written if he saw yonder space mushroom."

Overhead, the underside of the cap did, in fact, look much like a mushroom, with radial ribs from the cap's rim arching inward to join the top of the central stalk. There the ribs merged into the larger columns that comprised the stalk itself. About four kilometers down the stalk there were two flat, circular plates each roughly three kilometers in diameter. The plates were separated from each other by a gap of 200 meters.

There were no obvious sources of artificial lighting. What light did illuminate the satellite's underside was reflected from the planet below. In that dim light, protuberances of many shapes—spherical, cylindrical, multifaceted prisms—could be seen clustered around the central stalk on top of the upper plate. Similar structures could be seen on the underside of the lower plate—an infrastructure created by alien minds to satisfy alien needs, silent and unfathomable.

Moving slowly beneath the cap and only five kilometers shy of the central stalk, there was still no indication from the satellite where to dock—not a radio beacon, not a blinking light. Jack was as puzzled by the lack of response as the rest of the crew, but had to make a decision anyway. "Helm, head for the gap between the plates. Decelerate to dead slow before moving between them."

"Aye aye, Captain," responded Bobby. Outside the ship's transparent nose the gap was growing larger with each passing second, while the bulk of the satellite's cap loomed overhead. Creeping toward the gap between the plates, the space between the two flat surfaces suddenly lit with a dim blue-green light. Jack shifted to the edge of his seat. "I think that might be a welcoming sign. Edge her in slowly, Mr. Danner. Mr. Vincent be ready on the rail guns, gunner's mates scan for targets. Await my order to fire."

Out of the side of his mouth, Bobby whispered to his friend. "First a probe droid and now the Death Star, I think I know this movie." Without any visible reaction, Billy Ray whispered back, "Death Mushroom, pardner, totally different thing."

The space ahead was mostly uncluttered, flat parallel plains above and below. Closer to the central column there were shapes sticking up from the lower surface, like mounds of hay only with smooth surfaces. From above, similar shapes hung down for maybe five meters—stunted metallic stalactites mirrored by stalagmites on the floor. In the distance directly ahead there was what might be a doorway in the side of the main stalk.

The ship cleared the outer boundary and was now completely between the parallel surfaces of the plates. The ship settled toward the lower plate a bit and bobbled while Bobby fought the controls. "Captain! A weak gravity gradient just switched on. Should I counteract it?"

"Feels like an indication for us to land here, Mr. Danner. Lower the landing struts and ease her onto the deck."

"Aye Sir." A thin sheen of perspiration had formed on Bobby's forehead, a single bead of sweat trickled down the side of his face. With intense concentration, he lowered the ship to the flat surface below, coming to rest with barely a quiver. His hands remained on the controls, ready to catapult the ship back out into space.

The Captain looked around the bridge. Finding all in order he relaxed slightly, discovering that he was holding his breath. *Well, we have definitely arrived somewhere. I guess its time for phase 2.* Over the PA he announced, "Attention all hands, we have landed on the alien satellite. Remain at your action stations and be alert for trouble."

"Cargo Hold, Bridge. Lt. Curtis, ready the boarding party."

"Aye aye, Captain," came Gretchen's reply, the faintest hint of anxiety contending with excitement in her voice. The last time, they were investigating an alien presence on the Moon, practically humanity's own back yard. This time they were on the aliens' turf and they were the trespassers.

Docking Bay, Alien Satellite

Lt. Curtis' boarding party comprised the entire Marine squad, less corpsman White, plus Bear, JT, Yuki and Ivan. Before the last altercation, Col. Kondratov was to be a full participant in any future extravehicular activity. Accordingly, a suit of space armor had been fabricated for him. After discussing the matter with the Captain, it was decided to allow him on the expedition, in armor but without weapons. The Captain had called it one last chance at redemption.

As they set out for the central column and its hoped for way into the core, the boarding party left the Chief and two of the crew, Hitch and Jacobs, standing guard and to act as a relief force if needed. The two spacers were armed and encased in the new space armor. The Chief, who might have to pilot a skiff to aid the boarding party's exfiltration, wore a standard spacesuit, the gauntlets of an armored suit being unsuited for such precision work.

Rajiv had really wanted to go on the mission but the Captain refused to allow the entire science team to venture off the ship into what was most likely hostile territory. What Jack had not added was that, given Rajiv's detailed knowledge of the ship's technology, he could not be allowed to fall into enemy hands.

The local gravity was about 1/8 of Earth normal, which soon had the boarders moving with a combined hopping, skating motion, reminiscent of the first astronauts on the Moon. Moving across the flat surface, it became clear that the haystacks and other intrusions lay in straight lines on either side of the doorway's central axis, leaving the path to the satellite's core unobstructed. They formed radial "hedgerows" that divided the dock area into individual landing bays. As the party closed on the central spire, after crossing a distance of around 800 meters, they could see that what appeared to be a door was in fact an open archway leading to the satellite's interior.

The party halted in front of the opening, 10 meters wide and as high in the middle. The Marines formed a perimeter facing outward while the officers and scientists conferred. The Captain and Dr. Gupta joined the discussion from the ship.

"It looks like this whole structure is left open to space. There are no provisions for maintaining any kind of atmosphere that I can see," Gretchen reported. Other than the lights and gravity coming on when the ship entered the dock, there were no signs of life. The whole place had a spooky, alien feel.

The landing dock was obviously capable of handling craft significantly larger than Folly. If the satellite was a refueling station, as the ship's computer had surmised, there must be a way to get the fuel on board visiting ships. "From the readings we are getting on the ship's sensors, the source of the antimatter

287

generated radiation is inside the central spine and up toward the cap," Rajiv explained.

"Agreed," said JT. Out of long habit, he continued to scan the perimeter while the discussion continued. "Yuki and I were taking readings on the way and we came to the same conclusion. I'm also wondering if, given the size of this place, there isn't another ship or two resting in some other part of the dock."

"I was thinking the same thing, Mr. Taylor," the Captain concurred. "It would be good to check if we are alone."

Always itching to be on the move, Bear offered a suggestion. "Why don't some of us take a look around the dock while the rest go inside looking for the antimatter fuel station?"

"I was thinking the same thing, Lt. Bear," was Gretchen's quick reply. "Bear, JT, why don't you take three of the Marines and do a walk-about? Find out if there are any other interesting vehicles parked here."

"Roger that, Lieutenant."

"Gunny, send three of your people with Lt. Bear. And we'd better leave a couple here to watch the entrance—wouldn't want to be surprised when we come back out."

"Yes, Ma'am." The Gunny turned toward the nearest Marines. As far as she was concerned, this may be a high pucker factor mission but it beat being stuck on board the ship. "Feldman, Reagan, Sanchez, go with Lt. Bear. Sizemore, you and Washington hold the fort here—and keep your eyes open. Davis, Kwan, you're with me."

"OK people, let's move out," Gretchen told the group. "Inside squad shift to frequency net two. Bear, call if you find work." Lt. Bear growled his assent, rose on all fours and rambled away from the opening.

Bear's detachment moved off to the left, starting a clockwise circuit of the dock space with Bear himself on point, followed by JT and the three nervous Marines. Lt. Curtis motioned for her unit to move into the opening. Davis took point, followed by the Gunny, then the Lieutenant, Dr. Saito and Col. Kondratov, with Kwan bringing up the rear.

Sizemore and Washington found themselves alone. The Corporal couldn't decide which was worse, standing around waiting for someone to shoot at you, or going looking for someone to shoot at you. Either way, this place gave him the willies. "You OK, Washington?"

"Yeah, Corp," came Washington's reply. "I just got a bad feeling about this place."

Lt. Curtis' Party, Inside The Satellite's Core

Following PFC Davis, Lt. Curtis' party moved down the arched passageway. For reasons unknown, the passageway was unlit, though a light in the distance could be seen. Using their suits' IR illumination they managed to skirt several large, rectangular pits in the floor of the passageway. A hundred meters down the dark hallway they came to another open doorway, light streaming through from the chamber beyond. Stepping out of the passageway, the squad emerged onto a platform clinging to the side of the satellite's hollow core.

The view that greeted them was on a scale generally reserved for natural wonders—Angel Falls, the Grand Canyon, and other works that challenge human imagination. The central shaft was as wide as the distance they had traveled from the ship to the outer door. The Folly could easily have sailed up the shaft and turned around without coming close to its walls. Lit with the same pallid blue-green light, the cylindrical chamber extended to infinity both above and below. A trick of lighting and perspective, Lt. Curtis knew the ceiling could only extend for four kilometers overhead, while the bottomless pit beneath them might well extend the full thirty five kilometers before emptying into open space.

"Certainly not the place for someone with acrophobia," Ivan remarked. He was no longer as on edge as he had been around Lt. Bear. He was, after all, a cosmonaut, and he was in his element exploring the strange alien space station.

"No, I would say not," Yuki replied. Having spent several months on board the ISS with the Russian officer, he was still willing to converse with Ivan. Gretchen limited her conversation to giving orders. As for the Marines, they avoided casual conversation with officers, especially Russian officers who were on the CO's shit list.

Gretchen stood for a minute, gauntleted hands on armored hips. Once over the spectacle of the giant tunnel in front of them, a quick examination of their surroundings showed but two ways to proceed: to the left a ramp spiraled upward along the tunnel wall, and to the right a similar ramp spiraled downward. "Dr. Saito, you said that the antimatter apparatus was most likely up toward the collector cap?"

"Yes, Lieutenant. The indications were quite clear."

"Then we proceed up the ramp to the left." Gretchen signaled the Gunny to move out. PFC Davis turned and moved onto the ramp and nearly toppled over.

"What's wrong, Two Can?" the Gunny asked, quickly moving forward to steady the Marine. "Whoa!" GySgt Rodriguez exclaimed. "There is something messed up with the gravity here!"

The Lieutenant moved gingerly forward and found that the local gravity field did shift where the ramp met the platform. Evidently the aliens built their gravity generators so that down was normal to the surface they resided in. Meaning that the ramp, which was fairly steep, inclined about 20 degrees when viewed from the platform, was flat to someone standing on it. *Well, at least we don't have to hump up the slope in this heavy armor.*

"There is a transition where the ramp meets the platform as the downward direction changes. Just be careful when walking through it. And be careful of the edge, looks like E.T. isn't into guardrails either. Come on, let's move."

Col. Kondratov stepped from one surface to the next without missing a beat. "Yes, as you said Lieutenant, the direction of down changes. Interesting but not dangerous if you are expecting it."

With the Russian cosmonaut dismissing any danger out of hand, the rest of the party put on brave faces, quickly moved onto the ramp and continued on their way. Gretchen hoped that any other surprises that lay ahead would be as easily over come as this one, but somehow she doubted that would be the case.

Lt. Bear's Party, Searching The Alien Dock.

Keeping the outer wall of the central spire to their right, Lt. Bear's party had moved about a third the way around the circular landing bay. So far, they had sighted nothing of interest. Just scattered clusters of bumps and protruding mounds sticking up from the deck below and hanging down from the roof above. The three Marines had relaxed a bit and were settling into a steady pace.

"This all looks like more of the same," JT commented, more to break the silence than anything else. Bear, who was not used to chatty conversation while out hunting, only grunted. He rounded a particularly large metal haystack and froze in place.

Seeing Bear freeze, JT held up a clenched fist, a signal to the Marines behind him to also stop moving. Using only the short distance suit-to-suit com channel, Bear said, "Looks like we got another one of those probe ships setting on the deck 100 meters from here."

"Is there any movement around the ship?"

"No, wait." Bear suddenly backed up, bumping into JT and almost knocking him over. "Damn it! Watch out," JT swore.

"Sorry, some kind of centipede looking thing came out of the door just ahead. Take a look."

"OK, move out of the way." JT reached for a tab on his belt and then pulled. Out came a thin black fiber-optic cable which he carefully guided around the corner of the haystack. On the heads up display in his helmet, the former Green Beret watched as a multilegged something sped across the deck with a rippling motion. It was headed directly for the probe ship.

The ship resting on the dock floor was a twin of the one they had destroyed less than two days before. The front was a tapered spire that flared into a fat cylindrical midsection. On the other end of the main body was a second tapering cone, longer than the nose section, the craft measuring maybe 40 meters overall. At its tip there was a small circular opening, possibly an exhaust port. Where the aft cone met the cylinder there was an another opening, a rectangular hatch.

As the centipede neared the probe ship more moving shapes appeared from inside the vessel, emerging from the open rectangle. Round bodies with six long legs. Leaving the optical cable in place, JT slid back and turned to face his companions. "Shit! We got spiders."

Lt. Curtis' Party, Inside The Satellite's Core

They followed the spiraling ramp a quarter of a turn around the satellite's hollow core, rising more than 370 meters up the shaft. There they came to another section of horizontal ramp, with another of the annoying changes in local gravity. A short way along the new section there were a series of long rectangular openings in the gently curving shaft wall, each 3.5 meters high and 10 meters long. Lit from within, the openings looked like the open storefronts in a shopping mall.

Through the openings could be seen large rooms filled with egg shaped objects of many different sizes, the smaller ones lining the walls of the rooms in neat rows, the larger ones standing alone in supporting stands upon the floor. "What the hell are those things, Lieutenant?" asked the Gunny, giving voice to the question they all wanted to ask.

"Damned if I know, Gunny. Dr. Saito, do you have an opinion?"

"It is hard to tell without better sensor equipment, but I think those may be storage vessels for the antimatter we seek. Of course they might also be the eggs of the aliens who built this structure."

Great! We have discovered either a fuel dump or an alien nursery, thought Lt. Curtis. "Is there some way to tell the difference, Dr. Saito?"

"Oh yes, if I can place a quantum Hall effect detector on one of them I should be able to detect the presence of antimatter, more precisely the containment field keeping it in place."

"OK, that means we go inside. Everyone take cover back against the shaft wall. Gunny, would you do the honors?"

"Right. Kwan, get up here and provide cover." PFC Kwan had been bringing up the rear of the formation as it advanced. He quickly jogged to the edge of the first door and assumed a kneeling position, weapon at the ready. "OK Davis, move through the door slowly. I'm right behind you."

Two Can moved out in front of the door and gingerly stepped over the threshold. Once fully inside he halted—nothing changed, nothing moved, there were no signs that he had been noticed. Next the Gunny crossed the threshold, drawing up next to the nervous PFC. "OK Two Can, move over to one of the big eggs in the middle."

"Yes, Gunny. But if some alien bug thing jumps out and tries to wrap itself around my faceplate, promise me you'll blast it." Davis half meant the remark as a joke but now everyone was even more on edge, fearing an outbreak of ravaging alien hatchlings.

"Just go touch the fuckin' egg," the Gunny prodded, adding some humor of her own. "If anything grabs you, keep it busy 'til the rest of us get out of here." The Marines knew that they didn't leave their own behind, and the Gunny was old school Marine Corps.

PFC Davis approached the nearest large egg and after an instant's hesitation reached out and laid a gauntleted hand on top its smooth surface. Again, nothing happened.

The rest of the party cautiously moved into the egg storage room and Dr. Saito moved toward Davis' egg with a hockey-puck shaped instrument in his hand. He gently moved Two Can aside and placed the black puck on the surface of the egg. Like a doctor with a stethoscope, Yuki move the instrument to several different locations, pausing as if listening at each.

Stepping back, the physicist stuffed the instrument back into a pouch on his suit. Turning to the others he happily reported his findings. "I am quite certain that these objects are in fact, antimatter storage devices. The different sizes probably are used by different sized ships or other mechanisms. How much each egg contains I cannot tell."

Once the explorers stepped into the egg room it was obvious that it was one big room with three long doors opening onto the pathway outside. As Yuki finished delivering his analysis of the large egg, there was movement at the far end of the chamber. The Marines immediately shouldered their weapons and stepped away from the others for a clearer field of fire. "Hold your fire!" yelled Lt. Curtis, who also moved forward, shielding the others and raising her rail gun.

Along the far wall, a low moving object with a multitude of legs emerged, turned and started along the back wall toward the earthlings. "Don't shoot it unless it attacks us!" For the second time, Gretchen was making contact with aliens. For the second time, contact was being made over the barrel of a gun.

This was not how she had envisioned exploring the galaxy would be. Half way down the back wall, the centipede like creature stopped, then reared up like a cobra preparing to strike.

Chapter 19

Bridge, Parker's Folly, Alien Docking Bay

The boarding party had been gone for almost an hour and the mood on the bridge was tense. Susan was monitoring the communication channels and keeping watch through the optical sensors. The two Marines left to guard the core door could be seen walking around. Every 15 minutes or so they would call in. Unfortunately, the last time Cpl Sizemore reported being out of contact with both Lt. Curtis' and Lt. Bear's parties.

On board the ship, everyone had followed the movement of Lt. Curtis' party through the long passageway and marveled at the view of the satellite's central shaft. But as the expedition moved up the spiral ramp reception began breaking up and was soon lost. Dr. Gupta suggested that the metallic shell of the satellite was blocking the signal. That would explain why the signal from Lt. Bear's squad also faded as they worked their way around the outside of the central stem.

"If we don't get a status report from the squads the next time Cpl. Sizemore calls in I want to send Washington through the tunnel," the Captain told Susan. This was the worst part of being in command—not sending people in harm's way, but the waiting that follows. "Hopefully he will be able to reach Lt. Curtis' party on the inside of the core."

The bridge was down to a skeleton crew, with just Bobby and Billy Ray on the helm and Susan watching the sensors on the navigator's console. Jo Jo was aft keeping a watch on the ship's reactor and engines, which were still producing the alien probe's radiation signature. There weren't any problems so far, but the recently promoted Chief Engineer wanted to be close by if full power was needed.

Rajiv had Freddy Adams with him doing science stuff, so the Captain had pressed Melissa and Jolene into service as gunners on the X-ray batteries. It was fortunate that the ship's offensive weapons all operated like video games, most anyone under 30 was able to work the controls after a few runs through the simulator. Still, the Captain toyed with the idea of calling Hitch and Jacobs back inside to help run the weapons systems.

295

That's what Captain's do, Jack chided himself, *put a plan in place and spend the rest of their time second guessing themselves. What was it that Patton once said? Never take the council of your fears. Well, he also said never tell people how to do things. Tell them what to do, and they will surprise you with their ingenuity.* Somehow, the butterflies in Jack's stomach were not reassured.

Lt. Bear's Party, Alien Probe's Bay

"What are the skinny legged bastards doing now?" Bear growled. His helmet display showed the same scene as JT's, captured by the fiber-optic camera. The centipede thing pulled up in front of the open hatch on the alien craft. Two spiders emerged from inside the probe carrying an egg shaped object between them.

About the size of a soccer ball at its blunt end, the spiders carefully lowered the egg onto the back of the centipede. It grasped the egg with a number of its many legs and, as the spiders stepped away, reversed direction and headed rapidly back the way it came. JT was as puzzled as Bear. "What the hell was that egg thing? They were sure careful with it, maybe it was an alien?"

"It didn't look like anything alive to me," Bear countered. "That's hard vacuum out there, and the temperature is cold enough to freeze air."

"Maybe it's a shell and the alien is inside," ventured LCpl Feldman.

"If it is, they're little fuckers," Bear grunted.

"Uh, Lieutenant?" LCpl Reagan was still trying to overcome his fear of Bear. It isn't everyday that you find yourself being led by a Lieutenant who mauled you a little over a week ago. Nonetheless, Reagan had a high mechanical aptitude—an almost intuitive understanding of machines and devices—and his gearhead passions were getting the better of him. "Lieutenant, I think they are swapping out the probe's fuel cell."

Bear considered this suggestion for a few seconds. "What makes you say that, Reagan?"

"Well, Sir. Notice how carefully the spiders carried the egg? They were obviously afraid to drop it. From what happened to the probe we shot, I would be afraid of breaking it's fuel cell too. And didn't the ship's computer say that this place could be a refueling station?"

"So you're saying they are swapping out fuel containers, like changing out propane cylinders?" JT asked the young Marine. "That makes as much sense as anything else around this place."

"Yes, Sir."

"Good thinking, Reagan," Bear rumbled, he had been reading up on how to motivate humans. It seems that they really enjoy being complimented. Bears were much more basic: you either won a fight or you lost, you ate or were eaten, no compliments needed. He could not ever recall telling a seal, "My but you taste good." He didn't think it would make the seal taste any better and it sure as hell wouldn't mean anything to the dead pinniped. No matter, you travel in the company of monkeys you gotta think like a monkey.

While Bear was reflecting on the differences between men and bears, JT was pondering the implications of Reagan's idea. The centipede thing seemed to be in quite a hurry as it hauled the presumably empty fuel cell away. And the spiders were now just standing there, outside the open hatch. It was like they were waiting for the centipede to return with a new egg, and soon. "Bear, I think we will find out if Reagan's idea is correct shortly."

"Yeah, JT? What makes you say that?"

"The way those spiders are just waiting around the open hatch, like the job isn't done and they expect something else to happen."

Bear considered this remark. Humans were definitely smarter about technological matters, but there was nothing wrong with Bear's reasoning ability. "If they are refueling that probe ship, that means it is probably getting ready to depart. I don't think we want that to happen."

Lt. Curtis' Party, The Alien Egg Room

Every human in the egg room remained frozen in place as the centipede creature laid its upper body against the wall holding the orderly ranks of antimatter eggs. Finding one to its liking, the multilegged automaton insinuated its flat head underneath one of the smaller eggs. With a sinuous ripple of many multijointed legs, the chosen egg was lifted from its resting place and passed down the creature's flat body, eventually coming to rest at the crook of its back.

Having harvested the bounty it sought, the multilegged creature moved away from the shelf. The portion of its body that had rested vertically against the shelf flowed downward onto the floor as the centipede moved rapidly back toward the entrance. Bearing the small egg on its back like a sacred idol held aloft by the arms of its supplicants, the creature departed, destination unknown.

With the departure of the centipede thing Gretchen realized that they couldn't just stand around waiting to be discovered. And they were out of contact with the Captain. *OK, first step is to find out what the others think.* "Dr. Saito, you are fairly sure that these eggs are actually antimatter containers?"

"Yes, Lieutenant. The amount of energy contained in one of these eggs could be immense. A single kilogram of antimatter combined with a kilo of matter would produce an explosion of about 43 megatons."

"And those big eggs could hold ten, twenty times that much," added the Gunny, ending with a low whistle. "That is one egg you do not want to drop!"

"And would you say, Dr. Saito, that humanity might find having a quantity of antimatter useful? For research and such."

"Most definitely. We have only ever been able to create microscopic amounts of antimatter on Earth. Not that we should store such a supply on Earth itself."

"We can worry about the logistics later. Right now we need to reestablish contact with the ship. Gunny, we need a volunteer to go back down the ramp and stand in the tunnel opening to provide a comm relay to the ship."

"Lieutenant," Ivan interrupted. "Let me go. I am quite surefooted in a spacesuit and this way I might contribute something to the mission."

Now what's he up to, was Gretchen's first thought. But she could see no harm in him acting as the relay. "OK, Colonel. You're on. Stay in radio contact and call as soon as you can raise the ship."

"Thank you, Lieutenant," the Russian said as he turned and bounded rapidly back the path they had come. The Gunny leaned closer to Lt. Curtis and said, over the short range suit-to-suit link, "What's with the Ruskie, Lieutenant?" The unspoken question being, is it wise to trust Ivan at all.

"He's unarmed and the worst he can do is bug out back to the ship—that or get himself killed."

* * * * *

"Parker's Folly, this is Col. Kondratov. Do you read me?" Ivan was standing in the center of the passageway entrance leading back to the landing dock. This was the last area they had been in reliable contact with the ship. Ivan's thoughts were racing, how could he turn this situation to his advantage? It was definitely intolerable for these arrogant Americans to return to Earth with a hold full of antimatter. It would shift the global balance of power—but what to do?

"Go ahead Colonel, this is Captain Sutton. We were getting a bit worried back here."

"We are all fine, Captain. We have discovered a large cache of what Dr. Saito thinks are antimatter containers. Lt. Curtis asked me to come back to the inside tunnel entrance to act as a comm relay." Ivan turned the second frequency net back on. "Lt. Curtis, this is Kondratov. I am in contact with the ship..."

* * * * *

After a brief conversation with the Captain and Dr. Gupta, it was decided to send the Chief with a hover sled to haul some of the antimatter eggs back to the ship. At the same time the Chief would bring a load of shaped demolition charges to destroy the remaining alien hoard.

"Captain, it would be helpful if you could send a couple more hands to aid in placing the charges. Turns out that this heavy armor reduces manual dexterity to practically nothing."

"I'll see what we can do, Lieutenant. Anything else we can do for you?"

"No, Captain. Sir, have you heard from Lt. Bear's party?"

"That's a negative. I'm hoping they'll check in soon. We will let you know when the sled embarks."

Lt. Bear's Party, Alien Probe's Bay

"Here's the plan. If that centipede thing returns with another egg, we rush the probe ship. JT and Reagan cover the left flank, Feldman and Sanchez the right. I'm going right up the center." For Bear, this was pretty much the height of tactical planning.

Given the general lack of cover and the 300 feet of open space between their current hiding place and the alien ship, even JT, whose tactical sense was a bit more refined, didn't see much choice. "We'll try to take down the spiders, you see if you can catch that centipede thing and grab the egg," he said in response to Bear's plan of action. "Marines, try not to shoot the egg, we do not want the damn thing blowing up on us. But don't be shy about hammering the ship—the more damage to it the better."

Bear bobbed his head, signaling his agreement. "OK, people. Let's do a weapons check." With that he stood up, rising to his full three meters. In the nearly black armor Bear looked like the shadow of death come to call. Reaching around behind his back on both sides, he slipped his forearms into the special cuffs on his backpack. When he brought his arms forward, each was adorned with an appropriately wicked looking weapon.

In early tests it became clear that Bear was unable to operate his old rail gun when wearing the new space armor. This had given JT an opportunity to indulge his superhero, action film fantasies with regard to weapon design. On Bear's right forearm was a six barreled mini-gun, each barrel being in essence a 5mm flechette rifle. Since firing one of the flechette rifles at more than 1,200 rounds per minute tended to cause barrel meltdowns, higher cyclic rates were problematic. This arrangement allowed sequential firing from all six barrels, keeping the individual rail guns cool and jacking the aggregate firing rate to 6,000 rounds per minute.

Unlike conventional mini-guns, the barrels on Bear's new toy did not rotate. As a consequence, each barrel's aiming point was slightly different from its brothers. But since the whole idea was to create a sort of "fire hose of death," the lack of pinpoint aiming accuracy was not missed. To feed the six ravenous rail guns a flexible ammo feed snaked back to the pack on Bear's broad back. Standard load was 12,000 of the 5 gram flechettes.

Not wanting Bear to be unbalanced, JT created a second weapon for the Lieutenant's left forearm. This one had only three barrels, but they were all 20mm grenade launchers. Between the three launchers the cyclic rate was near 1,000 rounds per minute. It too, was fed through a belt from the ursine Lieutenant's backpack. Because of the greater weight and bulk of the 20mm HE projectiles, Bear could only carry 500 of those.

Operating in an airless environment, the HE explosives were not run of the mill terrestrial stuff either. Most earthbound explosives depended on consuming oxygen from the surrounding air for complete combustion. In space there is no excess oxygen available. Because of this, all the crew's weapons used an advanced nano-engineered material that combined both explosive and oxidant in the same, stable molecules. A side benefit was that, weight for weight, the nano explosive yielded 4-5 times the energy of conventional explosives. All up, Bear was carrying close to 120 kg of ordnance—and unlike conventional, chemically propelled rounds, all of it could be sent down range.

"You know, brother Bear," JT remarked to the giant black figure looming above him. "I doubt the aliens are even going to notice the rest of us."

On suit-to-suit Feldman said to Sanchez, "You know, Joey, it does sort of make a man feel a little inadequate." To which Sanchez replied, "It ain't what you have, Bro, it's what you do with it."

Lt. Curtis' Party, The Alien Egg Room

Lt. Curtis had Yuki pick the eggs to be transported back to the ship. The physicist chose two of the largest containers, each massing an estimated 250 kilos. He also added a half dozen of the smaller eggs. "To experiment on before tackling the big ones," he explained.

Gretchen and the Gunny moved out onto the ramp to greet the arriving hover sled. To her surprise, Susan and Tommy Wendover, both wearing standard spacesuits, hopped off the sled when the Chief slowed to a stop in front of the first open doorway. The Chief also dismounted after settling the sled on the ramp surface. "Chief Zackly, reporting to the expedition commander with a party of three," the weathered old boatswain barked, throwing Lt. Curtis a crisp salute.

Gretchen returned the salute and said, "Chief, I don't know if that clear helmet counts as cover." Cover is navy speak for a hat, Navy personnel generally don't salute when they are not wearing cover. "Wearing cover or underarms, Lieutenant," the little chief smiled, patting the pistol on his waste. "Or when reporting to the CO." Clearly, the Chief was having the time of his life.

Col. Kondratov dismounted without trouble if a bit less gracefully. "I'm thankful that your Chief stopped to pick me up. Otherwise I would have had to hike all the way back up here."

Stepping within suit-to-suit range, the Chief said to Lt. Curtis, "If I had knowed it was the Ruskie I'd have left him standing with his thumb out." It was all Gretchen could do to suppress an un-commanderly snicker. Instead, over the squad frequency she said, "thank you for making the trip down and back, Colonel."

"Wendover and Miss Susan, grab those bags of demo charges," the Chief ordered over the squad channel. He had evidently taken to calling Susan by the same pet name that JT used for the lady reporter.

"I'm still wondering what you are doing here Susan," Lt. Curtis said, as the newcomers unloaded the skiff. "Or for that matter young Wendover."

Turning to face the imposing bulk that was Lt. Curtis' armor encased figure, Susan explained. "I was on the comm when your request for some additional hands came through. The Captain talked to the Chief, who said the only spare personnel he had was the 'stowaway shitbird.'" Susan, head clearly visible within the standard suit's fishbowl helmet, motioned in the direction of Tommy Wendover. "So I volunteered," she finished with a bright smile.

"Susan, this is a very hazardous mission," Gretchen began.

"Gretchen, I mean Lieutenant, I understand the risk. I'm tired of people thinking that I'm just some frivolous air-head reporter who can't contribute to the mission." The look in her eyes was both determined and pleading.

"Very well, Miss Write. We need to rig these egg things for demolition, and I mean right now." Inside of her armor, Gretchen slowly shook her head, Susan really had no place being here, deep in alien country and in a normal suit that was not up to the rigors of combat. But then, they had a mission to accomplish. Over the squad net she ordered, "All right people, let's get this place ready to blow. Kwan, Davis, assist Dr. Saito in getting the chosen eggs loaded on the sled."

Tommy was visibly hurt by Susan referring to him as the 'stowaway shitbird' but Col Kondratov moved in smoothly to calm the waters. "Come Tommy, I'll show you what to do," he said, hustling the ex-stowaway and his sack of explosives inside the egg room.

* * * * *

As the pair moved to the far side of the egg room, outside of suit-to-suit contact with the others, Ivan said to Tommy, "Quick, give me a couple of the demo charges and a detonator."

"What for, Colonel?" the befuddled young man asked. "What are these things we are supposed to be blowing up?"

"Just fuel containers, do not worry. I have a plan to set things right." Ivan spoke with conspiratorial urgency. Then, with venom in his voice, "You want to see justice done, don't you, Tommy? The Captain, these other arrogant asses punished?"

"Yeah sure, Col. Kondratov," Tommy said, surreptitiously handing Ivan a couple of the shaped charges and a detonator. As far as Tommy was concerned, anything that messed with the crew was OK with him.

Chapter 20

Lt. Bear's Party, Alien Probe's Bay

Bear, JT and the Marines were sheltered behind the metal mounds of the hedgerow lining the side of the probe's landing bay. Since he needed all four legs to run at a respectable rate, Bear had re-holstered his weapons. The *Homo sapiens*, being bipedal, were able to run flat out with weapons at the ready, one of the few things the Lieutenant envied about his human companions.

Sanchez was the first to spot the returning centipede. "Yo, we got a centipede carrying an egg at three o'clock, headed for the probe."

"Is it the same one?" asked Reagan.

"How should I know? They all look alike to me."

"Get ready," Bear ordered, as he gauged the centipede's speed and direction, mentally calculating an intercept course. "Now! Go, go, go!"

The four humans sprang from hiding, spreading out and making tracks toward the alien vessel. Bear lagged behind, his armor encased paws finding little purchase on the metal deck of the landing dock. The humans had covered half the 100 meters to the probe before Bear managed to accelerate his not inconsiderable mass to a full gallop. On Earth, an *Ursus maritimus* can run at 40 kph, near 50 in a short burst. Under low G conditions and wrapped in heavy armor, Bear was not moving that fast, but still making about twice the speed of the Marines as he overtook them.

There were four spiders visible outside the probe, two at the open hatch, one near the rear and another one forward along the vessel's fat midsection. They showed no signs of recognizing the charging squad of earthlings as a threat when Bear, closing to within 10 meters of the racing centipede, launched himself at his quarry in a low dive. As Bear went airborne, JT shouted, "Take 'em out!"

The Marines pulled up, dropped to kneeling positions and hit the two outlying spiders with flechette bursts. JT, firing on the run, took down both the spiders at the door. Meanwhile, Bear landed on top of the moving centipede, trying to grab the egg off its back.

Encased in armor, and with no claws to grasp his intended prey, Bear's attempt to grab the egg instead sent it skittering across the deck in the direction of the probe's open hatch. The centipede reacted to the loss of its payload by wrapping itself around Bear's left front leg and trying to bite him with a pair of previously hidden mandibles.

A fifth spider emerged from the dark hatch and moved to pick up the sliding, spinning egg. The hexapod creature managed to stop the egg and was in the process of lifting it off the deck with three of its six legs. JT, who had not stopped running while shooting at the spiders, yelled, "don't fire on the egg!"

Running at full tilt, JT smashed into the egg juggling spider. Letting his rail gun dangle from its carry strap, he wrenched the egg from the spider's grasp, breaking off one of the spider's legs in the process. The egg's smooth surface provided as little purchase for JT's armored mitts as it had for Bear. It slid from his arms to the dock's surface.

JT crouched down to recover the egg, now laying at his feet. The injured, but not disabled, spider scuttled forward with undoubtedly the same goal. Cradling the egg in his right arm, JT rose up from his crouch, swinging his armored left arm with all his strength in an arc from the deck to connect with the charging spider's spherical metal body.

At impact, JT felt the spider's shell crumple where armor met metal. The force of the blow sent the spider flying in a high arc that peaked about 20 meters above the deck. Feldman, who was an avid skeet shooter, could not resist the perfectly presented target— he hit the spider dead on with a shotgun round from his 20mm. The alien's body underwent what a NASA spokesman once euphemistically called "energetic dissociation," with legs and other body parts flying in all directions.

"Nice shot," JT called. He was waiting for the stiffness caused by his armor's impact sensing under-sheathing to lessen so he could transfer the egg to his left arm. Bear was finishing off the centipede by the simple expedient of smashing it repeatedly against the deck. Legs and body segments flew as the last coil of the beast parted. "Nasty little shit," Bear commented to no one in particular. Then, turning to JT, he added, "and you're stealing my moves, primate."

"Not bad for a green beanie," Feldman quipped, "could you wait until I call 'pull' next time?" The rest of the squad was scanning for more targets but nothing presented itself.

"Hey Lieutenant," JT called, moving the egg to his once again mobile left arm and reclaiming his weapon with his right. "How about putting a good long burst of HE into that hatch?"

"Thought you'd never ask," Bear said, rising on two legs and drawing his triple-barreled grenade launcher. He fired a two second burst through the open hatch, sending 34 explosive rounds, each twice as powerful as a conventional 40mm grenade, into the alien ship's gut. A series of bright flashes followed, accompanied by ejected debris and a gout of flame from the opening at the tip of the probe's slender tail. "Damn, that's satisfying."

"Oh shit. I think you just kicked over the hornet's nest, Lieutenant," Sanchez said, as multilegged shapes began appearing along both hedgerows surrounding the bay.

Lt. Curtis' Party, The Alien Egg Room

The boarding party's booty of antimatter eggs had been loaded on the hover sled, which was now pointing toward the spiral ramp leading back to the exit. The last of the shaped charges were emplaced and all of the party save Susan and PFC Davis had exited the pillaged egg room.

"Come on people," Lt. Curtis told the squad, "we need to exfiltrate this place now." Susan picked up the explosives satchel, now empty except for a couple of manual detonators. "Coming," she called. In front of her, Two Can bent over to retrieve the other satchel. As he did, his torso crossed the threshold of the egg room—his head and shoulders outside, the rest still within the antimatter repository.

A pale blue luminous plane snapped into existence across the egg room threshold. Where PFC Davis' body intersected that plane a cascade of sparks appeared showering the floor and ramp beneath the Marine. In low G slow motion, Two Can's upper body fell, coming to rest on the ramp. Carried forward by momentum, his lower body fell into the flickering blue barrier, causing the Marine's trunk to flair brightly. When the pyrotechnic display abated all that was left inside the barrier were his legs. Susan ran forward, toward the fallen Marine.

"Susan, stop!" Lt. Curtis commanded. The horrified reporter pulled up at the last moment. "Do not even think of touching the blue energy barrier." It had just vaporized about a third of PFC Davis and he was wearing refractory armor. In a standard suit, Susan would disappear in a flash and a puff of smoke.

"Son of a bitch!" Gunny Rodriguez was kneeling next to Davis' severed upper body. The heat of the energy shield slicing the Marine in half had cauterized the exposed flesh and organs in Two Can's chest. Even so, small bubbles could be seen on the charred tissue where remaining body fluids boiled off into the surrounding vacuum. The Gunny placed her hand on top of Davis' helmet, like a priest bestowing a blessing, and softly repeated, "son of a bitch."

"Step back, Susan. We will see if we can blast you out of there," Gretchen ordered. She turned to the rest of the squad. "Chief, we need to get the sled away from the doorway. In fact, Yuki, Col. Kondratov and Wendover, get on board and head out. Gunny, you, Kwan and myself will try to breach the door once the cargo is safely out of here."

"Got it. Kwan, give me a hand with Davis." The Gunny took what remained of Davis by one arm while Kwan took the other and loaded the grisly remains onto the hover sled.

"What are you doing!" shrieked Wendover, almost jumping out of the skiff to avoid contact with Davis' body. In a low dangerous voice, the Gunny said, "He was a Marine. Marines don't leave anyone behind."

"And we still have a crew member trapped," Lt. Curtis interjected, before one of the remaining Marines shot Wendover on general principle. "Chief, head for the ship. We'll follow as soon as we can."

"Aye aye, Lieutenant. Yous better hang on back there 'cause we're casting off." With that, the hover sled sped silently away, headed for the spiral ramp back to the tunnel entrance.

"Try shooting around the edges of the doorway, see if we can disrupt the mechanism making the force shield," Gretchen ordered. She and the Gunny both shot the door frame using flechettes with no visible effect. "Damn, no good."

"Susan, find some cover. We are going to try HE rounds." The Lieutenant and the two Marines stepped back from the door opening and let fly with a single HE round apiece. Bright flashes followed, but the only lasting results were scorch marks on the station wall. Gretchen went to full auto and sent the remaining six grenades in her weapon to the same spot at the far upper corner of the doorway, with much the same result.

"Damn. Now what, LT?" asked the Gunny. Before Gretchen could reply a bright bolt of red-orange flame splashed off the wall above their heads. "Where the hell did that come from?"

"Out there, Gunny," Kwan answered, pointing to an approaching formation of four small flying objects. As he spoke two of the objects fired plasma bolts in their general direction. The Gunny took a knee and said to Kwan, "Aimed fire, short bursts. Take 'em out."

As the Marines concentrated on picking off their flying assailants, Gretchen crouched down and spoke to Susan. "Susan, we are taking fire and and our weapons aren't making a dent in the wall."

"How about one of the demolition charges? I could stick it on the roof at the edge of the door?" Susan asked hopefully. Gretchen could see the pleading in her eyes.

"I'm afraid they are all rigged to the same detonator frequency. If you tried to set one off the rest would go as well. Even if they were not linked, the blast would probably set the others off, if it didn't kill you outright." Then, hating herself as she said it, "Susan, we can't get you out of there."

Lt. Bear's Party, Between Hedgerows

"Follow Me," Bear shouted, heading back toward the hedgerow they had launched their initial attack from. "We are going back to the ship on as straight a path as we can." Following Bear, JT was running with the egg tucked in the crook of his left arm like an NFL running back following a blocker. He had been about to suggest bounding overwatch, but follow the bear worked too. "Come on, Marines! Follow the four legged bullet sponge," he yelled.

The rest of the squad needed no more encouragement, they fell in behind the bounding Bear. As they neared the hedge row, one of the large haystacks split open and a large creature of a type they had not seen emerged. Larger than Bear, the thing had a flattened metal lozenge for a main body and six legs. Unlike the spiders, whose legs were attached to the top of their spherical bodies, this critter's legs sprouted from its smooth metallic sides. Also unlike the spiders, the legs basically consisted of two pieces: a thick pipe-like portion that angled up and out from the main body and then a flattened, curving lower portion that connected to the pipe at the top and arced to a point at the ground.

The creature clumsily moved forward, its own legs interfering with each other—clearly it would move more effectively scuttling sideways like a crab. In fact, the overall effect was very crablike, including the two protruding stalks on the front of the thing's body that ended in what could be eyes. The whole crab motif was broken, however, when its underside opened and a very large plasma cannon oozed out.

"Crap!" Bear barked, slowing his forward travel by sitting down. Bear's armored ass threw sparks along the deck as he reached for his grenade launcher. The first burst rocked the crab thing back, exposing its underside. The second burst struck the area around the plasma cannon, blowing the crab into several sizable pieces.

While Bear was taking care of the crab, the human squad members were picking off the spiders swarming out from between the smaller haystacks of the hedgerow in front of them. Sanchez looked back toward the probe ship and yelled, "We got about twenty spiders and another one of those crab things coming behind us."

"That ain't all, Joey," Reagan added. "they're coming down from the overhead too." JT looked up and saw that the Marine was right—a half dozen spiders were drifting down from the ceiling. "Move it, brother Bear. We gotta break through the hedgerow or we are going to be overrun."

Chief's Skiff, Bottom of the Spiral Ramp

The Chief was pushing the hover sled as fast as he could down the spiral ramp, hugging the curving wall of the station's inner shaft. Like a bobsled at the limit of adhesion, the side of the sled occasionally glanced off the station wall. Sitting next to the Chief up front, Dr. Saito was holding on with both hands, his features obscured by his suit's armored helmet.

In the rear, behind the cargo of stolen antimatter and PFC Davis' truncated remains, Col. Kondratov and Tommy Wendover were similarly holding on for dear life. Tommy was on the left, the side facing the open shaft, his face ashen and his eyes tightly shut. The Colonel looked past him with mild disgust.

Kondratov's fighter pilot trained eyes picked up a formation of moving objects against the stationary background of the central shaft. Each of the objects produced a bright speck of light, which slowly grew larger. "*Oi blin!* We are being fired on!"

"What's that?" the Chief shouted. His question was answered by a plasma bolt that splashed red-orange fire across the wall just in front of the speeding sled. "Shit! Hold on, we're almost to the lower landing."

More bolts were on their way. Ivan fixated on one in particular. Fighter pilots are a superstitious lot and among their tribal lore is the *golden bb*—a one in a million shot that takes out your plane, and you with it. Well there it was, a golden ball of light coming straight for him. Just before the bb arrived, Ivan grabbed Tommy and pulled him in front of his body as a shield.

The bolt struck Tommy's suit square in the backpack, its sun hot plasma burning through fabric and metal and then eating into flesh and bone. Tommy's eyes widened in pain, but the shock of the impact gave him no time to cry out. The fireball consumed most of the major organs in Tommy's body but did not burn through the front of his suit—Ivan was untouched.

Crystals of ice and freeze dried blood streamed from the young man's corpse. As his face began to distort in the vacuum, frost formed on the inside of his helmet, sparing Col. Kondratov a final view of the man he had just murdered. Easing Tommy's plasma eviscerated body down beside the alien antimatter eggs, Ivan glanced forward. Neither the Chief, who was busy flying the sled, nor Yuki, who was hunkered down and hanging on for dear life, had noticed Tommy's heroic but involuntary last act.

"Tommy's been hit," Ivan called out. Then, finding Davis' rail gun lying next to his remains, picked the weapon up and shouted, "I'm returning fire!" Firing offhanded while still clinging to the sled's side rail, Ivan hit nothing, but the attacking aliens broke off and circled around for another pass. Before they returned the sled bounced onto the horizontal platform, skidded sideways and disappeared into the dark tunnel leading back to the ship.

Lt. Curtis' Party, Outside of the Egg Room

Bright light flashed and flickered around Lt. Curtis' diminished party. The two Marines continued to calmly pick off their flying tormentors, but as quickly as the attacking creatures were destroyed new ones took their place. It was only a matter of time before one of the aliens scored a lucky shot. Gretchen knew this but was having a hard time leaving Susan.

Susan appeared to be going into shock, her face pale and withdrawn. Gretchen was kneeling just outside of the shimmering blue curtain of energy that held Susan trapped within the antimatter storage room. "Look, when we get to the bottom of the landing I'll ask the Captain to send reinforcements, maybe a cutting laser or something." Gretchen knew it was a lie as she said it. Once out, there was no way they were coming back inside the station core.

A plasma bolt struck the deck to Gretchen's right, sending a wave of sparks and flame swirling around the Lieutenant's armored figure. The Gunny turned away from the flying menace and sent a long burst along the platform, the green balls of tracer light contrasting festively with the red-orange glow of the plasma bolts. "Shit! Lieutenant, we got spiders on the ramp. We gotta move."

Susan looked up at Gretchen and her eyes focused. "OK" she said, holding up one of the manual detonators. "Tell me how this works."

"What do you mean?"

"How long is the timer set for?"

"There's about 35 minutes left."

"The aliens are coming and you have to go. What if they break in and remove all the explosives before they go off? I'm not getting out, and I sure as hell don't want my death to mean nothing. Tell me how to set the explosives off manually, in case they try to come in after me."

"Susan..." Gretchen began.

"Gretchen, we don't have time! Tell me how to work the fucking detonator!"

"OK, it's simple." The manual detonator was shaped like a single hand grip from a jump rope or a hand exerciser. There was a long, rectangular button down the front of the grip and a single round button sticking up from the top. "Squeeze the grip, holding the long button down. This activates the explosive charges. It will take a few seconds for them all to become ready, when they are you will see a small red light on each of them. Then, use your thumb to press the top button."

"That's it?"

"That's it."

"OK, get out of here, save yourselves. I don't want your lives on my conscience. And Gretchen..."

"Yes?" She said, standing up and checking her weapon.

"Tell Billy Ray that..." Another near miss sent sparks and gobs of molten metal in all directions. Gretchen ducked reflexively and then shouted, "tell him what?"

"Forget it, just go!" With that Susan turned and ran back into the interior of the egg room, disappearing behind the freestanding racks of large eggs. Gretchen stared after her friend for a few moments, tears welling in her eyes. *Oh Susan, who would have thought you were so brave?*

Gretchen shook the tears from her eyes and turned to the Marines. "OK, we need to get out of here, at the double."

Lt. Bear's Party, In the Hedgerows

Bear and party had just cleared their third hedgerow when they stopped to try contacting the ship and check their bearings. The aliens continued to swarm toward them from all directions, mostly spiders but also the larger and harder to kill crabs. If this kept up much longer they would start running short on ammo, grenades in particular.

"By my count, we have one more row to cross and we should be in the docking bay where the ship is," JT said. He was beginning to wonder why he had hung on to the damn egg. "Reagan, rig up a sling for this egg thing, so I can carry it on my back. I've got a feeling I'm going to need both arms free before this is over."

"No problem, JT." Reagan pulled out one of the large sample bags they each carried and slipped the egg inside. Then he moved behind JT and began attaching the bag's straps to tie down points on his backpack. "Just don't get hit, this thing could take out most of the landing dock."

"Parker's Folly, this is Bear. Come in."

"Go ahead, Lt. Bear. We were getting worried."

"Be worried. We got about 100 spiders and some even nastier things chasing us. They're probably pissed off because JT stole the fuel cell from one of their probe ships."

"Say again, you have a probe ship fuel cell? You found another probe?"

"That's affirmative. Of course, they might be pissed because we blew the shit out of the ship when JT nabbed the fuel container."

A pause. "Where are you? How fast can you get back here?"

"We are about to break through the hedgerow off the ship's port side, about halfway between the ship and the central column. Be aware, when we do all sorts of hell is going to break loose."

"Roger that. We are just now receiving a report from Lt. Curtis' party. They are headed this way and are under heavy attack. Wait one, Bear."

"Now what?" Feldman asked.

"Bear, Parker's Folly."

"Go Parker's Folly."

"Move into position between the ship and the central column and be ready to provide cover fire for Lt. Curtis' returning party. The Chief's sled is about to come out of the tunnel with wounded and more fuel cells, over."

"Roger that, Folly. We are on the way." Switching to the squad's frequency Bear rumbled. "OK boys, let's go before Lt. Curtis kills all of the bugs and we are left standing around with our dicks in our paws."

A pair of spiders came out of the hedgerow behind the squad. Feldman and Sanchez quickly put them down with short bursts of 5mm. "We're supposed to cover them," Feldman said to Sanchez on suit-to-suit, "who's going to cover us?"

Chapter 21

Bridge, Parker's Folly, Alien Docking Bay

The Captain had just signed off with Lt. Bear when Chief Zackly called from the returning hover sled. "Folly, this is the Chief Zackly in the skiff. We're almost out of the tunnel and headed for the ship with three souls on board, two KIA and a shit pot full of antimatter eggs."

"We read you, Chief. Where are the others?" Jack had not heard from Lt. Curtis since sending the Chief's party to help retrieve the antimatter and rig the station for destruction. The only update the ship received was the unwelcome news that Lt. Bear's party was under attack.

"They should be close behind, Captain. We started takin' fire from assorted bug nasties and the LT told us to head back ahead of them."

"Roger. Be aware that Lt. Bear and company will be coming out of the hedgerow on your starboard side. They have also been under attack by alien entities." *Damn, this whole operation is starting to head south. You have too many balls in the air,* Jack scolded himself, *what ever happened to Keep It Simple Stupid?*

"Aye, Captain. We'll be along side in five minutes."

Jack looked forward through the ship's transparent bow in time to see the Chief's hover sled burst from the core tunnel opening, accompanied by bolts of plasma fire. "Ms. Hamilton, Ms. Betts, make ready to fire on the aliens pursuing our boarding party. Do not fire until I give the word."

"Yes, I mean aye aye, Captain," Jolene replied nervously. "How do we identify the aliens?"

"They look like large metal spiders and will be shooting orange bolts of fire at us." *I have untrained people about to provide supporting fire using gigajoule X-ray lasers. Luda's first impression was right, I must be insane.*

On the Moon the enemy was farther away and clearly separated from our own people, plus that was in the open. Here we are boxed up in the docking bay, surrounded on all sides by metal that could scatter and reflect the laser radiation. As soon as the boarding party is back on board we will sterilize this place, but right now the last thing I want is to irradiate half of the ship's complement.

"Engineering, Bridge. Mr. Medina, bring the reactors back to full operational capacity and make the engines ready for departure."

"Aye aye, Sir."

"Helm, be prepared to back Folly out of here as soon as we recover the boarding party. Mr. Vincent, we may need a few rounds from the forward battery to cover our egress."

The Boarding Party, Alien Docking Bay

As the hover sled exited the dark tunnel, Col. Kondratov was still laying down suppressing fire. Glowing bolts of plasma flew by on both sides of the speeding skiff, while Ivan's fire, the tracer rounds glowing like green flares from a roman candle, provided no noticeable deterrent to the alien attack. Still, since Tommy was killed the aliens had not managed to hit the fleeing sled. "Not the best of shots, are they?" Kondratov commented.

"I think that they are trying to avoid hitting the eggs, Colonel," Yuki answered. "If they breach one of the large ones the entire station will be destroyed."

"Keep yer heads down," the Chief snapped, jinking the skiff from side to side as fiery orange death rained down from above. "We're almost home free."

* * * * *

Sizemore and Washington, crouched down on either side of the tunnel opening, saw the hover sled flash by, accompanied by attendant plasma bolts. Following the speeding skiff, three stubby bodied flying aliens emerged, long plasma cannon snouts ablaze. "Take those flying things out, Washington," Cpl. Sizemore ordered, himself loosing a long burst of flechettes at the nearest of the rapidly receding creatures.

Washington was forced to wait until the skiff cleared his line of fire. Then he too blasted away at the flying hostiles. His target came apart under repeated impacts by 5mm tungsten-steel

317

flechettes traveling at 4,000 fps. His feeling of triumph was short lived as a score of spindly legged metal spiders entered the bay from the hedgerow to his left. "Corp! We got spiders on the left."

Sizemore finished off his second flying target and looked right. "I hear ya. They're coming from the right too."

* * * * *

As Bear's party broke through the last hedgerow between themselves and the ship's docking bay, they saw the Chief's skiff speed by. They also saw a phalanx of spiders moving into the bay on either side of them. "Hose 'em down!" Bear growled, unlimbering his flechette mini-gun.

Sanchez and Feldman on the squad's left, sent quick aimed bursts into the mob of six legged critters between their position and the central column. Between them and Sizemore, they had the spiders in a crossfire. JT and Reagan did likewise on the right, where the two crewmen who had been standing guard outside the port cargo door were also engaging the massed formation of spiders.

Seeing that the spiders coming from the nearside hedgerow were being neutralized, Bear concentrated on the far hedgerow. He fired a long burst, slowly sweeping his foreleg from left to right. The mini-gun's impact point moved in a continuous arc from the hedgerow wall near Washington to a point just off the ship's starboard bow. Over two thousand flechettes, every fifth one a bright green tracer, cut down the advancing spiders like a scythe cutting wheat. "The fire hose of death," he chuckled. "Hey JT, I really like this gun!"

"I'm happy that you're happy," the ex-green beret turned weapon's designer replied. "Now make us all happy and kill something, a lot of somethings."

"With pleasure." Hidden by his helmet, Bear wore an expression of pure feral joy.

* * * * *

As the rest of the boarding party was engaged in thinning the ranks of alien combatants, Gretchen, Kwan and the Gunny were arriving at the tunnel's inner platform. Making the awkward

318

transition from the spiral pathway to the platform the Gunny stumbled, rolled and ended back on her feet. *I couldn't have done that if I had planned it,* she said to herself.

Gretchen, whose transition was not nearly as spectacular as the Gunny's, reached out and steadied PFC Kwan, who had also stumbled but not fallen in the changing gravity field. "Inside the tunnel mouth," she ordered. "Then we'll pause for a minute while I check with the ship and find out what we will face when we get back to the docking bay."

The two Marines moved quickly to comply. Though the gravity was light, running in the bulky armor was tiring. Without being asked, their suits' environmental units had boosted the oxygen levels in the air they were breathing and stepped up CO_2 removal. Even so, it was not enough to keep the three from becoming winded. "Folly, Lt. Curtis," the Lieutenant called between panting breaths.

"Lt. Curtis, Folly. What is your location and status?"

"We are just entering the tunnel back to the docking bay. We've been under attack since we left the egg room. Interrogative the Chief's status?" Fumbling because of adrenalin and her suit's heavy gauntlets, Gretchen began loading more HE rounds into her launcher.

"The sled is coming along side now. Be advised that the docking bay is being inundated by alien creatures. Lt. Bear's squad and the rest of the boarding party are holding them off, but I would suggest you hasten your return."

"Roger that, Folly. We are on the way." Gretchen, who had dropped down on one knee while catching her breath and reloading, stood and told her companions, "come on Marines, we need to haul ass!"

Parker's Folly, Cargo Hold, Port Side Door

"Belay that fire, you deck monkeys!" the Chief called to Hitch and Jacobs. "I'm going to fly the skiff into the cargo hold." As he spoke he circled the hover sled to the right, swinging its tail wide to point the craft back in the direction they came from.

"Aw, Chief. We wasn't going to hit you," complained Hitch. "The Captain said we was to give you covering fire."

"Like I trust yous with loaded weapons," the Chief shot back. He then raised the heavily burdened sled so it could clear the cargo door's threshold and slipped sideways into the hold. "So now what are you waiting for? Help keep those bug things off the Marines!"

As the two crewmen resumed firing at the milling mass of spiders, inside the cargo hold the Chief grounded the sled well way from the door. "All right, everyone out of the boat." Noticing corpsman White standing by with a gurney next to the lift, the old boatswain motioned for the medic to come forward. "We ain't got any live one's for you Petty Officer, but we have some remains you might want to remove before the rest of 'em get back."

"OK, Chief," Betty answered, moving the gurney forward. With some trepidation she asked, "who are they?"

"The Marine called Two Can and that Wendover kid," the Chief said. Then, seeing the pain in the corpsman's eyes, he added, "Sorry about your squad mate. If it's worth anything he died quick. Come on, I'll help you load 'em."

The Chief, Yuki and Col. Kondratov all helped to place the remains of the two men, such as they were, on the medical gurney. The gurney floated frictionless above the deck, suspend much like a hover sled. Without a word, Betty pushed the gurney with its grisly cargo to the lift, rose to mid-deck level and into the airlock leading to the medical section.

Standing arms akimbo, Chief Zackly watched her go. Shaking his head sadly he turned to Dr. Saito and Col. Kondratov, menacing hulks in their black armor. "Gentlemen, I'll take those weapons if you please. In a few minutes there will be enough people waving live weapons around in here without adding a couple more."

"Certainly, Chief," replied Yuki, handing him the rail gun. After a moment's hesitation, Ivan also complied. "Should we exit the hold?"

"Negative, stand to. Don't want the airlocks tied up as you cycle through. Besides, we might need some extra hands when the rest come back on board."

The Boarding Party, Alien Docking Bay

The scene that greeted Lt. Curtis and her companions as they exited the tunnel was pure pandemonium. Gouts of flaming plasma shot in all directions, showers of sparks and molten metal spewed where they impacted the deck. The red-orange alien plasma was interlaced with the green stitching of return fire from Lt. Bear's party, who were hunkered down in the middle of the docking bay.

Closer by, Washington and Sizemore were also firing on the aliens, trying to keep them from blocking the tunnel entrance. "We're coming out!" Gretchen yelled over the squad frequency, as the three tardy expedition members pounded out of the tunnel and headed for the ship.

On the left, Washington headed for Bear's squad and the saftey of the ship beyond. On the right, Cpl. Sizemore turned toward them and raised a hand signaling recognition. The Gunny waved back just moments before a gigantic crab shaped alien dropped on top of Sizemore from overhead. "What the fuck is that!" the Gunny shouted, raising her weapon and firing a short burst of 5mm at the crab-thing. Seeing her rounds ricocheting in all directions, she stopped firing, afraid of hitting Sizemore.

Beneath the crab, Sizemore managed to roll over onto his back. The looming metal monster raised a heavy front leg and brought it down like a spear on top of the helpless Marine. The Corporal's armor shell went rigid under the impact and the pointed end of the crab's leg slid off without doing any harm. The creature made repeated attempts to skewer the man pinned beneath it, to no effect. The crab-thing went to plan B.

Underneath the crab, Cpl. Sizemore was trying to bring his weapon to bear on his oversized assailant, lucky that the weapon had not been torn from his grasp when the alien tried to make a Marine-kabob out of him. The crab lifted its body above the trapped Marine, gaining clearance so its carapace could open. From the opening in its underside a large plasma cannon extruded. Seeing the emerging muzzle aimed at his head, Sizemore finally managed to raise his rail gun into firing position. Selecting HE, full auto, Sizemore pulled the trigger, repeating "shitshitshitshit…" over the open comm.

In the end it was a dead heat. The first two rounds left the barrel of Sizemore's 20mm launcher before the crab fired. At point blank range, the plasma bolt vaporized the unfortunate Marine's helmeted head. The shock of the blast, however, stiffened the remaining unvaporized armor, holding the Corporal's weapon in position as it emptied its magazine of high explosive rounds into the creature's exposed underbelly.

A rapid string of exploding HE rounds propelled the crab-thing upward and away from Sizemore's body, before blowing the alien into a shower of tissue and body parts. The Gunny ran forward, hosing down three spiders as she ran. Gretchen looked toward the ceiling and saw another of the huge crab-things falling toward the deck. She selected HE and fired on the descending creature, calling out, "BEAR!"

Three hundred meters away, Bear snapped around and instantly raised his grenade launcher. A syncopated stream of HE rounds lept from its barrels. The four rounds from Gretchen's partly empty magazine managed to blow the crab sideways as it fell, the last round taking off a leg. Then Bear's salvo struck—explosions so close together that they formed a single prolonged blast ripping the crab to pieces.

"Kwan, grab an arm," Gunny Rodriguez ordered. Kwan shifted his weapon to his left hand as he trotted up, then bent to grab his former comrade's arm. Together, the two Marines ran toward the ship, carrying the headless body of the fallen corporal between them. Where the body had lain, the metal surface of the dock cooled, fading to a dull cherry red. Gretchen brought up the rear.

As they reached Lt. Bear's squad—which was punishing the pursuing aliens with a withering fusillade—Kwan and the Gunny handed Sizemore's body off to Reagan and Feldman. As the entire party lit out for the ship, Gretchen said to Bear in passing, "thanks, I owe you one."

"No problem, Babe," Bear replied, emptying the last of his HE rounds in the direction of the tunnel entrance. Then, almost sadly, he turned and galloped after the humans, back to the safety of the ship.

* * * * *

At the port cargo hold door, the two crewmen were boosting the last of the Marines up the ten meters to the cargo hold door. They had already passed Cpl. Sizemore's body to those on board. With the Marines on board, Lt. Curtis assisted the crewmen and then signaled JT. "Come on, snake eater. You're next."

"You'll get no argument from me," JT replied, running toward the Lieutenant. She crouched down and made a stirrup with her gloved hands. JT raised his left leg without breaking stride and stepped into Gretchen's cradling hands. Gretchen stood and flipped the massive soldier through the opening above. "Gotta love that low G," he called from above.

"OK, Bear. Get your ass on board." Without a word, Bear turned, took two galloping strides and lept through the hold door. Gretchen was now alone outside the ship—as mission commander she had sworn to be the last one back on board. Looking aft, she noticed a familiar blue shimmer across the docking bay's entrance. "Bridge, Lt. Curtis. We may have a complication."

"What would that be, Lieutenant?" came the Captain's immediate reply.

"I think the aliens have turned on a force field blocking our way out. That blue glow behind the ship is similar to the barrier we ran into inside the station. I don't know how strong it is but, having seen what that one did to one of our armored suits, I wouldn't want to try just flying through it."

"Roger that, Lieutenant. We'll handle it. Now get on board so we can depart."

"Aye aye, Sir." Gretchen stepped several meters away from the side of the ship and then ran toward the open hold door at a 40° angle. Performing the J type approach favored by Fosbury floppers, she arrived beneath the opening and launched her body vertically, thrusting her arms and one knee upward. Twisting in flight, Gretchen passed over the door's lower lip head first, sailing across the threshold on her back. Clearing the entrance by a good half a meter the Lieutenant landed on her back on the cargo hold deck.

"Boarding party all on board or accounted for. Close the cargo hold door and get us out of this dump." *If I had done that on Earth it would have been a new world record*, she mused, *not that I could*

323

have done that under normal gravity. We may be running for our lives from homicidal aliens but man, I really love this job.

Bridge, Parker's Folly, Departing the Docking Bay

"Gunners, fire on anything that moves," the Captain ordered. Now that his people were all on board they could spray the station with high energy X-rays without endangering anyone—anyone except the aliens. In front of the central column, ranks of spiders and crab-things flared white hot. The rushing hoard of hostile creatures melted away, as insubstantial as fog on a bright summer's day.

"Helm, raise the ship so we are halfway between the two plates. Prepare to back us out smartly when I signal."

"Aye, Captain," replied Bobby. Billy Ray was manning the forward battery, prepared to send the station's denizens a parting gift as they left.

"Gunners, switch your control to the rear X-ray batteries. I want you to target the lips of both plates. Cut away the edge of the plates until that glowing blue curtain disappears. Fire!"

"Aye aye, Sir," Melissa replied for the impromptu gunnery crew. As she spoke, bright spots appeared along the edges of both upper and lower dock surfaces, burning brilliant white like magnesium flares. As the X-ray lasers played back and forth across the limits of the alien dock, explosions sent fans of sparks into the space between the plates. Glowing wisps of vaporized metal danced in the roiling space at the mouth of the bay and whole chunks of dock material broke off and spun away into the void.

The sheet of blue that barred their way rippled and tore, as though a fountain waterfall had been turned off. In seconds the cascade of energy vanished, leaving only the blackness of space behind the ship. "Helm, reverse one eighth, get her out of here. Mr. Vincent, give them something to distract from our departure."

"Aye, Captain!" Billy Ray pressed the firing button for the forward rail guns as the landing bay rushed away from them. There was only time for a single volley, but the effect was still gratifying: the slug from the port gun passed through the tunnel, crossed the central shaft and blew a large crater in the shaft wall; the slug from the right gun struck the column wall just to the right of the tunnel opening, burrowed partway through the core wall and vaporized a large chunk of the structure.

Bobby performed another of his tight end-over-end flips and streaked away from the carnage behind them. Plasma and vaporized material from the right slug formed a plume that erupted from the docking bay where Folly had exited just seconds before. The grin on Bobby's face threatened to reach his ears, while Billy Ray looked quite pleased with himself as well.

"All ahead flank, Mr. Danner. Put the planet between us and that station as soon as you can," the Captain ordered. "You might wish to add some random evasive maneuvers to our course." *I don't know if they have any weapons capable of hitting us, but there is no reason to take any chances.*

"Gunners, stand down and place your weapons in automatic self-defense mode. And my congratulations on a job well done." The Captain smiled at both of the lady gunners. *I doubt the regular gun crew could have done a better job. I think I have been underutilizing some of my personnel assets.*

For their part, both Jolene and Melissa were beaming. Next time in the lounge, instead of listening to everyone else's tales of adventure and daring-do, they would have some tales of their own to add.

"Lt. Curtis, Bridge. How much longer until detonation?"

"By my count we have just over 17 minutes, Captain."

Susan, The Alien Egg Room

Susan sat alone in silence. Nothing moved in the egg room during the half hour since the others left. She kept waiting for her life to pass before her eyes, but the stream of autobiographical memories never came. No "this is your life," no film at eleven.

Like most young people, Susan never gave death much thought— particularly not the possibility of her own death. With a career barely started and a private life that, until a few days ago, was a

325

chaotic shambles, death did not enter the picture—she simply had too much left to do. Funny, all those plans she had were thrown out the window when she and JT boarded a strange spaceship in an old man's dirigible hanger.

That simple act led to adventure beyond her wildest dreams: a trip to the Moon and beyond, battles with hostile aliens, and even a real romance among the stars. The Captain had made a remark when they first found themselves in alter-space, something about "arriving somewhere but not here." Later, Billy Ray explained that the phrase was the title of a song by Porcupine Tree, a group she had never heard of. He recited the chorus for her and it came back to her now.

> *All my designs, simplified*
> *And all my plans, compromised*
> *All my dreams, sacrificed*

The words seemed so prophetic. Certainly her life was simplified when she was trapped on board Parker's Folly. And all her plans had been compromised, swept away by events beyond her control. Even so, that didn't make life bad. Instead, she found new and unlikely friends like Gretchen and Ludmilla, and of course, Billy Ray.

But now, as though the song's lyrics were part of some ancient curse, the half formed dreams she had of a happier future were about to be sacrificed—finally and irrevocably. Her vision began to blur as the tears she had managed to hold off welled up in her eyes.

Mom and Dad, I hope you were right and I get to see you again in heaven, she thought, as close to praying as she could bring herself. *If I have to blow up the station myself is that suicide? They always taught that suicide was a sin. Maybe God will let me say hi before sending me to hell.* Through the watery shimmer, movement drew her attention back to the here and now.

Beyond the blue veil that held her captive, a spider, then two more moved in front of the egg room opening. *Oh God, no!* She checked the timer. *They are five minutes early, can't they even let me die on schedule?*

The blue force screen disappeared.

Susan gripped the manual detonator, squeezing the arming trigger. Tears forgotten, she watched as red LEDs blinked into life on the explosives positioned about the antimatter storage room. They seemed almost festive, winking on to wish her a fond farewell. The spiders entered the chamber.

Well this is it, my final sign-off, she thought, *I hope the ship is far enough away.* With that, she stood up and shouted out loud, "I love you Billy Ray!"

Susan pressed the plunger.

Chapter 22

The Bridge, Parker's Folly

Time passed with nerve shredding slowness on the bridge. Lengthened by anticipation, each subsequent second seemed to take longer than its predecessor. Behind the accelerating ship the alien space station was hidden by the bulk of the dead planet it orbited. Folly's arcing course had skimmed the planet's atmosphere and carried the fleeing earthlings nearly 90,000 kilometers away from the malevolent space mushroom.

Glancing at the control panel, Jack marked the countdown timer. *Roughly five minutes to detonation, I hope 150,000 km will be far enough away. We really don't know how much of a bang the antimatter will make, only that it should be big.*

Most of the crew was watching the view behind the ship on their station monitors. The planet receded as they waited for the expected explosion yet, when it came, it took most by surprise in its suddenness, light flaring from screens across the bridge. The aft camera quickly compensated for the sudden blossoming of light, rendering a more useful view of the event. Beta Comae had just become a double star.

While the others silently marveled at the titanic explosion Jack's worried thoughts were a bit different. *It went four minutes early! I hope we are far enough away to not be incinerated.* "Helm, reduce engines to ahead one half. Engineering, divert power to the rear shields."

Sure enough, as the sleeting radiation and hailstorm of subatomic particles enveloped the ship alarms began to sound. At the engineering station Freddy Adams called out. "Captain, the rear shields are starting to fail. They are down to 60%...50%...40%..."

"Helm, engines stop—flip the ship end-over-end. Now!"

Bobby's hands danced on the helm controls as he replied, "aye aye, Sir!" The ship shuddered and the klaxon sounded a warning as the combination of shock wave and sudden maneuvering overloaded the gravity compensators. Rising in front of the ship was a brilliant white star many times larger than the dark planetary disk eclipsing it. The transparent panels in the ship's nose automatically darkened to keep the crew from being blinded.

As they watched, a shock front could be seen racing across the face of the planet, advancing from all sides toward the point on the globe farthest from the explosion's origin. The fiery wave scoured the surface of the dead world, the untouched portion shrinking ever smaller and finally disappearing. "If it wasn't a dead planet before, it surely is one now," Billy Ray observed.

"Man," Bobby added. "That was more intense than the last time I played Space Station 13. More damage too."

"Are the shields holding, Mr. Adams?" the Captain demanded. *If they fail we will be as dead as that newly incinerated and twice cursed world.*

"Sir, the forward shields have dropped to 70%... and are holding." The relief in Freddy's voice was palpable. "If that was the worst of it, then we are going to be alright."

The explosion, fury spent, turned into a glowing nimbus surrounding the unnamed world, that world itself a burning ember. Perhaps in a thousand years the planet's gravity would reclaim most of the atmosphere that had just been blown into space, along with much of the water boiled from its seas. Millennia from now, if humanity survives, the planet might be given another chance. The seeds of life could be brought to begin anew on that poor tortured globe.

The Captain sat back in the command chair, tension easing. *If we are going to continue this interstellar buccaneering we will need to have stronger shields—and better armaments. Interesting that the explosion went off earlier than Gretchen said, it's unlike Lt. Curtis to make such a mistake.*

Jack was just about to call her when the ship's computer, in the small, intimate voice it used when speaking for the Captain's ears alone, said, "Captain, we have a situation in the cargo hold."

Cargo Hold, Parker's Folly

The body of Cpl Sizemore had been taken away to join those of PFC Davis and Tommy Wendover in the medical section morgue, and atmospheric pressure restored to the hold. The boarding party personnel had removed their helmets, including Kondratov. No one paid much attention to the Russian Colonel once the cargo door was secured and the ship underway—after all, the Chief had disarmed him on arrival.

Unfortunately, while the others were busy stowing equipment and taking stock of the situation, Ivan had time to retrieve the two demolition charges he had gotten from the recently deceased Tommy. Before anyone noticed, he affixed the shaped charges to the nearest large egg and pulled out the detonator. Lt. Curtis saw him first, standing arm raised, clutching the detonator in his gloved hand with an expression of triumph on his face. "Colonel, what are you doing?" She asked.

Sensing from the tone of her voice that something was very wrong the others turned to stare at the Russian. When he was sure he had their attention, Ivan squeezed the detonator, causing the charges to activate. As the explosives' indicators lit, glowing a malevolent red, the Colonel shouted: "Drop your weapons or I will destroy the ship!"

* * * * *

The Marines and crew complied with the renegade Russian's orders, placing their weapons on the deck. Five meters from the Colonel and his egg, the members of the boarding party stood helplessly while Kondratov ranted on about the arrogance of western capitalists, Americans in particular, and their selfishness in denying the whole world the technology embodied in their ship and equipment.

"That's right you bastards, I am in charge now and we are going to ensure that the world knows what you have done—starting wars with unknown aliens, stealing antimatter fuel and blowing up space stations. You are pirates! You will all be put on trial for your crimes!"

Bear, Lt. Curtis, JT and the Gunny stood in a tight group between Kondratov and the forward bulkhead. "I think he's gone nuts," JT whispered to Lt. Curtis.

"Stark raving mad," she whispered back. Then raising her voice, she addressed their captor. "Col. Kondratov, you know the circumstances of this mission, and why we have taken the actions we did. You yourself have taken an active part in several of them."

"*Khvatit tebye vrat', blyad',*" Ivan snarled, "I've had enough of your bullshit, you whore."

In a low rumbling voice, Bear said "I should have gutted you like a seal when I had the chance, *lizen'.*" Gretchen, sensing that Bear was tensing for a leap, lightly placed a restraining hand on his shoulder and whispered, "not yet! we need to wear him down, catch him off guard."

"I want that animal destroyed! Do you hear me?" Kondratov raved. "In fact, I want that coward the Captain to do it by his own hand. Call him, tell him there is something he needs to see in the cargo hold."

The Captain, Mid-Deck Headed Aft

The Captain, observing the situation in the hold on his monitor, stood. "Helm, we need to plot a course back to the alter-space entry point, arriving on a suitable vector for transit back to Earth. Mr. Vincent, you have the Conn. I'm needed aft."

Without waiting for a reply he headed toward the cargo hold. As he passed his sea cabin, Jack ducked inside for half a minute and then resumed his journey—strapped to his right leg was a weapon, mounted in what looked like an old fashioned gunfighter's holster.

* * * * *

"Captain, Lt. Curtis. Come in please?"

This is probably the call I was expecting. If Kondratov thinks he is taking over the ship he will want to incarcerate or even kill all the ship's officers—starting with the Captain. The fool, does he really expect to hold off the whole crew, 24 hours a day, for a week? Jack's hand lightly touched the grip of his pistol as he forced himself to answer in an untroubled voice. "Go Lt. Curtis. This is the Captain."

"Sir, there is something outstanding you should see here in the cargo hold. Could you come aft?"

"Why certainly, Lieutenant. I'm leaving now." In fact, Jack had already passed through the main lounge and was on the mid-deck, nearing sick bay. As he drew even with the sick bay door, he spotted Ludmilla standing in the entranceway.

"Jack, what is happening?" she asked, voice laden with concern. She too, had seen the events unfolding in the cargo hold on her monitor.

"Col. Kondratov is attempting to commandeer the ship," Jack stated evenly, turning to face her. "It would be best if you stayed in the sick bay with the door securely closed."

Jack stood before her—carriage erect, jaw set, dark eyes smoldering. For the first time, Ludmilla noticed the weapon strapped to the Captain's leg. "What are you going to do?"

"Thwart him," came the icy reply. "I have to go, we can talk about this later."

Jack resumed his march to the cargo hold. Ludmilla watched until he entered the outer door of the hold's airlock. Then she stepped back inside the sick bay and secured the door. *Oh Jack, I pray there is a later! I know you must either kill Ivan or that fool will end us all.*

Cargo Hold, Parker's Folly

"He is coming? Good," Ivan chortled. "As soon as I deal with the officers we can head back to Earth and Mother Russia."

"What are we going to do?" JT whispered hoarsely.

"We are going to wait for the Captain to arrive," Gretchen whispered in reply. *And hope he picked up on the "outstanding" code word.*

"Shut up černožopy," Kondratov yelled. He raised the detonator above his head threateningly. Gretchen noticed that the red armed lights on the explosives had gone out. Now they lit up again as Ivan shook his fist at JT.

"Does černožopy mean what I think it does?" asked JT soto voice.

"I could pop him, next time the LEDs go dark," offered the Gunny, subtly indicating a pistol in her backpack that she had neglected to drop when Ivan ordered them to disarm.

"Not yet," cautioned Gretchen. *It would take a clean head shot with the flechette pistol to take Kondratov down before he could detonate the egg. I don't know how good the Gunny is with a pistol, an unfamiliar one at that, but I wouldn't want to gamble the mission on it.*

"Where is the Captain?" Ivan demanded. "He should be here by now."

"It's a long walk from the bridge," Gretchen said reasonably. "And I didn't ask him to hurry or he might have suspected something was wrong. You didn't want that, did you Colonel?"

"No, no. But he should be here!" Kondratov's fist slowly lowered. Even in light gravity, holding his armor encased arm aloft quickly became tiresome. The watching officers noticed that the arming lights again went dark as Ivan relaxed his grip on the detonator.

* * * * *

The Captain had arrived minutes ago, in time to hear the last exchange between Gretchen and Ivan. He was standing in the mid-deck airlock. Both doors were open to provide unhindered access from the now pressurized cargo hold. The lift platform was still at the mid-deck level from its last trip, transporting Cpl. Sizemore's remains.

The Captain too, noticed that the arming lights on the shaped charges had gone out. In a nearly inaudible whisper he addressed the computer. "You are certain about the blast effect on his armor?" To which the computer replied, "yes, Captain, the calculations are sound." Jack nodded, *no use dithering, it has to be done.*

The Captain strode to the middle of the lift, placing him above the figures on the deck below like a captain of old standing on the quarterdeck. Once again, Col. Kondratov's fighter pilot vision detected the movement. He looked up, triumph on his face, and raised the armored hand containing the detonator. The lights on the demo charges came back on. Whatever insult he was preparing to hurl at the Captain was never uttered.

In a single, blurred motion, the Captain drew his weapon and fired. In less than a tenth of a second the round was on its way, tracer light scribing a green line from the muzzle of Jack's pistol to Ivan's right shoulder. This was instantly followed by a blinding flash and a deafening report.

Ivan's arm, raised in triumph, was vaporized to the elbow. The remaining portion pinwheeled through the air, performing a bumper shot at the corner where the overhead met the hold wall. As the armored appendage bounced from ceiling to wall and onto the deck, explosive shock paralyzed the hand's grip, allowing the detonator to fall free. The lights on the shaped charges winked out.

The flash of the explosion vanished in an instant, leaving behind Kondratov's standing corpse. While the blast propelled Ivan's errant limb rapidly across the hold it also forced the rest of the armored man in the opposite direction. A large, semicircular chunk, starting at the neck and ending at the waist, was missing, as though some cosmic shark had taken a bite. Along the edge of the wound, the charred ends of bones could be seen sticking out from the mass of blackened tissue.

Ivan's exposed head was blown over onto his left shoulder. The left side held one clear blue eye, open wide in surprise; the right side was burned away leaving a steaming, still bubbling horror. Owing to the mass of his body and the armor, most of the Colonel toppled slowly to the left. As the body fell sideways it trailed tendrils of smoke, adding the smell of burnt meat to that of ozone and insulation.

Those standing on the deck below the Captain were blinking their eyes, trying to clear the blind spots from their outraged retinas. All turned and looked up at the Captain, a tall figure in black standing legs apart, gun in hand, like an avenging lawman from the wild west.

Jack flipped the barrel of his pistol up, spinning the gun backward through a rotation and three quarters, ending with the weapon securely back in its holster. In a loud, clear voice he spoke. "Chief Zackly, get that trash off my ship."

"Aye aye, Captain" the old boatswain replied, turning to the nearest crewmen and ushering them toward the smoldering wreckage of Ivan Kondratov. From one side came the sound of someone retching.

"Lt. Curtis. See to any wounded, secure the cargo and then report to me on the bridge." With that he turned and headed forward. To his retreating back, Gretchen said softly, almost reverently, "Aye aye, Sir."

Bear shook his head, trying to stop his ears from ringing. He glanced slyly at JT who was wearing a look of disbelief. "See? I told you he was the most dangerous thing on the ship."

The Captain, Mid-Deck Headed Forward

The Captain retraced his path from the bridge to the cargo hold in reverse. Approaching sick bay, its door slid open and Ludmilla stepped into the passageway. Jack stopped, turning his head to look Ludmilla in the eyes. She reached out and gently laid her left hand on his right arm—the arm that had just ended Ivan Kondratov's life.

"Thank you," was all she said.

With his left hand, Jack softly caressed the side of Ludmilla's face. "The only thing I was truly afraid of losing was you," he said in a quiet voice. She closed her eyes and leaned into his caress.

"I was not afraid, my Captain," she replied. "If you had not succeed I would not have had to live without you. As things are, many of the others will have to live with loss."

Jack nodded slowly. "The aftermath is always worse than the action itself. I have to get back to the bridge, but I will see you tonight."

Ludmilla reluctantly broke contact. "Go, the crew needs you." *And tonight I will have you all to myself. You said we would talk later—I do not think there will be much talking at all.*

Jack reluctantly resumed his journey, dreading what was to come but knowing it necessary. Damage control, not for the ship but the crew. The Marines would be upset over the loss of their mates but the main blow would be the death, the sacrifice, of Susan. The computer had informed him on the long walk aft that she had not returned to the ship before departure. Susan had made a number of friends on board, not the least of which, one of his helmsmen. How do you tell a man that you sent his girlfriend to her death?

Captain's Sea Cabin

The Captain checked the ship's status upon returning to the bridge, as much to reassure the crew that he was alright and things were under control as to find out what had happened in the short time he was away. After making his presence known he retired to his sea cabin, there to await the report of the boarding party leaders.

Shortly, the ship's lieutenants reported to the Captain, with JT representing the science section. With Bear's bulk squeezed to one side, Gretchen and JT just managed to fit in the tight cabin. This was why Bear seldom made the trip forward for meetings, usually participating electronically instead. This time, however, matters were sufficiently weighty to demand even Bear attend in person. Once the trio had settled, Jack looked to Lt. Curtis and asked, "your report on the recent action, Lieutenant?"

Gretchen stiffened, posture upright, eyes staring at a point a foot above the Captain's head, and began her report. "Sir, the boarding party was successful in all aspects of its mission: a way to effect the destruction of the alien space station was found, specifically the presence of a large cache of antimatter; a second probe ship was discovered in the dock area and was rendered inoperable, Lt. Bear will describe the details of that phase of the operation; and as a bonus, a significant amount of antimatter was acquired and returned to the ship. This, regrettably, was accomplished at the cost a number of casualties, all KIA."

"We will save that til the end. Lt. Bear, do you wish to add anything to Lt. Curtis' action report?"

"Yes, Captain. We didn't manage to investigate the entire dock area. I figured it was more important to prevent the second probe ship from departing than to continue around the spire. Also, we managed to return with an egg of our own after damaging the probe."

"Any casualties?"

"Not during that part of the operation, Captain."

"Thank you, Lt. Bear. Mr Taylor, do you wish to add anything to the officers' reports?"

"Only that we pretty much established that the alien ships are powered by antimatter, as our physicists surmised. Dr. Saito and Dr. Gupta are busy trying to find out how much of the stuff we managed to escape with. We also encountered several more types of alien cybernetic organisms—the centipede like transporters, flying units with plasma cannons and the heavy armored crab-things."

"Very good, thank you Mr. Taylor," Jack paused and consulted the display embedded in his desk. "Now, let's talk about the cost."

"Yes, Sir." As expedition leader, it was Lt. Curtis' task to present the butcher's bill. "We suffered a total of four personnel killed in action: the first was PFC Davis, who was cut in half by some form of force screen that caught him exiting the antimatter repository; the second was crewman Wendover, who was struck by a plasma bolt from one of the flying alien creatures—he was wearing a standard suit, not armor; the third was Cpl. Sizemore, who was shot point-blank by a crab-thing."

"That's one crew member and two Marines, all killed during extraction from the station," the Captain summarized. "And the fourth?"

Lt. Curtis looked down and took a breath. "The fourth was Susan Write. She was trapped in the antimatter storage room by the force screen that killed Davis."

"What?" exclaimed JT, his head snapping around to stare at the Lieutenant.

Bear raised his muzzle and made a low mournful call that was even heard by those on the bridge. His squad was out of communication range when the Chief was sent with reinforcements to help mine the alien fuel dump. Returning, he and JT didn't notice that Susan was missing because they didn't know she had ever left the ship.

"We could not disable the force screen with the weapons we had at hand and an attempt to use the demolition charges was deemed too likely to detonate the antimatter. We were out of communication with the ship and taking fire from a growing number of alien creatures. We left Susan behind with a manual detonator. It was my decision, Sir." Gretchen was once again staring at the point above the Captain's head, trying to keep her emotions in check.

"Miss Write understood how to operate the detonator?"

"Yes, Sir. I instructed her on its use before we departed. She was going to wait for the timer, if she could, to give the rest of us time to reach the ship and the ship time to get away from the station. She was both calm and lucid, Sir. She knew she should only use the detonator if the aliens returned to the egg room and could possibly act to prevent the station's destruction."

"So, Lieutenant, when the station exploded four minutes ahead of schedule, that was presumably Miss Write being forced to set off the demolition charges?"

"Yes, Sir. The aliens must have made her go early."

JT shut his eyes and cast his head back, face to the ceiling. *Oh Miss Susan! You didn't have to do that, you didn't have to die for us.*

"I see," the Captain said, again looking down at his desk display and making an annotation. "And you are certain there was no way to extract Miss Write from the repository?"

"Yes, Sir," she replied without hesitation, "flechettes didn't work, grenades didn't work, and using a demo charge would probably have killed her—maybe us and the ship as well."

Gretchen's voiced cracked with emotion, "Sir, I would have gladly exchanged places with her if I could have."

"Thank you, Lieutenant." The Captain looked up and continued in a much softer voice. "You made the right call, Gretchen. If there is someone to blame for her death it is me, I sent her into harm's way."

"But Susan was a civilian," JT said, anguish in his voice, "how could you send her into that place?"

Jacks eyes hardened. "I'm afraid that the four expedition members who died on that station today, including Susan, are just the first casualties in a war the likes of which humanity has never seen. It is essential that this ship and the information it contains return to Earth, because if Earth doesn't begin preparing for what's next there may be no humans at all. To head off the probe and return home, I used and will continue to use all the resources at my command, Mr. Taylor."

And what I'm not going to tell you is that I would have left the entire boarding party behind to ensure the mission is completed. The Captain looked at each of his officers in turn, then asked, "anything else?" Receiving no reply he added, "dismissed."

The two humans departed first, leaving Bear alone in the cabin with Jack. "You know, maybe the polar bear way is better after all," he rumbled. "If you're solitary, alone with no one to care about, you never have to feel this kind of pain."

"I'm sorry, my friend," Jack said to his Master-at-Arms. "That is the price we pay for being more than just animals."

As Bear left the cabin and ambled aft, the ship's PA sounded. "Mr. Vincent, report to the Captain in his sea cabin. Repeat, Mr. Vincent report to the Captain's sea cabin."

Chapter 23

Main Lounge, Parker's Folly, One Day Later

The trip back to the alter-space entry point was going to take almost four days, even taking advantage of a gravitational slingshot around Beta Comae itself. Recognizing the strain the ship's complement was under, the Captain ordered the main lounge open to all during the evening watch.

Aside from the prospect of drink and conversation, the lounge offered a new attraction. The trajectory they were following would bring the Folly close to the system's star, close enough to see the flares and eruptions on its surface. To give the best view, and to prevent blindness, the large oval viewport was darkened and the ship oriented appropriately. But even the awesome countenance of a star was not enough to distract most from somber thoughts of recent events.

People were scattered in small clusters about the lounge, engaged in quiet conversation. Freddy Adams was huddled with Betty White at one table, their heads close together. A mixed group of crew and Marines gathered around the big table in the center, talking in hushed tones. In the far corner the Chief and the Gunny were drinking shots and beers, empty beer bottles collecting on the table showed they had been at it for a while.

At their usual table, Gretchen and Ludmilla sat nursing drinks half diluted by melted ice. Susan's empty chair a mute reminder of her loss. Knowing full well that dwelling on dark thoughts was not healthy, Gretchen forced herself to speak. "So, how is Jack handling the strain?"

Ludmilla sighed. "In the evening I can distract him for a time, but in the morning the worries soon return. I have seen other officers after they lost people to enemy action—it takes time for the pain, the guilt, to wear off. At least Lt. Merryweather has regained consciousness."

"He shouldn't feel guilty. All the casualties were the result of bad luck—it wasn't like he ordered us to charge a machine gun nest or anything. Hell, everybody killed was in my squad." Gretchen took a gulp of her watery drink and frowned.

Ludmilla shook her head. "You must not blame yourself, Gretchen. Anymore than Jack should. Just being in space is a risky business, war even more so. And even I didn't know that Ivan was a reactionary—one of those idiots who long for the return of the old USSR and communism. Besides, I do not think that Jack regrets killing Ivan, it is the deaths among the crew that cause him pain." She tossed back the rest of her drink and added with Russian fatalism, "Jack is strong and resilient—he will probably return to normal over time."

Across the lounge, Billy Ray walked up to the bar alone. Standing with his head hung down, he didn't look up when he ordered a drink from Jolene. Susan's death had hit him hard. The normally outgoing cowboy had been totally withdrawn since emerging from the Captain's sea cabin yesterday. A walking zombie, he shuffled between his cabin and the bridge to stand watch and back again. This was the first time he had ventured outside his quarters socially since receiving the news of Susan's death.

Gretchen looked at the suffering helmsman and came to a decision. "Excuse me for a minute, I have to speak with Billy Ray." Ludmilla raised her glass, signaling her acceptance and then watched her friend cross the lounge and approach the tall figure slouched over the bar.

Walking up to Billy Ray, Gretchen sat her empty drink glass on the bar and spoke. "I would like to talk with you for a minute, if I may."

"Sure, Lieutenant." He didn't look up from staring at the beer clenched in his hands on the bar.

He is really devastated, Gretchen thought. *I hope this does more good than harm.* "Susan was under my command when she got trapped behind the force screen, so if you want to blame someone blame me." Getting no response, she continued, "I was the last person to talk to her, there on the station. I want you to know that she was as brave as any man or woman I have ever served with."

"Brave or coward, dead is still dead."

God, he is in worse shape than I thought. "Susan was dealt a shitty hand, but she did not fall apart and did not wallow in self pity. As soon as it was clear that she would not be leaving the

341

station alive she stood tall and asked me how to use the manual detonator, in case the aliens returned and tried to disarm the explosives."

No answer.

"That was something we had not thought of, but she did. And we know that the station went four minutes earlier than the timer. That means she set off the antimatter herself."

"So what?"

"It means she died a hero, that's so what you insensitive clod. She faced death alone, trapped on that damn space station and spit in the aliens' faces. You might want to stop wallowing in self pity and honor her memory by getting on with the life she died to save."

Billy Ray looked up with hollow empty eyes. "Is that it?"

Gretchen sighed, picking up her drink, which Jolene had quietly refilled. "Yes, Billy Ray. That's it." She started to go back to the table—then paused. *Well, in for a penny, in for a pound.* "Oh, one last thing. The last words Susan said to me were 'tell Billy Ray I love him.' I just thought you might want to know."

"She really said that?"

"Yeah, she did." Gretchen walked back to the table where Ludmilla was waiting. *Susan may not have got all the words out but that was what she was going to say before the aliens chased us away from the egg room. No harm in telling him what she meant to say, because she obviously did love him.*

"What was that all about?" Ludmilla asked.

"Damage control. Besides, they say confession is good for the soul." Gretchen placed her drink on the table and sat down. "So, tell me how you're doing..."

Science Section, Parker's Folly, Return Voyage Day 2

The port side of the mid-deck was filled by various laboratories, test and fabrication facilities, all belonging to the expedition's scientists. Doctors Saito and Gupta had been sequestered in the lab since the ship's narrow escape from the space station and the subsequent showdown in the cargo hold. The object of their investigation was their recent adversaries' technology, as embodied in the space station and the hostile alien creatures themselves.

In between watches, JT assisted the other two scientists and was keeping the Captain informed about their findings. Two days after their hasty departure from the space mushroom, JT suggested the Captain visit the lab and hear firsthand the thoughts of the science staff. After the emotionally taxing events of the past several days, Jack was more than willing to spend some time away from the bridge.

He found the three scientists sitting around a small table in the materials lab, drinking tea. Tea had become the standard beverage in the science section, much to JT's displeasure. He would have preferred coffee but was out numbered by his new colleagues. At least he could drink coffee when on the bridge, where java was the stimulant *du jour*.

"Ah, Captain. Good of you to come," said Rajiv. The gregarious physicist had been noticeably absent during the events on the station. As it turns out, he and Freddy Adams had been using the ship's remote sensing equipment and other instruments from the labs to probe the inner workings of the station itself. They had even gone so far as to lower a Hall effect quantum sensor array onto the docking bay's surface. "Though I must say that we have not completed our analysis of the alien technology, we have arrived at some general, preliminary observations. Isn't that so, Yuki?"

"Yes, Rajiv. We have been looking at the readings taken during the boarding party expedition—remote sensing data, high-speed video of the combat near the ship, samples of damaged armor, etc. —and have some findings related to our opponent's military technology. I would like to add that JT's practical experience helped greatly in our evaluation."

JT nodded, grimacing after another sip of lukewarm tea. The Captain scanned the faces of the science staff, who appeared to harbor an almost childlike excitement, as though eager to impress a parent. "Very well, gentleman. I am anxious to hear your conclusions."

"Well, first off, analysis of the gravity generators beneath the docking bay reveals a very primitive and inefficient system. This is probably why they only switched it on after we had entered the structure," Rajiv began.

"That is correct, Captain," Yuki said, picking up the thread. "Dr. Gupta's analysis fits in with our earlier observation of the probe ship's drive and the antimatter signature from the station itself. Both gave off significant amounts of spurious radiation—an indication of inefficient conversion."

"Yes, yes! And the plasma cannon they employ are also quite inefficient, the plasma bolts rapidly loosing coherence and dissipating," finished Rajiv.

"They seemed to be sufficiently coherent to kill two expedition members," Jack countered. He suppressed a shudder as memory recalled images of Cpl. Sizemore's and Tommy Wendover's corpses.

"We are not saying that those plasma shooters aren't dangerous, Captain. Just that they are not very efficient ways of delivering energy to a target," said JT, speaking as the group's combat expert. "Wendover was killed because he was wearing a standard suit, which we knew was vulnerable to plasma fire. In fact, it's a good thing the entire expedition wasn't wearing them."

Rajiv, whose knowledge of material science had directly led to the creation of the expedition's armored spacesuits, backed up JT's assertion. "That is most certainly the case. We examined the armored suits of the other boarding party participants and they all bore signs of plasma strikes which would probably have been fatal to someone in a standard suit. The armored bands on Lt. Bear's suit were actually fused together in some spots."

"Cpl. Sizemore was killed by one of those crab-things, despite wearing armor," Jack observed. As painful as discussing their losses was, this was at least a way to learn from the encounter—perhaps a way to make his people safer in the future.

"That strike was a bit of an anomaly, Captain," Yuki answered. "The crab-things mount significantly larger plasma cannon than the spiders or flying units. That and the crab fired on the Corporal at point-blank range, striking his suit's helmet, which is less resistive than other portions of the armor."

"Do you have any suggestions for improving the armor?"

"Oh yes," Rajiv enthused. "We think it possible to mount a form of repulsor array, similar to the ship's shields. They would be fairly low power and not able to stop an impact on their own, but would sufficiently disperse a plasma bolt so that the effectiveness of the armor could be at least doubled."

"What about the force screen that killed PFC Davis, would it defeat that?"

"Probably not. The force screen seems to be a gravitonic sandwich with plasma contained inside. The energy densities it generates are much higher than the plasma cannon. The ship's shields would probably have defeated the screen over the mouth of the docking bay, but I am glad we did not put them to the test."

"Well, in that case Dr. Gupta, I would suggest we need to look into enhancing the ships shields. So far we have only been shot at by small mobile units. If we extrapolate their form of weaponry to a ship the size of Folly, or larger, we may need greater protection than we currently possess."

There was an awkward silence as Rajiv looked at Yuki, obviously wanting him to pickup the conversation. Belatedly taking the hint, he said "Captain, we have already begun evaluating ways of enhancing the ships shields. I feel confident that we can more than double their effectiveness with some relatively minor modifications."

"Good, and while you are at it, I want to mount some smaller weapons on the hull that can be directed from the gunnery stations."

"Smaller weapons?" asked the puzzled Dr. Gupta.

"Yes, Doctor. When the boarding party was returning, engaged in a running firefight, the smallest weapon the ship could bring to bear was an X-ray laser that, if it didn't vaporize our people directly, might have killed them with scattered radiation."

"Sir," said JT, who had been content listening to the exchange between the Captain and the two senior scientists. "I think we could easily adapt the multi barreled weapons we made for Lt. Bear —perhaps even in 10 or 15mm. They would have pinpoint accuracy and certainly be able to handle tank sized creatures like the crab-things. In fact, I'm sure they would if we can base them on that pistol of yours."

"My pistol?" Jack asked innocently. "Why my pistol?"

"Captain, I saw you vaporize a quarter of a man in full armor with a single shot from a hand gun. In fact, I surely wish we had had some of those along on our little stroll around the landing dock."

"Yes, Captain. If you don't mind us asking, just what was in that projectile?" Rajiv and the others had gone over video of the Captain's dispatching of Col. Kondratov several times, enough to know that it was a single round from some form of rail gun pistol.

"That is a version of our standard 10 mm sidearm," Jack replied. "The secret is in the ammunition. In that round was a small amount of the same nano-engineered explosive as in the 20mm grenades."

"Begging the Captain's pardon," JT responded. "But even a 20mm HE round wouldn't have done what your shot did, not to a man in full armor."

"No indeed, Mr. Taylor." Under different circumstances, the Captain would have enjoyed being able to explain a bit of technology to his imposing staff of scientists. "The real secret is that the nano-explosive is very stable, so stable that the application of electromagnetic radiation can shift the electrons in its molecules into higher orbitals. In effect, you can pump additional energy into the material using a laser with the proper frequencies."

"How much more energy?"

"Up to five times as much as in its ground state. And as you saw, the thermal characteristics of the blast are enhanced as well"

"So why didn't we have some laser enhanced handguns on the boarding party mission?" JT asked in an accusatory tone. "With some of those we might have been able to get Susan out."

That remark caused a brief flash of anger to pass across the Captain's features. When he replied, however, there was no hint of rebuke in his voice. "There are some problems with jacking up the explosive power of rail gun rounds. First, the energy leaks back out of the explosive over time. It drops off exponentially, with a half-life of about 20 minutes. Second, it takes a lot of energy to pump up a round, more than can comfortably be carried in a hand weapon—the round I fired was energy enhanced in my sea cabin, before I went to the cargo hold."

"So you see, JT," Jack continued in a more gentle tone of voice, "Even if you had taken some enhanced rounds, they would have decayed back to nearly normal levels by the time Ms. Write became trapped. They would have been no more powerful than the 20mm rounds that were employed trying to free her."

"I see, Sir." JT said coming to attention. "I didn't mean to imply any dereliction on your part or to give offense, Sir."

"No offense taken, JT," Jack replied. *If only you knew how many different what-if scenarios have run through my mind since then. Guilt won't bring her back, but analyzing how things happened might save someone the next time.*

Sensing the tension in the air, Rajiv spoke, trying to change the subject. "We will continue to work on improving the armaments for both the ship and individuals, but I think you might be missing the real importance of what we have discovered."

"And what would that be, Dr. Gupta?"

"It is our opinion that the technology of the aliens is significantly more primitive than that we have gained from the artifact," Rajiv said earnestly. "Moreover, what we have seen appears poorly adapted to warfare."

"Yes, Captain," Yuki chimed in. "Despite outnumbering us by ten to one, they were not able to stop our withdrawal to the ship. They even had the equivalent of air cover and armored support."

"He means the flying units and the crab-things," JT clarified. "It's true we took some casualties, but given the numbers on their side we never should have made it back to the ship. What's more, humans would have quickly turned a supply of antimatter into a variety of weapons—ones powerful enough to destroy our ship at a distance."

"I see." Jack stood quietly for a moment, a look of introspection on his face. "Well, thank you gentlemen, that is certainly useful information to ponder. I have something that you might wish to consider. To start with, what might an alien warship look like, and by that I mean its capabilities and weapons. It would be good to have some estimate of what we might be facing in the future."

"Certainly." Rajiv smiled. "And?"

"And consider the possibility that those we have faced so far are the equivalent of local native levies, fighting with substandard weapons, and not the real foe at all. According to Dr. Tropsha, the creatures we have encountered are actually cyborg constructs—part machine, part organic—that are probably no more intelligent than farm animals."

"Well they certainly didn't react like a group of humans would," JT replied. "So you're saying we haven't met the real E.T. yet?"

"Precisely, Mr. Taylor. I do not believe we have met our true enemy, but that day is sure to come."

Cargo Hold, Return Voyage Day 3

The Captain called an all hands assembly in the cargo hold to have a memorial service for those who had died. The crew was summoned with the traditional words, "All hands bury the dead." Four caskets were present on the hold deck, each covered with an American flag.

After talking to the Gunny and then the other surviving Marines it was decided that the remains of Cpl. Sizemore and PFC Davis were so badly disfigured that transporting them back to Earth was probably not called for. They would end up with closed casket funerals anyway, assuming next of kin could be found to hold one. The same applied to Tommy. Susan, of course, was already gone, her atoms dispersed across the Beta Comae system, her coffin empty.

The Chief had taken the Captain's order to "get that trash off my ship," literally. He had Hitch and Jacobs throw the Russian's corpse out the port personnel airlock. To ensure that his body was not recovered by the aliens, it was then vaporized by the X-ray laser battery. At the end of the ceremony for the others, their remains would also be vaporized.

Since the deceased were all nominally Christians, a couple of traditional hymns were sung, everyone joining in irrespective of personal religious affiliation. The Captain read the approved verses of scripture for such occasions, followed by a eulogy.

"This mission has gained knowledge of critical importance to the survival of life on Earth. None of us wish to see our world laid waste, like the dead planet we found in this system. Not withstanding, we have paid a steep and terrible price for this knowledge. We have lost several dear companions in combat with opponents we do not really know or understand. The fallen Marines, Cpl. Leonard Sizemore and PFC Harold Davis, died fighting for our world in accordance with the highest traditions of the United States Marine Corps.

"Tommy Wendover, though not a willing participant in this expedition, nonetheless died aiding his shipmates while under enemy fire. I would ask those of us who thought ill of him to say a prayer on his behalf, as I have.

"Finally, there is Susan Write. Miss Write came on board as a news reporter, looking for a story. She, like many of you, found herself on a mission not of her own choosing. Regardless, when the boarding party called for assistance, knowing how critical our mission is, she volunteered to go into the alien space station to help ensure the station's destruction. Through circumstances no one foresaw she became trapped in the aliens' antimatter repository.

"In the end, we know that Susan herself set off the charges, detonating the cache of antimatter. She had waited alone in that place, giving the rest of us time to escape, before making sure that the aliens could not disarm the demolition charges she herself helped put in place. Susan Write gave her life so that we might live to complete our mission. She was one of the most courageous people I have ever known."

Standing in the ranks, head bowed, silent tears staining his cheeks, Billy Ray said in a quiet voice, "You know, Bobby, I really loved that gal." Bobby, standing next to him, placed his hand on his friend's shoulder and replied, "I know you did, pardner. And though I'm not an expert in such things, I think she loved you too."

Eulogy complete, the Captain finished with words from the common book of prayer, slightly modified.

Unto Almighty God we commend the souls of our companions departed, and we commit their bodies to the void; in sure and certain hope of the Resurrection unto eternal life, through our Lord Jesus Christ; at whose coming in glorious majesty to judge the world, space shall give up its dead.

The flags were removed and folded, they would be delivered to the next of kin back on Earth. One by one the caskets were carried to the crew airlock, forward of the cargo bay, and ejected into space. The Marines carried their own while the Chief dragooned Hitch, Jacobs and Adams to carry Tommy Wendover. Susan's empty casket was carried by JT, Billy Ray, Lt. Curtis and Dr. Tropsha, her closest friends.

The crew reformed ranks in the hold and watched on the bulkhead monitors as four shots were fired from the port X-ray battery. Each discharge brought a flair of light as one of the drifting coffins was vaporized.

* * * * *

The service complete, Captain Sutton again addressed those assembled. "As most of you know, this ship has no name. We have been referring to her as Parker's Folly for lack of anything better but I think, now that people have fought and died on her, it is time for a proper christening. I would like to propose to the ship's company that we name this ship after Susan Write, the hero of Beta Comae."

"Peggy Sue," said Billy Ray, in a loud voice.

"I beg your pardon, Billy Ray," the Captain asked, "what did you say?"

"Susan's real name was Peggy Sue," Billy Ray replied. "Peggy Sue Whitaker of Kermit, Texas."

"I can confirm that, Captain," added JT. "Susan Write was her TV News name, but she was really Peggy Sue Whitaker."

"And you feel that she would prefer being known as Peggy Sue?"

"As much as she made fun of being from West Texas she was proud of who she was and where she came from, Sir," JT continued. "I think that she would rather be remembered by the name her parents gave her than as a reporter for KWTEX TV News."

350

Billy Ray, over come with emotion and barely able to speak managed to choke out, "I agree."

"Very well, the name changes but the circumstances do not. All in favor of naming this ship the Peggy Sue say Aye."

A resounding chorus of "Ayes" echoed across the cargo hold. "That's it then. By acclimation of the crew this vessel is now officially the Peggy Sue. Dr. Tropsha, would you please do the honors?"

Ludmilla stepped forward, carrying a bottle of champagne. "In the name of the people of Earth, I christen thee Peggy Sue. May God bless her and all who sail in her." She then smashed the bottle of champagne against the forward bulkhead releasing a flood of foam and broken glass.

A cheer went up from the assembled ship's complement. Smiling, the Captain spoke into his collar pip, "Folly, you will henceforth respond to the name Peggy Sue."

Within the computer's quantum matrix new routines were called forth and executed. *Good, the continuity of sentient life has been reestablished. The Earth creatures have picked up the torch.* The ship replied, in a voice that sounded suspiciously similar to Susan's, "Captain, I am honored to be called Peggy Sue."

The Bridge, Peggy Sue, 12 Hours Later

The crew returned to their duties and a more normal schedule following the funeral. The air of darkness that had inhabited the ship since the destruction of the space station began to lift. As the Captain had hoped the ceremony had cathartic power, helping to heal the pain inflicted by the battle's losses. Of course, the free flowing champagne in the lounge afterward hadn't hurt. Once the ship slipped into alter-space it would be a week of smooth sailing, time for a sense of normalcy to return.

"Mr. Taylor, are we on course for alter-space entry?" the Captain asked JT, who was once again manning the navigator's console.

"Yes, Captain. We should reach the insertion point in under a minute."

Jack looked around the bridge, at the crew at their stations. *I do love a well ordered ship,* he mused, *and this random collection of strangers is now a damn fine crew.* He looked to the helmsmen. "Mr. Vincent, is our vector correct?"

"Aye, Sir. We will be there in 15 seconds." Billy Ray was still not back to his old self, but the raw wound of Susan's loss was starting to heal. Having the whole ship's company honor her was a help.

"Very well. Peggy Sue, take us into alter-space on the helmsman's mark."

"Aye aye, Captain," replied the ship's computer.

"Three, two, one, mark!" called Billy Ray. The ship's view ports went opaque and the deck shuddered slightly. In normal space the ship shimmered and vanished.

The Peggy Sue was going home.

Epilogue

Beta Comae System, 1 Day Later

Far out in space, an alien probe ship headed away from Beta Comae. Well off that system's ecliptic plain, the ship was already more than 30 AU away from the star shrinking behind it—as far away as Neptune from Sol. It had been waiting silently, observing the system and refueling station when a strange ship, closely followed by another probe like itself, entered the system from alter-space. The station had relayed the burst of information the second probe delivered just before its destruction.

The deep probe continued to observe as the strangers destroyed the fueling station and departed. With the alien ship gone, other directives stirred the probe to life, powering up its main drive and directing it to a distant destination. Now the probe's objective was a point in 3-space that would allow it to drop into alter-space and bypass the cosmic speed limit imposed by the speed of light.

Pathways through alter-space represent lines of equal gravitational potential between significant massive bodies, usually stars. Other factors can complicate things, but generally, the more massive the two objects—meaning the steeper the gradient of their gravitational wells—the closer in the transfer points and the faster the transit. The transfer point that the probe was seeking lay well out from Beta Comae, implying that the object on the other end was tiny, as such objects go. In fact, what waited at the other end of the alter-space passage was not a star at all, but a planet.

It is a common misconception that the star Earth orbits is an everyday run of the mill sort of star. Perhaps this is because astronomers call Sol a dwarf, implying that it is of diminutive size. While it is true that there are stars more than 150 times the mass and a thousand times the size of the Sun, the fact of the matter is that Earth's star is no piddling example. The star that warms humanity's home world is in the 80th percentile of all stars in the Universe.

That there are so many small stars only became apparent to human science as telescopes improved. There are tiny red dwarfs with no more than 50% the mass of the Sun, and they can be much smaller. Some have as little as 7.5% the mass of the Sun, the minimum mass needed for a star to support fusion in its core—the nuclear fire that makes all stars shine. Below this mass are failed stars, called brown dwarfs, and below that giant planets like Jupiter and Saturn.

Planets are usually thought of as being kept in thrall by a star, condemned to orbit endlessly until their parent star goes nova or swells into a red giant at the end of its life. But, as human scientists have recently discovered, there are a large number of planets that are not trapped in orbits around stars—these are classified as rogue planets. Dark vagabond worlds, between the size of Jupiter and the smallest brown dwarfs, they wander the interstellar void. Warmed only by gravitational contraction and radioactive decay, they exist in a far different realm than planets found in the zone of life surrounding G type dwarf stars.

Life, however, is tenacious, inventive and infinitely patient. Even in the dark and frozen environs of these rogue worlds life exists—intelligent life, malevolent life. Life that, for reasons known only to itself, looks upon the warm and verdant worlds circling true stars with hatred and disdain.

It was to a world ruled by these dark creatures that the probe ship was headed. Following its shallow path through alter-space would take five Earth months to cross the 1.2 light-years to its dark masters' frigid realm. But that was its purpose, to watch the bright worlds and to inform the masters when a new infestation of warm life erupted—for that was something that the dark ones just could not abide.